He Who Pays The Piper

By Alex Breck

1

to my family for their love and support

'If pain could have cured us we should long ago have been saved.'
George Santayana, The Life of Reason (1905)

Contents

Chapter One – All the leaves are brown...

The creature was clearly suffering under the unrelenting intensity of the midday sun. To look at the shrivelled facial features, incandescent white with black pinprick eyes, it seemed certain that he must have been cruelly evicted from the sanctuary of a nocturnal habitat. There were no obvious signs of injury on the outside of the body. But as he darted in and out of any available areas of blessed shade it was possible to hear quiet wailing sounds emanating from deep within, indicating the likely occurrence of serious internal injuries.

He had felt better, it was true.

Possibly, he could blame it on a popular excuse in these parts. He'd been abducted by aliens who had conducted depraved mental and physical experiments on him, leaving him this pathetic remnant of his past glory.

Unfortunately, he feared that he alone was responsible for his latest predicament. Plus, to sweeten his day further, he had just been fired.

Yes... *Again.*

As he emerged from the relative cool of the narrow, dusty Minna, onto busier 5th St, heading up to Market and home, he suddenly panicked at the hellish vision before him. The broad street wriggled wetly in the heat and the clear blue sky did nothing to dampen down the clamorous honking of the rushing vehicles. Stumbling at the litter-strewn roadside, he muttered various foul entreaties to the world and headed instead for the alternative existence of the 'Loch Ness'.

Downtown San Francisco on a Saturday afternoon was no place for a poor Scots lad with the mother of all hangovers.

Sliding through the door, he held his head low and found his way over to the bar as if possessed with some internal guidance system. He pulled himself up onto a stool with some difficulty and rubbed at the dried blood stuck to his unshaven cheek. His long pale fingers were shaking as he searched the pockets of his coat for a cigarette. Inhaling deeply, he finally raised his head and flint grey eyes looked around the bar measuredly, devoid of any interest. *Back again ...*, he said inwardly.

The Loch Ness was an 'Irish' bar run by two Thai women who wouldn't have been able to locate either Scotland or the Emerald isle on a map if their lives depended on it. Somehow though, in the crazy amalgam of life that typified this city, bars like these had survived every fad and they were a common habitat for sad-bastard runaway Europeans like Richard Walker Esquire. The best thing about the Loch Ness was it was always open and that his ethnic authenticity guaranteed him admission. The worst thing about it was that it was always open...

'Hi Ridge! You OK?

Look like shit today.
You wanna Jim Beam - no ice?'

'No Mama-san, just give me a Bud for now. You've got a hell of a way to go with that customer focused crap.'

'You be back again tomorrow. I know,' she stated with a certainty that shook him more than a little in his beleaguered state.

It was true he had popped in a *few* times in the several months he had been living in San Francisco. It was also true that he had the highest score on the antique arcade game against the wall there and that the pool table sitting in front of the long bar had earned him as much as any paid work he might have done.

The Loch Ness was an uncannily appropriate moniker for one such as him to gravitate to. Like its famous namesake, the bar was also murky and dark, frequented by deluded arseholes blindly searching for a 'thing' they could never understand which might lend some kind of meaning to their crap existence. If you knew where and when to look, there was also the wee matter of the Scottish monster attraction. Although this one was a tad puny and not a little bit *peely wally* when measured up to his more illustrious cousin.

As he sat, elbows propped up on the sticky bartop; Ridge surveyed the scene before him and tried to take stock of his present situation. It was only natural, he told himself, that when so far from home, he should feel the need to seek out solace from others like himself who were 'travelling'. In those situations it was important to socialise and get out and about as much as possible. There was no point in being half way around the world and then sitting in contemplating your belly-button fluff was there? After all, most of the jobs he had found had been through this hallowed emporium of the alcoholic beverage. Unfortunately he had been spectacularly unsuccessful at holding on to any of them for too long. He discovered that being a great computer programmer cut no ice when you were stuck 100ft up a ladder with a 40lb bag of sand over your shoulder.

He had applied himself to the social side of the task with some zeal, he had to admit, and if there ever was a spare place in the Manic Street Preachers line-up then he surely had the liver for it. Four years of university life in Scotland had prepared him well for this. The beer was weaker over here and the pool table offered easy prey after so many hours crouched over snooker tables in his Student Union bar back home.

He could see two lads over near the toilets who had 'gap-year tourist' stamped all over them. Gulping their bottles of domestic beer with barely concealed disdain whilst looking over constantly at their virginally clean backpacks, they were nervously trying to attract the attention of the pool players, unsure of the protocol. He thought for a moment, whether to fleece them or teach them how to survive the all important first few hours. But he turned away and gave up any thoughts of monetary gain as the floor swam and queasy Dali-esque memories of the previous day/evening hit him like a train.

There had been no presage of impending doom as he had sat here on Thursday with Eric. Just two regular guys having a quiet drink on the way home from work. Besides, Eric was, of all his acquaintances here, the most straight arrow of the bunch. He'd originally fled Switzerland to avoid military service and found himself in California, a place so screwed up, as he was so fond of recounting, that they said someone once tilted up America and all the crazies landed here. He was a carpenter and his mastery of wood had ensured him regular work at the construction company where his slavish attention to detail and unswerving good nature made him something of a paragon. However, apart from that, he was okay. So when Eric suggested they swing by a new sculpture exhibition down towards the Mission District with the promise of a beer and a *muy picante* burrito after, Ridge was all for it. He lost Eric about midnight

It was the same old story; meet people in a bar, get led astray, wake up wrecked. His memory of the first act was poor but by the time the final curtain went down he was strictly off-planet. The problem was, being a dashing young Scot, every time he opened his big mouth some dizzy Berkeley girl would say what a 'cool' accent he had, which would lead to horrible Sean Connery / Ewan McGregor impersonations and other embarrassing stunts. This time he'd fallen in with a bunch of art students, taken *way* too much coke for a Caledonian boy and been dragged to at least two clubs that he *could* remember.

He closed his eyes and could still feel the dull throb of heavy dance music and smell the sweet coconut of the swirling dry ice wrapping him momentarily in that sickly cotton-candy day-glo other world. A world where things were not always what they seemed. He had bounced off sweaty walls in one club doing his usual inane grinning at some gorgeous female who turned out on this occasion to be a 'he', in *transition*. At some party later there was still more coke and speed flying around and he could vaguely remember that warm feeling of supreme confidence and well-being and thinking that drugs really were not as bad as people made out. That feeling of confidence must have been what led him into a serious disagreement with two guys who were preaching the worthiness of the cause of the 'Irish freedom fighters'. After denouncing their respective parentage's in terms that they could understand, he discovered that he was sitting amongst a party of closet Republican supporters and that was when things went really bad.

Even now he could hear a siren shrieking in his head but then he glanced round in amazement to see other patrons of the Loch Ness moving out to the frontage of the bar where a myriad of flashing lights was reflecting off the old mirrors and cheap glass. Ridge shook himself hard as the fire services went about their drill on the opposite sidewalk, '*Bloody hell,* I thought that racket was in my head, I have *got* to sort myself out.'

He spun his head wildly round, saw that all eyes were out towards the front. 'I *will* sort it out, but not right now!' With that, he leant over the bar, grabbed a bottle of Jack Daniels, thrust it under his coat and lurched for the door.

The air seemed thick and clammy to Ridge as he walked quickly along Market Street, his pale face streaked with perspiration causing his hair to lie heavily across his eyes. He thought fondly of the grey skies and drizzle of Scotland and almost wished himself back there. To most other people on Market it was actually a pleasantly warm late afternoon and there was a light summer breeze gently blowing small debris across the city streets like tumbleweed.

Arnold Washington the Third had been called far worse names than 'debris' in his time and as he sat totally motionless and cross-legged on the sidewalk, only his opaque eyes followed Ridge with a faraway curiosity. Ridge knew that he was no stranger to anguish either but if he was in some way trying to reach out to the young man or perhaps to a fading memory of the man he himself used to be then sadly, today was not the day.

Men like 'Tres', as he was known to Ridge, were a common sight along Market. Straw hair bleached blonde and sullied skin turned to dark leather by the constant affections of the sun. Ridge had spent several interesting hours in the park, crashing cigarettes to his bitter friend who in return answered the thousand questions Ridge had about Vietnam. He was the delinquent progeny of an ignominious affair that even now haunts the US psyche. He had returned from war, not a hero, but to a perfidious coalition of hatred. Now he was left with only his cynical addictions to temper the madness at what he had witnessed. His milky blue eyes continued to track Ridge until he was lost from view. Only then did he lift his upturned hand and renew his familiar mantra.

Ridge slowed his pace a little but kept his head down and didn't glance up or sideways, not even once. The sweet aromas of pecan pie and cinnamon Danishes bowling out of the patisserie held no attraction for him today. The numerous strip joints and sex emporiums were equally repulsive to him and the usually forceful guys hustling at the doorways sensed there was little point in wasting breath on this deadbeat.

As always when he had too much time to think on his own, he began to flounder in a quagmire of self pity. It still took him by surprise some mornings. He would wake up wondering how he had got there, thousands of miles from home, slaving all day for pocket change then pissing it all up against a wall anyway. A lifetime ago he had been a successful, happily married, urban professional with a glittering career in a booming industry. He fully accepted that to look at him now, it would take a good stretch of the imagination to believe that less than a year ago it had all been..., *how would I put it*, he thought bitterly. *Yes, I've got it..., all so different...*! Healthy, fit and clean living, his life had been a cavalcade of rich and positive experiences revolving around family, friends, travel and the arts. But then the board got tipped...

He didn't exactly kick it over himself, he reasoned with himself for the millionth time. But he might have been able to catch hold of it, if only he had been a bit quicker off the mark.

Of course, he didn't really need anyone else to remind him of the cruel fact that this had not been the first time his failure to react correctly had cost lives. The lives of those dearest to him. So what else was there to do but waste another weekend attempting to blot out the pain with the assistance of his good friend Mr J Daniel.

He was soon on Post St and two blocks from home. Here long lines of Thai whores stood as if waiting for transportation to some garish lookalike competition. When he first arrived in San Francisco he was amazed at the vast number of these girls, so tall and skinny. It took him longer to notice the size of their hands and the inches of powder concealment applied to face and neck. They looked at him first expectantly from a distance and then with mock pity as he tripped up the steps to the door of his apartment block. Things are never what they seem.

Story of my life, thought Ridge darkly.

Huw shook his head sagely as Ridge staggered in to the sparsely furnished room and flopped artlessly on to a large bean bag.

'What the hell happened to you, Walker? Get into a turf war with the lady-boys out there did you now?'

'Oh you know Huw, hard day at the office and all that shit.'

13

He pulled out the bourbon with a flourish and the Welshman's tired looking face brightened up considerably.

'This'll be your second one of these today by the state of you I'll bet', the older man said somewhat more kindly.

'Huw, as far as the last 24 hours go, your guess is as good as mine, mate.
I swear to God even my pals on the street were givin' me a body-swerve today.'

Ridge jumped up quickly and headed for the far corner of the large room, which doubled as the 'kitchen'. He needed a knife to take off the plastic optic so as not to offend his friend, whose far from innocent habits didn't stretch to stealing. Eventually he prised the bugger off, grabbed a couple of mugs and a bottle of Coke and sat cross-legged opposite Huw. The bourbon bottle was placed strategically between them, centre stage as it were.

Just then the door burst open and immediately they could hear the strident tones of Sally from way down the hallway, Jamie coming in first with an apologetic shrug towards the lads. Obviously in the throes of one of their trademark rows, neither one of the seated men attempted to make eye contact with the warring factions. Sally marched straight through to 'their room' with an only a 'just for a bloody change' directed towards Ridge and his newly liberated plunder.

The couple had recently arrived from England, just north of Watford to be precise, and they were on the last dregs of their savings. That watershed stage had just been reached as they had to decide if they really wanted to stay in the place and work. Or just call it a holiday and go home. Unfortunately it was proving to be a difficult time for them as Jamie was up for staying, had a good bar job and couldn't understand why his girlfriend hated it so much. He was an easygoing lad whose prospects in the UK hadn't been startling whereas Sally was going to be a teacher and had no intentions of taking a menial 'McJob'.

Although there was only a little natural light in the apartment, the sky was beginning to darken and a warm glow permeated the now peaceful room. Night came quickly here and the two men seemed to settle deeper into the cushions, each one comfortable with the prospect of a relaxed slide into oblivion. Huw had by this stage produced an immaculate joint which he slowly lit with all the practiced control of an old craftsman. Ridge sat quietly and looked at him, nodding on occasion for the passing of the bottle or ashtray, but silent above that.

At first meeting, Huw had seemed a switched on kind of guy, heavily involved with recycling in the city and remarkably sane despite the drugs. Of a rangy build, he had the striking fair hair and blue eyes which were standard features for the Californian lifestyle although he was not normally known for athletic pursuits. But he loved to talk about his native Wales and seemed to display a real and deep knowledge of the country and its history coupled with a genuine sense of national pride although he had actually left over twenty years ago.

Initially, Ridge had been unaware of that and had assumed he was a relative newcomer like himself. He had mistaken his fevered excitement for this city for the passion of the new and exciting and it was only after seeing Huw in his come-down modes that he realised that most of his energy was coming from amphetamines, especially speed.

Ridge had inadvertently walked in suddenly on Huw, fairly soon after starting to room with him and had apparently disturbed him scribbling down something private. After Huw had scrunched up the paper quickly and tossed it into a corner, Ridge had felt it would have been too prying to say anything and so quickly forgot the incident. However after a series of similar episodes, often early in the morning as Ridge was awaking, he once sleepily asked him, any prior inhibitions still in slumber, what he was doing.

'Oh! I'm just writing a quick note to my love, Mary, back home.
Making some final arrangements for her to come out here, see.
We'll probably get a place together.'

That had been several weeks ago and neither of them had broached the subject since then. Ridge had caught Huw again and again however and had even begun to recognise the type of paper Huw used. He would often see the same screwed up balls of pale blue lightweight airmail paper thrown into the garbage bag.

Although he was extremely curious, Ridge would never have gone as far as to have opened out one of these sheets of paper but he had given the matter some thought. Sitting relaxed now and emboldened by the bourbon, he decided to go for it.

'So tell me all about this Welsh lassie then Huw, and when will I have to start bunking up with Sal and Jamie?'

Huw opened his mouth quickly as if to say something but turned his head to one side instead. When he looked at Ridge a moment later, his eyes had become filled with tears and his gaunt face flushed scarlet with emotion

'Oh I don't think you'll have to worry them about that just now.
To be honest, I think I've missed the boat on that one anyway.'

He then poured himself a large drink and told Ridge the whole story of himself and Mary and how he had landed up, middle aged, sitting in a dingy San Francisco apartment drinking himself to death with a mad Jock. Although much of the tale was fairly classical in content and Ridge had assumed something along similar lines, he was still disturbed by the waste of it all. Huw and Mary had been a typical young Swansea couple and they had enjoyed a carefree existence until Mary announced with an illicit gleam in her eyes that she was with child. Huw

17

talked quickly, unburdening himself of an anguish which had so obviously tormented him for half a lifetime. Ridge just listened patiently, saying little in return, busying himself with the provision of a constant stream of skinny joints and the odd line of Huw's speed.

He still didn't fully understand why he left, Huw said candidly, but he knows a part of it and it doesn't make things any easier. He had left Wales the very same night and had gone straight to London. Whilst living there he had heard through friends that Mary had lost the child early on and he had made up his mind to try and contact her and see whether she would have him back. Huw had matured quickly in the few months he had been away. He had poured out his feelings and regrets into several long letters but had stupidly kept them all, thinking always that he could word them a bit better and that maybe he might just appear on her doorstep instead and plead his case in person.

It was at this point that the miserable Huw found out that he was too late. The agonising loss of her child together with the bewildering desertion of her lover had driven Mary over the edge. With no one to turn to for help, she had taken her own life and had hopefully found merciful respite for her tortured soul at the end of a constricting rope overhanging a gloomy disused pit shaft.

Overcome with grief and poisoned by his own iniquity, Huw fled the UK and spent many years mindlessly moving from one place to the next, before ending up here, in San Francisco, with the other lost souls. Ridge wept silently as Huw confessed openly to his nightly ritual of writing the same letter to Mary over and over again and his subsequent addiction to the amphetamine drugs that helped him to stay awake. He spoke of the sporadic and fitful slumber he might have in the last few hours before daybreak in which they would be together again and then the crashing wave of self-condemnation that would engulf him as he awoke.

After a long period of silence, Ridge began to shake uncontrollably and the other man, exhausted now by his traumatic revelations, was convinced the boy was taking some kind of panic attack. He crawled over to hold him tightly in his arms. Huw had been taken aback by the intensity of Ridge's distress, which he had naturally assumed to have been powerful feelings of empathy.

He sat back down as now Ridge himself began to speak, in a torrent of mixed up words, as much to himself, as to Huw. It was now Huw's turn to sit speechless as Ridge avowed that he too was culpable in the death of the only woman he had ever loved. Much later, as the smoke filled room slowly became rent with the first shards of the light of a new day, the two men sat together in a newly forged brotherhood of wretched sorrow.

Chapter Two – The Killing Moon

Orla leant against the guard rail, revelling in the sea spray whipping lightly across her face as the bow of the ferry pitched and tossed in the rough swell of the spring afternoon. The waning sunshine still glinted warmly off her tousled thatch of flaming red hair and she looked up in wonder at the unsullied radiance of the full moon gradually asserting dominion over the pale sapphire sky. She had crossed this water many times in the past but never before had so much been at stake and her heart pounded as she scanned the horizon for the approaching Scottish coastline.

The very first time, her parents had been with her and they had all been very nervous. Her father still couldn't understand why Orla had passed up a perfectly good place at Trinity College, Dublin to come over to 'this godforsaken land' as he had put it. He had even tried to change her mind as the ferry began tying up at Cairnryan.

There was no one to help counsel her today. Not a single person on this earth who could advise what she should do next. That was a big part of the problem she realised, wincing slightly as she began to make out land ahead. Family was a definite no-no. For sure! She had good friends, trustworthy and true but if she spoke about all this to them she would be putting their lives at risk as well as her own. She was contagious, she knew it. *Worse than bleedin' swine flu*, she thought bitterly. The only person she had tried to tell some of it to was Richard. *That went well...not!*

He had been the best thing about Scotland. He had made her supremely happy that she had undertaken that first voyage. Orla chewed the inside of her mouth nervously as she remembered all the good times they had had. But now, they had lost their way. She accepted that somehow she had allowed circumstances and events to reshape her life into something alien and cold. Although she knew she still loved him and hoped he felt the same, she was also aware that love would probably have to take a back seat in all this. It was bigger than the two of them. Unless they could work things out today there might not be a 'two of them' ever again.

The throb of the engines changed register and Orla knew that she would soon be back on land. She shook away her negative thoughts and tried to focus on the present situation. Despite the anxiety, she grinned cheekily as she thought, 'sure, I'm only going to meet me husband for a cup of tea!'

As Richard drove slowly into the little seaside town he realised with annoyance that he was far too early. He had many happy childhood memories of this place however and so he decided to take a wander about. Making sure the car was securely locked and wishing he had brought a coat, he left the breezy promenade and headed for the centre of town. The main street had changed considerably since his last visit and he struggled to find any recognizable features.

Perhaps he had been too young to remember, but the hideous amusement arcade, which had swallowed half the street, certainly seemed new to him and he began to be concerned that their hallowed meeting place had itself become a victim to progress.

Eventually, having found his bearings, he came upon the Pantry, the old cafe, its cream and sea-green painted frontage bleached by the elements making it somewhat incongruous next to a flamingo pink DVD and game rental shop. As he stood staring in the café window, a flood of warm, dream-like images took Richard back to the holidays he and his brother had spent here visiting his grandparents. Suddenly, gripped by self-doubt, he wondered if he was about to do the right thing. He pulled himself back into the present and quickly looked round the corner for the old narrow wynd that would take him, if he remembered correctly, back to his car.

An hour later he was to be found sitting in the Pantry, fiddling nervously with the salt and pepper and looking furtively up at the door every time someone walked past the window. He tried to console himself that this was, after all, his own idea. He was here to meet his wife of two years to see if there was a relationship worth saving. It was a month since she had left him and gone home to Ireland and despite everything he had missed her like crazy.

He glanced over to see an elderly man pour tea into his wife's cup and then silently add milk and sugar. He then picked up his newspaper again with one hand and reached down automatically to scratch his old Labrador dog with the other. Tears welled up in Richard's pale sea blue eyes as he thought bitterly, 'Will we ever have that level of contentment and togetherness, distilled over the years shared? How can we ever have a normal life after the things she's done?'

He wished she had just been unfaithful. That would have been easy. You can pick up dozens of magazines for advice on cheating partners; you can see a hundred counsellors who'd be happy to talk it through. You can watch it daily on Jeremy Kyle. Richard's problem was a little more delicate than that. He had no grounds to suspect his wife of infidelity but he *did* have a strong suspicion that she was involved in something more explosive than that, literally.

When they first met, at college, he was completely smitten by her feisty Irish charm and her refreshingly irreverent outlook on life. Orla had openly mocked his closed Presbyterian values whilst stealing his way too serious heart and transforming it into one drunken with love for her. She had opened up a whole new world to him, a world of literature, travel and politics and she would tease him often that until she had come along, he'd been '*a bit of a Jim Corr.*' Eventually he found out from some Belfast students he knew, that it had been a common expression over there for someone who was maybe a loner, or who just wasn't cool, the guy who'd find himself standing on his own at a party. This was simply down to the fact that at that time, Jim Corr had been an ordinary kind of a bloke who just happened to have been in a superstar band comprising of himself and his three identical looking, totally drop dead gorgeous sisters. Ask 99% of the male population of the planet at the height of the Corrs' fame and they would have said Jim *who*? He just couldn't win. Richard was crestfallen though, as he had secretly hoped it was somehow a play on '*phwoerr!*'

They spent itinerant summer holidays hitching around Europe or over in Ireland putting the world to rights over a few beers and he had read voraciously the kind of books that would not have been found in his parent's home. Orla introduced him to the finest works of Irish prose and had alleviated the concerns of his father by presenting him with a signed copy of *Catching Trout* by Rivers Carew. She had given Richard a fine birthday present of the works of Scots poet Tom Leonard and his repayment was to reduce her to a hysterical puddle on the carpet as she listened for the first time to a live rendition in the authentic patois. As he sat there morosely, he remembered one of her favourites;

> '*nuthnlik disperr*
> *keepsyi gawn*
> *a hawf boatl*
> *ur behtr stull*
> *a fuhll wan*'.

He was no stranger to despair now that was true, he thought sadly and then he gave himself a shake. He was here to make things right, to get the old Orla back again. He tried to focus on happier memories.

Orla had taken him to the Guggenheim in Bilbao and then after hitch-hiking through the grandeur of the Pyrenees, together they had watched the running of the bulls in Pamplona. They had spent gentle, romantic, smoky weekends in Amsterdam and wild chemical nights in the neon bright full-on madness of Berlin. Richard had drunk himself sober at the Rose of Tralee festival in County Kerry and for Orla he had suffered the kissing of the Blarney Stone. After graduation, it seemed a natural progression to marry and settle down.

As was tradition, he had told her he and the men from his side would wear the kilt tartan of his clan and this had caused a right furore! Apparently a distant cousin of Orla's had once married an ill-bred broth of a boy from Greenock. The Irish side had been nervous about the whole thing and had over compensated by making sure it would be a wedding that no-one would forget.

Orla admitted that she had only been a young teenager at the time but remembered the occasion as feeling expensive and tasteless. It was only evident a couple of months after that there had been a delicate timing issue at stake but it would have been hard to predict this as the bride had been even heavier than her lardy beau. Orla had poetically described the bride in her diary entry that night as looking like a 'pregnant sow.' This proved to be remarkably prescient.

The actual ceremony was fine apparently but it was during the wedding photographs that it all kicked off. The gallus groom had worn the kilt and unbeknownst to the Irish contingent had elected to 'go commando'. The entire bridal party had been drinking heavily since before the ceremony and they were just warming up for the speeches and some serious liver damage. The photographer had instructed the groom to sit gently on the ample lap of his new spouse. In his inebriation, the gauche fellow slid off her chubby thigh leaving an indelible brown skid mark six inches along her white designer dress. That was it. Game on! Hair-trigger emotions already provoked by a surfeit of cheap cava, spilled over into a violent fracas. Then the men also became involved, several of whom spent a hungover night in Greenock prison.

Thankfully Richard had assuaged the doubts of Orla's parents and their beautiful Dublin wedding went off without any problems. After honeymooning in Morocco they had returned to their new flat on the Southside and life had seemed perfect. It was only then that he started to feel something was going on and now, looking back, Richard could see that he had perhaps been a little naïve.

In the months leading up to the grand event, Orla had begun travelling back and forth to Ireland every other weekend and at first Richard took it to be wedding preparations and then after the wedding he put it down to homesickness until he found out that she was rarely seeing her folks. He didn't think twice about the way he seemed to be singled out for searches every time he travelled back over himself. Then, after recounting to her strange older brother Colm, how an over zealous Garda officer had even forced Richard to open wrapped Christmas presents, Colm helped him compose a salvo to the authorities to complain. The resulting letter of apology ensured that Richard sailed through every checkpoint or airport baggage check no matter how many parcels Colm gave him for long lost pals over the water. The two of them had become a team and Colm had even taken him away camping on a fishing weekend. The fish didn't bite however and Richard had got toothache. He liked the calm methodical way the man went about things and he was totally at home in the outdoors which suited Richard who missed his own brother greatly. Although he didn't see Colm often as he worked away a lot, he did enjoy hanging out with him when he could. He had thought to carefully explore his worries concerning Orla when he next bumped into him but he realised it was already eighteen months since they had last met.

The surprisingly strong anti-Republican stance taken by the newly independent Scottish Government after the continual breakdown of the 'peace process' had clearly rankled with Orla and Richard found himself increasingly questioning her motives whilst privately wrestling with doubts about his own judgment.

It was the 6 am visit by the Special Branch that finally brought things to a head. Both he and Orla had been taken away separately for interrogation and after many hours were finally released. Whilst grudgingly conceding that Richard might be innocent of any actual criminal actions, the police did not spare him any details as to what they thought his darling wife and her family were up to.

The next time he saw Orla was the following day when he confronted her over the police allegations and his own increasingly strong fears. She had in turn accused him of emotional cowardice for so readily siding with the police but after many tears and painful recriminations, she eventually admitted 'flirting' with some of the ideals of the Irish republican movement.

Richard looked around the small tearoom nervously, his scarlet cheeks betraying his emotions as he remembered his overwhelming relief when Orla had told him that she hadn't personally committed any serious crimes, although she knew many who had. Unfortunately his subsequent inglorious readiness to overlook whatever she had done in order to 'clear the decks' and start afresh had only added fuel to the fire. Orla didn't look at it like that at all and the purpose of this meeting was to try and find out whether their common future was as bleak as it seemed or not.

As he sat shuffling his feet nervously, giving a good impression of someone on a first date, the waitress approached him yet again and asked impatiently whether he would maybe order some food after all this time. Just then, the bell above the door jangled discordantly and the woman laughed nervously as he jumped out of his skin.

Orla breezed in through the door, her radiant eyes directed straight at him. Richard stood clumsily, momentarily rendered dumb by the power of her beauty and they embraced stiffly. He noticed as they sat down that Orla had no luggage with her and she couldn't help but see the look on his face.

'I'm after leaving my bags at the terminal for now.
Don't know if I'll be needin' them, do I now?' She said defiantly, 'That depends on you.'

The old waitress ambled up and took their order. She winked at Orla and proceeded to tease Richard with a professional familiarity.

'She's worth waiting for eh?
Now why don't you be like her and have a wee scone or something, you'll fade away there!'

And so to all the world they looked like another young couple spending a perfectly pleasant hour together drinking tea, the strikingly tall, tanned woman contrasting markedly with the pale boy with the intense eyes. Orla had evidently thrived over the last few weeks, Richard noticed sadly.

'You're looking well, despite everything, I mean...'

He was not able, or willing, to hide the rancour in his voice. Orla's eyes shone with an evangelical zeal as she laughed back at him, trying desperately to keep the conversation as upbeat as she could.

'Sure, I'm really grand, so I am, 'cept missin' *you* of course.
But you know how it is.

When you're actually doing something
you feel is important, something that you
have a *passion* for, something that makes
a difference, then it fair fires up the
blood, so it does!'

'I have a passion too, Orla…and I'm
looking right at it!
But I don't suppose that's enough for you
anymore?'

'It's not just about us, my love!
I HAVE TO DO THIS! IT'S NOT A
CASE OF WANT TO OR DON'T
WANT TO!
Jeez, I wish I could make you
understand!'

'Tell me then!' Richard struggled to keep
his voice in check.

'It's like when we first met…, how you
always said that it was me who seemed
to see the bigger picture.
What was it you said…, it was like in the
song. I saw *the whole of the moon.*
I used to rip it outta you 'cos you didn't
have a bleedin' clue what was going on
outside your precious Scotland!'

Richard nodded in acquiescence,
blushing slightly. He reached across the table
and stroked the back of her hand gently.

'OK, fair enough. I admit I wasn't as
worldly as you back then.

I've changed a lot.
But so have you…
There's still no way you'd get me mixed
up with a bunch of cretins like the IRA!'

Orla pulled her hand away, eyes blazing!

'You don't have a bleedin' clue what
you're on about!
Is that what you think of me then?
A cretin? Do you…'

'No. Of course I don't! But that's what I
just cannae get into my skull!
WHY?'

'It's easy for you! Nothing ever impinged
on your cosy wee island life, now did it?
Oh! I'm sorry! I never…'

'Just Gav! That's all!'

Richard had slammed his hand hard on
the table and the waitress glared at him furiously
as the other customers whispered and tutted to
themselves.

'You know I didn't mean that, Richard!
I meant the decades of poverty,
repression and resentment that we all had
to live with.
It ground you down, so it did, you
couldn't escape from it. After a while, it
gets to the point where you just can't
stand passively on the side lines.
Believe this when I say it, Richard.

31

I don't have any choice now, in any of this, neither I do.
I have to see it through.
But if you still love me, as I love you, then please trust me and try to understand what I am doing. Come on over for a few weeks and maybe you can come to terms with what we're doing over there.'

Richard could feel a deepening sense of unreality closing in around him, like he was watching himself on film and was unable to influence what was happening.

It was late afternoon now and the tearoom was deserted. It must have been obvious for a while now that the young couple were not exactly having a dream date and Richard had scared off several customers with his wild eyes glaring around the room as he struggled to come to terms with what Orla was saying. He was also having difficulty getting her to keep her voice down and, as usual when people are trying too hard to keep other people quiet, he was making things even worse. He had to ask her the question that boiled painfully deep in his stomach. The question he knew he wouldn't like the answer to.

'I'm sorry Orla.
I am not coming over for a 'terrorist break'. Why won't you stay here instead? If you won't stay, what are you going to do after this?'

He saw her big green eyes flicker for a moment before they lit up with a fierce pride.

'If you're saying no to me then I'm straight back on the boat, so I am.
I love you Richard Walker and I want you to remember me sayin' it.
You've broken me heart and that's the truth.
What am I going to do now?
I'll carry on and finish with what I have to do and that will be the end of it.
I hoped you would be there for me then but if you're too weak to handle me then it looks like goodbye, my love.
And you won't be strong enough for this, neither you won't...'

Richard felt the life blood drain out of him as he sat and listened to the woman he once loved, still loved, tell him how she and her friends were going to personally blow up the 'turncoat' Scottish Parliament whilst in full session. His head spinning, he stood up and made for the door, the acrid taste of bile rising up his throat with every step.

Sitting here now, in a San Francisco coffee shop, he was still deeply ashamed at the way he had run away from the situation and his guilt-ravaged brain ached with the realization that he had failed not just Orla but also himself. His feelings of culpability over what had happened following his encounter in the tearoom permeated every atom of his worthless being and he wanted to scream out 'It was me! I did it!'

He had spent the last few months here, trying to run away from himself, with drink and drugs his wayward companions. Somehow, last night with Huw, he had reached his lowest point and yet he had also cleansed his soul in some small way that gave him a glimmer of hope for a future. It was time to sort out in his head what had happened and try to draw a line under it. His face was a blank as his mind travelled back across the ocean and he completely missed the warm smile of the young woman who handed him a fresh tall glass of latte.

His first reaction upon leaving the seaside tearoom had been to return to the bosom of his family back over on the small island of Sorsay, one of the many islands comprising the Inner Hebrides, in his case not far from Mull and a short boat ride from Oban. His family had not been overly demonstrative with each other since his older brother's death. Like many Scots males he had never talked with his parents much about his emotions, however he felt loved and comfortable there for a while.

He had taken extended leave from his job over in Glasgow and such was his standing in the small software company that he was under no pressure to return immediately. He had helped set up the business, 'OK Computer' and after designing too many opinion survey websites he had become a leading light in the new wave of 'augmented reality' gaming platforms.

Most days were spent sitting down at the busy little harbour, watching the clamorous gulls circling over the rusty fishing boats as they came alongside the pier. He spent hours with his dad, silently fishing from their wee dinghy, *Am Mol*, with maybe the odd word passed concerning the quality of the bait or the likelihood of rain. His mother, sensing the deep-seated distress in her son's heart, tried to cheer him up in her own ways, showing him endless black and white photographs of family gatherings and holidays. She teased him about his early speech impediment when he struggled with even his own name and called himself Ridge, a pet name that would stay with him through most of his school days. A college girlfriend had once remarked on the appropriateness of this sobriquet, given his naturally lofty aloofness and his tendency to live life on the edge, even in those innocent days.

Richard had been edgy though and gladly took up the offer of a weekend jaunt over to Holland from an old pal working in London. He took the early train down to Euston station and suddenly overcome with the unfamiliar tumult of the city, he took refuge in the large and anonymous station bar.

Looking back now, he winced as he remembered feeling a bit down at that point and how he was delaying the call to his friend while he considered whether or not to just go back up to Scotland. *If I could only go back to that point now*, he thought bitterly. Sitting up at the chrome and plastic bar, his eyes were drawn to a TV screen just above his head. Although silent, he could tell the lunchtime news was just about to start. As Richard was just about to turn his eyes elsewhere, his world was abruptly and catastrophically substituted for the alternate universe he now inhabited.

It seemed to happen almost in slow motion and he felt as if there were hundreds of huge flashbulbs going off right in his face as he watched grainy footage of a wrecked van, blown apart, in the murky light of dawn, alongside surreal photos of what looked like some 1970's Baader-Meinhof terrorists.

Only…, one of the two faces was Orla.

Richard heard himself shout, almost as if underwater,

'Turn…the…fucking…volume… up…! NOW…! '

The barman took one look at Richard and complied. The whole bar went quiet as the newscaster told how two alleged Real IRA terrorists had blown themselves up with their own bomb in an empty car park alongside the newly independent Scots Parliament building in Edinburgh.

Richard was in Amsterdam within two hours and in New York by the following morning, his vomit streaked clothing ensuring him an undisturbed flight.

'Are you OK my friend…? Hello ?'

The waitress touched his shoulder and he jumped back into real time with a start. 'Is everything OK with you, can I get you another coffee or something?' She spoke softly to him while he just stared at her plaintively, her huge brown eyes wrapping him up in a soft warm envelope of safety. 'No, I … I mean, yes! I'll have another coffee…, thanks' he stuttered. She glanced at him sideways as she walked away 'OK, no problem, this one's on the house,' a look of concern crossing her face.

As he watched her preparing his latte, he pulled himself upright and smiled ruefully. 'I'm still here', he thought, 'it's in the past now…, all that, just history…' It was true in a sense. His worst fears had been realised, it *was* Orla who had been killed. The other bomber, a man, could not be identified. Blown to smithereens, they were struggling even with his dental records. Orla always did have great teeth, and Colm too. He had wondered at first if her brother had been the other guy. The force of the explosion had scattered body parts and debris over a wide area. Blood and brain fragments were even found on the very steps of the Parliament. Her leather jacket, however, was one of her most favourite items of clothing and it must have been folded up in their van as it apparently had been found relatively undamaged with her purse and wristwatch in it.

He had stopped reading about it after a couple of days but had sent his folks a postcard, via his friend in London, to say he was all right. He had given them no forwarding address though. There was little point sending them a text as there was no reception on Sorsay and so consequently his folks rarely ever switched their mobiles on. He had also dumped his beloved Blackberry in a bin at Schipol before embarking for New York. He didn't remember why he did that although it had seemed a good idea at the time.

The midday sun streamed across the tiled floor of the coffee bar as the girl came over with his drink. The lunchtime suits were just starting to filter in and Ridge smiled broadly and said, 'Cheers, thanks, tell you what, give me a piece of that pie there as well, but I'm paying for it, mind!'

Chapter Three – Dancing in the Rain

The cool evening air brushed the restless pages of his paper as Ridge sat near the elegant doorway of '*Le Jardin*'. He had read the San Francisco Chronicle from front to back and had found himself laughing aloud at some of the weirdness of contemporary American life. It was a weirdness that he could relate to though and the very fact that he was finding amusement in the great scheme of things was testament to his dramatic recovery, a fact that he was acutely aware of.

Most of this born-again bonhomie was the product of an unexpected and refreshingly easy development in his life. It was also the reason why he had a perpetual smug bastard grin all over his face. He was beginning to feel edgy though, and glanced down again at his watch. *Only a few minutes more,* he thought to himself, then looked up suddenly to see an attractive dark-haired girl bound out from behind the bar and race over towards him and he leapt up with open arms, awkwardly embracing the whirlwind that was Juanita.

They stumbled backward laughing and Ridge said, 'Let's get out of here before I get you sacked!' Gripping each other tightly, they ran for the BART. In what seemed like moments later he was chasing Juanita up four flights of stairs trying to smack her pert little bum without dropping the bottle of Napa Valley wine tucked under his arm.

It had been a few weeks since they had got together after he had jumped to help her pick up a tray load of plates which had cascaded spectacularly onto the tiled floor of *Le Jardin*. The quietly spoken girl had touched a chord with Ridge. Her kindness to him over many visits had not gone unnoticed and in truth, he had welcomed the opportunity to repay her. They had got talking and after Juanita had laughed at his plate stacking skills he had swallowed hard and asked her out.

As they tumbled into bed, Juanita tugged at his clothes urgently and he felt, with wonder again, her taut brown body writhe beneath him, her slim arms and legs far stronger than his. She wrestled him onto his back and Ridge gasped as she took him inside her and pushed down hard against him. He had been nervous initially of proceeding too fast with Juanita, his largely false notions of her Mexican-Catholic, 'look-but-don't-touch' attitude combined with his own feelings of first time jitters. So, instead, he had taken her sightseeing. They were both new to San Francisco and the raw energy of their mutual attraction fuelled a hectic marathon any holiday-maker would have been proud of.

It was Juanita who had taken the initiative in the end. She had been initially impressed with his polite manners towards her and his comfortingly laid back attitude towards getting to first base. Ridge had seemed to understand that she needed time to get to know him but she had soon found herself melting under the gentle warmth of his tender care. But a girl couldn't wait for ever! He was hot, she was hot and so on a sun baked afternoon, half way up Mount Tamalpais, she grabbed him by the crotch and pulled him behind a tree and onto her.

She smiled broadly as she remembered Ridge scrambling like a clumsy teenager to get a footing in the shallow sea of dust and pine needles before he lifted her up and against the rough bark of the tree. Heading back down much later, they had met a strange assortment of older far-out types and earnest yuppies returning from some kind of a 'hug a tree' day out.

'Ah'm telling you man,' one of them was saying as they walked off the hill, 'You ain't lived until you've got real close to them trees'. Ridge bit his lip hard and nodded mischievously as Juanita stared furiously at him, her eyes wide with horror at what he might say. Tears rolling down his face, he held out until they were safely out of earshot before erupting with laughter. As she tried half-heartedly to grab him, Ridge darted and swerved around Juanita giving her mocking peace signs and twirling her panties around on his little finger at he same time. They had both felt on top of the world.

Ridge looked down at the sleeping head rising and falling with his chest. It had been a long time since he'd had any meaningful physical contact with a woman and it felt good. *It almost feels too good*, he thought. He tried not to think about what had happened in Scotland but it was still there, gnawing away at him, reminding him that things weren't always as they seemed and that he'd thought he was so happy in the past and look how *that* had turned out.

'In that case', he thought sleepily, 'let's just take things one day at a time and have as much fun as possible'. He stretched his right arm out of their mattress bed to pick up the wine bottle, hardly touched, and moving slowly so as not to wake Juanita, took a long drink at the bottle. The dry wine caught his throat and he struggled to stifle a cough, without success. Coughing deeply like only a Scotsman can, he sat up a little, letting Juanita's head slip gently onto the bed and reached for the crumpled pack of Marlboros on the floor. She turned grumpily away from him, still sleeping and curled into a foetal position.

He had definitely cut down on his drinking excesses since meeting Juanita; in fact he had lost his taste for all that kind of stuff completely. 'Except maybe the cigs', he had to correct himself, as he exhaled deeply across the small room.

Sitting back contentedly smoking, Ridge gazed down with fascination at the sleeping woman. He drank in every feature of her face, her perfect skin and high chiselled cheekbones giving her the look of an exotic priestess. She was his own Amazonian princess he thought absentmindedly. Her left shoulder had a vivid white scar which exhibited a singular lack of surgical skills, looking as it did, as if it had been crudely drawn on her umber skin by a five year old boy with a Frankenstein fixation. Juanita told him she had recently been involved in a car accident in which someone's driving ability had been on a par with the subsequent medical aplomb.

Stubbing out his cigarette and returning his gaze he noticed her high forehead had become creased with lines and pricked with tiny beads of sweat. Her tiny right hand had balled up so tight her flesh looked white and bloodless. He let her writhe silently for no more than a few seconds before gently stroking her face and speaking softly to waken her. Juanita jumped like a startled animal; her contorted face turned to him and, just for an instant only, her dark eyes blazed with an unrecognizable fury to be replaced with a look of blank desolation. In seconds, she recovered and her eyes shone out at him warmly as if she was seeing him again after a long, long time away.

Ridge tried to make light of the matter and quickly proffered warm wine and even warmer passion in an easy double-act that passed several hours. Interspersed with their strenuous bouts of lovemaking, in the normally quiet moments between dissipated lovers, Juanita dreamily played with the sparse hairs on Ridge's white chest while he entertained her with stories he had read in the newspaper that afternoon. Her command of written English was not that good and so Ridge had some leeway as to the levels of artistic licence he could employ in his renditions.

'You know the 'New Meat', on Jones? *You know*…the one that really freaks you out, round the corner, 'The New Meat Campus Theater' to give it its proper name!'

Juanita pulled a face and Ridge knew she had remembered it. She had a big problem with the vivid, poster portrayal of explicit gay sex that assailed pedestrians unfortunate enough to have to walk past the 'One-stop shop for gay live strip 'n' porn video' venue on a daily basis. It wasn't the gay sex part that upset her, she would say to

Ridge when they talked about some of the more unseemly first impressions they had had on arrival in the city; it was the cold-hearted brutishness of the whole sex industry that upset her.

'Apparently, there's been loads of homeless people sleeping in that big alcove at the front, the bit with all the subtle 'art work' that you like so much. The owners were getting pissed off at these people scaring off the classy clientele in the early part of the day and they had tried everything to get rid of them, bar extreme violence.
What worked in the end was a speaker that played music to them every night, not angry rap music, not even loud music, just Mozart! Plain and simple.
So much for *Rock me Amadeus*!'

Ridge then spent a while trying to persuade Juanita to join him and Huw on an 'ecological project' he had allegedly read about in the paper earlier. In truth he had only made up his story as they lay there but he had her going for a good while anyway.

'It's true! Seal Rock used to be a haven for sea lions and seals. Now they're all down by Pier 39.' He tested the muddied waters carefully. 'Is that down where we got lost last week, near the docks?' Juanita asked sleepily.

'That's right, when we tried walking back from the Embarcadero. Anyway, its proper name is 'Seal Rock' but most folk call it 'Shit Rock' now 'cos it's pure white with sea bird droppings and there hasn't been a seal or a sea lion seen there for years. There's a hotel on the headland called the Seal Rock Inn and the guy who owns it doesn't really fancy the name change option and so has asked Huw to clean up the rock and he'll help pay for it. There's a petition here in the paper to get enough signatures to persuade City Hall to cough up some cash as well. Let me grab a pen and we'll do it now.'

'Smart idea, dumb-head! Two illegals, making it easy for them! Just sign here now..., then pack your damn bags, straight to *La Migra*'!

Juanita gave him a pitying look and thudded her head back onto the pillow.

Ridge hadn't completely forgotten that he had overstayed his tourist visa. It just hadn't seemed important before, so many people he knew were in the same boat and it wasn't a problem for them. Of course he knew some who had bought a marriage with someone to help get a Green card but for most it wasn't even worth going to that much hassle. But, as Juanita had pointed out wearily, his cool European pals all had one thing in common – they were white.

It was barely dawn when she woke, cold and stiff after such a short sleep. Dressing quietly, she left the apartment and walked quickly through the chilly morning air. Tired and somewhat crotch-sore after their strenuous night together, she was glad to see an approaching cab.

It was unusual for her to rise so early, Ridge had worriedly thought, several hours later. Since they had got it together, it was rare for either of them to make an appearance before lunchtime and Juanita didn't start at the coffee bar until 2pm. He realised of course that he had been a tad uncool in his WASP outlook and hoped he had not offended Juanita. It also hit him how little he knew about her and how much he had just assumed.

He was still in a melancholy mood a few hours later when he bumped into his pal Thad and meekly let himself be taken to one of his former haunts much to the delight of his friend. As he held open the door to the 'Flesh Exchange', the tall dark haired man had the opportunity to look closely at Ridge's face as he brushed past and he couldn't help seeing the old pain in those pale eyes.

'Thad! Don't fuckin' look at me like that OK! You know I hate it when you give me that 'deep down into my soul' look.'

'You don't wanna know what I see boy, you don't *wanna* know', his friend said coyly.

They found a seat easily, as every other customer preferred to stand. In fact there were only four small tables in the whole bar. The 'Flesh Exchange' was a gay bar comprising a large square room with minimal décor apart from a double layer of plasma screens encircling the top quarter of the each wall. The clientele, all men, all standing completely still, took up every available square foot of floor space. No one was speaking and they all looked up at the screens which showed an eclectic mix of music and 'art' DVD's to the accompaniment of a thumping techno sound system.

When Ridge had first come here he had not noticed what was really going on until Thad had pointed it out and from then on, he was entranced. Ridge had then similarly educated Juanita on her one and only visit. If you looked very carefully at the throng of mostly young guys, they were only half-looking at the screens and every so often one of them would approach another and after the very briefest of communication they would abruptly leave the bar together.

It was, in effect, a completely efficient pick-up joint, where all parties knew the rules of engagement and there were no ambiguities. Juanita's only comment had been that she had never seen so many good-looking men in one place.

Thad was handsome and he knew it. He was openly gay but did not look like any of the other slim shorthaired guys in this room. Tall at over 6'3, he had a long mane of jet-black hair and unfeasibly broad shoulders. A genetic product of at least three continents, he appeared to emanate the relaxed self-assurance of a man who could have anyone he wanted, male or female. He was, as he liked to describe himself, a *'sexual Bedouin'*, prodigious in his sexual appetite and he made no bones about it. Ridge could never be sure whether he was making up stories or not but if so, he fell for them every time.

One thing they had in common was their shared musical obsession with David Bowie and Iggy Pop. Neither had ever seen Bowie live and Ridge had only seen Iggy once in Scotland but Thad had been to see him dozens of times in the US. But Ridge reckoned there was no-one on the planet who could match his own knowledge of Bowie songs and lyrics and his big friend had been in awe after vainly trying to catch him out on several occasions.

Thad had confessed that his life had been changed by listening to Bowie and that he had long held a secret desire to emulate an American performance artist, Chris Burden, who had been the basis of a much vaunted Bowie song, 'Joe the Lion' from the 1977 'Heroes' album. The two of them had gripped each other like star-struck kids as Ridge, in turn, told Thad how he had actually met and worked with the guy back in Scotland of all the unlikely places. Between them they became the Chris Burden fan-club.

The guy had taken part in some pretty controversial 'performance art pieces,' predominantly in the early seventies, including one where he allowed himself to be shot in the arm. The particular incident which had gripped Thad's imagination and which had become such an integral part of 'Joe the Lion', had been a 1974 performance where Burden had had himself nailed onto the back of a Volkswagen Beetle and driven out of a garage.

Thad had drooled in envy as he heard how as a young IT student, Ridge had volunteered to help Burden put together an onboard computer system which operated a crewless self-navigating boat all the way from the Shetland Isles, situated far to the north of the Scottish mainland, down the east coast to Newcastle on the north east coast of England.

Thad was pleased to see his strange Scottish pal again. They didn't often move in the same circles these days, since Thad had started modelling for Levi's commercials and was frequently out of the country on shoots. They had a long-standing joke between them that Ridge was actually gay but didn't know it and he just needed Thad to unlock the gates to a whole new world of sexual happiness. As Thad had said to him a hundred times, usually after too many tequila (*it makes you happy!*) slammers.

'Think about it my friend. How can a woman know what you *really* want in bed? How can she know what it *feels* like? But me! I'm a man too...I know! I can give you *everything* man!'

At which point Ridge would always say 'thanks but no thanks' and the pair of them would laugh their heads off. Today however, Thad's tale of his recent snorkelling in the team bath of the Miami Dolphins was not eliciting the usual spluttering beer responses and so he knew something was up. He listened to his pal's concerns about Juanita shooting off so suddenly and not being at work that afternoon. With his far greater experience of both romance and the big wide world, he advised Ridge to just take more time and get to know her better.

'Simple as that, you fuckwit', he said. 'You don't even know a goddamn thing about Mexico, do you? But give you a couple of beers and you're a friggin' Scottish tourist agency!' Ridge nodded in glum assent as his friend laid on the gentle sarcasm.

'You're always mouthing off about your *Edinboro Castle* and your *Bonnie Prince Charlie* and all that queer '*Highlander*' shit man.
Hell! Who's the *gay* one here? Hairy mother-fucking soldiers in skirts!
Even I couldn't make that one up!
Just don't go there OK?
Lay off a little, be more '*tranquilo*' and let the poor broad get a word in.'

Ridge cheered up a little with a positive plan of action ahead of him and they had a few more beers, shouting over the music, ignoring the crotch level view in front of them. Ridge knew his big friend had his own demons and he didn't always pay as much credence to Thad's advice as he made out he did. But right now, he did trust him more than anyone else on earth. Of course he didn't know at this point that he would not see his girlfriend again for a long time. Or that in the near future, trust was to become a fluctuating and ethereal commodity, the safekeeping of which he would have to put into the hands of many more people than he could ever imagine.

Arriving back at his apartment several hours later and somewhat the worse for wear, it still didn't take a moment to sense something was not quite right. Ridge stumbled into the only bedroom to find amongst his few scattered possessions the odd neatly vacant space where Juanita had removed her things.

She had gone!

As he sat staring, on the edge of the dishevelled bed, now a memorial, he could hear the faint sounds of some demented bagpipes in the distance and wondered vaguely whom it could possibly be, playing the pipes, in this godforsaken land.

He could still hear the pipes as he woke up to find himself on Thad's sofa. His head pounding in tune, his first instinct was to look down and he gasped with relief. He still had his jeans on.

'Hey dude! You're alive...*almost!*'

Thad handed him a mug of steaming hot espresso and with his mobile clamped into his ample shoulder, turned away to continue his phone conversation. By the time Ridge was fully awake he discovered that Thad had contacted every airline and bus company in Northern California. None of them had any records of a Juanita Huarez on their manifests for the preceding day or the next week.

How he could find out such confidential information so fast, Ridge didn't understand, but figured it must be something to do with his father's business connections. He vaguely remembered that Thad didn't like his dad as he had often ended their drinking bouts railing against him. As far as Ridge could remember, Thad had always considered his dad to be one of the skeletons in his overfull closet. The two of them hadn't spoken in years and his mother had died very young in a traffic accident. Thad didn't drive.

Thad Senior was a businessman and back-room politician and was a self-made millionaire several times over. He had initially made his pile during the Vietnam War by being the main contractor for the building of massive concrete beachheads. What were glorious battles won for Uncle Sam were just more engineering projects for Thad's dad. His concrete mix was just a bit more unusual; one part concrete, three parts sharp sand, two parts blood and bones.

So they knew she hadn't left town. Ridge decided, on the advice of his pal, to clean himself up and once he was in half decent shape he would nip down to the café and see what was what.

Ridge was correct in his assumption that Juanita hadn't left town at this point in time. She was, in fact sitting in *le Jardin* hoping that he would come through the door. After a sleepless night at a friend's during which most of her worst fears had been realised, she knew she had to go. *Before anyone else was hurt.* Her beautiful mouth was pinched tight and her face was pale with fatigue and apprehension. Against her friend's advice she had come here to find

Ridge. She had argued it was better she stayed on the move, one step ahead at least.

It was 4pm on a hot afternoon for this time of the year. Ridge had just stepped into the all-embracing cool of the *Loch Ness* for a restorative draught on his way down to *le Jardin*. Just at that exact moment, Juanita was beckoned by one of the other girls and told there was someone waiting outside to see her. She darted up, her heart beating furiously like a trapped bird. She still hadn't worked out what she was going to say to Ridge but felt that whatever she said it was still fairer that just leaving town. She clutched a letter that explained things better, just in case words failed her. As she stepped out into the bright sunshine and bustle of Market Street, Juanita shielded her eyes with one hand and scanned the street for Ridge.

Instead, her gaze fell onto two squat men in dark suits, dark glasses and a demeanour to match. For a brief second she considered running. The closer of the two men read her mind and lifted a forefinger slowly wagging it as if gently scolding an aberrant puppy. The other opened a car door and gestured that she should get in. Not a word was spoken and the faces of the two men remained completely impassive as she walked over and climbed in. They didn't see her letter, torn into pieces and dropped into the gutter, the door slamming with an unfeeling thud.

Chapter Four – Deeper into the Night

There was no reason for Ridge to have noticed the dark sedan speed past him as he sauntered along Market Street and he was in good humour, his face slightly flushed with anticipation and more than a little alcohol. Scuffing carelessly at litter, drop-kicking the odd crisp packet as he walked along the empty street, he probably wouldn't have seen Juanita even supposing the car had had a flashing neon arrow on the roof saying *I'M HERE YOU IDIOT!* Even then, he'd probably have looked the other way. Ridge had a particular dislike for flashing neon signs after the experiences of his very first night in the States.

Arriving late evening from the airport, Ridge had headed straight for downtown San Francisco. Exhibiting a naivety almost to the level of it being an art-form, he had sort of expected a 'flowers-in your-hair' kind of a place and completely bereft without his Blackberry, he had not considered booking a hotel.

Vaguely picking up unpleasant vibes on the street, he was glad to see a 'Cheap rooms to let' sign and had headed in. The male receptionist had looked up from manicuring his long slim fingers and his lizard eyes bored into the peach skinned out-of-towner. Unfazed, Ridge had thought it a bit strange that the wee guy was in a wire cage, but nonetheless appreciated the free rooms and didn't put all the pieces of the jigsaw together until he had to make a visit to the toilet. *Bit crowded for 3am?* he had thought, although room was quickly made for him, and seconds later there was a queue of men bidding $50 and more to have Ridge pee on them.

Barricaded back into his room, he spent the rest of the night sitting bolt upright in bed, hand protectively over his balls as if one of the cockroaches scuttling across the floor would jump up and try it on with him. Just outside his window a red neon arrow flashed on and off and on, all night, until he was blinking in unison, as if his eyelids were somehow flicking the switch themselves.

He had learnt a lot since then and it was a street-smart dude who walked into '*Le Jardin*' late that afternoon. Smart enough to notice something was real fucked-up.

As he walked up to the bar he found it impossible to catch anyone's eye and the whole place had gone quiet apart from a couple of small kids goofing around under a table. He shot his usual winning smile at Shelley, one of the waitresses he knew best, and asked if Juanita was about. The girl visibly paled and muttered down to her feet that she thought Juanita had taken a vacation that afternoon and wouldn't be back for a while. But 'she wasn't sure 'cos she'd not been on duty that early and she didn't really know and maybe someone else would know.' He had stopped listening by then. He didn't believe a single word of it. Besides which, he knew Juanita was as skint as he was and there was no way *he* could afford a holiday right now.

As the nervous waitress poured Ridge a double shot of bourbon, he shouted through to the back bar to attract the attention of Joseph, the weekday duty Manager.

Joe was a good bloke, if a bit on the slow side. One of the other wise-ass guys who worked alongside him had once joked to Ridge that he wasn't saying that Joe was stupid, but if you stood real close and put your head near his ear, you could hear the ocean. But Ridge liked the big guy, he had always been protective towards Juanita if she was getting any hassle plus he had slipped Ridge the odd buckshee drink.

Ridge went over to a table and gestured for Joseph to come over and join him. As Joe ambled slowly over, the sheepish look in his eyes was not difficult to detect. Ridge knew that if there was something going on here, this was going to be his man. Joe sat down facing Ridge, his big freckled hands sitting flat on the table, the fat sausage fingers somewhat at odds with the delicate furniture. He looked like he was awaiting a firing squad and so Ridge decided to shoot the breeze with him instead for a while.

'Shit man, why am I always totally broke these days?
I need to find me a rich old lady!
You must see some broads in here?'

'Sure I do Ridge, sure I do…' ventured the barman nervously, not sure at all where this was going.

'Today's pay day for you guy's, s'at right Joe?'

56

Ridge knew the answer.

'Sure is Ridge, but I got rent to pay this week and all. I guess I could give you a ten.'

'That's cool man.
I'll get some from *Neeta* later.
She picked up her pay, right?'

The big man scratched his head. He was the only one who would have had access to the safe today. He didn't understand what Ridge was getting at and didn't see any point in lying to his friend about it anyway.

'No man, she's not been through to get it today, not yet anyway, that is. I thought she was takin' a few days off or sum'n.'

OK. Ridge thought. *She's not away on holiday that's for sure*.

He went to see Huw, partly because he had neglected him of late but mostly because he needed a change of scene to help him think things through.

Ever since their anguished night of self-revelation together, they had a bond between them that was not dependent on regular contact or on any normal platforms of friendship. Each of them truly felt that they owed the other a debt of gratitude for saving their respective lives. Ridge would definitely credit Huw with turning his life around to the point he was able to ask a girl like Juanita out, and Huw certainly hadn't been a slouch either. He now had a responsible position in the city's recycling and waste management industry and had been responsible for much of the dramatic improvements over the Bay area in recent months. He still had their old apartment, all to himself nowadays. It was also furnished for the first time in years and a dejected Ridge sank down into the comfortable old Chesterfield.

After enduring an initial slagging about only coming over when he had women trouble, Ridge explained the missing Juanita story as he saw it and asked the genial Welshman for his take on the situation. Huw was typically relaxed about her disappearance and didn't even view it as such.

'Jesus, the poor girl's just buggered off for a few days.
Give her some peace!
How do you know she's even left San Fran? If Thad was right then Juanita must still be here in the city, for God's sake don't suffocate her.
I never took you for a clingy wee shite!'

They had a enjoyable evening together with Huw doing most of the talking and Ridge was duly impressed with the dramatic improvement in his friend. As Huw himself pointed out, there was a lot Ridge could learn from him in terms of taking control of his life.

'You're still a youngster. It's all very well getting yourself a bird and a navvie's job

and thinking you've made it, but you should be
doing more than that.'

Ridge wanted to explain that going out
with Juanita had left him with precious little
energy to do anything after he's crawled out of
her bed. However, as celibacy was one habit that
Huw still hadn't managed to kick, Ridge just
nodded quietly.

After a tortured night's sleep however,
Ridge's more paranoid nature was beginning to
assert itself and he decided to go back to the bar.
It was the same again when he walked in and
this time he decided to cut the bullshit.

When he saw Soterrana behind the bar,
he thought he was in luck. The beautiful Latina
was one of Juanita's closest friends and she had
got Juanita the job here in '*Le Jardin*'.
Unfortunately, the girl had never taken to Ridge
and had constantly mocked him, referring to him
as 'the English conehead…,' in front of Juanita.
He hadn't really bothered about it as Juanita
would vociferously defend his mediocre
physique or lack of transportation or whatever
and he always enjoyed that a lot.

Soterrana fixed her withering gaze on
Ridge as he pulled up a tall chair alongside her
and leaned across the bar conspiratorially.
'Hey…, *leech*,' she hissed slowly, her huge dark
eyes flicking rapidly over his pale face,
searching for signs of what he might know or
might ask. As he flicked a match and lit his
Marlboro with a theatrical deliberation, he could
almost feel the hot breeze from her long black
eyelashes as they swept the smoke back into his
face.

It was the right time for acting. Soterrana was tougher than Ridge, two times tougher. It suited him that there was no love lost between them as he could play a part and not feel sorry for the other players. He thought he knew himself well, but that didn't mean everyone else would see through him. Inhaling deeply, he leant back on his chair and smiled very slowly.

'Listen up, Sugar, I *know* what's been goin' on here.
I know you don't think I'm too 'woo-hoo' but I got a few surprises for you. Just tell me where the two of them have gone, that's all I want and I'll be out of your face, *muy pronto*'.

Ridge was bullshitting like mad but he could see to his dismay that this story line was not too far off the script. Soterrana began posturing and gesticulating wildly.

'*Jack shit* is all you know, you fuck-up! If you *know* she's with him then you don't *need* to ask me where the fuck she is. *Entiendo*?
Ask any prairie-dog south of Nogales if he knows who Ramon is and he'll either cut out your heart to give to the man on a fucking plate or beg to you on their knees not to tell anyone you've spoken with him about the son-of-a-bitch.'

This was not going the way he had expected and Ridge was struggling to keep a grip on himself. *Who the fuck was this Ramon*

'OK, Soterrana! Keep cool OK!
All I know is she's with some wise-guy
called Ramon but I just need someone to
cover the waterfront for me and you were
putting her up at your place, last night,
right? Yeah? Well that's good! I'm real
happy that you've been such a friend to
her. All I want to know is where exactly
she went *next*.'

Ridge somehow manufactured his most
sincere smile and at the same time slipped a
couple of folded bills across the bar top. The girl
seemed to relax her aggressive stance and, after
first looking pointlessly around an empty room,
gestured for him to come closer. She could tell
him more, sure thing, she had whispered to an
increasingly confused Ridge, but not here. If he
came round later that night to her apartment, in
the Mission District, not far from Juanita's
place, she could help him out.

Ridge left quickly and broke a rule by
jumping a cab in daylight. For some reason, it
had suddenly felt colder and he was dog-tired.
Stumbling into the apartment, he fell into bed
fully clothed and slept fitfully. As he came to, a
few hours later, he remembered he'd been
dreaming of being in a garish 70's style
nightclub watching Juanita forlornly dancing on
a stage whilst a handsome Antonio Banderas
type guy in a pink tuxedo clapped proprietorially
at her. The music, still in his head, was that
weird bagpipe sound again.

He quickly showered and headed over to

Soterrana's place stopping briefly for some enchiladas on the way. He felt as if he was going to need all the strength he could muster that night. In his state of mind he was really just going through the motions. Had Juanita run off? Did she have a *heid-the-ba'* boyfriend back home in Mexico? He hadn't a clue what was going on but *what was new,* he thought sourly.

Unfortunately, there are times in a young man's life when no amount of bullshitting is going to get you out of something and this was one of those times. When looking back at the events shortly to unfold, Ridge often smiles wryly. He maintains that it was one of the watershed moments of his life. Hopelessly unprepared for what was about to happen, he was so *embarrassed* by his own stupidity, that never again would he allow himself to walk into a situation so mentally ill-equipped.

He had run up the steps to the top storey of the two-storey block, being only a couple of minutes late and was striding purposely along the long exterior landing. The sky was twinkling brightly on an unusually clear night but Ridge was oblivious to the charms of the Californian evening vista. His mind was on other things. He was also oblivious to the two shaven-headed men leaning over the balcony just a couple of yards before Soterrana's door.

As he approached, they turned quickly and the nearest one flicked out his arm and stopped Ridge. They were boys really, certainly under twenty, but they had probably been bigger than Ridge by the time they were twelve.

The white guy was the taller and seemed to be in charge although he seemed very nervous. He had an impressive amount of roughly inked tattoos which looked like he'd done them himself…, *prison* tattoos. So he'd been in jail awhile and he didn't want to go back. Ridge could sense that the other guy, an overweight Hispanic, was spaced out on something and the fluff on his upper lip was wet with sweat. The white guy pushed back his Giants cap and recited what was obviously a poorly rehearsed script.

> 'You've been asking too many questions, guy, so we're here to give you this message.
> Back off and don't fuck with stuff you don't have no call to fuck with. OK?'

Ridge shook his head up and down quickly but silently, his heart was thumping so hard in his neck that he was seeing stars in front of his face. He tried to say *you've got the wrong guy* but couldn't get his mouth to work properly and just said *sorry, sorry* over and over again to himself. The white guy then turned to his accomplice and gestured with a theatrical deliberance towards Ridge.

'Oh yeah, right.' The smaller youth mumbled, 'OK guy. Arms or Legs?'

Ridge just stared at him, eyes popping out of his head. He saw the guy had what looked like a tiny baseball bat in his right hand, which he now proceeded to wave in front of him accusingly. '*Arms* or *Legs*, man?' He now realised what was about to happen. This had been commonplace over in Ulster during the Troubles and even after, *but he never expected it to fuckin' well happen to him.*

Without making any rational decision, Ridge waved his left hand limply in the air as the tears began pouring down his face. The two men were getting jumpy and they both looked at each other quickly, the taller nodding to the other and like lightning the little club snapped out and Ridge felt a hot current of electricity emanate from his left elbow. Somehow galvanised into action by the tremendous pain, Ridge jumped forward and did something he had seen often in his youth. Right then it seemed to be almost instinctive. He pushed up strongly through the back of his legs and headbutted the guy hard on the bridge of his broad nose. There was a sharp sound of bones breaking but then Ridge couldn't stop his forward momentum and he careered full onto the squealing boy. Falling backwards the guy momentarily lost his balance then fell completely over the balcony. He landed fifty feet below with a stomach-turning crunch. Ridge turned quickly to the bigger man, his face stricken with sheer terror; his eyes screaming, *Kill me then! Just kill me now!* The two men stood for a fraction of a second in silence then the taller man pushed Ridge aside and ran for the stairs.

Ridge crumpled to his knees, quietly sobbing, but then as the pain brought him round he felt a hot wave of nausea surge over him and as he leant forward he could see through the railings. Praying that this was just some absurd dream, he looked down into the darkness, wanting there to be nothing there. All he could see was the distorted shape of the body on the ground. His stomach heaved and Ridge threw up violently. The hot mixture of vomit and half digested Mexican food splattered across the corpse below, mingling with the dark pool of blood slowly spreading across the rough tarmac of the car park.

His heart beating double time, Ridge hauled himself painfully up with his right arm and stumbled off into the dark night, his terrified eyes darting this way and that. As he ran, his heightened senses assaulted him at every turn and the cruel intensity of the pulsating streets seemed to stretch out menacingly all around him, a spinning vortex of horror. The city, in turn, only spasmed briefly, just long enough to assimilate yet another tragic death into the fetid miasma of an ugly night. In his anguish, Ridge couldn't see that no one else was remotely interested.

Chapter Five – Sits like a man, smiles like a reptile.

The next few days became a bit hazy. To Ridge it seemed as if he was reluctantly watching his life being played out as one of those ubiquitous 'reality' type programmes that are so popular in the UK. The ones where everything is jerkily filmed in soft focus, with a hand held camera pointed, for the most part, at someone's feet. The kind of car-crash TV which pretends to have lofty ideals about raising a semblance of awareness concerning some particular plight of the moment. A never-ending cavalcade of vomit inducing faux-concern where we are presented with a measured and insulated exposure to some hitherto unknown festering of our society. Thus allowing each of us to privately revel in the vicarious pleasure of other people's misery. Each sad exploitation worth only a momentary spike in the minds of armchair slobs for whom it is only, at best, a minor depressant until the next ad for The Shopping Channel. At worst, a positive affirmation that their own sad and useless lives may, in fact, be enviable compared to those other poor bastards on the other side of the screen.

He woke up from his nightmare on Thad's sofa again, somehow he *always* ended up here when things got all fucked up. However, he remembered that it was Huw who had sorted him out this time. Thad had been out of town when Ridge staggered to his apartment door, his left arm hanging limply at his side, a dark crimson elbow patch staining his tatty suede jacket. Scared shitless to go home to his own place, Huw had been his only other option.

Huw took one look at him at he sidled along the wall into his apartment.

'*Jesus!* What the fuck have you been up to now, boy?
Look at all that claret on your arm.'

Ridge tried to make up a story about falling down some steps but his level of anxiety was a dead giveaway that something serious was going down. The pain had only been slumbering before but now vicious spasms were tearing through his body relentlessly.

'Easy boy. Easy does it now. Let's have a look at that arm.'

Ridge winced as his friend gently pulled the sleeve away from his elbow.

'You've broken it, you daft bugger!
You'll need to have that seen to.
Come on.
Keep your jacket on, I'm taking you to the hospital.'

It only took a few minutes for Ridge to come round to the idea, as Huw poured a neat bourbon down his throat. His head spinning, he

67

stumbled outside with his good arm wrapped over the shoulder of his worried friend. Neither of them had a clue where the hospital was and so for the second time in a week, Ridge found himself in a taxi.

Huw handled everything at the hospital Emergency Department. Ridge had collapsed and gone into shock and so they had to put him on a saline drip and keep him in for a few hours until his condition stabilised. Huw allayed any fears that the staff had as to how Ridge was injured as with his Welsh accent it was easy to convince them they were on vacation. Unfortunately, he was too honest about the fact that they had both overstayed their tourist visas and it was delicately suggested to Huw that it was maybe a good idea to go home soon.

Sitting in the 'Loch Ness' the following day with Ridge proudly displaying his plaster cast to the world, Huw drank deeply from his beer.

'I'm sorry mate, if I've fucked it up for us here, I don't know what I was thinking of.'

Visa problems were the last thing on Ridge's mind at that moment but he could see that Huw had maybe jeopardized a long term future here in California, all because of him, He was not going to let that happen. He pretended to make light of their predicament.

'Don't sweat it, we'll fix this easy enough.

Come on. Let's see if that big poof is back in town.
He'll know what to do…'

Ridge was thinking more about his other problems. Shit, all Huw has to do is marry some lassie and that's the problem solved. It's about time he buried his ghost anyway, he thought. Meanwhile my malignant spirits are real and they are fucking well marauding through San Francisco!

Thad was home and with the aid of strong drink and gentle words, he soon had Huw cheered up and on his way. Smoking a large joint, purely for medicinal reasons, Ridge then attempted to unfold events since they had last seen each other, to the best of his scant knowledge. Thad scrutinised his friend's face as Ridge poured out his feelings on what was going on and what he should do next. The big man said little in return but sat deeply into his comfortable seat and nodded slowly when required. To Ridge, it all seemed a bit mad by then, sitting there in beautiful sunshine in this peaceful sanctuary. After a few hours, Ridge passed out again, the effort to stay awake just too much. He didn't hear Thad go out shortly after, or the carefully disguised steel reinforced door of the apartment being triple-locked and deadbolted.

As Ridge lay sleeping, his strained and aching brain blissfully resting in neutral, someone else's head was speeding into the red zone.

Soterrana quickly counted the wad of notes again. *Wow!* She thought, *ese tipa esta loco!* The strange girl had only just left her apartment but already Soterrana was wishing she had really taken a note of her mobile number after all. She has said she would come back again, but who knows. *Mucha pasta, that's for sure!* But, she still had a shift to do at the bar soon and had a shower to take yet. Crazy to think she'd just made two months pay for ten minutes talking! She'd always liked Juanita, bit of a mouse, but cool enough, but she couldn't see why everyone was making such a big deal. First, that skinny prick from England and now this big dyke!

Soterrana grabbed a towel and began to undress. She knew that it was stupid to get involved in anything to do with Ramon, but all she had told the stupid bitch was common knowledge. *Mostly...*, she thought, suddenly nervous. Now naked, she felt an uncommonly cool breeze play over her damp skin and she realised she had broken out in a sweat whilst the girl was here. She laughed to herself quietly as she thought, not for the first time, about what a turn on money could be!

Standing under the hot shower, still shivering slightly, she had a gnawing feeling inside that the girl had somehow wheedled more out of her than she had intended, never mind the dough that was on offer. *No te comas el coco,* she told herself as she switched off the shower. Don't sweat it girl! This has been one lucky day for sure.

As she stepped over the edge of the bath and put one wet foot onto the cane matting, Soterrana quickly realised her luck had deserted her just as quickly as it had arrived. Her second foot never made it onto the floor as a large pair of gloved hands gripped her neck from behind and she felt herself lifted into the air. It was over in seconds, her last thought was how filthy was the fetid cigar breath that rasped in her ear and then she herself became breathless and still.

An athletic looking girl bounded up the steps to the main apartment door in a quiet residential street, her long coffee coloured thighs clearly visible under her short summer dress. It was warm even in the elevator and she was looking forward to the cool comfort of her air-conditioned apartment. She disarmed the sophisticated alarm system and quietly entered, going straight to her bedroom where she showered and slipped on a pair of jogging pants before checking on her guest.

Ridge jumped up startled from a fitful sleep as Thad gently shook his shoulder.

'Hey! Rumplestiltskin! How's that arm? Come on through and I'll fix us some breakfast.
You must be hungry!
You've slept nearly 20 hours!'

As he struggled off the sofa and staggered through in the wake of his big friend, Ridge mumbled darkly that it obviously wasn't enough 'cos he was still knackered. He hauled himself up onto a stool at the breakfast bar and with a heavy head propped up by his good arm, surveyed the industrious proceedings. Coming slowly to life he could see and smell the fresh breads and pastries that Thad was laying out on trays for them. He had assumed Thad was only just recently awake himself, particularly as he was only partially clothed.

'Oh no, my one-armed *bandito*! I can't sit around baby-sitting you all day. I've had my own adventure!'

His dark eyes were twinkling mischievously and Ridge could tell by the coy smile that Thad was just dying to tell him something. Problem was, Ridge wasn't in the mood for one of his stories today and his sullen demeanour was not to be easily overlooked. Breathing deeply, his massive chest tensing visibly, Thad remained composed and his voice took on a more serious and controlled edge. He stopped for a moment and looked Ridge directly in the eye.

'Listen you little douche-bag, let's get one thing straight here, what I did today was for your miserable ass, not mine OK? Now do you have *any idea* what the fuck is going on with your life right now?'

Ridge shook his head, intrigued and slightly scared by the steely composure of his normally laid back friend. Thad unwrapped

72

some imported smoked bacon as he spoke, 'well I might just have a few answers for you if you're interested. Hold on 'til I get a T-shirt 'tho, I don't want any hot fat ruining my skin tone!'

Over the next hour, Thad explained, between mouthfuls of breakfast, how he had been to see Soterrana.

'How the hell did you manage that?' Ridge spluttered into his English tea.

'Well, that's a long story, but you know how I like to dress up every now and then? I think this time I pulled it off like a real trouper!
She bought it totally and I even got a pat on my fanny from some heavy dude hanging around outside, one of your amigos, I guess.'

Ridge was utterly speechless. Despite the gravity of the situation, he made a mental note to explain to Thad one day, the subtle difference in meaning between the US and UK for the word 'fanny'. He assumed Thad hadn't taken the gender bending *that* far!

The rest of what Thad had to say, however, was not what he wanted to hear and he was picking up loud and clear the underlying message he was being given. It seemed that Juanita and this Ramon guy went back a long way and were practically married for Christ's sake. His worst fears about Ramon were entirely justified. He was some big time drug smuggler who operated all over Central America and was well connected with the underworld in the States and possibly overseas. He commanded fierce loyalty from his people and was known to have very bloodthirsty habits. Soterrana had told Thad that his pet name was *El Cocodrilo*, the crocodile. When, with his reasonable handle on Spanish, Thad had suggested more in hope than anything else, that this was a play on *coco* or bogeyman or maybe just *contrabandista* as in smuggler, she just looked at him with one of her cold, withering glances. 'But, of course, you must have never seen him smile'.

Apparently things were not going too well in the court of the big lizard and Thad had got the impression that Juanita was seen as being a talisman for Ramon and that was why he wanted her back. Soterrana also made it clear that Juanita was not just in love with Ramon, she was completely in thrall to him. This she had greatly exaggerated to hopefully throw off her earnest interviewer who appeared, in her impression, to be an infatuated and rather muscular lesbian. Thad had cottoned on to this but he, in turn, had laid it on even thicker for Ridge's benefit, somewhat in pursuit of the same goal.

Scratching furiously throughout all this, Ridge was barracking him with questions and cursing him in turn. Thad explained that Ramon was continually on the move as there was a vicious war between the main Mexican drug cartels and the security forces. He was rumoured to have a power base in Oaxaca, in southwest

Mexico where he was practically the government and his influence was spreading further south into Guatemala and Panama.

To make matters worse, he was probably involved with the military as Guatemala was in the midst of the bloodiest civil war since the 1980's. Thad explained as kindly as he could that the guy is bad karma and that Ridge was probably the luckiest SOB to get away with only a fractured elbow and a broken heart. Soterrana had implied that Juanita had been more or less kidnapped, as opposed to her returning under her own free will, but Thad had been fairly economical with some of this and so left Ridge, he hoped, with the feeling that she had left him willingly after her 'holiday romance' and there was nothing more to be done about the situation.

Ridge was in a morose mood for the remainder of the day. Thad felt bad about deceiving him and wanted him gone soon in case his own resolve broke and he told him the truth. The real truth was, he told himself sternly, that what he had done had been the right thing to do and he had helped his friend out of a particularly crap situation. He had also received a call that afternoon about a photo shoot on the East Coast the next day and so he would need an early night. But Ridge was in no hurry to go anywhere.

Looking back, Thad realised that what he did next was monumentally stupid but, you know what they say, hindsight is always 20/20. He had left Ridge sitting up late, drinking hard and so early next day, with Ridge crashed on the sofa, he had left a key by the sofa with a note to say let yourself out or stay here and I'll be back in two days. When he returned from New York the apartment was empty. He was tired and didn't notice anything was amiss. Next to his note was a scrawled piece of paper that said,

'Gone fishing … Richard'.

Chapter Six – The Prisoner

The late afternoon sun had forced them to move from the baking heat of the little square to the relative cool of the old courtyard. Still, Charlie refused to talk. They had tried everything but in the end had all walked off into the shade, muttering death threats under their breath and stroking the warm barrels of semi-automatic pistols slung loosely around their damp bodies. It had been a trying day for the men. Not that it was an unpleasant place to spend a few hours. With a small green-roofed bandstand in the centre and a circle of small fountains enclosing the outer edges of the town's central meeting place, the Zocalo was quietly buzzing as people began to ready themselves to go back to work for the remainder of the day.

The shoeshine men moved up now from their kneeling stations and climbed high up onto the garish plastic chairs recently vacated by their steady stream of customers. In these dentist's chairs, enjoying a relaxed cigarette now, they could sit for hours extracting the hottest snippets of gossip from their counterparts. The occasional tourist would nervously approach them and, with a great flourish of hands and cloths, the men would usher them into a chair and carelessly shine up their expensive sandals for as much as they had made so far that day.

It wasn't just Maximiliano's shoes that were shining. He was a big man, over 240 pounds and his hot face dripped sweat. As Ramon's right hand man, he had been given the responsibility of looking after the girl, *and* now Charlie. He paced the broad courtyard from North to South and then across from side to side. As he turned on reaching a wall he would smash his huge fist against the old wooden beams that helped support the stone building.

He wasn't used to this. He preferred action to this baby-sitting. If he actually thought the girl was in any tangible danger, then it would be a different matter. He would be happier if she was under threat but he knew in his heart that this was stupid as there was no way any new friends she had made in California would be able to trace her, even if they were crazy enough to try. Xavier had assured him that he had taken care of any loose ends in San Francisco. Meanwhile, he, Maximiliano, '*The Hummer*', was supposed to look after the boss. That is where he should be. Bad shit was going down and they didn't need any more fuck-ups. They had good men working for them, for sure. He respected Xavier a lot but no one was a match for Maximiliano! He spat onto the large flagstones in irritation, narrowly missing his expensive Italian shoes.

Juanita was pretending not to notice Max's bad humour. She was enjoying herself tremendously within the boundaries of her situation. Needing a friend to talk to, she had persuaded Ramon, over the phone, that the macaw would stop her feeling lonely. It had been bought the day before and Juanita had been tormenting her keepers that unless they could get it to talk before Ramon got back he would be furious with them for buying the wrong type of parrot. Charlie, for her part, (yes, 'it' was in fact a 'she'), was not playing ball. Juanita had her face perilously close to the rim of Charlie's old wrought iron cage and could almost discern a soft crooning sound whenever the goons left the two of them alone together.

To look at, Charlie was an impressive creature, standing over a foot and a half tall and resplendent in bright red feathers over her body and head with feathers green and yellow at her wing tips and electric blue at her tail. Closer up though, Juanita looked at the pale lizard like skin around her sharp black eyes and huge hooked beak and decided with an instant delight that this was a bird with attitude.

Having had a very down to earth upbringing where sentimentality was a luxury few could afford, Juanita was not usually one for anthropomorphic notions but she felt a genuine bond with this bird, which seemed to share her antipathy towards the men watching over them. Maybe it was just the situation she found herself in but she could swear to it that Charlie's eyes would twinkle when looking at her, replaced by a steely glare when directed at their captors. The men seemed to feel this also and they had retreated to regroup and work out what to do next. She had already drawn blood on two occasions, which only Juanita had found hugely entertaining. 'You and me girl', she spoke quietly, 'we are going to be great *amiga's* I think'!

Since being forcibly repatriated to

Mexico, things had been not too bad for her so far. Ramon was still away on business and she had been kept away from the vast majority of the clan, particularly Ramon's wife. Luisa had reportedly been ecstatic at Juanita's disappearance thinking that she would at last be re-instated to her rightful position in the affections of Ramon. But her flight only served to underline the gulf that was between husband and wife and seeing Ramon so tormented, Luisa had understood now more than ever that she could never be loved by him in that way again. Before Juanita fled, the illicit romance had been relatively private. You didn't live too long spreading stories about Ramon. At that time there had been tacit understanding between the two women. However, he himself had made the relationship public property in his obsessive quest to find her and he had not considered the feelings of his sorely wounded wife for a moment.

With the recent very public killing of his much older brother Arturo, at the hands of the newly empowered authorities, young Ramon was a crocodile who had to swim a lot harder against the current these days. As much as he wanted to see Juanita, he was fully occupied with more pressing matters.

It was Arturo who had been the real brains behind their criminal empire. The death of his brother was a huge blow for Ramon although he would never had admitted that to any of his men. But worse than that, at a pivotal time when he least needed to swell the ranks of his many foes, he had unwittingly created a bitter enemy more dangerous than he could ever have foreseen. Juanita, for her part, was unaware of any of this, but now knew instinctively that she must forever be on her guard.

Towards Juanita, Ramon, of course, had been at his most charming. He phoned her many times a day, begging forgiveness for the heavy handed method of her return and promising over and over that he had turned his back on violence and had his heart now set on political office and the establishment of a solid base of legitimate business.

She didn't doubt his sincerity for a second. That was never the problem. When he took her hand softly and looked deep into her eyes, she drank deeply the words that he spoke. She believed that he believed in what he was saying. *That* was the real problem. He would be genuinely feeling remorse for his actions on a Tuesday and then be ripping out someone's throat the following Thursday. It was simply in his nature. She knew inside that he would not ever be the man that even he said he wanted to be. This was what she had been unable to reconcile before. This was what she still had to overcome. Could she not turn a blind eye to his shortcomings? Half of Central America appeared to have mastered this ability.

Can she?

Many thought of him as a great man, *es casinadie*. Most respected him but all feared him. He had a proud history – they both had, that was one of their initial bonds, before her naive idealism became mired in the foul stench of reality.

Juanita settled comfortably into the large

cushions that were distributed generously over the cane furniture and gestured across the courtyard that she would like a drink. A strong drink she thought, a *Cuba libre* perhaps.

She had been only a teenage student the first time she had met Ramon while visiting an aunt in Chihuahua. It was 2004 and the country was in the grip of an austerity programme implemented by the government since 2002 in an attempt to reverse the catastrophic economic situation. Ramon was already a successful smuggler and racketeer by this time but he was also testing the water in the local political arena, following in the footsteps of his forefathers.

Juanita squirmed slightly in her chair as she remembered that it was in the smuggling rather than political context that first brought them together as her aunt was haggling over a contraband portable television. The chemistry between them was intense from the start. Barely sixteen, Juanita had been heavily politicised at an early age by her parents after her mother's own parents had been killed tragically in a political demonstration when she was not even a year old.

Although his personal motivations upon meeting Juanita were more primal than political, Ramon could readily be loquacious about his political convictions and found an easy mark in the impressionable teenager. It was not difficult to find fault in the political system. With inflation rampant and the country massively in debt, vast shanty towns were disfiguring the edges of the large cities, particularly Mexico City where Juanita lived.

As he talked, so she drank in his words, her face flushing passionately as he would draw closer and his words coming faster and yet more intense.

She was already aware of the great social tension in Mexico and had been schooled by her parents in the great socialist nationalism of the Institutional Revolutionary Party, (the PRI), with its three tenets of agrarian justice, social equality and economic sovereignty. But in the last few decades the urbanisation and industrialisation of Mexico had meant rural society was in decline and the peasants had fled to the cities and shanty towns.

In Juanita's lifetime, the government had borrowed money to solve their problems, leading to vicious inflation and a massive inflow of imported goods. The apparent salvation of oil discoveries in the mid-seventies only made matters worse with more borrowing and ever accelerating inflation. Endemic corruption ensued, attracting sharks like Arturo into the feeding frenzy of politics and business. In 1981, the Mexican oil company Pemex borrowed $10 million dollars from the state. The same year saw oil prices plummet and in 1982, Mexico became the first country to suspend interest payments on international debt. From there the situation had gone from bad to worse.

Ramon railed powerfully against the system and Juanita could feel herself yielding to his presence, unconsciously offering up her young body to this strong and bitter man as if to say *Yes! I'm with you, make me one with you!* All the time he was mentally licking his lips with delight at this most unexpected outcome and it was all he could do to stop himself lifting her onto his straining lap right there in front of the old bag and her new TV!

He could afford to be patient however, and he smiled broadly as Juanita asked him of his proud inheritance. He could trace his family back over a hundred years, he announced defiantly. He swung a thick arm out towards the window and told her how his papa's own father had been among the railway workers building the great Chihuahua railway who had protested at the far better wages of US nationals working alongside them. He had gone on to revolt under Pancho Villa in 1910 and further south he fought and died with the great Emiliano Zapata. Juanita stared open mouthed when he told her how his grandfather had become trapped in Mexico City with the rebel leaders in a ten day bloodletting which became known as '*La Decena Tragica*'.

The country was riven by the political battles between the *cientificos,* the progressive liberal technocrats, businessmen based in Mexico City, who favoured a national ruling party and the *caudillos*, who had traditionally strong provincial roots and were an old style power, run on a personal basis with broking between regional barons and clans. The *caudillos* feared institutionalization as it threatened their basis of power in their home territories. However, after complicated and violent struggles, the *caudillos* from the north-west state of Sonora finally emerged as the victors and despite their provincial origins they succeeded in building a nation-wide authority, which proved to be among the most enduring and stable in the turbulent history of Latin America.

His eyes shining with mock emotion, Ramon told her how his family became an important part of the *caudillos* power base which also spread to include many of the dispossessed peasants and industrialized labour of the cities. He explained how this period became known as the 'Mexican Revolution', and brazenly attempted to link it with the more well known progressive watersheds of the French Revolution and the Bolshevik Revolution. The implication here was not lost on Juanita, that this was a break with the corruption of the past, a new future where the people are united behind a common identity with the spirit of the revolution being the equivalent almost of a divine will.

Unfortunately his family didn't quite get the hang of all that, Ramon proving to be just another chip off the now very old block. It had not taken too long before they lost position due to the old problem of the law and other minor details. So although his family had been disgraced by the time of his birth, Ramon and his brothers still counted themselves to be the *caudillos*, and they had built up their criminal organization very much on the old style with many brothers and cousins controlling various areas both legitimate and otherwise. This had taken a lot of the pressure off the still young Ramon and freed up more of his time for him to pursue his true calling, as he saw it, not that of political office, more the physical education of young girls such as the exquisite flower who was fragrantly poised by his feet at this moment.

Juanita was transfixed. Ignoring the frequent grunts of disapproval from her aunt as Ramon delivered his well practiced lines, she felt a strange warmth deep down inside that threatened to well up and envelop them both. His story had struck a particular chord with her as her own family had also been enmeshed in the violent history of the last century. In Juanita's case it was very much more personal. She struggled to keep her composure as she gazed up at Ramon and poured out the story of her grandparents' untimely end. She had never met them. All she had were some photos of a couple always touching or holding hands, both tall and slim, both with long dark hair and patently much in love. Only twenty eight years old when they died, Juanita thought about them every day of her life.

Her grandmother was conceived in Spain and born in Mexico in 1940. Her maternal great-grandparents were staunch republicans that had come over to Mexico in 1939 along with thousands of others, after the Spanish Civil War. Intensely political, she had met Juanita's grandfather at university in Mexico City and shortly before the most tumultuous period of protests and activities throughout the globe they had married and Juanita's mother was born.

The student Left had been demonstrating vociferously in the run up to the autumn of 1968 and with Mexico hosting the Olympic Games, the PRI had been over anxious to present a flattering picture of the country to the world at large. There had been a series of confrontations between students and the army over a period of weeks and it was getting to be an embarrassment for the government.

On the second of October, Juanita's mother was left with her great-grandmother for the day as her parents and grandparents made their way down to the Tlatelolco district of Mexico City for a student rally. As there had been increasingly violent demonstrations they vowed to stay out of trouble and promised to return well before dark. They all waved up brightly to the young baby as they sauntered off arm in arm. There were a great many people gathering together and at some point the two generations became separated. Her mother had tearfully told Juanita this story many times. She would always feel guilty that after a few hours she and her young husband began to feel unsafe and decided to make their way back to Juanita and the family. Later that afternoon, at the *Plaza de las Tres Culturas*, Juanita's grandparents along with many students and fellow liberals were herded up on all four sides before being shot or bludgeoned to death. It must have been difficult, her mother had said to Juanita, many years later, for the government to have painted a flattering picture of Mexican life when the word 'BLOODBATH' was the caption underneath that picture.

Ramon was suitably consolatory and he could see it would not be difficult to find a way into her heart, and more, if he could only just get rid of the old aunt. His high hopes were soon dashed however, as Juanita's uncle entered the house abruptly. Still strongly built despite his age, Rafael threw a look of disgust towards the young interloper. He knew Ramon by reputation and being a man himself, he had summed up the present scenario in a flash. 'The TV looks good, but now you can go, *biutre*!'

As Ramon quickly scuttled out, Juanita called sadly after him but he didn't even look back for a second. Scowling up at her uncle, she stormed off into another room. She understood that not everyone felt comfortable with the black market but she was still taken aback by the raw intensity of Rafael's obvious distaste. It was to be many years before she set eyes on Ramon again, although there were many stories and many times she had defended his name as if, in some way, he had already become her lover.

If only she had kept him contained him in her romantic imagination, then how different would her life be now? Sitting here like some grotesque B-movie princess, guarded by apes with guns, awaiting the return of her monstrous lover! She didn't dare to hope that he had really changed. She knew in the depths of her soul that he was not capable of changing any more than she was able to resist him. She thought of the beautiful boy she had met on her brief escape! In her memory, he would be always smiling and the pale sun would be glinting off his tousled blonde hair. It was such a perfect moment!

But it had been only a dream, a seductive taste of transient bliss. A kiss. Ridge was not the man to right her world, and she knew how closely she had come to shattering his, how near she had been to pulling him over the precipice and down into her empty hell.

Chapter Seven - The Hitcher

He hadn't eaten anything in two days. If the huge woman seated next to him was to press against him any harder, Ridge felt that he would have to succumb to the inexorable force and let himself be squeezed out through the numerous holes in the bone-jarring metal body of this suffocatingly hot bus. The pop rivets must have failed under previous ordeals and any second now he was going to turn into foul half-cooked Scottish mince, spewing out through the tiny holes onto the blistering roadside. His grimy body was soaked and any parts of his clothing that were pressed hard against his doughty companion were heavy and transparent with their commingling sweat. He was just hanging in there... *just*... it would be okay... if only the fucking bus would *move*!

This had been the pattern of his journey from Tijuana. Endless stops, each one ushering in a frantic melee of street vendors and passengers along with a fetid unremitting heat that sapped all energy. He was still optimistic at this point, despite a weariness bordering on hallucinatory, because he knew he was only a short distance from the boat that would take him off the Baja, away from this oppressive heat and out into the fresh, clear blue sea...

It had been only three days or so since he had left Thad's apartment in San Francisco but already that seemed a lifetime ago. For some reason, probably still drunk, he had decided to hitch down the coast to Mexico in order to preserve his limited finances. The real truth of the matter was more to do with the fact that he didn't really know where he was going or what he was going to do when he got there and so there seemed to be no real hurry at all. He had thought it would also give him time to think things through, which he later decided, on balance, was maybe not such a good idea after all. One positive thought was that he would try and stay straight for a while. There were too many crazy things happening in his life right now and he was going to have to be more on the ball. He had no idea how prophetic a statement that was.

The hitching got off to a good start when a woman picked him up only moments after he had speculatively stuck a thumb out on Van Ness. It turned out to be the plaster cast. Her own daughter had recently broken her arm and so she had felt sorry for him. It was only 7am and they quickly shot through Redwood City and down past Los Altos. In a different life I might have done well here, he thought ruefully as they sped past the glittering mirrored-glass palaces of the great software houses. On her way to Monterey for the weekend, she dropped him off at Salinas and he promised faithfully to send her a postcard from '*Edinboro Castle*' when he got home.

He barely had time to stuff an Egg McMuffin down his throat when a small van stopped with two young guys in boiler suits and back-to-front baseball caps. In high spirits and heading for their first ever job for a new decorating business, they could take him all the way down the coast road to Los Angeles.

Spotting his now grubby, but nevertheless virgin, plaster cast, the older of the two, Zack, who was driving, asked if he could be the first '*dude*' to autograph the cast. Ridge was happy to agree until he realised the guy meant to do it whilst he was at the wheel and the van slewed violently across the highway as he turned round to append his name. Ridge was struck by how beautifully it was written. The younger guy, they turned out to be brothers, thought this was funny.

> 'Cool bro! Wicked! Next time try keepin' yo eyes to the fuckin' road! We're gonna need *another* fuckin' blast after that, man. Say! You partakin' of some marching powder my friend?'

To his jaw-dropping astonishment, Ridge watched as the kid liberally sprinkled cocaine onto a flat area in the centre of the plastic steering wheel whereupon his deranged brother then sniffed up the entire lot, *without* swerving this time. Only half-listening to their incessant gibberish, a prickly sensation quickly overtook Ridge as he realised these two pop-eyed painters inhabited their own, alternate universe.

As he stared out helplessly across the flat desolate highway towards the rugged beauty of the Pacific coastline he felt himself becoming increasingly disconnected from the unchanging serenity of the landscape. Fearing for his life, it was therefore, with unalloyed enthusiasm, that he encouraged them with their new plan.

Fast approaching the turnoff for Big Sur, they had vaguely decided to 'go check out the waves and the babes'. Bouncing around in the back, with more beer tins than paint tins, this meant Ridge had a valid reason to extricate himself from their company and keep hitching south. Graciously deflecting their requests to help them paint the seascape onto the side of their van, Ridge thankfully stepped out and back onto Planet Earth.

On the re-bound from the crazy crew, Ridge hardly gave the next guy a second look as a battered old Chevy pick-up pulled over slowly. Looking in, all he could see he was an older guy with a wild moustache and the ubiquitous cap, the *right* way round this time, which Ridge interpreted as some semblance of normality.

'Going South at all?' Ridge shouted in through the window. 'Kinda'… get in…' the man said gruffly, in a take it or leave it manner.

In a horrible déjà-vu moment, Ridge realised the entire floor of the truck was ankle-deep in beer cans.

Different driver, same shit.

The driver in question stared straight ahead at the road, but silently passed Ridge a beer, which he took. Christ! He would have taken anything at that point. The man said nothing for a long while which was a relief after the last ride, but the way he passed his beer can up to his mouth in a steady slow rhythmic manner, every forty five seconds or so, as if this somehow was directly connected to the movement of the wheels, (*a beer-o-meter?*), wasn't so relaxing. On the plus side, most of the cans around his feet were still full. Ridge guessed he obviously couldn't have been travelling for too long. It was still morning on his first day out of the big city and he was starting to think that his wild sybaritic existence over the last few months had only been 'big girls blouse' stuff compared with the die-hard proclivities of the indigenous population.

The silence between them gave Ridge an opportunity to glance over at the man every so often. He had a craggy skin loosely covering an expressionless face carved out of granite. His thick greying blonde hair and huge moustache gave him a Joe Walsh kind of look, a 60's Mount Rushmore face, which reminded him of some old album cover of his brother Gavin's. John, as his name turned out to be, was heading for somewhere called China Lake and would drop Ridge off at Bakersfield which he said was due south. Ridge had no idea where Bakersfield was but wasn't too bothered as long as he was going in the rough direction of Central America.

'Are you off to do some fishing?' Ridge ventured innocently.

The man smiled slowly and without taking his eyes off the road, took a long draught from his beer before crushing the empty can in his heavily tattooed hand.

'No son, there ain't many fish left up at the lake… on account a there ain't much water up there either. It's a dry lake. A desert, if truth be told, hot as hell and flat as a grandmothers' tit.'

Ridge was momentarily silent as he racked his brains for an intelligent reason for wanting to go to a desert, to no avail. Luckily, John was loosening up.

'I guess you're wonderin' what the fuck makes a guy want to drive all day to get to a dried up ol' lake.'

'Archaeology?'

'Hell no!
I got me a little Indian woman. Loves me dearly, bless her soul. I'm going to hold out there for as long as I can. Mebbes the rest of my damn life!'

'Me too.' Ridge volunteered quickly. 'I mean…, I'm going to Mexico to find *my* girlfriend, if I can, that is…' he trailed off miserably.

'Hey! A little *mammasita*!
You be doggoned careful down there! She give you that?'

He laughed and punched Ridge gently just above his plaster cast.

'Long story…' Ridge muttered quietly.

This seemed to brighten up his driver and the sense of a common bond between them livened up the conversation as they traded bad jokes and related stories back and forth. Just as

Ridge was beginning to think he had been a tad paranoid on first meeting John, he started to come over all heavy again. They had been talking about 'women' and how they were the cause of so many of men's' problems. It was the usual bullshit repertoire, 'can't live *with* them, can't live *without* them' and so on. John had gone quiet for a moment, as if he was deciding whether or not to let his passenger in on a secret. Then he pointed away over to his left.

'D'ya see that building over there, beyond the scrub?

Ridge stared hard and could just make out a long and low anonymous looking modern building. It was still way ahead and a good mile from the road, he would never had noticed it if it hadn't been pointed out to him. It looked like the admin block for a factory or maybe a small research facility.

'That's Corcoran. I spent fifteen years of my sorry-ass life in there. That's where I got this...'

With that, John turned slowly and looked at Ridge with his face straight on for the first time and the dumbstruck Scot saw that he had a black eye-patch over his left eye. He couldn't understand how he hadn't seen it before; it was a real Long-John-Silver fuck-off pirate's eye-patch!

He had never heard of the place but assumed it was a prison of some kind. It was as if an inflatable question mark now hung in the air between them, gas-filled to bursting point, one wrong move and it would blow sky-high. *Why the fuck was he in a prison, for 15 years?*

'You don't know what in the sam hell I'm talkin' 'bout, do you son?'

Ridge shook his head mutely.

'Corcoran is a prison. California's thirty-third state prison. The shit-hole of the universe'.

'Did you work there...or... were you... I mean did you...?'

'Hell yes! I did time there! Sure did! Maximum security! Pre-meditated murder, all the way! Could've been the chair, almost!

He could see the colour drain from his passenger's face.

'Don't you worry none! I'm a *reformed* son-of-a-bitch! It was a one-off. No fucking way would I ever want to go back there again!'

Without any prompting from Ridge, John opened another beer and told him the story. He had been a wild kid, running with the Oakland Raiders who were a particularly tough chapter of the Hell's Angels in the late sixties. 'It was a crazy-ass time', he admitted.

'The whole country was going up in flames or so it seemed at the time.

The government was all fucked up and the people were looking to Haight-Ashbury more than to DC.

And the acid!

Hell, that and some other good stuff was freaking out the whole West Coast.

Come on in, Jim, my friend. The West *is* the fuckin' best!

Break on through!

So, anyways, we were hanging out at a bar over near Berkeley, few beers, some grass, being cool and stuff.

I was on a real downer. I'd had some 'ludes and they'd depressed the shit outa' me all morning.

I noticed that Bella, my woman, had disappeared and she didn't have a bike of her own, she *always* rode with me so I was real pissed that she'd just took off like that.

Then the old paranoia jest started fryin' my head, sizzling away 'til I had to go outside and see whose bike was missing.

Straight away, I saw big Boomer's new Harley had gone and I could see them together, clear as I'm looking at you now with this old eye of mine.

Before I knew what I was doing, I was settin' my puddle-jumper for Boomer's place over at Piedmont.

I never expected to see nothin', but there was the bike outside his yard an' I pulled up half a block away. So I sneaked up,

real fuckin' quiet and looked in the front
window. I couldn't believe ma own eyes!
That fat bastard was givin' Bella a good
dickin' in full fuckin' view, man!

I totally fucking froze, man!
They didn't even see nothin!
I slapped my goddamn face so hard!
But they were still there. I turned and
walked back to my bike.
I wasn't even mad at that point, just
numb.
As I climbed onto the bike and fired her
up I had this vision of me flying right
through the window like some avenging
son-of-a-bitch angel, some fuckin' dark
horse of the Apocalypse, y'know, some
real evil shit like that.
Then it just came to me!

People say they don't remember shit like
this, like it's some kinda' excuse or
something. Messed up I rightly was, but I
recall what I did with supreme clarity.
My lawyers got me to say I was totally
trashed and stuff like that, but it wasn't
the truth at all, no way.

I had a bottle of gas in a saddlebag.
I just walked up to the house, lit the
bottle with my Zippo and tossed the son-
of-a-bitch through the window.
It was like fuckin' Nagasaki man!
'Course I'd not realised what a dirty cunt
Boomer was and that he had engine parts

sittin' in oil trays, cans of gas and lube
oil all over the goddamn room.
The explosion carried me all the ways
across the street.
Woke up in hospital with my friggin'
legs cuffed to the bed!'

Ridge had been speechless through all of
this, alternating between shaking his head sagely
and nodding it quickly in assention. He coughed
and cleared his throat before blurting out, 'So
the bastards were dead then!'

'No, man!' John looked at him,
surprised at the intensity of the youngster's
outburst.

'Boomer was for sure.
His ass was grass!
Bella was pretty much OK on account of
the fat bastard on top of her soaking up
most of the blast. She was a bit deaf
though, I mind she had some kinda
hearing aid at the trial. Sure as hell put
her off from fornicating for a while!'

'So you kept in touch with her?'

'Sure did, man!
Bella wrote me every week for 'bout ten
years or so but then she got married an' I
kind got the feelin' her husband didn't
get off on it much. She don't even know
that I'm outta prison.'

John continued to scare the pants off Ridge for a while longer, relating how he had lost his eye and other choice tales. He had eventually taken part in a pioneering substance abuse treatment project, which had helped to establish Corcoran as the world's largest correctional centre for substance abuse treatment and sliced six years off his sentence. He was now training to be a community outreach worker.

Ridge would have loved to relate his own personal 'explosive theme' experiences but he thought it was probably better to leave the subject on a positive note. They were apparently getting close to Bakersfield and it was a good time to find out where the hell he was. He had been hitchhiking, John was telling him now, along the most dangerous stretch of road in the whole country.

'You've been real lucky, *amigo*. There's some crazy S.O.B.'s out there and most of them use this coastal route! I'm going to drop you at the bus station and I strongly suggest you get the 'dog' to San Diego.'

As they pulled in to the Greyhound station, Ridge quickly fingered the few notes he had in his back pocket. It would hopefully be enough, he thought, but he knew he would need to buy food at some point soon. He grabbed his bag and jumped out of the huge old pickup.

John had nipped round to see him off and it was strange to see him straight on again. He did look pretty scary, but Ridge was sure a lot of that was on purpose.

'Come round the back here, boy. I've got something for you.'

John sounded serious and immediately Ridge's heart began to pound in his chest. He cautiously looked round the truck to see John closing up one of his own dusty old bags. He fixed his one eye hard at Ridge, which gave him a slightly angled head position and a wary look about him.

'Here. Come take this.' He held his closed right hand out towards Ridge, palm facing down.

The look on Ridge's face must have betrayed his feelings for the man laughed and then physically reached out and took his small hand into his own much larger bear-like paw and forcefully stuffed what felt like balled up paper into Ridge's hand.

'Take this, you'll need it if you're ever gonna find yer little lady!
You hang loose, my friend!'

With that, he turned with a wave, climbed back into the truck and was off in a haze of petrol fumes and dust. It was a couple of minutes before Ridge could look down and open up his clenched fist to reveal almost one hundred dollars in scrunched up notes.

Within twenty minutes, he was on the bus for San Diego.

Chapter Eight - Falkirk no more

The ice-cold bus was a welcome relief. Ridge, completely wired after his recent encounters, sat up at the front, found an old school techno playlist on his Nano and turned the volume to max. The purple and red sky was rapidly darkening, something he would never get used to, and as they sped towards the myriad lights of Los Angeles, his racing heart played its own frantic bass line to the thumping sounds in his head. This was bloody brilliant! Sitting bolt upright, feeling like some future-world urban nomad, he alone was piloting this fast-cruiser through the sparkling neon highways, pulsing red to green, red to green, leading inexorably to the brightest light of the mother ship.

As he reviewed the day, especially his time with John, he felt he had somehow received a valuable lesson, one that may take time to sink in. He thought about Orla, without rancour, for the first time in ages and some of that dragging weight of futility that he had been burdened with seemed to have been left behind in Bakersfield. He never made it to the sunshine of the mother ship however. He had been running on empty for too long and, inevitably, once the adrenaline rush of the last few hours wore off, the weariness hit him like a locomotive. He slept the last hour into LA, all the way through and on to San Diego, where he awoke, frozen stiff, disorientated, and with the sweet remnants of a past life fraying into nothingness with every cruel second.

Past hunger, he was so tired that all he could think about was finding somewhere to lie down and crash out again. As he stumbled through the foyer of the station, giving the best Bela Lugosi impression seen in Southern California for many a year, he saw an ad for an international hostel down by the beach. Safe place to hide 'til the morra' he thought wearily. He stayed for over a week.

If the peeps were a tad weird in San Francisco then at least they were interestingly so, whereas Ridge found the locals down here to be more vacuous than the worst teen frat movie ever made, *like..., OMG! Totally*, dude! He *did* have blonde hair, which was good. But surfing was out 'cos of the arm and his genetics ensured that not only did he have terminally crap deltoids, he would be incapable of ever gaining a suitable tan and so the poor Scots lad didn't really fit the stereotype in La La land. However the hostel was really friendly and he quickly picked up some good tips from other travelling types and even found a much needed job for a couple of days.

As everyone knows, where ever you go in the world, you always find an Irishman or a Scotsman and in this happy case, Ridge found a fellow countryman just when he needed one most. A rank pisshead – of course.

Crawford was *'fae Falkirk like'* and a more authentic Scots bloke you couldn't meet. But a new improved version…, with added sunshine. He drank his vodka with Irn Bru, a wonderfully teeth rotting bright orange fizzy drink which was advertised as being made from steel girders and which, back home, engendered a brand loyalty that Coca-Cola would die for. He was still rabidly following every Glasgow Rangers game, albeit a week late, through the back page sermons of the Daily Record, received weekly along with his case of Irn Bru.

Best of all though, was that he smoked fags the right and proper way; all the way down to the end, drawing hard, right through the cigarette into the brown filter. This he would then squeeze between two nicotine stained fingers until, with a screwed-up-eyes last desperate gasp, he would finally finish what must have been the very last cigarette on earth. He was totally oblivious to the aghast looks from the locals as he polluted their precious air space. Ridge himself had perfected his Dennis Leary routine if anyone tried to curtail his own impressive smoking activity but Crawford; he just never seemed to notice.

His live-in girlfriend, Larni, was an impossibly thin, beach blonde, nail technician from Colorado. Ridge had never seen a lassie with such tight jeans since those hazy teenage afternoons watching Daisy in re-runs of The Dukes of Hazard. Although not really his type, he couldn't fail to be impressed with anyone who would even contemplate running 3 miles along a beach each sun-drenched morning before work as she invariably did. But, after a few one-sided conversations he quickly realised she had the intellect of Flipper and he came to the conclusion that she would probably run or even crawl, over broken glass every day as long as it meant she would remain THIN!

But Crawford thought he'd died and gone to heaven as she was several stratospheres above the level of talent he would have been able to pull back home. She was also pretty horny too and apparently '*hud a pure tap on her vadge, like*'.

Larni was a mass of contradictions however and although one of her more impressive talents was her ability to drink both of the Scots lads under the table and still look great the next day. But if you offered her a cigarette she would look at you as if you had just suggested asking her mother to dance naked on YouTube. It was hard to square this with the fact that she was living with a walking ashtray, but *hey*, that must be the seductive power of the Scottish personality. It was infuriating for Ridge who was relying on his wee joints as an emotional crutch at that time but both her and Crawford were very anti drugs and even although they could spend entire weekends completely polluted with alcohol they just couldn't see how sanctimonious their attitude was.

All the same it was great to hang out with the big C and talk crap about back home, get to take out and polish some of the gems of Scots vocabulary like 'jobbie' or 'crabbit' and be able to shout 'Get it up ye' proudly without having to hastily explain that there was nothing inherently offensive about this most favourite of Scottish toasts. They would endlessly play 'good guy – wanker' games with all the famous people they could think of, then argue which Scottish news-reader they would like to shag the most.

Like most Scots abroad, Crawford was good at finding ways of earning money and what did he spend it all on but a massive, increasingly augmented, fuck-off stereo for his 'wheels'. You can take the man out of Falkirk, but you can't take Falkirk out of the ... most refreshing.

So after two days and an unfortunately steep fall from the wagon, Ridge found himself sitting on a hostel sundeck with a whisky in his good hand whilst Crawford sawed audaciously through his other arm to the horrified fascination of an assortment of backpackers.

Suitably anaesthetized to any possibility of pain, he was quite comfortable about his erstwhile new friend's gung ho approach. He tried to mumble an explanation to a stunning Finnish girl that in Scotland it was considered unmanly ever to consult written instructions when constructing or dismantling any items of equipment, particularly in the home and especially in front of womenfolk. He went on to patiently explain that the general idea was just to wade in without any undue hesitation and then vainly try to make the best of it when it all went pear-shaped. On seeing that little common ground was being forged between the nations, Crawford tried the more direct approach.

'We just dae it cos' we're pure radge like!'

Ridge added that this was also our main tenet for the tactics of the national footie team. Thus, Crawford was simply following the Scots credo when he drunkenly agreed to cut off Ridge's plaster cast with a rusty chisel and a Swiss army knife.

Following his successful debut surgical procedure, Dr Crawford was therefore able to secure Ridge a job alongside him on a construction site a mile or two up the coast at San Clemente. This job was initially made for Ridge as it involved skulking about in subterranean darkness whilst all his fellow workers were baking in the heat of the glaring sun.

However, much as he fought it, he was promoted from waterproofing foundation trenches on his first day to painting sun decks and flat roofs on his second day. From this, much improved vantage position, he was then able to see quite clearly the events that were about to unfold, but was to understand none of it.

The site was going to be a large high value piece of real estate with select waterside properties and a marina. However at present it was an ugly piece of arid scrubland made into a veritable dust bowl by the activities of Ridge and his colleagues. It was the presence of this all pervasive dust, *and* the camouflaged vehicles obviously, that gave the enemy an element of surprise when they attacked in a well planned pincer movement.

Looking up from the glaringly bright silver decking, Ridge had become dimly aware, in the periphery of his vision, of a group of khaki coloured tank-like vehicles and what seemed to be soldiers pouring out of them and through the dust towards the site. He was only just starting to wonder why the army were conducting an exercise so close to them. He'd dreamily invented a bizarre scenario where the property developers had been sold an army testing ground by unscrupulous types when all hell broke loose around him.

'*Immigracion*'!

'*La Migra*'!

Ridge could not believe what he was seeing! All the wee guys who had, until moments ago, been working away quietly beside him were now screaming their heads off and running for their lives from these soldier type guys who were brandishing rifles and looking extremely mean. He was still rooted to the spot when he saw Crawford over on the far side of the site, running like a hare also. Just then he stopped, looked round at Ridge and made a neck-severing hand signal, eyes popping madly, before legging it again.

It was too late to do anything at this point as the Immigration men were all over the place and Ridge watched in horror as an older Hispanic guy raced past him and jumped down what must have been a thirty foot drop to evade capture. Obviously injured, he pulled himself up and tried to limp desperately on but to no avail. He was dragged off without ceremony back through the dust towards the vehicles. Incredibly, no one even looked at Ridge twice and he stood there, along with a few other white Europeans and Americans, all looking suitably bemused or relieved depending on their respective employment validity.

Back at the hostel, they all had a laugh

about it but it reminded Ridge sharply of Juanita and his reason for being there. There had been several hostel residents working at the site, all illegally and all white. Not one of them had been picked up by the authorities.

There were a few local guys hanging around that evening, as seemed to be the norm; a fairly reliable and constantly replenishing supply of cute European girls being the primary motivation for their attendance, rather than a deep seated desire to further the aims of pan-global understanding. *Like flies tae shite*, thought Ridge ruefully, not forgetting that he had fallen into that category himself, back in San Francisco. Already that seemed a long time ago, he thought, as he listened to some of the conversations relating to the drama of earlier.

The general attitude of the Californian guys was of a light hearted antipathy towards the Mexicans and the other more obvious immigrant communities. They spouted some pseudo economic reasons for not allowing them across the border along the lines of; sure, they brought in a substantial monetary benefit from their cheap labour but 'alongsides that you gotta look at the vastly increased welfare bill and crime rates'. To Ridge, it sounded like they were just regurgitating the same old crap they must hear from their parents, day in and day out.

But to some present, it had set off alarm bells and the dialogue had become more heated. Most of the Europeans had encountered a far greater ethnic diversity in their own countries than these local guys would ever see, but it did seem to ring true that nowhere else would you see such an obvious disparity between just two distinct groups of people. The 'wetbacks' and the *gringos*.

As back-packers, even some of the white travellers admitted to feeling a slight taste of discrimination when working in California and some of the more longer term expatriates had noticed that there did seem to be an increase in the number of exclusive developments or rather, whites-only 'gated communities', steadily insinuating their way into urban life here like an unstoppable and remorseless moral cancer. A quiet young guy from Jo'burg described to Ridge what it had been getting like back home in South Africa where it was becoming unusual *not* to want to stay in a protected area, guarded by men with guns day and night.

Ridge felt so foolish now, thinking of the last time he had been with Juanita and he wanted to hold her tight in his arms and tell her she had been right to be angry with him and that he was starting to understand now a little of what she had been talking about.

Crawford gave him his Swiss army knife as a memento and Ridge left before dawn for Tijuana and Mexico.

He had wandered through the pandemonium that was the border control without even having his passport stamped or being subjected to any official scrutiny and so he wasn't sure at which exact point he had actually entered Mexico.

The heat and bustle of early evening Tijuana was intense, confusing and hostile and he was soon under no allusions that this was another country. Completely bewildered by the frenetic noise and activity around him, he recognized that his main priority was to get out of there *muy pronto*.

Standing alone and still amongst the hectic pushing and shoving of the crowded bus station, he had the strange sensation of being like a tethered sacrificial lamb. With the atmosphere darkening as the daylight faded he could imagine the hungry coyotes circling in the shadows and so he jumped an ancient old bus heading for the Baja California with vague instructions corkscrewing around his jangling brain from a girl at the hostel about a bus, then a boat, then a bus again.

Chapter Nine – Paradise Lost

Whilst a weary and sweating Ridge was silently praying to himself for his destination to miraculously appear, another man was also sweating too much and offering up his own prayers for a swift and robust resolution to his own predicament. The man was not used to feeling like this. He was no saint, that was for sure, but he usually preferred to leave the higher level machinations to others, to those who had no trouble sleeping at night. He was *not* sleeping well. His nightmares were invading his waking thoughts too and people were starting to notice that he wasn't on form. In his line of business it didn't do to have people think you were losing your grip.

Sitting here in this expensive air-conditioned suite in an expensive hotel in an expensive part of the city did not lessen his anxiety one bit. He was a large man, well able to handle himself and he had the command and loyalty of an army of men who would kill to order and ask no questions, however, today, he was on his own and it did not feel right.

Of course, the reason he was on his own was because he was not supposed to be here at all. He fervently hoped no one else knew he was here except for the party he was sitting nervously waiting for. *Where the fuck were they*, he thought desperately, trying to affect an air of calm while inwardly panicking. He was experienced enough in these matters to be able to run several possible scenarios through his mind in rapid succession, none of them involving any long term future for him. If it *was* a setup, then he was dead already. It could go the other way too and he would be incarcerated for the rest of his days, unless someone got to him first.

At last, the door opened, heavy with wood and leather panelling and three men in suits came in, each with two bodyguards carrying barely concealed automatic weapons. The three men stood in a line in front of him as each was frisked in turn and then subjected to an electronic sweeping device before he too was made to stand up and do likewise. Not a word had been spoken up until now and with the security contingencies now in place, one of the men smiled impassively and gestured for each of them to take a place on the cushioned leather seats around the dark wooden table.

The ferry from the Baja peninsula, with its cooling sea breeze, had been cruelly quick and short-lived compared with the slow and never-ending bus journey before and afterwards but somehow he had made it to Acapulco where he decided he just had to have some time away from buses. He wandered through the early morning town as if in a dream and found it impossible to reconcile what he was experiencing here to what he had seen or heard about Acapulco on television or other media. He was sure he could remember his father saying that it was one of the 'wonders of the world'. Well, *not today*, thought Ridge.

As he walked along what must have been

a major road into the town centre, the early morning mist was swirling around his feet and to his horror he saw a large dead animal lying in the middle of the road. Not believing what he was looking at, he stopped and stared. Sure enough! There was a dead donkey on the road, the buzzing of insects and the stench of dead meat overpowering.

He quickly walked on trying to look up instead and all he could see were dilapidated old buildings and run down shops. It looked like Benidorm on a bad day. After a few hours of milling about hoping to find a 'nicer' part of town, he gave up and went to sit on the beach. He saw a couple of backpackers who had been on the same bus as him and he plonked himself down beside them. Chatting easily, they had been equally horrified when they had arrived.

The beach was fairly impressive, Ridge had to admit, but he had no energy to walk any further and was quickly dozing in the heat of the sun. He awoke to finding himself being poked abruptly in the ribs and jumped up with a start. One of the Dutch couple he was with was pointing down the beach somewhat where they could see a phalanx of soldiers moving across the beach towards them. The long line of uniformed men effectively cut off the beach and it seemed no-one could get past them without their permission. Ridge was unperturbed, particularly as his two companions said they spoke good Spanish.

As the soldiers reached them, it became apparent that they were actually some kind of police and all they wanted was to see a passport. The couple had theirs handed back without a word and then they scrutinized Ridge's. Instantly, there was a lot of loud gesticulating and shouting down at him and he jumped to his feet nervously. The Dutch couple tried to intervene on his behalf and the problem seemed to be that his passport hadn't been stamped at Tijuana nor anywhere else since then. As if in a grotesque Orwellian nightmare, they were accusing *him* of being an illegal immigrant! Ridge had laughed and told them to fuck off which, in hindsight, had probably not been a great idea. With his two friends trying their best to rescue him, he was escorted off the beach and into the back of a festering hot police car. The station was all of two minutes drive where he was led into a dark old office and made to sit down.

He was put on one of those stackable plastic chairs which have to be the most uncomfortable chairs in the world and at best only suitable for short sits and probably better suited to those with a more ample posterior than the one he possessed. The large open-plan office was hotter than Hades and most of the men working there had a fan of some description blowing tepid air onto them. Ridge could feel the life force draining out of him and he fervently hoped that he would not be there for long. Regretting his foolish behaviour earlier, he was amazed that out of that huge sweep of the beach, he was the only idiot that seemed to have been picked up.

On most of the cluttered desks he could see big old PC's that belonged in a museum and in most cases their primary function seemed to be to help prop up unfeasibly large heaps of paperwork which otherwise would be scattered on the floor. Not that this would have made a great deal of difference to these guys, thought Ridge.

The guy nearest to him was leaning over his desk, unable to sit down as his chair was piled with official looking paperwork. His saggy and tired eyes stared listlessly at a screen which seemed to be stuck onto the end of what Ridge imagined a cathode ray tube would look like. Sweat poured down the contours of his weary face as he attempted to type in a faltering one-finger-one hand style onto the filthy looking keyboard. Every so often it would bleep angrily at him and he would curse darkly back. He would then scratch his thick moustache for a while then try again.

As an IT professional, Ridge might have found this laughable if it wasn't really happening. He could see another policeman appear to print something out, write onto that piece of paper, take it to another printer, feed it into that and finally print more stuff on top of it. Each segment of the operation involved walking from one end of the room to the other more than once, all the time bumping into other poor souls doing similar stuff and all of them ducking and dodging wall fans, desk fans, ceiling fans and a whole host of other electrical bear trap devices designed to impede the progress of whatever the fuck they were trying to achieve.

Three hours later, he was still there and every time he made to stand up, he would be shouted at to remain seated. He could see his passport still untouched sitting on the desk nearest him. The room was so airless that he started to feel as if he was going to pass out. Then, realising that most of the men had become engaged in an energetic discussion at the opposite end of the room, he quickly reached across and retrieved the incriminating document. Emboldened by the success of this recent action and desperate beyond any logical reasoning to get out of that stifling room, he slid out of the chair and walked out of the door, all the time waiting for a barrage of abuse or even a hail of bullets.

Nothing. *Nada.* He was outside! The balmy evening air, fragranced by the fumes of a prehistoric old truck passing by was nevertheless as beautiful as any air he had ever gasped and he walked fast in the opposite direction with his head down and avoiding any eye contact with anyone.

Weary and hungry, he decided it was time to bring out his secret weapon, only to be used in direst emergency. His cash was almost non-existent and despite being a complete shit-hole of a place, Acapulco was not the cheapest. Into the first dive of a hotel and out with the American Express courtesy of Mr T LeGrange! The room was foul, overpriced and the 'steak' he had was suspect enough to make him fear for any other donkeys that might be daft enough to stray into these parts.

The incredibly noisy air-con was at least working, after a fashion, and he attempted to sleep with his hands clamped tightly over his ears. He felt sure Thad would understand and he would pay him back later once he was safely back in a land with flushing toilets. He could hardly believe it himself to think that he was actually enjoying air-con after slagging it off so much up north. He drifted off to a restless sleep, soaring over the sea to distant Sorsay, suffering inside the deafening roar of the coastguard helicopter. He awoke a few hours later, even more tired and straining to hear the last haunting peals of those bagpipes again.

Chapter Ten – Higher

When he finally arrived in Oaxaca the following day, Ridge was suddenly at a loss. It was a miracle that he had found his way there in one piece, of that he was in no doubt. The intensity of his fatigue however, had momentarily erased from his disorientated brain the actual reason for being there in the first place. Sitting by the front of the bus at the edge of the dusty road, Ridge lifted up his knees and let his head fall heavily onto his folded arms. Struggling to find the strength even to lift his head, he suddenly felt a hand roughly shake his shoulder and a surge of lightning arced through his body, searing his tired brain with one word... Juanita!

'You OK, ma friend?' the man's voice said.

Propelled to his feet, he stared at the young guy who had shaken him back to life, recognizing with relief that the two of them had been on the same bus since Mexico City. With his pallid complexion and shock of peroxide blonde hair, the guy stood out even more than Ridge.

'Yeah..., yeah, thanks. Just a bit shagged after the bus y'know', Ridge replied, trying to sound more chilled out than he really was. The guy just grinned and introduced himself.

His name was Marcel; he was French and was on holiday from University. His English was excellent and he offered to buy Ridge a coffee across the street from the dingy looking bus station, whereupon Ridge saw that his Spanish was pretty fucking good as well. Ridge could only raise his eyebrows, unable to disguise the fact that he was obviously impressed but Marcel just laughed quickly and explained that he was a languages student and that he was majoring in Spanish.

Neither of them seemed particularly chatty and Ridge was more inclined to find a quiet shadow to crash in than in furthering the cause of European fraternity. But he had become a little more skilled in the art of survival lately, and as he had little hard cash and even less Spanish, he could see that his Gallic chum could be handy. Luckily, Marcel was on a tight budget anyway and was looking for someone to share the cost of a room, the offer of a coffee not being as altruistic as it had first seemed.

They found a cheap room which Marcel agreed to pay for, two nights up front. Ridge mumbled quietly about planning to stay for a week or so to which Marcel replied that as he only wanted to stay four nights then that would be fine, Ridge could pay for the other two nights.

It was only after he was positive that Marcel was asleep at the other end of the small stifling room that Ridge allowed himself to relax his aching limbs and fall into a long restless sleep.

His fevered brain critically reviewed the last few days as he dozed fitfully and the inevitable headline was 'So where do we go from here?' He had got to Oaxaca that much was evident. So far so good – the boy done well. However, he had also managed in three short days to become an illegal immigrant and a fugitive from the police. So, just a normal weekend for a Scots lad on his holidays then?

It was a whole day later when Ridge woke up, his stomach cramping with hunger. Marcel was not around and so Ridge stumbled out into the early evening sunlight desperately looking for something to eat. He felt very weak and the narrow lanes were chokingly claustrophobic and he eagerly dived for a seat near the more airy fringes of some kind of square.

It was a bistro style outdoor café, he figured and probably too expensive but he was in no state to start conducting price comparisons. The wafting aromas were making him want to heave and he sat stock still staring at the silver tabletop until a young woman came over. By a series of grunts and gesticulations and not a few smiles, he settled for some kind of egg dish which turned out to be ballsier than he'd hoped for but he wolfed it down nonetheless.

The food was cheaper than he expected, and emboldened by his success with the café, he sauntered farther along to a busy bar underneath the welcome canopy of some huge trees. Populated entirely by men, the conversations were loud and manic and the air thick with cigarette smoke and emotional outbursts. Ridge was doing his best to become quietly invisible but was surprisingly pleased to see Marcel saunter past. Another beer was purchased with little persuasion and soon the two of them were having a pleasant and relaxing evening. Ridge had barely noticed that there were a few other tourist types about but as time went on there were fewer locals and more travellers.

Inoffensively, a tall thin guy in a Beatle jacket slipped into a seat at their table whilst shouting farewells to friends and moving out of the way of some others who were leaving. He didn't even glance at either Marcel or Ridge and seemed to be looking for something in a pocket.

Ridge and Marcel carried on talking. The chat was idle and lightweight, but they were both enjoying the experience of being able to sit and talk safely without any great pressure or effort. The thin guy suddenly pulled out a fresh hard-pack of Marlboro Lights and chapped them on the table in a theatrical manner. Ridge gazed longingly at them as he only had some cheap local fags in a mangled soft pack. The guy clocked this in a nanosecond and launched into his routine.

'Gee! Why do I always lose my fucking lighter man? Shit! I must'ah had it two minutes ago. Hey, my friend, you give a guy a light uh'?

Ridge met his imploring look and judging him to be harmless, reached out with his Bic lighter.

'Can I offer you a cigarette in return'? The man said. But Ridge and Marcel both had a hand out already for the reward.

'Sure, sure, no problem, guys... my name is Joaquin, but most people call me John, as in John Lennon'.

He brushed his hand down his face and jacket, as if in some way explaining his last

123

statement. Ridge and Marcel looked at each other for a brief second before introducing themselves, Ridge only just beating the temptation to call himself Elvis, as in...

It was true though; Ridge had to admit grudgingly, the guy did bear more than a passing resemblance to his holiness, the mighty Mr. Ono.

His patter was brilliant and within an hour, the Marlboro packet was looking pretty flimsy and Marcel had headed off for bed, not before giving Ridge a stare that was only thinly disguised as a 'be vigilant' look.

Ridge wasn't that daft and he could see that this was leading up to some scam or other, but as he had already been robbed, he couldn't see what else there was to worry about. Nevertheless, he would have been ten minutes behind Marcel if something very strange hadn't happened. He never saw Marcel again.

John had already gone through his routine about being a John Lennon look-alike in Mexico, and how he had been on T.V. and had his own website, his family originally fleeing Europe after the war and so on. He was talking about how many people he knew in Oaxaca and that nothing important happened here without him hearing about it, legal or otherwise.

'In fact', he leant closer to Ridge.

'In these very seats, just a day ago, sat the biggest gangsters this side of Panama City. And some of them had seen my show! It is true, my friend, and the girl, what a princess! She said my English accent was terrible! And who am I to

argue with such a sad beautiful creature,
Juanita was ...'

'WHAT DID YOU SAY?' Ridge shouted
out, just managing to choke his outburst into a
hissing rasp. John had jumped back, genuinely
startled. Ridge started to cough uncontrollably.

'Shut up! Please, amigo!
You don't know this girl, I promise you,
she is from another world to yours, believe me.'
John looked at the poor boy with a mixture of
pity and fascination.

But Ridge could feel that familiar feeling
and knew he was on to something. More beer
came and then tequilas and soon he had the full
story. He was positive it *was* Juanita, and he
listened intently. She was portrayed by John as
some underworld concubine, willing or not, John
suspected the latter, resting in Oaxaca before
some great gathering further south. The rest
confirmed his worst fears. The shadowy Ramon
Beltran had reared his head again.

It was too much of a coincidence! John
intimated that it was not too healthy to speak
about *El Cocodrilo* too much in public but he
told John he was involved in a lot of serious bad
shit including smuggling, narcotics, guns and
people trafficking. John had never ever seen him
personally but his reputation was formidable.

Throughout the one way conversation,
Ridge sat glumly, nodding at the appropriate
moments to ensure the other man kept talking.
He discovered that John was actually on
speaking terms with several of the Crocodile's
gang and even supplied them with small

quantities of primo hallucinogenic mushrooms which only he knew the location of. 'Magic mushies! For fuck's sake!' Ridge blurted out.

'That's what we're doing tonight, my friend,' said John casually, waving his hand limply in the direction of five or six other young traveller type guys sitting around the adjacent tables. 'We're off up the mountain to collect the finest Psilocybin mushrooms, maybe some Peyote, have a ball and then come back and sell them for big bucks, even to these jackals I was just telling you about'.

A distinct frisson of cold dread ran up his spine but still Ridge listened.

'Yes, my friend, it is guaranteed money, keeps you travelling for many months more. All you need is to be young, fit and hungry for some easy cash'!

Ridge gulped slowly as he realized how close he was to signing up for this mad adventure. He got John to confirm that the gangsters were passing through Oaxaca in a few days, where they would be staying over, like before, and John was to sell some mushrooms to one of them.

'When do we go'? asked Ridge. The man laughed. 'By the light of the midnight moon, my friend!' Ridge looked down at his watch. 11.50 pm.

With barely time for any introductions and no time to pick up the rest of his stuff, they were on their way, a strange line of earnest looking young backpackers setting off for a walk, in the middle of the night. After a short while they squeezed into a couple of taxis which quickly took them to the outskirts and the start of their trek. The other guys were mostly like him, or on the surface anyway, up for a good laugh, taking nothing seriously. Three were German, two Dutch and one teenager from Uzbekistan. The walking was not particularly arduous, particularly for Ridge as he wasn't carrying anything and the 'mountain' seemed more of a gentle upland at this point. Oaxaca is already almost twice the height of Ben Nevis, Ridge learned and so he was a little worried about whether he would need oxygen or not.

They came to a cave after three hours, which John had kitted out like a base camp. It was huge but they were only allowed to doss down around the outer chamber, 'for security reasons'. However, John lent him a sleeping bag and they all got totally stoned on some of the most incredible weed that Ridge had ever tasted.

Early next morning the young travellers were abruptly wakened out of deep slumber with strong coffee and within a short time they were off again. It was a beautiful morning with gentle mists lying in the hollows and reminding Ridge of home. The air was fresh and cool and they seemed to be moving quickly across the landscape. The terrain was becoming rougher and the men could feel the gradient begin to incline steadily.

Whilst being totally unfit, Ridge found himself to be enjoying the rhythm of walking which he hadn't experienced for a long time. The sheer effort of watching where you put you feet and keeping pace with the others had that particular meditative quality that he remembered well from his jaunts with Gavin. He hadn't been near a mountain since he was young and memories were flooding back of some of the good times he had with his brother; when Gav had taught him how to swallow dive from a seemingly cathedral-like rock bluff into the river Dee, or when, one spring camping trip on the island of Arran, tucked up in the warmth of their sleeping bags, he had tried to verbally convey to his mystified young brother the exquisite revelation that was the 'wank'. Ridge couldn't help smirking now at his own innocence and how on that same trip he had crushed up bright yellow celandines into a glass jar with water so that he could pretend he was drinking the same Strongbow Cider as his cool big brother.

He suddenly felt a sharp pang of guilt for the life he had had since and the way in which his brother was robbed of that chance. Here was Ridge now, being a fucking idiot, mixing drugs and mountains just like Gav. He hoped fervently that his brother wasn't looking down on him just now or that he could appreciate that there was a higher purpose here, no pun intended. They *were* high up now and as he gazed down across the tree tops he couldn't stop himself thinking out loud, 'Here's to you, mate. You'd have fuckin' *loved* this man'.

They slowed to a stop behind John and he bid everyone to sit around him as he explained they were now in the right area for harvesting the mushrooms. He passed around some tortilla bread, explaining the finer points of the Psilocybin as they ate and then they drank some water from a cool stream and rested in the shade while John collected a few mushrooms for them to use as a reference.

The German guys were total fiends for ganja and they rolled some more killer joints which were quickly dispatched leaving most of them completely spaced. It must have been the combination of altitude, fatigue and the hash but Ridge felt very serene and on the cusp of something important and special. The sense of camaraderie was tangible as they sat awaiting their final mission instructions and it was as Apollo astronauts striding across the gangway to their ship that they each set off in a different direction to begin their search.

Ridge walked for quite a while before he saw anything that looked promising but once he found one mushroom, he found a lot more in small clumps. After a while he found himself crawling through the grass and rough brush land on his hands and knees as he felt he had been missing too many before. The heat of the day was overbearing now and there were little bright green lizards darting around and over his hands as he foraged in the undergrowth. John had given them all a thin canvas shoulder bag which they had to fill before returning to the shaded area by the stream when they were ready. He had given them a rough timescale of meeting in the evening, sleeping there until first light then heading back to the cave in the morning and back to the town by the evening. As long as they returned to the stream by first light then they would be okay but he refused to wait for them past that time.

Ridge reckoned that gave them a maximum of 14 hours before being abandoned and he felt sure he would be back long before that. He had been away for less than three hours so far and his bag was half full already.

John had seemed very relaxed about them sampling the mushrooms as they were picking them assuming they were collecting enough to bring back over and above that. He actually promoted the idea that you can find them easier if you are a little high as your mind becomes more focused and you develop a relationship with the plant as you learn more about its' habitat preferences and so forth.

Ridge had never partaken of magic mushrooms in Scotland but he had few reservations about it after his chemical excesses in San Francisco. He lay in the grass, propped up on one arm, and set out a dozen or so mushrooms in front of him. Most were two or three inches long and thicker than the ones he had seen people take at home. He selected three or four of the least bruised and brushed them clean before throwing them into his mouth. The taste was stronger than he anticipated; an earthy metallic taste and he ground them in his teeth briefly before swallowing. They were slightly gritty and he wished he had taken a water container with him. Finding a stream would be cushy, he thought.

He had carried on looking for mushrooms and after his rich harvesting period he was now experiencing a drought and started to feel a tad guilty about the few extra mushrooms he had munched. John had showed him pictures of a Peyote cactus and explained how to cut off the relevant button-like pieces from the small white tufted plants if he came upon any.

He had stumbled upon a large clump of

them and so cut a substantial quantity before stuffing a few pieces into his mouth. The taste was less pleasant and he moved off further with the ulterior motive of finding some water. The drugs had still not taken any effect as yet and he actually felt full of energy and extremely healthy and at one with his surroundings. After a short time he could hardly believe his luck as he realized he could hear running water nearby and it was as he started to move more purposely towards the sound that he suddenly felt the ground move abruptly under his feet.

It was exactly as if someone had pulled a rug sideways under his feet. He quickly sat down in the undergrowth and apart from his heart pounding faster, he felt fine, besides, the water sounded very close now. He jumped back up again and almost immediately went sideways again and he grabbed quickly at a slim tree branch next to him which could not support him and he fell face first into the brush. 'Shit' he muttered. 'I'm off my face already. Holy fuck! Where's that water?' He pushed some branches away from his face and as he did so he could see trailing images of his arm and the branch as if in slow motion. He laughed. 'Bloody hell! It's really going off now! Och well, bring it on, baby!'

Ridge lay back for a while and let the experience take hold of him, so he could get a measure of just how wasted he was. Then he would get a drink of that cool water, which sounded good, very good. He started to crawl forwards, bit by bit, occasionally lurching to his feet on easier terrain before stumbling again. He stuffed a handful of mushrooms into his mouth to give him an energy boost just until he found the water. It was so close he could smell it! He bumped into a tree with a welcoming canopy of leaves and decided to sit there in the cool shade for a while. The sun had started to blister his skin in the midday heat and he could feel the mosquitoes biting through his thin shirt sleeves.

As he sat propped against the tree, he could see something move towards him in the distance. His vision was becoming more affected and he was picking up vibrant colour changes now but he was positive there was somebody walking through the tall ferns towards him.

He shouted.

'Hey! How's it going! Hi'!

He still couldn't be sure who or what it was but he felt only warmth and empathy towards this thing and he had no concept of fear or danger in the slightest.

Suddenly he could see the face of a girl, smiling at him and waving as if she knew him. No doubt. It was a girl. A dark haired girl in a rough cotton dress and she walked over and sat beaming at him! He guessed she was Mexican, and tried to blurt out some basic communication but somehow the words just didn't come out. She had the most beautiful smile! Her teeth were so white and he just felt loved by those large brown eyes.

She spoke softly to him but he couldn't understand what she was saying. It was not Spanish but some other language he was not familiar with, perhaps a Mayan tongue; the words were pleasing in their sound and he imagined he could see them flash briefly in the warm air in vibrant colours like floating technicolour graffiti. She took his hand gently and rubbed along the top of his knuckles and as she did so, pulses of warmth radiated up his arms and across his shoulders.

She looked deep into eyes and smiled knowingly. He knew she was wanting him to love her but he could do nothing but grin inanely back to her and he tried to tell her he was powerless to move. She nodded and removed her hand and he felt a sharp sense of loss as profound as any he had ever experienced. He continued to stare at her as she gazed into his eyes and then suddenly her face changed into Juanita, then a girl he had met recently at the hostel in San Diego, then another girl's face then another and another. Her face became a flickering image of everyone woman he had ever known and before he could even register them all. His mum. All the faces seemed to smile at him and although he desperately wanted them to slow down long enough for him to communicate something to them, he just couldn't. Orla was there and then gone in a flash. She looked beautiful and he ached for her to reappear.

The girl started to move away and the faces grew older and older. He could hardly bear to watch as he saw the faces become more distorted and faded and before he knew it the girl had moved off and suddenly she turned away from him and was gone.

Ridge didn't understand what had just happened but he was overcome with emotion at the profound nature of the experience and he just sat and wept for a long time.

He drifted off into a strange waking sleep and found himself thinking about his old job back in Scotland, what now seemed a strange alien world of computer programs and network systems. He determined that he would stay here on the mountain and set up an IT laboratory. A satellite link up was all he needed and then he could design a new family of software, DNA based systems that reasoned like humans but which solved complex problems better than us because they worked organically along the lines of this fantastic mushroom he had just ingested. He would bring in bio-chemists who could breakdown the constituent chemical structures and relationships and then he could model them into his programming.

He woke up, spreading his arms wide and pushed off the ground gently to glide down over to the edge of the mountain as if it were the most natural thing in the world. This was fantastic, he was actually flying! There had been no water flowing near him. That must have been the drugs, he told himself. He could see hundreds of little animals scurrying around, their little eyes brightly reflecting upwards to him and he gazed down at them with a beatific smile across his face.

He swooped down fast and low now across the landscape. He had *always* wanted to do this! But, suddenly, he was too tired to continue and he quickly landed in an untidy heap and curled himself up into a ball. He felt cold and shivery now and he needed to sleep. Scooping up some leaves and brush from around him, he was soon snuggled underneath and fast asleep.

What seemed like minutes later, he could feel a strange wind against his face. For a split second he thought it was the girl's breath. He quickly opened his eyes and jumped as he saw a tiny little bird hovering right there in front of him. It was like a hummingbird and the wind was from its' little wings flapping so fast. Ridge lay still and looked right into the eyes of the little bird. It just returned his stare hovering without moving an inch. It seemed to be trying to tell him something, to get him to do something. In a flash, Ridge knew he had to get back to Oaxaca. This was crazy, all this mucking around with mushrooms!

He jumped up and realized with some relief that he was still beside the tree where he had seen the girl, or thought he had, the previous evening. He was sure he could make his way back to the meeting spot and all being well he would still be in time as it was not yet fully daylight and hopefully the others would still be there.

Chapter Eleven – The Return of the Thin White Duke

The meeting spot was deserted and Ridge couldn't see any sign that people had been there recently, no flattened grass where anyone had slept, no rubbish lying around. He tried to convince himself that he wasn't too bothered as he greedily scooped up handfuls of the cool fresh water from the stream. The effects of the Peyote were still evident; the cold water seemed to be racing through his entire body and he could feel little stabbing pains up and down his spine as if someone was practicing acupuncture on his back. An emergency evacuation of his bowels followed and it was a considerably weakened Ridge who set off forlornly for the cave and hopefully the others.

He was determined to catch them up, if they were indeed ahead of him, although he half hoped that the others had got even more messed up than him and that he would be the advance guard, the tough Scot who wouldn't let a mere hallucinogenic mushroom slow him down. He remembered a club he had been to once with Orla, called FUBAR, and how they had naively asked someone what the name had meant. He certainly qualified now;

Fucked up beyond all recognition…

The going was easier than he had remembered on the way up and the drugs were probably acting as a painkiller for his knees as he plodded heavily down the mountain. There was a cooling breeze and although weary, Ridge felt positive about his situation and was resolved to finding Juanita back in the town. He still had the canvas bag of mushrooms over his shoulder which was more than half full and he hoped this would realise enough cash to fund an escape for the two of them.

It was by chance he came upon the cave as it was not where he had thought and he blundered up to the entrance, shouting his head off. 'Anyone here? Hullo!' There was stuff lying about unsecured so he guessed they couldn't be far away. Curiosity got the better of him and he took a little look deeper into the dark mouth of the cave. He could see a heavy steel door had been fitted and it had even been painted to blend in with the rock. There was a small spotlight inset into the roof of the cave just above the door and the light was on; a narrow beam playing down over the locking mechanism. Whoever had set this up certainly had spent a load of dosh, he thought to himself.

He was a lot more interested now and couldn't resist the temptation to try the door. It wasn't as heavy as it appeared, probably had some weighted assistance, Ridge thought, as the door swung easily open. His heart missed a beat as he looked through into a massive area, all lit up with professional looking studio lights, mirrors and video equipment. He had just noticed a huge US-style fridge which was promising when something else took his attention.

He heard a muffled sound coming from a large expensive leather sofa which was turned away from him. Ridge walked over to the back of the chair and found Fabio, the youngster from their trip, naked and trussed up, legs wide apart, leaving no room for doubt as to what the intention was. A fucking great camera was set up pointed right up his arse. The lad was conscious but heavily doped by the glazed look in his eyes. Ridge untied him as fast as he could, struggling with the well tied knots, as the boy sobbed uncontrollably.

He helped Fabio put some clothes on and the boy began to pour out the story to him in graphic detail as to what John had been doing. Ridge didn't need to hear it, it was pretty obvious but he let he boy get it out of his system as he raided the fridge and forced him to have some food. Fabio was sick at first but gradually managed to keep some down. Ridge couldn't do justice to the quality of produce either but ate enough to spur him into action. He was pretty scared that John would come back and while he appreciated that they would not make a great team if they were caught either inside or outside the cave he instinctively knew they stood a better chance out there. The fact that he wasn't very sure where the fuck he was didn't make for a promising prognosis.

But one thing he was sure of was that the sick fucker wasn't to get away with this. He found out from Fabio that John had gone back into town to pick up a wealthy client who was coming back up here to have his way, candid camera- style. They guessed roughly that he could feasibly be back within a couple of hours and so Ridge tried to get Fabio to rest up for the trip ahead. The boy was crazy though. He wanted to smash the place up and Ridge could not offer up a valid reason why not to. First, he wanted to take some evidence back with them. He found a video and DVD library, each disc or tape with a boy's name on it. He asked Fabio to check outside to see if the other lads had appeared yet. He wanted to have a quick look at a disc to make sure there was something on it.

The boy just laughed however.

'They won't be back, for sure. They were never coming back.

They only came for the mushrooms, not for money. As soon as they got the stuff they were going back to town. Me and you were the only stupid fucks to fall for his game.'

Ridge slapped himself on the face, hard. 'Fuck, fuck, fuck…!' He looked up and apologised to his brother and to Orla for being such a miserable idiot. Fabio told him how John had said he would go looking up the hill for Ridge next, hoping that he too would be too spaced to resist.

'Yeah, man! He fancied you too! You were next for Fuck-TV man!'

Fabio also told him how the story about Juanita and the thugs was manufactured to suit the game too.

'She never left Oaxaca, man! The *amiga*…that you told me about!

She *was* there, sure. He knew who they
were, so did a lotta people. She could be
there now, but I guess not.
All that stuff about selling to them was
bullshit man, just to get you to come on
the trip! He told me that they were fixin'
to go over to… I think he say,
Guatemala, Antigua.
He told me they be long gone by the time
we got back.'

'Come on, Fabio… let's get the fuck out
of here right now.' Ridge grabbed the nearest
DVD and stuffed it into his mushroom bag.

'Come on, COME ON!'

Ridge implored the lad to leave with him
but Fabio had found a bottle of tequila and was
determined to wait for John's return.

'I'm gonna kill him, for sure.
No problem. You just go man, good
luck, but leave me here.'

As Ridge was stashing a water bottle into
his bag he noticed a huge stainless steel bowl of
what looked like dried mushrooms. Fabio saw
his look and he spat, eyes blazing fiercely.

'Yeah, they're the mushrooms man!
Dried ones are ten times as strong.
You can put them powdered on your
pecker!'

Ridge hesitated for a moment then

140

grabbed the bottle of tequila. There was no time for niceties. He picked up a large handful of the mushrooms, stuffed them into his mouth before pouring the tequila down his throat. 'Rock'n roll!' he shouted, before giving Fabio a slap on the shoulder.

'Take care, pal.'

Back outside it was very bright after the gloom of the cave and it seemed hotter than ever. He walked quickly, the brief rest and food having helped him physically but his mental state was shaky however and all he could focus on was getting back to town as soon as possible. He realised he had had yet another lucky escape and he hoped that Fabio too would somehow extricate himself from the situation safely. But it would be a long time before he could ever listen to 'Love me do' again he thought bitterly.

He tried to sort through in his head the bits and pieces of information he was gradually finding out about Juanita and Ramon, hoping that if he could get it into some semblance of order he would be able to make better plans and avoid so many cock-ups along the way. At least he now had it from more than one source that Juanita was likely to be in either Oaxaca or in Antigua, Guatemala, wherever the hell that was.

The first energy rushes of the mushrooms had started to flush through his bloodstream again and he began to feel a sense of nervous impatience overcoming him. Ridge swung the bag over his shoulder and tentatively broke out into a slow loping run. He fell a few times at

141

first, it was rough ground and not easy to find a footing quickly, but he soon found himself in an easy rhythm. Although it had been a long time ago, it was not as if running was completely alien to him as a former Scottish under-16 AAA's champion.

His family had never been particularly sporting, but had always enjoyed the outdoor life and his father loved to go fishing. Richard and his brother Gavin were considered to be too young and boisterous for serious fishing and they got bored quickly anyway but they would tag along with their dad for weekend trips or longer in the holidays.

The two boys were at their happiest camping and climbing. Richard adored his brother Gavin, who was six years older than him and they were very close, the age difference being just wide enough to put them in two separate social scenes thus avoiding any fraternal competition or jealousy.

Gavin was very different from his wee brother. He was tall and slim with thick dark hair and he was a gifted artist with a love of music. It was Gavin who educated Richard in music and they spent many evenings listening to Gav's extensive record collection so much so that in the years to come, Richard was always regarded as something of a music guru by his own contemporaries.

Richard was just eleven when they went over to the mainland for a camping weekend at Loch Awe. It was on the Saturday morning, with their dad content to fish on his own, that it was decided the two boys would be allowed to climb an easy local mountain, Ben Cruachan, which cast a dark shadow over much of the loch. It was a particularly fine day and they were not going to be too far from their dad. Gavin was experienced on the hills and the two boys were considered very safe within certain boundaries.

They were dropped off at Cruachan Power Station early in the morning with arrangements made to meet in the cafeteria later in the afternoon. If the boys were quick or the weather turned nasty then they could go and visit the hydro-electric power station which was built inside the mountain and was a popular tourist attraction, 'The Hollow Mountain'.

Right from the start, Gav wasn't his usual self that day and for the first hour or so, the boys hardly spoke. Ben Cruachan is over 3,000 feet and although an easy mountain in many respects, it has a very steep initial section, which tends to inhibit free flowing conversation to a certain extent between all but the super-fit. The steep gradient notwithstanding, Gavin was still very quiet.

Richard was just so happy, initially, at the prospect of spending a whole day with his brother on the hills, with the added bonus of the 'Hollow Mountain' power station thrown in as well! He scrabbled up the hill, finding it difficult to keep up with his brother and hoping he hadn't done something to annoy him or make him angry with him. When Gavin put on a set of earphones after a while, his wee brother became despondent but followed him meekly anyway.

Once the hill levelled out a little and they could see the full majesty of the mighty dam rising up in front of them, Gavin thawed a little. They had some crisps and water and Gavin took a couple of pills. Richard assumed he had a sore head or something like that and they had a good laugh taking photos and imagining the dam breaking on to them.

They set off again at a breakneck pace, Gav with his music on again, some new acid house stuff that Richard hadn't had a chance to hear yet. He could hardly keep up with his brother and wasn't enjoying himself when they slowed suddenly and Gavin switched off his walkman and started chatting away just like his old self. He was talking about going to Art College and starting a band and he was very expansive about his life and plans. Richard as usual listened in awe and just thought his brother was so cool.

High above the reservoir now, they worked together closely as they neared the summit, helping each other scrabble up a couple of massive snow-covered rocks to reach the top. As they stood looking at the views, shivering in the cold wind, Gavin pointed to a further peak some way off and suggested they try that before heading down.

The mountain looked like a huge molar from some angles and there were actually two peaks, one being the summit and the other one just slightly lower but harder to traverse and much less travelled. There were too many tourists on this track, he had said. Richard wasn't so keen to veer off the plan they had agreed with their dad, but he wanted to keep in with Gav and it didn't look too far away.

At least Gavin was still on good form

and they chatted about all sorts of things. They were both looking forward to Gavin getting a driving licence in the summer and the adventures they would have. It was after an hour off the beaten track that the going became tougher, lots of loose shale that made it difficult to stay upright and necessitated a half walk half crawl kind of movement which was very tiring. They stopped for a drink and a bar of chocolate and Richard noticed his brother had gone very pale and was sweating heavily despite the cooling breeze. He kept on rabbiting about the Scouts and learning to ski while his big brother became quieter and paler and less interested.

After a long period of sitting in silence, with the biting wind providing a chilling commentary of its own, Richard was becoming seriously worried. He poked Gavin and asked him of he was alright. His brother turned slowly and looked at him straight in the eyes and said,

'No, I don't feel well at all, I think we need a doctor...'

With that, he slid straight off the rock he was on and dropped down onto his haunches and it was only his wee brother's quick reactions that stopped him keeling over flat on his face. Richard was scared stiff now and he propped Gavin up hard against the rock and looked at his eyes. They had gone all funny looking and his face was white and clammy. 'Stop mucking about Gav!' he said, 'this isnae funny.' But Gavin just started weeping and he cried out,

'Ah'm not kiddin' you twit, go and get

145

some help. Please!
I don't know what's going on but
something doesn't feel right!
Please hurry! I can't stand up!
Get dad, will'ye! I'll be OK sitting here,
go on! Run!'

With that, Richard darted off as fast as
his little legs would carry him. As luck would
have it, there were no other walkers in sight and
not knowing where any rescue stations were, he
thought the best thing was to keep going on and
back down to the bottom and if he met any
doctor or whatever on the way down then so
much the better. There was no obvious short cut
down from where the point they were at and he
head decided that the safest thing was to retrace
their route all the way back. Too make matters
worse, there was a slight drizzle now which he
hadn't noticed at first as his face was soaking
wet anyway with his own tears.

He ran and ran and successfully traversed
the worst bit back on to the main drag but even
that was quiet now as most people were either
higher up towards the proper summit or had
headed back from the lower sections due to the
change in weather and the time of day. He
stopped one couple who were not much help but
who promised the frantic young boy that they
would try and find Gavin and keep him warm
with some hot soup until help arrived.

He was not far from the bottom and he
had slipped and fallen so many times he was
covered in scratches from head to foot but still

he charged on, wiping the tears away as he ran. Suddenly without warning he caught a foot in a heather root as he had done a hundred times before, but this time he fell awkwardly and his thin frame, already exhausted, had not the strength to stop him crashing heavily. His left ankle hurt like mad! He couldn't see any blood or anything and he knew enough not to take his boot off in case the ankle became madly swollen and then he wouldn't be able to get it back on again. He lay for what seemed like ages in the cold wet heather and the pain subsided a little. He pushed himself back up and started on down the hill. It was getting steeper now so he knew it couldn't be more than two or three miles at most.

The ankle was now piercing agony but he couldn't let himself slow down and so he pushed himself on and on. The rain was heavy now and the hill was deserted. He could still remember reaching the black puddle road and stumbling out across it, oblivious to any traffic and then falling into a dark void of nothingness. In fact, he had run into the arms of a hill walker coming out of the power station café at which point he had passed out.

It was several days later before his parents could bring themselves to tell Richard the whole story. His own ankle was badly broken in two places and his running on it had caused other complications but they said he would be out of hospital in another couple of day's time. That would be the day of his brother's funeral.

In all probability, Gavin had been dead by the time Richard had reached the power station. By the time the couple with the soup had found him he was unconscious with a very weak pulse and he had died in their arms not long after. There had been a post-mortem and the family were told that Gavin must have had a weak heart which he would have had from birth and there was little anyone could have done about it. They were told that there was a strong likelihood that he could have had a heart attack at an early age even without the added strain of climbing mountains.

However, this was not yet known when his parents were telling him in the Oban hospital and of course Richard blamed himself totally for taking so long to realise something was wrong and for messing up his dash down the hill for help. His poor parents tried to dispel this notion immediately but they were so grief stricken and confused themselves that they could not quite adequately reassure their son enough that he had done everything that anyone could have done.

There would never be the closeness between them as a family as there had been before Gavin died and Richard had still never really forgiven himself. His mother withdrew from the world and lived the rest of her life in another separate, paler and less substantial existence. Richard himself walked with a limp for over a year and he spent most of that time sitting forlornly in his room listening to Gavin's records and wishing he could put the clock back. After two lonely years he could recite every word of every song Bowie had ever recorded.

But then, thirteen by this time, he emerged from his gloomy isolation to face the world. He took up running and he became very good at it. He had such a powerful edge over the competition. His kung fu was strong! Whenever he became tired or his ankle became sore, he just thought of his brother and the anguish only pushed him on, stronger and faster. He welcomed the pain and he learned to savour, to almost relish, the agony and with this unique ability to punish himself, to go that much deeper into a dark well of suffering, he became very hard to beat.

His father was naturally proud of him but Richard sensed deep down that both his folks would probably have preferred it if he had just left it alone. He eventually became a Scottish schoolboy cross country champion and for three years in a row he competed against grown men in the arduous 'Ben race, leaping down through the mists to the eerie echoes of the Lochaber Pipe Band and into the safety of Glen Nevis. Each new trophy in the house just served to remind them all of their loss.

When he was sixteen…, he just stopped.

His mum and dad were probably the only parents on the island who were relieved when their son discovered cigarettes, alcohol and girls. This was also the age when he, alone, finally put the pieces of the jigsaw together and realised his parents had been spared the real truth of Gavin's death. His brother must have been one of the first ecstasy related fatalities in the country.

149

So, here he was running and crying all over again. This time he would not fuck it up. He couldn't afford to stop now. If he even tried to look down at his watch he was off into some twirling vortex and so he had to keep moving. He had become the human equivalent of Sandra Bullock's bus in the film 'Speed' – slow down and it all goes Pete Tong. So what if he fell, so what if he breaks an ankle, he's done it all before. He had bought the tee-shirt.

Then he had a better idea. Sod the running, it takes too long and hurts too much; he threw himself into the air and soared high up into the protective coolness of the soft clouds. Here he could make up some time and before long he was swooping down into the fringes of Oaxaca.

He came back to a semblance of reality as an old bus honked its horn angrily at him and he kept on running as the driver's exclamations became fainter.

He had just enough presence of mind to circle the Zocalo from behind, so he still had the cover of the trees and shrubs. He would wait there for her and if she didn't show then he'd track her down to that Antigua place if he had to. He was almost there now and he had to force himself to walk as slowly as he was able to. The drugs were still pumping through his body and he imagined that he could see for miles and hear conversation from a distance. But he had still frozen with shock when he saw Juanita sitting at a table, surrounded by gorillas in suits. With his

150

heart pounding so hard his vision was blurry, he crouched in the undergrowth and tried to move slowly forward behind a tree to afford a clearer view. Just then, she looked up and their eyes met for an electrifying instant in time. Her sunken and tired face paled visibly but otherwise betrayed no unnecessary outward emotion. Even from a distance Ridge could see the horror in her eyes. She gestured all around her with her head and knowing she was warning him, he ducked his head down.

He looked up again after a few moments but she had gone. He sunk back down heavily into the foliage and passed out completely.

Chapter Twelve – We can be Heroes

'You ran *how far?*' exclaimed the girl incredulously.

'About twenty miles or so. It's okay. It's what we do in Scotland, 'cos we have no TV and stuff.
We just get completely shitfaced and then run and run.'

If he was being totally honest, he didn't feel too sharp at this moment in time, but now wisnae the time for introspection. He was filthy, bruised, sweaty and bleeding from several nasty cuts on his legs, arms and head. But hey! He wasn't going to let that get in the way of a bit of patter with a bonnie wee lass. Not when his life may actually depend on it, that's for sure.
The wee lass in question was from Auckland and so technically was about as far from home as he was. But Kim was shaping up a tad better than him it seemed. After waking up the following morning in the bushes across from the square, Ridge had stumbled around for a while until he found himself sitting at a table in the cool shade of a quiet off-street looking down across the main thoroughfare. Luckily, there were few people around and those that were about were too busy scurrying around in the interests of commerce and they paid him scant heed. They were used to the hippy *gringo*

tourists who had underestimated the strength of the tequila the night before or who had lost daddy's credit card and were working their way back to the US as best they could.

Ridge wondered how many other shaken backpackers had sat here after the 'John Lennon Experience'. He reached into his canvas bag to grip the DVD tightly as if to prove to himself that it had not been the chemical invention of a deviant mind. He shivered as he wondered what had happened with Fabio and he hoped the boy had got out in one piece.

Kim was being very chatty with him and she gave him a coffee and some kind of egg and rice dish on the house. She loved his accent and was planning to visit Scotland on the European leg of her world tour. Ridge made light of his current predicament and said he had just been having too wild a time and he needed calm down a bit, sell some mushrooms and get himself down to some place in Guatemala.

Kim was able to confirm that the 'Juanita gang' had suddenly departed and that they always tended to stand out a bit as the bodyguards were very obvious and they did not try and hide the fact that they were the tough guys. They should be easy enough to track down in a small town like Antigua. Kim said she knew nothing about any of it but she had read in the local paper that there was a lot of internecine violence in the area and that the authorities seemed to be just as bad as the gangs. She advised Ridge to go to a local hippie hangout called Zipolite beach where she was sure someone would buy the mushrooms.

'Just, like, don't take any more yourself, because Zipolite is at the bottom of a huge cliff!
That's why it's so popular with backpackers because there are no oldies down there, or cops.
It's like in the movie, y'know, 'The Beach', but even better…it has killer waves!
You like to surf, right?
These waves are awesome!
Every bit as good as Puerto Escondido but without the Yanks!

Ridge nodded mutely as he wished he could be just going there for a surfing holiday. What was he really doing here at all? Should he not just head back to the relative safety of the States? Or better still, why not go home? He felt his guts wrench as he thought of his parents and of Orla. If he had not thrown away his phone a lifetime ago he would have texted his parents right there and then. But he wasn't even sure that that was such a good idea. He had no sanctuary to return to now. This was as good as it was going to get.

As he sat glumly and listened to the pretty New Zealander talking about all her travel plans, he bit his lip hard and resolved there and then to finish what he'd started and to hell with everything else. Juanita had tried to escape from something that had scared her, something malevolent and evil. He knew she wanted a different life and he vowed that he would help her.

It was not about him and her, he realised.

154

She was a beautiful girl but he hadn't had the time or the emotional resources to fall in love with her. But no-one was going to wrench her away from him just like that, like a toy to be played with, to be dragged from one play-mate to another. He had lost enough in his life and he would not roll over on this one, not again, not ever. A cold chill came over him with the realisation that this foray into the unknown could well end up costing him his life. He shivered as he knew deep in his heart that he was ready and willing to offer up his life to the altar of redemption.

Kim realised he wasn't really listening to her travel itinerary and she saw him shiver. Hauling him to his feet, she pushed him off down the street in the right direction for the bus to Puerto Angel and onwards for Zipolite. With her email address hastily scribbled on a dollar bill and scrunched into his pocket, he made his way, somehow fortified by their encounter.

The bus station was the usual mad rush of people and animals all charging about, with a seeming lack of purpose or any conclusion but more than a little confusion. After a great deal of pointing and nodding, Ridge was on the bus for Zipolite beach. The stationary bus was wickedly hot and airless, even with the door and all the windows open, but Ridge hardly noticed because to his delight he saw a fellow backpacker with a union jack tee-shirt sitting on his own near the back.

He sat down unceremoniously next to the guy and introduced himself. The bloke was called Bert and was from Woking near London.

He had only been in Mexico for a few days, was milky pale and spoke no more Spanish than Ridge. Strangely relieved at having some innocent company for the trip, Ridge relaxed into some easy banter. The bus was filling up quickly with all the remaining customers being local people and the noise was deafening.

Just then, they could hear a man shouting up to Bert from outside in a mixture of Pidgin English and Spanish. Bert leaned out the open window and ascertained with some difficulty that the guy was asking what time the bus was to leave the station. He turned to ask Ridge who replied with some pride 'tell him it's just going to leave now, three o'clock, *a tres hora*'. Both of them were leaning out at this point and the guy eventually gave them a highly theatrical thumbs up and made to go towards the front of the bus. They sat down and continued to chat, both feeling more like well seasoned travellers after successfully communicating some useful information to a fellow would be passenger.

The old bus coughed into life and everyone settled back into the uncomfortable seats. Bert suddenly jumped up and shouted,

'Where's my bag! It was right here under my seat! It's gone...!

The two of them frantically looked under all the adjacent seats, but to no avail. Ridge had been subconsciously holding onto his small rucksack on his knees, by luck more than by judgement and so it was only poor Bert who was really starting to freak out.

'It's got all my travellers cheques in it! Oh Christ! My passport too! I'll need to get off! Shit, shit shit...! What will I do?'

It was at that point that Ridge guessed what had happened and he smacked himself hard on the head before telling Bert.

'Duh'oh! We've just been robbed like a couple of muppets! That wee shite outside didn't give two fucks about what time the bus was leaving! Look around you, is he on the bus? Is he fuck! I remember a guy brushing past me, up the aisle, going too fast, now I thing about it, as we were leaning out the bloody window. It was a scam! Get the dopey tourist to lean out the window while yer mate comes onto the bus, goes up the middle, dips under the seat from behind and scarpers with the fucking bags...!'

It seemed so easy, but it looked like Ridge was right. Without time to say more than a brief goodbye, Bert was up and off the bus as it rumbled towards the station exit. With his heart still racing, Ridge sank down into his seat, strangely lonely, one hand over the body-wallet under his shirt and one eye on the remaining passengers. It was a tired and weary lad that arrived at Zipolite many hours later as the light was beginning to fade.

Unreceptive as he was, Ridge had to

admit this was a great spot. He stood at the top of the cliffs and looked down and across a beautiful stretch of beach and further coves to each side. It really did remind him of the film, as Kim had said it would, but also of a beach holiday he and Orla had had in the western area of the Algarve, a mini-Thailand, they had called it.

He safely negotiated the cliff path down to the beach and was met with a posse of little Mexican women who were all prodding him and attempting to lead him one way or another. It was like being surrounded by a flock of noisy geese. He tried to shrug them off and wandered further onto the sand where he could get his bearings. All along the beach there were makeshift wooden structures with Robinson Crusoe-type roofs made from massive leaves and a kind of thatched material. No walls, just a roof and rough beams strong enough to support rows of hammocks. Behind each of the large beach huts was a little breeze block building and Ridge could make out what looked like showers and maybe some chest freezers and the like.

He kicked off his trainers and felt the warm sand under his feet as his now very tired legs struggled to carry him along the beach. The waves were crashing heavily onto the shore to the left of him as he trudged along the beach to his right, trying all the while to look like he knew where he was going. He was succumbing very quickly to the exhortations of a bustling wee lady of impressive dimensions and a voice like a black-headed gull on a stormy day. Lucia, led him away from the sea and over to her hammocks and before he could protest, he had rented himself a hammock and a berth for $5 for the rest of the week!

With nobody else very interested in him, Ridge fell into a hammock and after a few hairy moments he was sleeping. He slept until late the next day and awoke, still tired, aching all over and with a raging thirst. He dimly remembered falling out of the hammock several times during the night. He hoped fervently that no one had noticed and he vowed to practice during the day and not to wear so many clothes that night.

His hammock training took a step backwards almost immediately, however when he was approached by a huge bearded guy with the most impressive dreads that Ridge had seen outside of a reggae club. He was the welcoming committee, he told Ridge as he proffered him an enormous cone shaped joint. His name was Winston and he said he had been at Zipolite for five months and he did not see himself leaving for another five at least.

'Why would you wanna leave man? That there is the most beautiful beach in the world, look at those waves will'ya. There are fish out there that anyone could catch, Lucia will sell you Corona for next to nothing and she'll cook for you too, man.
It's a paradise...!
And if its chicks you're digging then just look around, man. That's what I'm talkin' about, man, that's what I'm talkin' about...!

Ridge could not find any flaws in the

man's argument but unfortunately due to the serious potency of the spliff he had just smoked, he would not have been able to speak any words at all in reply. He drifted off into a happy doze for the next few hours.

On awakening, he dragged his dead body to its feet and wandered up the beach. As the affable Winston had said, at first looking, it truly was a paradise. Everyone was young and all were smiling and waving at him but no-one was overly pushy or seemed too interested in him. More impressive than anything else though, were the waves. They were so much bigger than anything he had ever seen and he found it difficult to pull his gaze away from the crashing surf.

He sat in the sand for a long time watching the rise and fall of the sea and he marvelled at the way the huge waves rolled in one after another. Ridge was an island boy himself, and no stranger to the sea, but where at home you may get the occasional big wave, the 'seventh wave', here they were all just charging in like trains. He was amazed at the way people were throwing themselves into the surf and then emerging minutes later, seemingly unscathed.

Making his way back to Lucia's, he was soon furnished with a tasty burrito and a beer. Cheap cigarettes too, they tasted awful but who was he to complain? He lay in his hammock watching the sky turning crimson over the water and almost forgot all about recent events as a calmness came over him.

Snapping out of his reverie, Ridge fell out of his hammock ingloriously and then

160

ventured off to make some progress in his quest for Guatemala. He sought out Winston and was soon talking amiably with several others who were berthed nearby. Most were sitting with the upturned necks of broken Corona bottles stuffed full of grass. Using the silver paper from cigarette hard packs or whatever, as a plug to stop the grass from falling out, they had lit the grass from the jagged top end and hey presto you had your very own chimney pipe! Ridge took tiny puffs that night to break himself in gently and in conversation he quickly found out that, as he suspected, grass and beer were cheap and in plentiful supply. Other drugs were not much in evidence but what everyone seemed to want was something more than the grass, maybe a little more psychedelic. When Ridge broached the subject of mushrooms and Peyote, there was universal agreement that that was the kind of thing they needed down here, especially the Peyote, which was hard to come by apparently.

It would have been churlish to wait any longer and within a short time, he had sold all of his recent harvest and had been paid especially well for the 'Devils root' which had made him the hero of the hour. He declined to join in himself and was content to get quietly stoned and plan his next step. The small amount of cash he had just raised probably wouldn't get him far but would it get him to Guatemala?

The following day, he awoke late again and discovered his hero status had now achieved mythical proportions and he was delighted to find the main reason was down to the most recent arrival to the beach, the irrepressible Fabio!

There was a circle of people sitting all around Fabio as he was retelling the story of his abduction, torture and escape to freedom. Ridge listened in and smiled as he discovered that Fabio was not letting the facts spoil a good story. He decided that it could only be a good thing that he was letting everyone know what had been happening and to warn them not to be taken in like that in the future. He had already told the amazed group that Ridge had rescued him and so there was nothing else to do but accept their praise. Truly, it was tempting to stay here for ever! But as soon as he could, Ridge pulled Fabio aside to find out the truth about what had occurred after he had left.

He hugged the youngster hard and asked him how he had managed to get away. As is often the case, the true story was very simple and straightforward. Fabio had lain in wait for J.L. and he had been frugal with the tequila, which had been the main thing Ridge had been worried about.

As our erstwhile Beatle impersonator had entered the cave, wee Fabio had banjo'd him hard across the head with the still half full bottle. Only once, but that had been enough. Before John regained consciousness, Fabio had dragged him outside, stripped him and tied him, spread-eagled, over a large rock.

'And I got you a nice present, amigo! Very nice present...!
I wanna to kill him, right there, you know that yeah? I really did, but I did better than that.

162

I killed him two times, two times I killed him. I tell you.'

Ridge gulped as he could imagine Fabio whipping out a plastic bag with J.L's cock and balls in it.

'So, what the fuck happened, Fabio, tell me you didn't actually kill him, please…'

'I tell you, I kill him two times. Listen to me.
He sleep when I hit him hard, then I say to the fat man he bring with him, I say, 'Give me the money you had for this guy or I gonna kill you too', so he gives me the money quick and I chase him away fast as his fat fuck legs can go.
I tell you it was very funny!'

'But you didn't kill John?
Fabio, Fabio!
I know he was a perverted wee fucker but murder and robbery? They'll get you for this.
You can't stay here!'

'Listen to me, you mad Scottish guy!
Listen to me… I tie up Mr Queer Movie, like I say, then he starts to wake up.
I count the money from Fat Fuck and I think – Fabio! Use your head! This is not the first time this has happened!
Are you thinking too Ridge? I tell our friend I will cut off his balls and feed them to him 'Medellin-stylee' unless he

tell me where the money is!'

'How did you know, he had any more money?'

'I dunno! It was message from God, I think! Anyway, he tell me to look in underground hole at back of cave and I find bag full of money, big money Ridge, big money!'

It turned out Fabio had reduced Mr Lennon's cash reserves by something in the region of six thousand dollars, half of which he wanted to give to Ridge. He had then simply left him, tied to the rock.

'He will not be dead yet, I think, but he will be dead soon.
If the sun don't kill him, the raptors will.
If the raptors don't kill him, some big animal will.
If they don't, then maybe some other sad bastard will do it to him for us.'

They opened a beer and toasted absent friends, then they hosted a party on the beach that lasted until sun up and that would be talked about from Zipolite to Ibiza and back for a long time to come.

Two days later, Ridge left for Guatemala.

Chapter Thirteen – Wild is the wind

It was hard leaving Zipolite behind and he had met some really nice people there. The night before, he had found it gratifying but increasingly awkward fending off the repeated pleas from those who wanted him to stay on the beach. He grew tired of listening to himself continually trying to explain to them what he was about without making it sound like a cheesy movie and he knew if he had left it any longer, he would never have got away. He had left many there like that, those who would be there for the duration, living in a blissful state of suspended animation, an outrageously agreeable extended holding pattern, flying so very high above the altogether much harsher existence of 'Airport Real Life' far down below. *And why not*, he thought as he trudged upwards, in the relative coolness of the dawn.

He turned only once at the top of the cliff, sad to leave this temporary cocoon. He knew he would take some small piece of it away with him, just as he also knew he would never again look upon these towering waves.

Armed with the knowledge gleaned over the last few days and nights from more experienced travellers than himself, some of whom had come to Zipolite from Guatemala, Nicaragua and further south, he had decided to try and hitch-hike his way down to Antigua. The general consensus was that the buses were crap, painfully slow and unreliable, which he was well used to being from the West Highlands of Scotland, but that they were relatively safe and very cheap. The other argument was that you could travel on your own much quicker by hitching and, after all, he had already hitched through the most dangerous part of America unscathed. He only partly heard the story from a couple of Germans at the beach who had said they wouldn't go back through Guatemala right now as the country seemed to be fixing for a fight with someone.

The bus to Puerto Angel was miraculously on time and soon he was off again and really on his way to Guatemala. It was still very early but the heat was overpowering as he stood by the edge of the road. There was little traffic but every time something went past, it delivered another cloud of dust onto Ridge, and he coughed his lungs out, spitting phlegm down into red dirt balls at his feet.

When the old camper van suddenly stopped, Ridge jumped up and dusted himself down quickly before leaning in the side window. The little man at the wheel had a round red face and a wispy white beard giving him a saintly look. When he heard that Ridge was from overseas he was quick to offer him a lift.

> 'Why, I'm goin' right the way down
> through to Panama, sonny. We'd be
> rightly honoured to have you ride with us
> some ways.
> Jump in quick now!
> This old bus don't take too good to
> standin' still in this heat!'

Ridge quickly hopped in behind old father time before he could change his mind and he gave out a small yelp as he realised there was someone else occupying the bench seat behind the driver, whom he had just clattered unceremoniously with his rucksack.

'I'm so sorry!' apologised Ridge to the lithe young girl who uncoiled her slender limbs from underneath his dusty pack as best she could in the cramped cabin. She must only have been about sixteen and barely dressed in what looked like pyjama shorts and a vest top. She didn't utter a word but just looked straight at him with piercing blue eyes. He was taken aback somewhat by the intensity of her stare. She seemed to be probing deep into his soul and he felt a wave of guilt as if she could read his thoughts which had momentarily imagined her without a stitch of clothing. She was still a child, he quickly reasoned with himself yet her eyes were imploring of him and few had ever looked at him like that, even with their clothes on. He had found himself almost hypnotised and he could sense a deep tension behind those eyes, a haunting hurt of some kind. He wriggled himself backwards as far from the girl as possible and tried to focus on what the old man was saying to him.

'As I was saying, you don't need worry about AJ here. She won't say boo to a goose! Likes to keep herself t' herself, isn't that right girl?'

The eyes stayed locked onto Ridge and

there was the faintest of enigmatic smiles visible through her tightly drawn lips, immature as yet, but still strangely captivating. Ridge remained distinctly unnerved as he listened further to his other travelling companion.

'We'll be heading a kinda' long ways down if you don't mind.
I like to keep myself kinda' private too so we'll avoid the main routes in for a while and anyways, that's how we picked you up, isn't it?
You just set back there and don't take no mind of AJ, she won't harm you.
Tell me about that cotton-picking country of yours! Is it true you don't have no negroes there?
And why'd you let that darned rag head Iranian bomber loose? Should'a died in jail, not at home. He not murder some a' your own kinsfolk along with all those innocent Americans?'

Ridge chatted easily with the old man. His name was Jeb and he had no idea where Scotland was although he claimed some long lost ancestry 'on ma grand pappy's side'. He enjoyed talking about his home, the beautiful islands of the West and he tactfully explained that there were people of all hues and nationalities in Scotland and he horrified him with the story of when the first black man came to the island in the 90's, a doctor from London and how the local women all swooned. The poor man was swamped with customers and he had had to bring his reluctant wife up from the metropolis earlier than planned whilst also advertising for a female doctor to deal with the sudden epidemic of 'women's issues' on the island.

He had been only half listening to the old man telling him about his own life. In the background he was far away, back on Sorsay, daring his friends to dive into the dark waters by the old abandoned slate quarry as they stood high up on the cliff. It had been a rite of passage for all the island children since anyone could remember. Only once you were heavy enough could your body overcome the unrelenting cold of the deep water.

Ridge remembered watching his big brother and his pals when he himself was too wee to manage it. All he had wanted was to show Gavin that he was growing up too. At the highest point on the island, he would feel the strength of the wind on his face and body as he ran full pelt towards the cliff edge and then at the last moment as he launched himself up into oblivion he grudgingly allowed himself to be blown backwards down onto the safety of the springy heather.

Apparently the old man's general racism stemmed from a store robbery in Detroit, where they hailed from. His wife had been run down in broad daylight in front of their daughter, as the raiders sped off in a stolen car. All four suspects were young black men and they were never apprehended. A nine year old AJ had cradled her mother's head in her little arms and watched helplessly as her life blood ebbed out into the dirty street.

It turned out that AJ was nearly twenty

now, but something had gone wrong inside her head after her mother's death and she had never really moved on emotionally or educationally. In effect, she was still just a frightened little girl. Ridge felt even more guilty for his earlier thoughts but felt that he at least partially understood some of what she was going through.

Old Jeb had lost it himself after that and the two of them had wandered aimlessly for months. Bitter, raw and living on the very edge of societal norms, Jeb had eventually drifted into the life they had now. 'Saved by the Lord Jesus', as he put it. He was in actual fact a smuggler, guns being his particular speciality. His modus operandi was to disguise himself as a preacher and he quickly reached under the steering wheel before deftly fitting a dog collar on with one hand.

He had business all the way down through Central America and as long as he steered clear of the drug cartels, no-one seemed to care. The poor old priest with the afflicted daughter in the ramshackle van, spreading the love of Christ. Not for the first time the Bible and the gun thought Ridge ruefully. Jeb boasted that the van had been re-fitted by some Columbian expatriate friend in Florida and it could carry a considerable payload. That, he explained was the reason for the lack of space for non-profit making passengers.

It was getting late now, and he felt himself drifting off, dreaming of the sanctuary of Sorsay, of his brother and again, of Orla.

He awoke suddenly in the cramped darkness as the camper van rattled over the rough back roads. His nostrils were immediately assailed by a strong-smelling and strangely familiar musky aroma and as he wriggled upright he realised with shock that the cab was redolent with the smell of sexual activity. He pulled back his knee which unbeknown to him had been pushing hard against the moist pubis of the young girl as the van had rocked rhythmically over the bumpy ground. She leant back, her hands still cradling the offending leg. Her eyes were on fire and in the dim light Ridge could see a sheen of sweat over her luminescent skin. He instinctively slapped her hands away and she cried out once, the sound raw and guttural, like that of some cornered animal.

Jeb quickly turned around and slamming a foot on the brakes, he instantly took in the situation as he saw it.

'You dirty little fuck! She's just a child! Get the fuck outta here!'

The van door was torn open and Ridge was hauled out and thrown to the ground while all the time he tried to protest his innocence in the matter. He cowered in the dust as a small grey pistol appeared in the darkness. Ridge looked up at the stubby barrel pointed straight at his head, the old man standing over him, shaking with fury.

'Honestly! I didn't do anything! I promise! I was a-fuckin-sleep!
It was just ma leg!
Don't do anything daft, ask her?
Ask her!'

171

Jeb pivoted round to his daughter who had dropped to her knees, gripping her father tightly around his middle, her whimpering face buried deep in the folds of his ample waistline.

'Well? Can it be true girl?
Was he not touching you?
Did he put his filthy fingers on you?'

The girl looked up at her father and her face broke up into an anguished sobbing. One look into her eyes and the old man could see that the boy was somehow telling the truth, that he had been an unwitting conduit for the girl's path to adulthood. He knew a large portion of the blame lay at his own door too. He had her cooped up in this jalopy for days if not weeks at a time, she had no friends, no peers, and what use was he anyway to her for broaching all the taboo areas in the life of a young girl. He dropped heavily to his knees, the girl still clinging on to him and his head fell as the tears rolled down his face onto the already wet cheek of his daughter. 'I'm sorry, girl...I'm so sorry' he repeated over and over.

They all sat in the dark and the dust and they all cried. Ridge wept for the girl but he also shed tears of gratitude for the chance to continue breathing for a while longer. He understood once more how fragile his existence was while he continued this wild adventure and he thought again of Sorsay, that safe life he once had. He realised immediately, that to return there as before could never happen. He was irrevocably changed and his life could never be the way it was nor ever be the way he would have chosen it to be.

There was no way Ridge was getting back in the camper van again, not that he was particularly welcome, but the good news was that they were actually inside the Guatemalan border and not far from a road where a bus could be found to a nearby town, Huehuetenango. All he had to do was follow the road and as long as it follows the river, Seleguá, Jeb told him, he would end up on the right road in no time.

He was in the hill country apparently and it was not particularly safe, but if he jumped on any bus he should be fine and would be in Guatemala City later the next day. He proffered the gun to Ridge, 'as a peace offering, from a man of God'. Ridge felt that that kind of peace he could do without and anyway he was good enough at finding trouble, without carrying a loaded weapon to boot.

A cold and dark wind whipped the cruel dust into his eyes as a grubby and increasingly weary Scotsman trudged along the rough road to meet with the river and hopefully a bus, destined to take him deeper into uncharted waters.

Chapter Fourteen – A game in two halves

After only minutes sitting at the roadside, Ridge was back on the road, *safer on a bus*, he thought. Of course, he was in a different country now and had no currency for the bus but luckily the Yankee dollar was always good to go. The handout from John the biker was still lasting, but for how much longer?

The bus was slow and seemed to stop whenever possible. It was pretty much full up now and it was not even mid morning. Ridge had presumed that most people would be going to the capital and so once full, the bus wouldn't be stopping much. The heat was intense and with his tiredness, Ridge just couldn't stay awake.

He arrived at Huehuetenango in a sleep deprived trance. With his poor grasp of the language he managed with difficulty and subsequent deep disappointment to find that there was no ongoing bus until the morning. However, he followed a couple of people from the bus station to what looked like a discount bunkhouse across the road and decided to splash out and get a good nights sleep or at least what was left of it.

He was ushered in by a tiny woman with deep dark features and bright bird like eyes. She took some change from his open hand and pushed him into a small room with a rough bed. Heaven!

He fell into the bed fully clothed and was

lost to sleep in seconds. It seemed like a short time later that he was awakened by the most fearful moaning that he had ever heard and he jumped up with a start. He initially imagined that it was some animal in his room and he tried to resist the temptation to climb up the walls.

It was at this point, in the harsh orange glare from the crudely positioned street lights outside, that he realised that there were no walls really. They acted as divisions between rooms, but they were not solid walls in the conventional sense, more like the felt partition screens which make up those cubicles in call centres, only these were not nearly as nice. They looked as if they were made of rough canvas or old sailcloth and they were obviously second hand or worse. The 'wall' which his bed was against had a metre long brown stain diagonally up it as if the room had possibly been a Halal butchery in a previous existence. Come to think of it, Ridge thought, it smells like that too. These makeshift walls were only six feet high at best and to add to the ambience, Ridge noticed from his bed, that there wasn't even a door in his 'room'.

These interior design facts he could appreciate in a second. The other features of his temporary haven were slowly making themselves known to him. The 'bed' was literally crawling with smaller non-paying clientele and he desperately wished he had not let that Welsh tosser purloin his sleeping bag back in San Fran, although he would have been way too hot in here.

But it was the grim soundtrack from next door that had really freaked him out. Ridge had never been a big fan of horror or gore-fest films and even had had nightmares from seeing 'Alien' as a kid. Orla had taken him to see 'Hostel' and the images of young backpackers being slowly dismembered by plier-wielding Austrian nut-job escapees from a Kwik-fit from hell was far too vivid in his imagination right now.

The poor sod *must* be ill, thought Ridge and even allowing for the 'it is late at night which makes every little noise seem much more dramatic than it really is' factor, he spent a long and feverish night drifting in and out of a series of dark nightmares. Each time, when he thought the guy had eventually drifted off to sleep, the moaning would resume. There was a gradual and ominous progression to moaning and shaking as night painfully moved towards morning and Ridge could feel his whole body quivering in reluctant unison.

It was just after dawn when Ridge was awakened suddenly by a tumult of noise and movement nearby. He jumped up and grabbed his clothes, cast off, in the red hot heat of his travels through Dante's inferno. Stumbling through his 'door', he collided with a makeshift stretcher with a covered corpse upon it. Looking blankly at the assembled helpers, they could obviously read his confusion and they all shook their heads with a contrived melancholy, 'Malaria', they muttered and pushed past him and down the corridor.

Without really understanding but at the same time not wanting to know any more, Ridge made his way out to the relative fresh air of the early morning darkness. He could already see a long line of people waiting for the bus, some of whom he thought he recognised from last night's bus in to the town and he wondered what kind of a hairy night they had experienced.

Within five minutes of getting a seat on the first bus out of town, Ridge was fast asleep. He awoke after an hour or so, the bumpy road not being conducive to a sound sleep. The bus was full and didn't seem to want to stop at all and, becoming more used to the old buses now, he settled back into a half-awake, half-asleep dream like state for what seemed like several hours. He only realised the bus had stopped when the noise from passengers became more strident than normal. He glanced out of the mud stained windows to see what looked like armed soldiers shouting and pointing their guns at the hapless passengers who had begun filing down the steps at the front of the bus. He figured that whatever it was, it had nothing to do with him and so he took advantage of the fact that the bus was stationary and promptly fell asleep again.

Anyone who has been prodded awake by the muzzle of a gun will probably tell you it is an unforgettable feeling and after initially jumping upwards, Ridge was frozen rigid with fear as he stared back along the barrel of the semi-automatic rifle which had unceremoniously interrupted his slumber. The soldiers were barking orders at all the passengers, and clueless to what was happening, he duly filed out into the central gangway and off the bus.

It was only at this point that he realised they were in the middle of nowhere and that there seemed to be a degree of segregation going on. Many of the passengers were just walking off to sit in the cool shade of the trees while others, including him, were being shepherded back against the wall of the bus, under the full glare of the noon sunshine. The metal of the bus was painfully hot against his back, yet Ridge hardly noticed as he stared incredulously at the scene unfolding in front of his eyes.

There must have been seven or eight men in military uniforms, aged between 15 and 50 and to call them soldiers was probably being a tad flattering. Knowing absolutely zero about anything military, Ridge instinctively knew these wee guys were not regular soldiers and the sweat quickly grew cold on his skin as he realised he was standing in front of what was effectively, a firing squad.

He slapped himself hard across the face and glanced surreptitiously around him, to confirm his worst fears – each of the five men standing against the bus was a *gringo*, just like him. Ridge could feel his legs shake uncontrollably and he was suddenly gripped with an urgent need to pee. The soldiers were shouting at them all and Ridge wished he could understand what was being said but he couldn't catch a single word.

A young guy, maybe German or Dutch, who was standing two down from his left, seemed to have a good handle on the lingo and was talking loud and fast with the bandits and the one who seemed to be in charge gesticulated sideways with his gun at which the guy beetled off, quickly followed by two others. As Ridge didn't know what was happening, he just stood there feeling like a spare prick at a hoors' wedding.

There were only three of them now, and

Ridge was closest to the soldiers. The chief sidled up to him and poked him hard in the ribs. The man was sweating worse than Ridge, and judging by the thick vein beating visibly up the side of his neck, he was almost as keyed up too. Ridge stared down at him helplessly and whimpered, half to himself, that he was just a tourist, just on holiday, from Scotland.

Just as he was saying that, he saw to his utter astonishment, that the soldier had an old Scotland football top on as an undershirt!

'Hey! I'm Scottish man! *Escoscia*! *Escoscia*!'

The effect was electric! The whole gang became extremely animated and gathered together in front of Ridge appraising him anew whilst laughing and shouting loudly at each other and at Ridge.

'*Si*! *Mi Escoscia*!' Repeated Ridge, again and again, all the while pointing to the guy's filthy old shirt.

'Tartan Army, man!
Fitba' crazy! Fitba' daft!'

The rest of the soldiers seemed to revert back to school playground age and started doing mock headers and penalty shoot-outs to either thunderous applause or hysterical booing. The old chief just stood staring intently at Ridge as a small child might stare at a strange looking animal in a zoo. Then he spoke the first words that Ridge could actually understand. '*Glasgow Celtic*? *Si*? *Jeemy Jardeen*? *No*? *Archie*

179

Guemmal!

Ridge chanced his arm big time, but hey, when you looked at the alternative!

'*Si*! I know Archie Gemmill! *Mi amigo, mucho amigo…*!'

The bandit, grinning from ear to ear, dropped his weapon, divested himself of his army shirt and began demonstrating football moves and whooping with delight. Ridge likewise started playing an imaginary football game while racking his brains and shouting out the names of great Scottish football stars from a time when he was barely born.

'Kenny Dalgleish!'

'*Si*! *Keeny*! *Keen Keeny*! The chief bowed in a 'we are not worthy pose,' and all the others aped him like some weird parody of 'Wayne's World'.

It was true, Ridge had been a babe in arms when most of the players they seemed to like had already passed their sell by date but Ridge quickly figured out it was the period around the Argentina World Cup in '78 that they were most fond of, perhaps some of them had actually been to the games.

Argentina has been a big deal for Scots but Ridge had a particularly strong card to play here. Growing up, whilst visiting his granny in Ayr, he used to spend many hours during long hot summers, listening with his Dad to their famous but beaten down neighbour, Ally Macleod rambling on about 'how we wiz robbed' over the garden fence when they all should have been cutting the grass.

It was difficult here in the heat and dust of Guatemala, to comprehend what superstars Ally Macleod and his team had been back then. Ally had become Scotland manager in 1977 and had then taken the team to Wembley where they had ripped England to pieces before the fans literally ripped Wembley to pieces during an infamous pitch invasion. It was a rare victory over the auld enemy but a low point for the reputation of the 'Tartan Army'. It became the stuff of legend and almost everyone back home knew someone who 'allegedly' had a wee piece of Wembley turf.

So, it was off to Argentina the following year and with a heavy weight of expectation, Scotland reverted to form and were beaten 3-1 by Peru and then scraped a measly 1-1 draw with Iran. Most sane folk would have written them off at that point, but in Scotland, they were past masters at working out, often without the aid of a calculator, the arithmetic gymnastics required to remain in a contest. In this particular case, Scotland only needed to beat the mighty Holland, the clear favourites in the group, by three clear goals!

Despite the Dutch taking the lead, Scotland fought back tenaciously to win 3-2 with a goal from King Kenny Dalgleish and two from Archie Gemmill, the second of which is considered by many to be one of the greatest World Cup goals ever. Gemmill skilfully beat three Dutch defenders before lifting the ball right over the keeper and into the net. However, as was usual with Scotland, they were cruelly eliminated on goal difference and it was a shameful early return for the Scots.

The other two passengers who had been standing with Ridge had just stood gawping in amazement at the crazy scene in front of them. Thinking back on this bizarre scene much later on, Ridge had thought they would have been better served to have got down and dirty with the rest of the 'team'. As it was, Ridge had rifled through his backpack to haul out and ceremoniously present an old Scotland 'away' shirt to the main guy.

This seemed to bring the festivities to a natural close and after lots of macho hugs and high-fiving; the passengers were all chaotically ushered back onto the stifling bus. Moments later they seemed to be back on their way, none the worse for their ordeal, barring, for Ridge, the unexpected unearthing of a painful national misadventure.

It was very many hours later, after a long wait in Guatemala City, that a filthy and slightly homesick Ridge arrived in Antigua.

Chapter Fifteen – The Hunter

He stood stock still. Undetectable to all but the most alert of night creatures, his luminous white pelt glowing eerily in the misty light from the half moon high above the Sierra Madre de Oaxaca. White skin was unusual in these parts, particularly when it covered a long and lithe body as strong and tightly muscled as his was. Dark weals marring the pale perfection gave evidence that this was the body of a warrior. The head upon this alabaster statue did not move and the eyes seemed to be closed as first, his left hand began to slowly swoop downwards towards the ground as, moments later, his right arm gently glided upwards. Again, he was still, very still.

His ears were not closed however, and he had heard them coming a mile off. They would not be expecting him; in fact, they would never have come upon a physical specimen such as he, ever before, especially one standing here, naked in the dark, in the squatting single whip position.

He knew all about them. He had been warned not to travel in these parts at night as it was very dangerous and he would be easy meat for them. They always preyed at night and their reputation was fierce. But they did not know who he was; they would be totally unprepared for what they would find. He had chosen to be here precisely because of them; because their presence would help ensure that he would be able to rest here in peace, undisturbed by too many idiot tourists.

A low rumbling sound emanated from deep within the earth and for a brief moment the clanking of lamps and the incessant chatter from the men abated. Then, as if nothing had happened, the noise returned as the bandits resumed careful combing of the thick jungle in search of their usual midnight feast. *Volcan Pacaya* was a semi- dormant volcano, but had of late begun to shower forth a small amount of volcanic material.

The heat that she produced, even at 2000 metres above sea level, made for an attractive alternative sleeping location for the adventurous backpacker keen to add '*slept the night on the side of a volcano*' to their gap year cv. This, in turn, made for an equally attractive and somewhat easy harvest for the bandits who appeared out of the darkness armed with guns and machetes, demanding cash and passports from sleepy, terrified and defenceless young tourists.

He was neither sleepy nor defenceless, and terror…? Well, terror *was* his business, but he preferred giving rather than receiving. However, tonight he did not feel like killing anyone as it did not serve his purposes and he needed to conserve his strength as it had been a tough old year so far and he had much bigger fish to fry in the coming days. Oh yes.

He was still. All that moved were his eyes. They opened with a bright flash of intense aquamarine, even in the half light they seemed to shine like powerful torch beams through the misty night. They took in everything around him with one sweeping glance.

184

He needed to be safe for a few hours, just until dawn. Then, he would resume his own hunting expedition. He was a creature well used to being hunted; being hunted by vicious animals looking for him, specifically, whose sole function was to flush him from hiding, and who would take sick pleasure in ripping him limb from limb. However, he was eternally grateful to those who had chosen to punish him, for they had unwittingly provided him with the very best survival training. They had given him a mental arsenal of weapons more powerful than they could imagine.

It was only a matter of time before the shadowy, elusive quarry had become tired of hiding and then, all of a sudden, the tables were turned. The hunters became the hunted. Those unfortunate enough to have made themselves known to him would never again sleep easily at night, although many would bless the Lord when they saw the sweet light of a new morning. He would play with his prey; at times his vengeance was powerful, and swift, sometimes he would be merciful. Often it paid a higher dividend to allow his prey to limp away to add further to his fearsome reputation. For this was a highly lucrative, if dangerous, way of life he had embarked upon and there would be no pension plan waiting for him, when and if, he chose to play his end game.

This time, though, he was here F.O.C. This time it was up close and personal.

Looking up, he could see his sanctuary. A raw animal intensity poured from those wild

185

eyes and his body lowered for a moment, every muscle tensed, every ligament taut. He leaped up, two metres or more into the tree and nimbly scaled another twenty metres through the branches until he found a berth to his liking. Pausing only for a moment, he wound his lower body around the tree branch and swung upside down, quickly becoming motionless and almost invisible, hanging like some grotesque albino bat. His eyes surveyed the surrounding area and then they closed as he relaxed into a deep sleep.

Chapter Sixteen – Agent of Despair

Ridge woke up abruptly to clamorous clanking and banging noises and an ominous other-worldly deep-throated moaning sound that seemed to pervade every wretched atom of his being. He had slept fitfully with terrifying dreams of playing football for his life. There had been firing squads at Hampden and he had been on the pitch in bare feet.

The game with England, *of course*, had gone to penalties but there were hardly any players still able to stand. Rooney had just missed a penalty for England and had been dragged to the edge of the pitch and shot through the forehead. Ridge was up next and the noise from the stadium was like standing under a 747 on take off. As he stood shakily to his feet, the whole place had suddenly gone silent.

Ridge stepped forward to take his kick and at that, Rooney jumped up from the sidelines and came running straight for him, his dead eyes staring lifelessly, an eerie whistling sound coming from the clean hole through his head as he sped across the park.

Then he awoke.

Not sure if he *was* actually awake, Ridge covered his sweating hands over his ears and tried in vain to screw shut his eyes as the cacophony intensified. He fell out of the bed and staggered over to the flimsy wooden door. As he pushed it open, still with one eye shut, he jumped back in horror as thick sweet smelling mist overpowered him and he fell heavily to his knees as a line of ghostly figures paraded slowly past in a macabre procession.

He *was* dead, he thought quickly, and now he was watching his own funeral.

'He had definitely been pushing it, he knew that. But he had gone too far. He had been a stupid wee prick and should have just gone back to Scotland and got a fucking job. Once you start dreaming you are playing football for Scotland, then you should know you are just wanking yourself in hell.'

Then he came to a little more and sat watching in amazement as the purple-robed mourners slowly filed past his door through the haunting fog. He saw incense carrying children and women dressed in fine black dresses and as he heard the slowly beating drums, clapping cymbals and doleful tubas he eventually realised it was some kind of parade. A bit more fancy than your average Orange Walk down Duke Street, *'nae neds though'*, he muttered. Maybe just one, mind you.

He had to get away from this racket and give himself a chance to think straight. He pushed out into the narrow cobbled street and gave himself another scare as the procession had suddenly hushed. He thought he had somehow done something to make this happen. The thick incense was stinging his eyes and his throat was aching. As the drumming and cymbals resumed their rhythmic torturing, this time with some profound sounding chanting he decided what he really needed was a drink.

Ridge staggered forwards and tried to get into a gap between the groups of marchers. They walked slowly and he easily found a space then looked down in abject terror as he saw he was walking over a beautiful tapestry-like carpet made of flowers and other stuff. His feet were messing it up but the bona-fide marchers were mucking it up even more and nobody seemed to give a toss so he kept going and quickly nipped off into a broader street where he could see a pavement café.

There were throngs of local people everywhere and everyone was yakking away, the noise reminding Ridge of the black-headed gulls on the high cliffs back on Sorsay, when he and his brother used to dare each other to climb up and try to steal an egg.

He saw through the incense fog a table with a tourist sitting alone, an empty seat alongside and so he dived for it and plonked himself down unceremoniously. He quickly ordered a beer and a tequila chaser but with all the noise he was having difficulty asking for a double. The tourist leaned over, 'I'll join you in that if you don't mind' and quickly organised the drinks for them.

Ridge was grateful but not overly chatty with the guy, who in contrast seemed to be glad of an ear.

'I've been toying with having a drink for a while, but it's a little early for me' he said, 'but under the circumstances, it would be rude not to, I guess.'

The guy was called Ed and he seemed to be living in the area, recently retired and fairly bored with his existence, by the sound of him. It turned out he had just fallen out with his wife who had gone off to stay with a friend and so Ed was doing what all guys anywhere in the world would do, contemplating getting completely rat-arsed. Well misery loves company, thought Ridge and if there was a drink to be had then he was only to happy to oblige. They chatted freely after a few drinks and Ed explained that there was a festival in full swing and he had been lucky to find anywhere to stay last night even if it was a flea-pit.

Ridge sat and watched the stream of marchers, many of them carrying huge floats on their shoulders, at times silent and then singing or chanting. Most were wearing dark purple robes and some of the floats had scenes from the Bible such as Jesus carrying a cross and Ridge saw a float carried just by women with a huge Virgin Mary upon it with dozens of small children scurrying about underneath it. He learnt from Ed that within a few hours of this procession ending, the beautiful tapestry-like carpeting, *alfombras*, would be recreated, before being walked over and ruined again in a further procession.

Ed had a local paper tucked in his jacket pocket and he had remarked with a discernible degree of bitterness on how lucky or maybe just *'plain stoopid'* Ridge must have been to be travelling alone in these parts. He hadn't said anything earth shatteringly new to Ridge at that point but upon seeing the crumpled front page complete with fuzzy but graphic photos and hearing the rough story of what had happened, the blood began to chill in his veins.

The pictures showed two bodies, arms

bound behind them, lying apparently dead at the side of the road and although the photos were poor quality and in black and white, it was obvious there was blood coming from their heads. Ridge stared at the grainy pictures and struggled to understand what exactly he was looking at but with some additional news bulletins from Ed, he realised the men had had their throats cut and then their tongues had been pulled out through the gash in their necks, '*a Mexican necktie*'.

Stunned, Ridge listened in horror as the story further unfolded and then he himself added the dramatic ending. The two men were, in fact, US journalists, and it only took Ridge a short but hot moment in hell to work out that they were his recent bus companions.

After hearing the whole story pour out madly, Ed looked at the quietly weeping boy and decided there and then that this rag-tag idiot tourist must be very special and that their meeting could not have been by chance. Their encounter was fated and in saving this boy from an undoubtedly nasty end, he would in turn find the salvation he now realised he so desperately needed. Perhaps Mandy would look at him with something more than resigned pity. *Or was it revulsion,* he thought sadly.

They sat quietly for a while over a couple of strong drinks, had a wander and a few more drinks. Ed instructed his young friend in the art of selecting and purchasing some fine local street foods although Ridge couldn't help thinking that in no way could it ever compare with the Mission back in San Fran.

Somehow, after a doing a quick arse-bandit calculation, Ridge let himself be persuaded into coming back to Ed's place to crash and so they collected his stuff and Ridge staggered off behind Ed as they looked for his car, *'while ah'm still drunk enough to drive it'*.

They walked up to a beautiful gleaming black pick-up truck, some big Ford job, literally twice the size of anything else parked along the whole street and Ridge jumped as Ed activated the remote alarm.

'Fuck me, big man…! Is this yours?' Ridge exclaimed as they climbed into the enormous vehicle. Ed looked over at him with obvious pride in his eyes but then Ridge saw something else flicker across his face, an emotion he couldn't place just then.

'Yup, it was a…, a present… to myself, call it a mid life crisis or somethin' like that!'

It turned out Ed lived a few miles away in a small village called Panachachel and he explained that when Ridge sees Lake Atitlan tomorrow he will see why someone would want to rest here awhile.

'Mind you, the whole place has been near totalled a couple of times by mudslides and last year the whole area was cut off by road, so y'see the truck is not just for show!'

And so Ridge just settled quietly into his comfortable big seat and half listened, half dozed, whilst Ed steered his beast of a car over the rough roads and talked, almost to himself, it seemed, about who he was and what he was up to. He had been some kind of US Government customs agent or something like that and he and his wife, Mandy, had lived mostly in Texas, near the Mexican border.

'It was a goddamn hell hole! Murders or drive-by shootings every few hours, every goddammned day of the week. We came down here to escape all that shit.
It was like a paradise to start with but the shit seems to have followed us and now we have our very own deathsquads, as you now know, my friend.
You will like Pana though. Real nice. Too nice mebbes, too many goddamn Yankees, movin' in all the time. Local jokers call the place *'Gringotenango'*, place of the gringo!'

They soon arrived at a modest house set alone into the hillside and all in darkness. Ed wasn't expecting his wife back anytime too soon. A bottle of Mescal was quickly unearthed and Ridge was awake enough to notice the huge Scorpion on the label and he naively hoped it didn't mean anything too sinister…

He needn't have worried as they worked their way through one of the finest bottles of liquor that Ridge had ever experienced. Feeling better than he had in ages, Ridge laughed and wisecracked through the night with Ed as they took it turns to tell bad jokes and dark stories each one worse than the one before. Ed was impressed with the fact that Ridge was still alive. He spluttered his drink several times as his companion related some of the spectacularly daft situations that Ridge had inexplicably found himself in.

'Holy Moses!
It was no accident, my friend!
You are on the primo suicide trip to Hell if there ever was one!
You must have a guardian angel!
Before you move on from here, you an' me are gonna have a little talk about survival tactics down here, else your momma will be walking down the streets of your town just like you seen today, and puttin' you in the cold earth.'

Ridge quietened down as Ed outlined some of the wiser ways to keep himself safe for the remainder of his adventure. 'First off, keep the fuck away from those goddamn chicken buses...' He went on to advise Ridge to carry a dummy 'throw down' wallet with a little cash and a couple of dud cards that he could use if needed and so protect his real one which should be under his shirt. He was speechless to find that Ridge didn't even have a basic Spanish guide book. 'When, not if, you get in more shit, you need to have the basic lingo or you will be truly fucked over! You can't rely on a old football shirt to save you next time!' His number one recommendation, however, was that Ridge got back to GC and caught the first available flight home.

The rest of the night it was Ridge who gasped as Ed gave him a true-life insight into the mad world of the war on the drug gangs. It seemed that Ed too, must have had a guardian spirit watching over him as it seemed that not too many survived contact with these guys.

It was when Ed told him more people were dying every year than had ever died in the war in Afghanistan or Iraq that a cold chill spread through his bones. It also seemed that they had the kind of cash available that made the North Sea Oil boom look like a kid's monopoly game. After a while, the drink began to affect him. Right at the point where Ed's account of millions of dollars getting buried underground just because the cartel chiefs couldn't get rid of it quickly enough began to seem normal, instead of bizarre, then Ridge knew he had had enough for one day and passed out on the floor.

Much later the next morning, he found himself propping up his head at a noisy café called The Last Resort. It was actually pretty quiet compared with the bustle, noise and fumes of Callé Santander round the corner, but any sound was too loud for Ridge that morning and his head hurt so much he had already vowed never to drink again. The bar was not especially busy, a few locals it looked like, but to increase his already extreme agitation, there were two boys playing table tennis just a few metres away and the *thwack-thwack* of the little ball on the table might as well have been a baseball bat across his forehead.

Trying vainly to focus his aching eyes on

a crumpled copy of the local paper from yesterday, Ridge was determined to understand better what had happened to his former travelling companions from the bus. In the absence of any working synaptic connections between his eyes and his brain, he gave up trying to understand the article and chucked the paper across the table to a surprisingly sprightly looking Ed. He hoisted a flag of surrender and promptly buried his aching head down into his arms. But despite himself he could not stop his brain turning over. A muffled request for help came up from his folded arms as he slowly turned his head sideways and squinted across the table.

'Ed, please, please tell me why these guys are dead and what's going on with those neckties and bits of, is it paper…, stuck to them?'

It was paper, apparently. It looked like the two journalists had fallen foul of a cartel based further north, around Morelia, an area the bus had passed through, a few days before Ridge had got onboard. 'In a fucked up world, these guys are the real nut-jobs', Ed explained, shaking his head sadly. You can't make this stuff up, he said. The two men had written some less than complimentary pieces about Nazario Moreno Gonzalez , a drug baron known colloquially as '*El Mas Loco*' or 'the maddest one'. Ed looked directly into Ridge's red eyes as he went on and Ridge realised once again how lucky he had been to get so far relatively unscathed, barring self-inflicted brain damage

196

and a broken arm.

This gang were known as '*La Familia*' and by Ed's estimation they controlled or had some involvement in about 80% of all businesses in the Michoacán state. Their leader was a master in controlling people and he had even published his own bible. Although they ran a drugs empire, including the usual other criminal activities that go along with that, they espoused a quasi-religious ideology which strongly discouraged gang members from using alcohol or drugs.

> 'Therefore, just *by being you…*, a half-drunk, drugged-up *gringo…*, wandering about, sticking his nose where it don't belong…, you might as well have painted crosshairs on the back of your goddammned fool head!'

Ridge gulped and had to focus hard on not throwing up. Ed told him the pieces of paper were in fact notes pinned to each body which were a trademark of *La Familia* and each one was a hand signed message that the dead were victims of 'divine retribution'. When Ridge asked the usual obvious questions like, 'why not just arrest the guys if you know who they are' etc, Ed just snorted.

> 'Yeah, we know who they are but we can never find the top guys and anyway, they are almost everyone at some stage. Picture the scene, *amigo…*
> A guy comes in to your poor village and gives you enough hard cash to build a

new school, a church and fund a drainage
project which will improve the life of
hundreds of your townspeople.

Then, the kicker.

He asks if you will hide Senor Gonzalez
for a couple of weeks.

What would *you* say?

Before you answer, bear in mind that to
say no, would almost certainly mean the
death of you and your family...'

Chapter Seventeen – The Freakiest Show

It was still relatively quiet in the Last Resort, although there was a persistent group of Taiko drummers beating monotonous pain through the head of at least one poor gringo. Ridge was still ashen faced and he had not been able to eat any food yet; his stomach was queasy enough without the gruesome tales from Agent Foster, (retired). He summoned up the courage to try a coffee and listened on, enthralled, despite his weakened state.

'The drug war is getting worse', said Ed.

He went on to patiently explain how over the last couple of decades there had been significant progress, mostly US led, against the established cartels from Colombia who had been trafficking drugs up and across the Caribbean and Florida. This partially successful clampdown had resulted in the cartels altering their strategies and pushing their drugs up westwards through Guatemala and especially Mexico. This had then brought into prominence the Mexican cartels who now controlled around 70% of all drugs that flow into the States. The Colombian cartels such as the Medellín and Cali were still very powerful but they had weakened under intense pressure from the US and the hunting down of leaders like Pablo Escobar.

'All of which', said Ed sadly, 'has made the local guys become even richer, more powerful and more deadly.

Then the stakes got higher and higher. President Felipe Calderón, who is from Michoacan, and then Obama, have both vowed to clean up this mess. But, for me, they have made it more dangerous to live here and in my experience the deaths have certainly increased...'

Ed told him that what prompted him to retire early were the 110 deaths in only six months in his town Nuevo Laredo on the border.

'I did not want to be next', he said grimly.

'Calderón has sent in over 50,000 troops since he came to power and Obama gave him 5 military helicopters and the pressure on the cartels is increasing', which, Ed explained, has meant that our home-grown Mexican gangs are fighting among themselves with new alliances springing up and a general atmosphere of bitter fighting and widespread bloodshed.

'My old bosses and the Mexican government will say outwardly that the increased violence is a reflection of the success of the hard-line policy against the cartels and that what we are experiencing at the moment is brutal infighting between leaderless cartels for fewer and fewer spoils.
But in my last few months I was seeing more and more people being killed as the

gangs fought against each other and against the army.

As they became more desperate, or rather, as they became greedier, then so the violence, intimidation and corruption increased'.

Ridge asked him why he seemed so pessimistic about the whole situation and to try and cheer things up a bit he bravely ordered up the first drinks of the day.

'That didn't last long…!' said Ed wryly.

'It's purely medicinal, honest' replied Ridge with a fairly good likeness of a look of distaste on his face, 'I dinna want to do it, but like you say, it is survival we are talking about. This is war!'

Ed took a quick gulp of his beer and went on.

'Why do I think things are getting worse? Well, listen here, sonny, I spent the end of my career helping to put down one of the worst of the worst, Arturo Beltran Leyva, who incidentally was based very close to Oaxaca, so pay attention if you think you will ever see your Juanita alive again.'

Ridge was paying attention.

'So, we were after Arturo who controlled his own cartel, the Beltran Leyva Organisation, the BLO, and these guys would make the goons that nearly popped you last week, look like altar boys!

The BLO had split a couple of years ago and the offshoot gang are now known as the Sinaloa cartel and to give you an idea of how big this 'offshoot' is, their boss, a sorry ass called Shorty Guzman is reputed to be a billionaire already.

These two groups fought intensely and we had to bring them down. To make matters worse, not only did the BLO control a massive business empire they also teamed up with another vicious bunch of low-lives called 'Los Zetas'. Now, get this!

Los Zetas hate the Sinaloan cartel, so far so good. But Los Zetas are no ordinary drug gang. Just a few years ago, they were the elite military troopers in Mexico, but the money was too tempting so they turned 'to the dark side' and operated firstly as a private army for one of the cartels then becoming more ambitious, they formed their own drug cartel.

They have better weapons than we do! They even have Kevlar body armour for Chrissake!

When we eventually found Arturo, in Cuernavaca, just south of Mexico City, we had Special Ops, Delta Force, over 200 troops and police.

It was a real battle, just like in the movies; grenade launchers, remote control drones and everything, the whole nine yards.

Then, the day after we shot him, the severed heads of six of our policemen were found in plastic bags outside the local church with a note saying this was a direct result of the previous day's shooting.

So, my friend… Are we really winning..?'

'But surely, it would save lives eventually, when you keep getting the bosses, the leaders, the ones who have the brains to lead others?' Ridge was grasping for some signs of light.

'Yeah, yeah, sure it will…Listen up! Arturo had brothers to take his place at the head of the cartel, lots of the little freaks.

Next to them, old Arturo could almost be considered a moderate influence, but now he's gone there is no one strong enough or fool enough to try and keep a lid on the caboose. We've popped a couple already but the one you've got to be worried about is his youngest brother Ramon.

Yes! The Crocodile!

He is the freakiest of the freak show so far presented for your delectation today and you, you little dipshit, have got yourself into something of which you have no comprehension!'

Ridge could not think straight. His head began to spin and he felt as if the bar was revolving around his head. If what Ed had been saying was true, then the guy who was responsible for the kidnapping of his girlfriend, the guy that *yours truly* had been happily going out of his way to provoke, is only the head of one of the most powerful drug cartels in the world! *I am so dead...* he thought morosely. He stood unsteadily, turned and walked away as if sleepwalking.

Ed sat for a moment and feeling bad for the kid, wondered if he should have kept his big mouth shut. Mebbes I could have sugar coated it a little, he thought, then quickly he realised he *had* sugar coated it. It was exponentially worse than that and it would take more than a few hours to get that through to the dopey Scotsman. And anyway, he was trying to do him a favour as had others before him, apparently, but maybe this time the message had been received and understood.

He hoped so. He had seen way too much bloodshed, some of it, admittedly, on his own hands. So now he wanted to attempt to wash some of it away. This was no place for naïve tourists. Copy that.

At that, Ed heard a chair leg scrape behind him, and as he turned, Ridge was there, plonking down a wooden tray filled with a cornucopia of Mexican junk food and four large drinks.

'Right then, pal! If this is going to be as

tough as you say, we'd better get some fodder in us, 'cos where I come from an army marches on its stomach!'

Many hours later, they wended their weary way back to the house where Ridge launched himself onto the couch and into oblivion.

Some time later, he awoke to some bizarre voice in his head asking him to breathe deeply, to focus on his floor muscles and the like? Thinking, not for the first time in recent weeks, that he had again died, he was scared to open his eyes, but he did so, cautiously, and was witness to such a most peculiar apparition that he had to blink fast to prove to himself that he wasn't still dreaming.

Mandy, as she turned out to be, was lying flat on her back with her legs straight up in the air with her exposed rear facing Ridge. Her head was arched back so she could still watch what was going on with some bizarre TV exercise show. Ridge felt like a peeping Tom and decided to pretend he was still asleep but he must have moved and the old sofa gave him away. The legs came swiftly down and the torso came up correspondingly quickly as if by some cantilever action.

'Caught you!' she said, smiling coyly.

'Really sorry,' blurted Ridge, 'Ah just woke up, didn't know anyone was even there,
I 'hink Ah'm still a *wee bitty* pissed to be honest'.

He mumbled on and on, feeling more stupid by the second. Mandy was an immaculate looking woman, smaller than him and he would guess in her early 40's although she looked a lot younger. Dressed, almost, in a loose vest top and tiny pair of tight shorts, with toned limbs and a full head of auburn hair, she smiled broadly at him before jumping up onto her knees to introduce herself. Before Ridge could even raise himself up, she had bounded over and she stood and leant over for a faux formal handshake, her vest hanging low enough so he could not avoid the sight of her perfect cone shaped breasts, firmly in place, only inches in front of his face.

'I'm Mandy, but I'm sure you guessed that', she smiled a perfect, maybe just *too* perfect smile as an embarrassed Ridge only managed a sheepish grin, barely conscious of the blood rushing to his groin. 'I hear you're from Scotland, is that right?' Ridge muttered in the affirmative still incapable of getting his mouth and brain to synchronise effectively.

'Well, you just stay there and relax. I gather you've had a wild time with that fool Ed.
He has gone out and won't be back until tonight. So, stay put and let me finish my Pilates class, won't you.
A girl has got to keep herself in shape after all!'

Incapable of resistance, Ridge crumpled back along the sofa and watched this perfect doll-like apparition go through various stretching and toning exercises. He couldn't help but notice how toned she was and how easily she could achieve and hold the various positions. He was a typical bloke when it came to stretching and even when he was a champion runner he had rarely stretched and had only ever warmed up under duress.

He was warming up now though. In that hazy half-sleep his imagination was definitely getting the better of him and he lay there fantasising about this complete stranger prostrate in front of him. As he drifted in and out of sleep, his stiffening becoming more obvious, he imagined he could feel hands rubbing on the outside of his jeans and he found himself moving rhythmically with the strokes. It was a pleasant feeling and it was a short while before he realised it wasn't a dream.

He opened his eyes to see Mandy right there at his crotch and before he could say or do anything she had unbuttoned his straining fly and had taken him in her hand. 'There now, that's better, isn't it? You've been through a tough time. Let me make it all better.' He started to sit up and was about to attempt to protest when she opened those perfectly crafted lips and pushed down over his member. He sank back, not believing what was happening.

Mandy sat up after a few seconds and pulling him up by his manhood, she guided him onto his feet and he allowed himself to be led meekly to a nearby bedroom.

Within seconds, she had removed her clothes and wrapping those perfectly waxed legs around him, they fell onto the bed. Any reservations now dispensed with, Ridge ran his lips over her taut body before entering her and their lovemaking was very strong, almost too strong for Ridge. Mandy quickly took control, pushing him onto his back and sitting astride him, lifting her pelvis up and down. The benefits of her exercise routines were all too evident.

It was over fairly quickly, but not before Ridge was already thinking that this was maybe all too much like another exercise workout for this woman. Was he just another piece of apparatus that she was using to help release her pent-up frustrations? They must have been strong emotions, given the ferocity of her advance. Even in his battle fatigued state he was surprised at his own feelings, or more his lack of feelings at this moment.

Normally, for a single guy back home, a situation like this would be considered a stroke of good luck. In the right place at the right time, a 'consolation shag'. But he didn't feel like 'shagging' women at all, he thought with an unexpected realisation. The real shock advanced upon him slowly like the cold mists back home as he understood that the painful truth was he just wanted *to make love* again. Make love like he hadn't done for a long, long time.

He was not thinking about Juanita either, the girl he was currently putting his miserable life in jeopardy for. He had only ever 'made love' with one girl and she was the one he would never, ever hold close to him again, at least…not in this life.

They lay still together for all of a second or two then she thanked him for his performance before jumping up and out of the room. Ridge was still in shock and badly in need of a cigarette. Clumsily pulling on his clothes he staggered through to the main room and rummaged through his jacket for fags. Feeling like he had just stolen something or broken a taboo he sparked up the cigarette and inhaled deeply, considering whether or not to just leg it as fast as he could.

Just then Mandy came back in dressed in more appropriate clothing although still unable to disguise that inherent horniness that she most certainly possessed. Handing Ridge a beer, she took a slug of hers and then seemed to go into a meltdown right there beside him.

> 'You probably think I'm some kind of 'Desperate Housewives' nympho or something. Far from it!
> If you knew how long it's been since I had an orgasm like that!
> Ed and I just don't do it anymore. To be honest, the sight of his flabby, flaccid ass doesn't do much for me anyways, but he hasn't seemed interested in my needs for a long time now, no matter how much I would try to encourage him.
> So now we just don't bother.
> We could never have kids and I guess that was a big problem for me for a long time but he also blamed himself and although the doctors could find nothing wrong with either of us, he took it real bad that as a former college quarterback, as a man, he had failed to do his time-honoured duty in the marriage.

I'll never say anything to him, I promise, and I won't hound you either! I'm really not like that and I've never done anything like this before!'

Seeming happier after her outpouring, Mandy flashed him a nervous smile and Ridge simply shrugged back, saying little and feeling distinctly uncomfortable. The only thing for it was to get more pissed and hope that he had passed out before Ed got back.

The strident tones of the phone rang out across the open plan office and the man hesitated for a brief moment before going to answer it. Sure, he was about to leave for the day, but maybe this could be the break he was looking for, after all he was due one about now.

'Hello? Well, hi there! I wasn't expecting to hear from *you* any day soon…! You do know that we are onto you, don't you? It's only a matter of time you know…'

'*Listen hard,*' the caller said quietly, '*is this a secure line? Good. Now I have a deal for you. Do you want the biggest apprehension of your miserable life? I can get you 'El Cocodrilo'…on a plate… Are you interested? Good. I want only two things in return.*
One, you give me complete immunity from all that bullshit from the past and two; I need a favour, a very big favour! What do you

say? Ok. Here's the deal...'

The man placed the phone back on the receiver some minutes later. He smiled slowly. This maybe was going to be his day after all. He picked the phone back up again and dialled.

'Hello... Never mind that, I need to speak to Xavier...now *por favor.*'

Chapter Eighteen – A Worm Turns

Xavier was in a quandary, there was no escaping it, and the longer he thought about it, the deeper and more deadly became the hole he was digging for himself. *A burial hole,* he thought morosely.

He had always considered himself a loyal soldier. As a key player in the bloodthirsty and cruel games of the drug cartels where callous indifference to the normal rules of human conduct was the default condition, he was widely considered one of Arturo's most feared *sicarios*. It had been only last year, as the new wave of US funded federal authorities had begun to close the net on Arturo, that he, Xavier, had been the man who uncovered a DEA informer amongst their own men.

For his reward he had been allowed to determine the method by which, after prolonged torture and interrogation, the hapless agent was to meet his final end. It had been inspirational, he had thought at the time. Only Arturo had known the original idea had come from stories about the *gringo* Capone way back in the days of Prohibition America.

As befitted an informer, a traitor, *a rat...*, the man had been left in an abandoned warehouse, tied, naked, spread-eagled and bleeding. Still conscious, he had been made to watch as a large bucket of hungry rats had been deposited onto his body. He could only scream in unimaginable agony as the voracious rats first ate into his belly and then the soft flesh of his cheeks before their sharp teeth and claws sliced into his eyes.

Widely reported in the media, as expected, the result of his murder was the immediate bailing out of many previously unknown informers and a general air of being seen to show allegiance to the cartel.

It was Xavier who had been with Arturo right until the end. He had pulled the boss away from the tapped phone call that cost him his life. He had shouted at him for breaking his golden rule of keeping all calls short. With an acute sixth sense for survival keenly developed after months on the run, they had hidden together in the secret chamber built under the hotel by Arturo's men in preparation for such a situation. Whilst the battle was raging above, Xavier waited patiently, confident that they would escape as they had always done.

That was until the agent kicked down the door single-handed and disarmed Xavier with a devastating blow to his body, breaking three ribs in the process. The agent was in a black Special Forces uniform and he only carried a small handgun.

Arturo had lunged forward, screaming obscenities but the gun spat silently and Arturo dropped to his knees, his fat little face suddenly slipping downwards. By the time he had fallen half way to the floor, caught by Xavier, *El Patron* was dead and the man was gone. Ever since that day, Xavier had felt he must have had a guardian angel watching out for him and he looked upon this foolish world with new eyes. He knew Arturo had died instantly and he had felt sick to leave him like that. Somehow he had found himself outside and away to safety while behind him he could hear the beginnings of gun fire and celebrations to mark the successful demise of the once feared Arturo Beltran!

Now he owed his fealty to Ramon, the wild and wayward younger brother. He looked up into the rear view mirror at his new boss, dozing fitfully in the back, as the large black SUV charged through the countryside, the fading light casting ominous shadows across the rough road. Xavier only felt revulsion towards the man.

Ramon had cause to be tired as he had just been asserting the cartels control over a low ranking member who had been light on his payments recently by the use of a little intimidation from Xavier. The poor man had been made to smoke one of Xavier's trade mark cigars, but with the lit cigar the wrong way around in his mouth. Whilst this was going on, the man was being made fully aware that Ramon was upstairs forcibly deflowering his 16 year old daughter.

Xavier had been lucky to escape with his life back in Cuernavaca and ever since then he had been feeling most peculiar. He had realised, out of the blue, that he was in love for the first time in his life and he couldn't think straight at all.

He knew it was folly. No matter how he felt or how she felt, he had become infatuated with the one woman in the whole wide world that he could never be with. Not only that, if anyone ever found out how he felt, he would be a dead man, straight to hell. But despite that, he knew deep down, that hell would have to freeze over twice before he would change the way he felt about her.

He had lost the taste for torture altogether and he was avoiding killing people where at all possible. If it was a specific order from the boss then it had to be done, like that recent business up in the north, but he didn't feel so good about dealing out death anymore and he was sure that one of the men was going to guess something was up sooner or later. That would mean he would have to waste them too, and so it would go on.

He would not go so far as to say he was woefully unhappy however. There was this perpetual underlying feeling of inner warmth that he had never experienced before and, sure, he had felt great at many times in his life; at the conclusion of a successful op or even after *mucho* tequila, but that would wear off quickly whereas this sensation was like the generous light of morning sunshine flooding through every atom of his entire being. If he thought about it too deeply then the light would fade for a short time and he would feel extremely edgy and uncharacteristically vulnerable. At those times, he couldn't see any way out of it that didn't involve one or both of them dead.

And now he had just received credible intelligence from one of his paid informers in the DEA that sometime soon they will be going to put the hit on Ramon but for a fee the informant will be able to keep the brakes on it for a short while.

That meant he, Xavier, will have some more killing to organise and if Ramon gets to find out about it, a whole world of torture and pain for some poor fucks before they will be allowed to depart this earth. The details were sketchy at this point and Xavier would not have the time to investigate further until he could deliver Ramon to a safe house in Chiapas for a few days before they would meet up with Maximiliano and head further south.

One thing the informer did mention, which troubled Xavier, was that a non-negotiable condition of the deal had to be that before the exact circumstances of the attack would be conveyed to him, his boss Ramon would have to give up the girl, Juanita. Once she was released, Xavier would be informed of the location and timing of the authorities' operation. Now *that* Xavier did not like at all. He could give a damn about the girl but her existence and more presciently her importance to the boss might be very important to Xavier's situation. This was a complication that he didn't need right now.

Some time later, as Ramon woke abruptly from his slumbers, cursing Xavier for his poor driving, he was unaware of the reason for the sudden unintentional increase in the velocity of the SUV. The large car had speeded up in direct relation to the increased heart rate of the driver and Xavier's mind was racing even faster! *Maybe losing the girl might not be so terrible!*

His fevered brain was busy chasing down every possible outcome as a hungry coyote would hunt a ground squirrel or a rat. *If he, Xavier, handled it the right way; it would have to happen almost immediately to suit his purposes, but maybe, just maybe, it might just be what he was waiting for!* As he sped down the highway, with his grand plans becoming ever more aspirational, his spirits soared alongside him until he remembered who was in the back seat. He glanced nervously up at the mirror and carefully brought the car back down to a sensible pace.

Chapter Nineteen – The Problem These Days

It was a cold wet morning in Dublin and *not the best of weather to be after having me fookin' car break down*, true to form, bleedin' miles from anywhere and him after leavin' his bastarding jacket at home after storming out the house the night before last with her words still ringing in his ears.

'Yer always tellin' me yer a poor bleedin' student so what the fook are ye pissing off to Galway fer in such a bleedin' hurry?'

It was a fair point, the wife had, mind you, thought Jimmy O'Rourke as he walked into the city bar, squelching across the worn lino. He *was* fookin' poor! There was no argument there, right enough. But as for being a student, did he look that daft? Well, mebbes today he could pass for one of the scruffy work-shy wee nonces but normally he would be dressed smarter than your average college kid and he was quite old-fashioned about liking to have a wee shave before going out of a morning.

But the last couple of days had not gone to plan. He was tired, grubby and still soaked through from the inclement weather. The special privileges afforded to him enabling him to call up some vehicular assistance at 2am with no questions asked had been tempered by the fat bastard and his filthy truck which had bounced him back to Dublin.

That was the problem nowadays, he thought angrily as he waited for his contact to appear. The quality just wasn't there anymore. The so-called fookin' 'peace process' had transformed many of his number into politicians and statesmen but those who had been left behind, the flotsam, now had to stumble onwards, forced to work with all these pathetic wee tossers who couldn't organise a piss-up in the proverbial brewery. Too fond of a fookin' pint, they were, most of them anyways.

Jimmy was teetotal now, something of a rarity in these parts. He had run with a wild crowd of ruffians in his youth and he quickly realised that a slack tongue or other symptoms of a lack of self control could and usually did result in at best a severe beating or ultimately in your kneeling down in a roadside ditch, the Act of Contrition and a bullet in the back of your head.

Mind you, I was in a fookin' ditch last night..., he thought ruefully, looking at his watch for the hundredth time since he sat down. Just had the brakes looked an' all. You just can't trust any bastard to do anything right these days. Looking down he could swear there were faint swirls of steam coming up from his damp jeans. *Jesus, where the fook was Mickey?* He was already twenty minutes late and this was exactly the type of thing he was on about. Mickey was a top man in the organisation, his 'mentor' and the two got on pretty well but Jimmy was still nervous about this meeting and he was growing increasingly disenchanted about the whole deal.

Privately, he thought men like Mickey exercised too little control compared to days of old, and he feared that the Real's were becoming better known for their cock-ups and touts rather than the taking of enemy lives. They were just another gang of criminals half the time and while he was looking forward to making some decent cash from these newest ventures, he felt that most of them had missed the point of it all and he looked forward to better progress when two of the most hardline old school Provo men completed their sentences later that year.

Eventually, Mickey appeared and Jimmy jumped as the large man thumped a huge bear like paw on his shoulder.

'Jaysus, James! What the hell happened to you boy? You look like a feckin' dogs' breakfast!'

Jimmy looked askance at the severely overweight man sitting opposite him. Mickey had a massive overhanging beer gut which must have taken years of investment and dedication to develop. His food stained jumper had long since given up the hopeless task of meeting with his dirty jeans and a hairy swathe of blue and pink blubber fought to see the light of day like some albino whale surfacing in a polluted oil field. His yellowish jowly cheeks sagged down each side of his thick stubbled face pulling his sad dark rimmed eyes even lower. As he laughed at Jimmy, his thick lips parted just enough to reveal brown stained broken teeth reminiscent of an abandoned graveyard.

'Yeah, well…car trouble y'know. Next time I'll be after calling the fookin'

AA!
And anyways, Mickey, the words pot,
kettle and black spring to mind, if you
don't mind me saying!'

The big man laughed again, brushing an
oil stained hand through a mat of unkempt and
thinning hair.

'Fair play to ye!
Some of us have been working while you
were off gallivanting over to Galway, so
we have.
Oim' still after trying to work out what
the blazes is going on.
Had the bleedin' balaclava over me head
the last 24 hours in a poxy farm over by.
Thought we had a wee grass, so we did,
but I don't think the wee shite knew toss
all.
Took us two feckin' fingernails to find
that out, mind.
So, tell me what's so urgent and why you
couldn't feckin' tell me on the phone.
I'll have a glass over here if you please,
Liam!
I don't suppose you'll be after wanting a
drink ye big pair o' lassies knickers!'

Exasperated, Jimmy told him this was
too important to talk about on a mobile and
anyways that was against the rules these days,
you never knew who was listening. He went on
to remind Mickey that it was unusual not to have
had any contact from the two boys for so many
days and that this incident in Galway must

somehow be connected.

By a stroke of luck, Jimmy had a source within the authorities over there who he had worked with at Warrenpoint many years ago as the police were keeping tight-lipped about the whole thing.

'They've arrested a Yank, so they have, name of Bobby Goldsboro.'

Now suddenly Jimmy could see he had Mickey's undivided attention as the big man placed his Guinness back down on the bar without taking his doleful eyes off him. As far as his source could tell, Goldsboro was a big shot ex-con from Florida who had made a pile of dosh and he was actually apprehended in his own private plane. The cops were searching it naturally but at this point they had come up with nothing. The official pap was that they would probably be letting him go with nothing more than a slap on the wrist for paperwork irregularities and possession of a gun for which he had a US permit for.

However, his source had said there was definitely more to this that meets the eye as over the last 24 hours there had been a constant parade of Brits and Yanks in and out the station, no names, no uniforms.

'I heard it said that the guy was singing like a budgie but about what I've not a notion…'

Mickey had a pretty good idea and deep in thought, his hefty elbow thumped down on the bar top as his thick fingers scraped up his face, sounding like a tractor turning in heavy gravel. After an agonising minute, he turned to Jimmy.

'We may be after havin' a wee problem. This is what I want you to do...'

Chapter Twenty – Relief and Release

Ridge had spent most of the next day hiding away in a spare room either sleeping or pretending to be asleep and he was in a deep melancholy. He was trying desperately to avoid either of his two hosts. Whilst he had been reasonably successful in this, intermittently sloping off to the bathroom like some unkempt ninja, there was an appalling inevitability to the fact that he was going to have to confront them sometime soon. He had heard Ed and Mandy arguing loudly a while back and had felt that he must be wholly responsible.

Despite burying his head in a blanket, he was still unable to suffocate himself sufficiently to end this horrendous situation. Fearful of what would imminently occur, Ridge was mentally preparing himself for a hasty evacuation. He was trying to work out what he would do next, assuming he escaped in one piece, when his worst fears were realised and a pale and drawn looking Ed came through into the small room closing the door firmly behind him.

Attempting to get up, Ridge was pushed, albeit gently, back down onto the makeshift bed and Ed hunkered himself down on the floor beside him. Bringing out two small beers and thrusting one upon a bewildered Ridge, Ed looked at him with an immense sadness in his eyes.

'I have something to tell you, son.

I got to make a confession to you and I want you to shut up 'til I get through with it, ok?'

Ridge nodded silently, the stench of hypocrisy oozing out of his every pore.

'I've come to a kinda crossroads in ma life, son.
Talkin' with you, listenin' to your story, has made me realise that I have been a worthless piece of shit for far too long now and this is my chance to put some stuff right!'

Ed took a long draught from his beer, wiping his mouth with the back of his big hand before continuing, his face turned away now.

'Fact is, my friend, some of these assholes you've been talkin' about are not totally unknown to me.
You have no fuckin' comprehension of what they will do to get their way.
When I said I retired early so as not to end up on my back with a tag on ma goddamn toe, I was dead cold serious.
But, if truth be told, I've already bent over for the bastards and on more than one occasion. That shiny SUV outside didn't come outta a pension that's for damn sure and this little vacation home neither!
And I'm sick to my stomach of trying to square all that stuff away and still look at my face in the goddamn mirror of a

mornin.''

Ridge sat impassively, not knowing what to say and sipped his beer slowly. Ed had finished his bottle and he took a huge breath and sighed deeply.

'I know my wife doesn't love me the way she ought to. Don't you say nothin' now! I've seen the way she goes on and I'll betcha she's been makin' eyes at you!

Time passes so fast and somewhere down the line our train got itself derailed and it's kinda hard to know how to get back on track again.

I guess she knew I was a bent cop, but in my screwed up head I kinda thought that if I could provide better for her then things would get better, know what I'm sayin'? So, I ain't got nothin' more to lose by takin' a chance on you son, if you wanna listen.

Bottom line, kid, is that with what you've told me plus what I already know, I think that I've come up with a plan for you to get your girl back from those goons. I ain't givin' you no cast iron guarantees mind but you're not lookin' at too many options right now!'

So there it was that several hours later Ed was parking his enormous SUV in a quiet side street in Antigua. He had been getting several calls and texts on his mobile during the trip and he now seemed to possess an air of confidence and assurance, like he knew what he was doing, this was his arena and he was ready for the fight.

Ridge, on the other hand, was quietly shitting himself. It had seemed easy enough back in Pana, and when Ed said it quickly, it didn't sound too bad.

Across the cobbled street there was a high quality restaurant with tables out the front, mostly empty, and a large cooler looking tree lined courtyard along one side and at the back.

The only customer sitting in the baking heat looking onto the road was, Ed informed him, one of the apes who were tasked with keeping Juanita safe but in confinement. A large man in a too-tight suit, the guy was clearly baking under the merciless heat of the afternoon sun. His fleshy oleaginous head was bowed as if he was almost asleep and he didn't even glance up as Ed crossed the road and quietly and efficiently put a small bullet hole through his fat skull. As the man slipped imperceptibly forwards, Ed gestured over to Ridge and the two of them walked through the front entrance of the restaurant.

Standing inside the small room which was totally open along the back, the two men had a good view through and into the courtyard behind. Ridge stood stock still, as if hypnotised, as sitting alongside the side wall under the shade of trees he could clearly see Juanita, quietly reading and completely oblivious to their presence!

Shaking uncontrollably, Ridge knew that he was shortly to play his part and he clenched and unclenched his fists nervously waiting for the second act.

Right on cue, a wandering troupe of actors, jugglers and other theatre performers

227

entered the courtyard from the other side and with a fanfare of trumpets they began to tumble and dance in front of the astounded customers.

The three thugs who sat by Juanita looked at each other in bewilderment as they decided what to do and when one of the dancers grabbed Juanita by the arm and entreated her to dance, the largest of the men jumped up, throwing his chair across the floor and barked loudly at the poor little street artist. He backed off slightly while all the time singing and smiling at Juanita. The girl spat back at her massive captor and she allowed herself to be waltzed into the centre of the courtyard. This was too much for the bald headed giant and he strode off in fury towards the interior of the restaurant and Ridge!

The next few seconds were a blur of activity as Ridge turned himself away from the rapidly approaching thug. Then as he could hear the restaurant owner being vociferously attacked and the theatre troupe whirled away towards the road, with Juanita in their midst, he darted out. Before he knew what he was doing, he had gripped Juanita by the arm and they were out into the bright sunshine. The powerful engine of the SUV revved loudly and with gunshots echoing in the narrow street behind and hapless tourists diving clear in front of them, they were away! Juanita was free!

Bouncing around in the back seat like small children on a trampoline, they initially hugged each other tightly but soon after that an awkward shyness overcame them and a polite distance was maintained for the remainder of the journey. Not much was said but it was clear from their eyes that a lot was going on in each of their heads.

Ridge had been as high as a kite when they first sped off but this feeling of elation was quickly replaced by exhaustion and a despondency fuelled by the weary realisation that he had no idea what to do next. It was fantastic to look into those beautiful eyes again but the longer he looked the more he realised that she had come to the same conclusion as he had; that their time together in San Francisco had been a wonderful few months but in the grand scheme of things it had been just that, a holiday romance of sorts.

Juanita was frantic with fear. She was not sad to leave Maximiliano behind but she never would have wanted *this* to happen. That Ridge was still alive at all was a blessing and proof that her prayers had been answered. But now he had put himself back into danger for her and she felt an enormous weight of guilt and expectation crushing down upon her. She could never have a life with this boy, this beautiful crazy *gringo*!

The interminable days of captivity had given her time to think long and hard and she knew that once Ramon had tired of her, once her looks had faded, if her life was spared, then she could perhaps return to her people, what was left of her family, get a simple job and see out the remainder of her life as quietly as she could.

As she searched his wild eyes for answers to the thousand questions careering around her brain, she thought she could see something different within Ridge also; the last few weeks had changed him too, a look of considered resignation crossed his face as he gazed back at her. Maybe there was a chance for him to live!

They sat staring at each other, their clammy hands, bridging the gulf between them, gripped tightly together like school sweethearts and in those moments came a mutual understanding.

'This can *never* work, between us', she said quietly.

'I know', he replied wistfully.

Juanita thought suddenly of an old aunt who had recently passed away and how guilty she had felt for not visiting enough in the old woman's twilight days. As a penance, she had reluctantly agreed to go to the house and help clear away her few possessions. It was several weeks before she could summon the courage to go but she remembered the feeling, when opening the door and bright sunlight flooded into the dark and dusty house. It had felt like a cleansing, a spiritual exculpation, a sense of relief and a release from the wearisome burdens of the past and perhaps even humble optimism for the days ahead. She felt a little like that now.

'Hey guys!
How we doin' in the back there? I can't hear you too good but we gotta' keep this baby gunning hard all the way home. The name's Ed by the way, I'm very

obliged to meet your acquaintance little lady!'

'Thank you very much sir' Juanita whispered back. 'But where are we going and what are we going to do now?'

'Hey! Don't you two lovebirds worry 'bout a thing.
That was just the first quarter!
We got a ways to go yet before this little game is over! What you say?'

Ed was pleased that everything had gone as planned, more or less. He wished he had taken the chance to pop that evil brute Maximiliano, whether he had eyeballed him or not. With any luck the theatre troupe will have managed to vamoose before he had worked out what had gone down.

There was something else though that was not so good. Ed could not be positive but he would swear that just as he had screwed the big car across the road to collect the two runaways, he had seen the reflection of the bright glare of the late afternoon sun from the lenses of a pair of binoculars. From a roof a hundred yards or so along the road. Big lenses, looked like military grade Steiner's or the like. Who was watching them? In this business you never knew who was going to double-cross who and with the end-game still some way off, there was a lot to go wrong.

Back at Ed and Mandy's place, they were all having a celebratory beer or two although the atmosphere was less bubbly than the beer. Juanita sat quietly looking up at Ed with big brown eyes whilst he in turn could not take his gaze away from her as he paced up and down the room. Not sensitive enough to see there was a problem, he waded in several times with totally inappropriate comments and Ridge was becoming mightily embarrassed. Mandy was also building up a good head of steam.

'Hey Ridge! You never told me how beautiful your girlfriend was, *amigo*! No wonder you battled so hard to find her. I'll bet you won't be letting her outta your sight from now on, eh?'

It was probably post-gig euphoria but Ridge thought Ed was acting really weird and whilst both Ridge and Juanita were appreciative of what he had done so far, he was in danger of blowing it massively.

It was Juanita who would repeatedly bring them all back down to earth with her genuine fears about the aftermath of today. But then Ed knelt down and took her slender brown hands into his huge paws and told her that before long there would be no Ramon, period.

He told his rapt audience that the second phase of this operation was the elimination of Ramon and his gang, with extreme prejudice. When Juanita cast doubt on this, looking around the room at just the three of them, Ed explained that it would not be themselves who would be carrying out the final operation, that would indeed be too suicidal for words but rather it would be the authorities both local and *norteamericano.*

It was all in motion, they just had to sit tight and do nothing. Then, he said, they would all be free of the stain of Ramon and they could all have their lives back again.

They all wanted to believe Ed and he certainly seemed sure of what he was saying, so much so that Mandy took one of his hands and squeezed it tightly and looked afresh at the husband that she had doubted for so long. Ed acknowledged his wife for the briefest of moments before returning his gaze to Juanita like some love-sick Labrador.

For his part, Ed felt immortal at this point. He had taken on and defeated one of the most feared men in Central America.

He had rescued Beauty from the Beast!

As he continued to pace the room expounding his plans, he felt the blood race through his body in a way he had not felt for a long time. Looking down at Juanita, right now, he felt that he could do anything and he what he felt like doing was to lift her right off the chair and carry her away on a shining white horse.

They ate a feast that night and drank the finest wine that the village could provide but eventually the day took its toll and they all went to bed, Ridge gallantly giving up his bed for Juanita and crashing on the sofa clutching a warm beer for solace.

Ed could not sleep. He thrashed for an hour or two, tormented both by visions of death and anarchy and also of the beautiful enchantress Juanita, dancing and twirling before him.

As he thought of her, he felt himself

stiffening; a physical response that he had long ago believed had permanently forsaken him. For a moment he considered awakening his slumbering wife. Fearing the situation would not last, he eased out of bed and paced the floor for a while, gently stroking his member. He was enjoying that powerful feeling of being hard and unyielding.

Without being aware of any conscious thought, he found himself padding through the house and into Juanita's room and he stood there quietly, hardly daring to breathe. As he tugged away he imagined her naked body under the thin blanket and he dared himself to waken her. He could see it all now, how she would reach up and welcome him down to the warmth of her brown body, but then he stopped himself abruptly. This girl was rescued to help a friend and through his actions he had begun the redemption that his life so sorely demanded.

Unwilling to tear himself away from her, he listened to her quiet snoring and in the dim light he could see her chest rise and fall. Lying on the floor at the foot of the bed he saw her small panties. Instinctively he reached down with his spare hand and grasped them up to his face, sniffing and tasting the musky fragrance like a pack animal. Rubbing the soft material against his swollen manhood he felt dizzy and from the remnants of a long distant sensation he realised something was about to happen. Pulling the pants over his head like a grotesque mask with the thin gusset covering his nose and mouth, he felt his legs buckle underneath him. As his knees gave way and he collapsed to the floor, his hips jerked and a jet of warm liquid sprayed across to the blanket. He lay for a few seconds, his sweat-drenched body still writhing spasmodically and his breathing heavy and damp through the underwear. As the pounding in his ears began to subside, he drifted into unconsciousness.

Waking late from the deepest sleep he could remember, Ed found himself lying in his own bed and he could hear music and laughter through the wall. He broke out into a cold sweat as the memory of the night hit him like a tidal wave. He remembered waking with a shock, freezing cold on the floor, the damp panties still over his head. He had jumped up, relieved beyond imagination that the girl was still asleep and had staggered through to his own room dimly aware that the first rays of dawn were edging pink and grey into the sky.

In his fragile state, he hadn't seen anything untoward. If he had been more aware he might have noticed the green glare of all seeing night-goggles sweeping back and forth across the house.

He could hear Mandy's voice clearly and he felt comforted by the natural banter, the alarm bells in his head gradually subsiding. Rolling over to get up, Ed recoiled in horror as he saw the pink frill of underwear sticking out from under his pillow! *Jeez*! He still had her panties! Feeling nauseous and unable to think straight due to the pounding in his chest, Ed had to get some fresh air.

Bumbling through the house, he burst into the living area where he was met with three astonished faces and a burst of laughter. Sitting himself down quickly, it was a shaky Ed Foster who listened with grateful relief at their humorous observations about his bedraggled appearance and lack of ability to hold his drink. In turn, he observed that Juanita was paler than yesterday and still quiet as a church mouse but he was cheered up to see that she was wearing a fresh top *and* jeans donated from his wife.

Feeling the need to get far away from the scene of crime and vaguely conscious of a odour of illicit sexual activity emanating from his body, Ed jumped up and proposed that they all needed some fresh air to clear the head before making any decisions about the future and so they should accompany him on a day trip to explore the beauty of Lake Atitlan. Nobody was too keen but eventually all but Mandy agreed to go. Juanita was feeling very strange but she liked Mandy and tried to stay but she was outvoted and so reluctantly trotted behind the other two towards the big car.

They only drove a short distance, picking up some food on the way and soon they were looking across the calm blue water of the lake. Instantly reminded, apart from the intense heat, of many Scottish lochs back home, Ridge was in his element. They left the car in a small village and began trudging up dusty hot tracks behind the striding tall figure of Ed.

The way became steeper and piercing black eyes watched them every step of the way. The inhabitants of San Marco all appeared as tiny, dark shapes, sitting in the relative shade of their tin roofed little shacks discussing the endemic insanities of the *gringos* as the three of them worked their weary way higher and higher.

Climbing through the dry brush for a short time, they found the shade of an ancient tree overlooking some useful looking flat rocks and flopped gladly down to rest. It was then that they looked down at the panoramic vista before them, the whole lake now resplendently laid out in all its glory.

Above the tree line mostly now, Ridge looked down at the tiny buildings of the village each one of them manifestly fragile and temporary. He thought sadly of recent disasters around the globe and it seemed to him that this had always been the way of things. The only substantial building in sight was, of course, the majestic church, standing tall and proud, and gleaming white in a sea of rust, concrete and dried mud. All around the lake there was a ring of huge mountains masquerading as benign sleeping volcanoes; little wisps of cloud replacing fiery lava smoke the only blemishes in an otherwise perfect blue-white sky.

It was an idyllic few hours spent sleeping and snacking on spicy meats wrapped in flour tortillas and washed down with warm beer. They spoke about many things, insignificant things mostly and the atmosphere was light and airy as befitted a mountain-side picnic.

Later, as Ed and Juanita dozed in the shade, Ridge sat out upon a large warm rock and surveyed the scene. He missed home painfully at this moment and he had more or less made up his mind to steal a little more from Thad's credit card and book the nearest flight back to San Francisco to say his goodbyes before cadging a little more cash for his flight back to the UK.

Then what? He had no idea right now but

237

one thing that was certain was that he could never just go back to doing what he had done before. Without Orla it would be different anyway but he had changed so much since those days that he doubted anyone would know who he was.

Looking down toward the lake, Ridge suddenly noticed a tiny figure striding up towards them purposefully. The man was moving quickly and seemed to be dressed entirely in black which was unwise in this heat and it looked to Ridge as if he was looking up directly at them, stopping every so often to look through what might have been binoculars perhaps.

Ridge sat up and felt distinctly uneasy. This did not fit with the quiet tourist scenery all around him.

'Ed! Wake up will you!
Have a look! See? Down there!

Ed slowly came to his senses and eased himself out of the shade and over into the intense heat of the rocks.

'What's the panic *amigo*?
So…, it's some dumb-ass *gringo* tourist out for a walk without a hat!
Looks like a red head too! Dumb son-of-a-bitch gonna have a sore head damn soon!'

Ridge stood up straight now and rubbed his sleepy eyes. Ed was right! The guy did have a thick head of red hair. *That's pretty unusual round here,* he was thinking and at the same time he was also thinking the unthinkable. *There is something familiar looking about that shape, the way he walks, but it can't be!*

The man was closer now, only a couple of hundred metres away and Ridge was suddenly aware that he was shaking with emotion. He felt tears welling up in his eyes and he brushed them roughly away as he began to run quickly down the hill.

There was no doubt in his mind now… The two men collided and toppled over into the dust as Ridge unbalanced them both, his arms wrapped around the other, tears pouring down openly now, the deep hurt of almost half a year bursting forth like the collapsing of a mighty dam.

Chapter Twenty One – Shadowplay

Ridge wept on his knees as his brother-in-law stood up impassively, brushing the dust and leaves off his black clothing. As he looked up through his tears, Ridge was struck by how pale Colm was and he thought that he had never seen him look so cold and hard. Suddenly a hand went out and Ridge was pulled roughly to his feet.

'Come on! You and me need to have a wee chat! Will you give your friends a wave and shout up you'll only be a minute?'

Colm walked quickly along the side of the hill with Ridge struggling to keep pace with him or to make any sense of anything else.

'What the hell are you doing here? How did you find me? What is going on?' The words spilled out of Ridge like a stream of consciousness. He couldn't think anymore, he would never understand. His first feelings had been of unreality and fear for his life, for his sanity even.

But almost immediately, even now as he chased after him, still confused and scared, he began to feel something else. He could not explain it yet but something about Colm exuded an aura of control and calm.

They found some shade and Colm ushered him down onto the rough ground and stood towering above him, his back to the sun, his face shadowed, dark and grim. *Like a vision of Death*, Ridge thought ominously.

'Ok, Richard! You are going to have to just hold your wheest for a wee while and let me do the talking!

There's a hell of a lot that I need you to know, but we haven't got the luxury of time at the moment.

I'll fill you in on the important stuff now and I'll be after telling you the rest as and when we get the chance.

The first thing you have to know is that I am on your side.

I *am* here to help you, but I am in *no way* the pleasant fellow that you think I am.

Second thing is that you and your friends are in an extremely dangerous situation and it will be touch and go whether or not you survive the next 24 hours!

You will only make it if you listen to me very carefully and do *exactly* as I tell you.

Do I make myself clear?'

Ridge nodded in quiet assent, his polluted brain backing up with the congestion of a hundred thousand questions.

'Ok, good. Now, Jeez!

Where to start?

Ok, you're going to hear a lot of stuff you won't like and things that you just don't get, but, trust me, you need to go along with this for now if you want to

241

live.

Here goes!

Right, you have known me since you and Orla became an item and you thought I was a Customs fellow for a while, working for the government.

Well, I did work for the government alright but not that one.

I was an undercover agent for the Brits for years and I have learned many things I wish I had never known and I have committed crimes and done lots of other stuff I'm not proud of but it was a job, a dirty job in a dirty war and for a while, at least, I thought I was doing the right thing.'

Colm went on to quickly explain what he meant by undercover agent. He reminded a stunned Ridge how he had dropped out of law at Queen's University in Belfast and then gone on to walk into a job as a Customs Officer. Ridge had only been dimly aware of this as it was long before he had come upon the scene.

What nobody had known was that Colm, an Irish Catholic, had been recruited into the Force Research Unit, a beyond-top-secret wing of the British military intelligence forces through one of his lecturers at Queen's. He was a gift to the security forces as his family had no republican leanings although he himself, as an idealistic young man with a passion for Irish history and politics, had already been in contact with many who held IRA sympathies. Ever since the Omagh bombing way back in 1998, the British had been determined that nothing like

242

that would ever happen again.

Colm explained how they had gone all out to bring down those who were thought to be responsible, particularly a splinter group calling themselves the 'Real IRA'. The FRU had been working with agents in both the republican and loyalist paramilitaries and if they couldn't catch people under their own auspices then they often fought one lot off against the other in a gruesome government-backed game of tit-for-tat.

Initially, he said he had been fair flattered by the attention and he told Ridge about being spirited away to an army training camp in County Down where they taught him among other things, how to use weapons. They had told him he was a 'natural.' He was taught to shoot AK-47's, M16's Sterling sub-machine guns and his favourite; he lifted his black shirt at the front to reveal a small handgun tucked into his trouser waistband, a Browning 9mm automatic pistol.

He had worked away quietly for a while and began to drink in the 'wrong' bars and hang out with the 'wrong' people. He made good friends with a guy whom he knew was keen to become involved with the republican movement and so had become more open about looking to do the same thing.

One night, he met his friend as arranged in a bar and the man was in a high state of agitation. He had been picked up earlier and questioned by men in balaclavas as to his intentions regarding the IRA. They had kicked his arse a little and asked him lots of questions including some about Colm. They had suggested that if he and Colm were serious about being useful to the Real's then they needed to prove it.

Later that night, after a few too many glasses of the black stuff, Colm began his double life in earnest as he and his pal stole a lorry full of DVD players!

Working in Customs was ideal for Colm as he could smuggle in and out of the country with ease and he only had to don his uniform to get waved through any police or army checkpoints.

'So that's why I never got any more hassles from the airport guys!
But, were you using me?
And what about Orla?
How does she fit in?
Were you involved with her death?'

Once the questions started, they poured out like rain from a leaking gutter on a black winter night.

'Listen!
We don't have time right now to talk about Orla, Ok?
Let's get through this and then we'll maybe have a chance.'

Colm stared directly at him and he spoke with such conviction that Ridge could not doubt him for a moment.

'I was not involved in my sister's death, I promise you and that is all I can tell you right now.

But I do have some very bad news for your friend up there and then we have to get away from here as soon as possible! Now, keep quiet about all of this will you. Get up and come on up with me.'

As they walked quickly back up the hill, Colm pumped Ridge for information about Ed, Juanita and what they had been doing for the last day or two. Dumfounded, Ridge discovered that Colm knew most of it anyway as he had been watching them closely since they had rescued Juanita.

'Have you been *looking after us*?' Ridge asked, more in hope than belief.

'Sort of... but I've made a right arse of it so I have.'

'I still don't understand how you knew where I was anyway *and* you still haven't told me WHY you are here.'

'It's not important why I am here.
Finding you was easy enough.
I knew you had been to Schipol and I even got your mobile phone back.
From lost property!
Not that it helped me much.
But I had another method, so I did!'

He smiled briefly and tapped his front teeth.

'D'ye remember having that god-awful

toothache when we'd been fishing?
Did you no think it was a wee bit strange
that I was so insistent in taking you to my
own dentist rather than the nearest one?
I had her fit you with a radio transmitter
location device.
Yep! Right there in yon big molar!
Jeez! It wasn't *you* I was interested in, so
don't be getting too big-headed, it was
my wee sister, God love her, and I had
thought you two were pretty inseparable
around then so where you were, she
would be too!
Mind you! When you scarpered off like
that, after the bomb in Edinburgh, you
did set off a fair few alarm bells I can tell
you!
I've been 'officially' retired for a while
now but I've my ways of keeping tabs
and there was a buzz going around that
you had been part of the bombing.
I even wondered meself for a minute or
two if you were the other body from the
van! I thought you might be daft enough
to go along with her but then I realised
that you were too much of an eedjit for
anyone to let you be part of an operation
as important as that!'

Fuck you, ya big wank, thought Ridge,
his eyes swimming in the heat and dust as he
struggled to keep his emotions under control.
'Well, I thought it might have been YOU ya
bastard!' Ridge retorted forcefully.

'Fair play to you!
246

I could understand why, but, here we are now. I need you to shut the fuck up for a bit and see if you can't be a help here'

They arrived back up to the others and Ridge could see that both of them had been straining to see what was going on, the worry clearly evident on both faces. Juanita was tired and frightened and she did not like the look of this *pelirrojo* man at all!

Colm quietly and politely introduced himself as Ridge's brother-in-law and then gently took Ed to one side and put a hand on one shoulder. Ridge had a very bad feeling as he looked over and then he saw Ed crumple to the ground, his arms curled up and over his head as if to ward off a mortal blow. Cries of anguish emanated from his huge quivering body and then his fists pounded into the dirt.

'WHY...?
What did she ever do to deserve that?
I'm the goddamn guilty one!
It should have been ME...!'

Ed sat for a few minutes more and the others left him to it. Juanita sobbed quietly into Ridge's shoulder, his shirt soaking. Ridge himself just blinked and looked imploringly into Colm's stony face for some kind of answer.

Juanita whispered that this was all her fault and she should just go now or they would all die and Ridge wrapped his arms around her and held her tight as much for his own solace as for keeping her from escaping.

Colm began to look impatient, glancing

over to Ed and then back to the other two every few seconds. 'I'm sorry guys! He said loudly. 'But we have to go!'

Ed leapt up; his eyes a fiery red and tears streaming down his face. 'You're goddamn right we gotta go!' he shouted. 'I wanna find and kill these son's of bitches and I mean now!'

       'I did that....' Colm replied flatly.
       'I just wish I could have been quicker at it. I was too far up the hill to stop them.'

       'Did you hurt the motherfuckers?'

As Colm's jet black eyes penetrated deep into his very soul, like some evil necromancer, Ed felt his blood freeze for a moment and a demonic vision from hell itself, a certain and absolute panoply of death played across his mind. He was left in no doubt as to the fate suffered by the men who had killed his poor wife.

Chapter Twenty Two – Escape From Atitlan

It was a crazy 5 hours, 3 cars and 2 cell phones later, after a desperate race, propelled ever faster through the clammy darkness by Kafkaesque wraiths, that they found themselves sitting shattered and fearful on the harbour wall. They had travelled 200 dusty miles of Highway CA9 to Puerto Barrios. The three of them stared blankly out over the Bahia de Amatique as the anaemic early dawn rays began to gently caress the grandiose cruise liners inducing a reluctant blushing, slowly spreading across the antiseptic and unsullied white of their voluptuous bodies. Fuelled only by a high octane terror as to what may be rampaging after them, they had simply run out of juice.

Colm, Ridge considered, was off no doubt stealing them another old van or acquiring yet another pay per go phone. Sitting up front throughout the journey, Ridge had absorbed a great deal of new information about his erstwhile relation. Over the noise of the straining engines it had been hard for the others to have conversed with Colm, even if they had wanted to. Ed had been catatonic ever since he had been told about Mandy. Meanwhile Juanita had just gazed unseeing out into the blackness, flinching every so often as she foresaw the inevitable fate that awaited all of them.

They now sat motionless as the first cargo ship workers began to appear, bustling around them, shouting and waving to each other, oblivious to the personal hell inhabited by the crumpled *touristicas*.

Ridge nervously replayed portions of their journey; fragments of hoarse conversation, the confident way Colm had hotwired a vehicle, the easy nonchalance as he used a mobile for a short while then threw it out a window and overriding all of this, the unyielding, piercing eyes that held him fascinated in their icy embrace as he told his compelling story.

Over the complaining noise of engines and suspension joints, Colm had told him he was no longer part of the security services nor was he involved with any paramilitary or terrorist groups back home. 'You could say I'm a wee bit *persona non grata* with both sets of eedjits'. He told an astounded Ridge how for a time he had been a key player in the grotesque game of cat and mouse being played by the intelligence agencies and the Real IRA.

He had not been the first double agent and so the Real IRA were always on the lookout for 'touts' which ultimately meant that his British handlers often had to let him commit real crimes to avoid exposing him and others like him. He guessed there were maybe a dozen other agents, from both sides of the religious fence, all feeding information back to their handlers. He himself had been forced to take part in bombings, shootings and other activities which had often injured or killed innocent civilians as well as paramilitaries and security personnel.

In a bizarrely ironic situation he had even at one stage been a member of the Real IRA 'nutting squad', which was responsible for the torturing and killing of suspected informants.

He had wanted out from early on but this was an occupation that few ever escaped from and not many ever saw a pension. 'In that line of work, when they said you were gettin' the bullet, they meant it!' He had been interrogated once himself by one of the top Belfast hard men who was concerned that he seemed to have lost heart in the great struggle. He had been accused of doing 'a road to Damascus job', developing a sudden case of conscience, and after three long days, strapped to a chair sitting on a roll of plastic sheeting, he had narrowly avoided a bullet. This of course meant that he was required to throw himself deeper into the mire in order to shake off any doubts. His handlers were content to let Colm walk this tight-rope every day as they were confident he would save more lives than he would take.

In another surreal situation, Colm had been caught out in a RIRA informer sting operation which had been targeted at another agent who had been hitherto unknown to him. By pure bad luck he had been meeting this man to get some information to pass on to his handlers concerning the location of a state-of-the-art horizontally-fired mortar device. They had been attacked at a small country house, near the border, deep into what many still regarded as bandit country.

After a protracted and well fought gun battle, they were both wounded and trapped like rabbits in a snare. Drenched in his own blood, Colm had made his peace with the Almighty and had held on grimly, knowing in the pit of his stomach that they would never escape alive.

They had sat waiting for RIRA reinforcements to arrive followed by a slow painful death, when confusingly, they heard the unmistakable deafening sound of an army helicopter flying low overhead. It had landed nearby and the two weakened men braced themselves for the end. There was the sharp crack of a brief fire-fight outside and seconds later, they found themselves being led, dazed and lurching into the aircraft.

With the blood from their wounds hardly congealed they were back on the ground and whisked off into a private jet. When the pain woke Colm up less than an hour after take off, he was being stretchered into a military ambulance in London. The jet, he found out later, had been Prime Minister Blair's. 'I still don't know who this other fellow really was but he was obviously a lot more bleedin' important to the authorities than I was!'

That had been the tipping point as far as he was concerned. His cover was intact but his career prospects had been blown. Officially, his handlers still employed him and they would not hear of him walking away from the job, but deep down he knew his days were numbered. His counterparts in the Real's had no idea he had been involved in the incident as he had told no-one where he had been going that day. His temporary absence had been conveniently explained by an urgent case of appendicitis and subsequent peritonitis – he even had an authentic if somewhat messy scar, courtesy of a shotgun bullet.

Increasingly worried by now and struggling to function effectively through excessive drinking and consequent sleeping difficulties, Colm had begun to bring forward his plans to escape. 'Funnily enough', he told Ridge, 'I had been waiting for your wedding anyway before I made any moves as I didn't want to bugger up Orla's big day!' Ridge shook his head in wonder as he remembered that Colm had been absent from the stag night due to 'some work thing' that had 'cropped up suddenly in London'.

He had not been at all surprised, he said, when they tried to check mate him. He had been waiting for something and barring actual death, he had a few moves up his sleeve himself before they would reach end game. His handlers obviously thought he had outlived his usefulness and with the rapidly changing political situation, men like him were becoming an embarrassment to the authorities.

'He who pays the piper, calls the tune' he said bitterly to Ridge.

They had instructed him to go by car to Belfast with two other Real IRA men as part of a reconnaissance team for an imminent hit on a prominent lawyer.

Just outside the city, on a bleak and dank morning, the car was mysteriously stopped and the three men arrested. 'But yon Brits had seriously underestimated the survival instincts of yer' man here', Colm said and it appeared the two young policemen had only been told to look out for that particular car and they had not been briefed on who specifically they were to arrest.

'To them we were just two spotty wee
wanks and some skinny ginger Provo
sheep shagger!'

The police car was found a few hours
later, with two highly embarrassed policemen
handcuffed to the steering wheel and two dead
youths in the boot, shot by a police revolver.

'Did you...?'

'I had no choice!
This way I was out without any official
come back.
I had been wearing gloves and the two
cops had sworn on their families' lives
that they would give a false description
of me. The authorities covered the whole
incident up, naturally.
Obviously I haven't been back to see the
folk's too often since then either!'

The sun was becoming warmer now and
Ridge decided to wander around the harbour and
try and find some food. 'Shouldn't be too hard'
he thought, as he looked around warily. They
spoke English here, Colm had told him, and
apparently the British Army have been here a lot
over the years. 'Wonder where the hell he has
got to' he mused, 'hope he's not off killing
anyone...'

By the time Ridge had found his way
back towards the harbour wall, with only a poor
repast of fried and dried pork meat to offer his
companions, he could see that Colm himself had

also returned and the three of them were tucking into fresh bread, cheese and bottles of ice cold cola from a large stuffed army style rucksack. 'Hey! Glad you could make it!' Colm shouted over sarcastically as Ridge weaved his way through the increasingly busy port traffic. He sat down heavily beside the others and winced. 'Christ my arse hurts!' He then laughed to himself as he grabbed thirstily for a coke bottle.

'If only Thad could have heard me say that one!' No-one else seemed amused and he didn't notice a strange look crossing Colm's face.
'What's next boss?
Not another roller-coaster car ride? I'll need to get my piles looked at first!'

Colm actually laughed and just for a brief second, Ridge could see the man he had once known. He was the bugger that had hid a farting cushion under the seat that he had then so politely ushered the young and bashful Richard Walker to sit upon, on the nervous occasion of his very first visit to meet Orla's mother and father. Juanita and Ed were still very quiet and they chewed resolutely at the tough bread, stomachs growling from the sudden breaking of their weary fast.

'No! Your arse is in luck, for a wee while anyways. We're going to sea in a boat! And a mighty fine boat she is too! So, come on let's look lively about it! We sail North, me shipmates!'

At that, Colm jumped to his feet, shouldering the heavy rucksack with ease and the others scrambled less gracefully to their feet and staggered after him as he strode along the quay. Mouths still valiantly chewing as they walked quickly behind Colm, the dizzy trio didn't have much opportunity to ask the many questions that arced between their newly recharged imaginations.

Ridge knew only that they were in Belize, a country he knew almost nothing about apart from his experiences that morning. He figured the sea must be the Caribbean and he hoped fervently that if they were headed north then they must be going back to the States and that this perilous adventure of his would soon be over. Somehow, deep in his heart, he knew that there would have to be some final reckoning before this could ever end and he steeled himself to be strong enough to see it through.

With the skirl of pipes playing surreptitiously in the yawning depths of his subconscious he thought fondly of Orla once again and he prayed that he would have the fortitude to honour her memory somehow by surviving this ordeal.

He stared wistfully at the back of Colm's head, the thick red hair a heart-rending identical match to that of his younger sister. He was determined to get to the truth about all of this. Why had Orla's brother come here to Central America? Was it simply to save him? He should be flattered, he knew that, but perhaps Ridge was just a small vestige of the memory of a lost sister that had to be protected at all costs. Or was Colm doing this all to save his own tortured soul? That, he could identify with, for sure...

The boat was a real beauty. For someone like Ridge, who had grown up around small boats on a remote island, they had always been just a practicality, often the only means of transport when the weather would be too rough for the ferries to run.

But he had never been on one like this! Despite the circumstances, his face beamed as Colm proudly escorted them onboard, pointing out the classic features of the 33 foot Nauticat cruiser. He could appreciate the vessel without a guide but he laughed as Colm explained to the others how the vessel had been built by a famous Danish boat builder, Klaus Baess and when he showed them the teak decking and mahogany interior. It was a fair age, Ridge reckoned but he could see modern Garmin GPS monitors and she seemed to be in excellent condition.

The boat belonged to an army friend, allegedly, who was on holiday in Florida, hence the free availability. Although Ridge was dubious about this tale the other two couldn't care less and immediately flopped onto bunks in the aft of the boat.

Ridge helped Colm with all the practical matters like filling the water tanks and purchasing fuel for the trip. He had managed to coax out of Colm that they were not headed for America just yet but were in fact going to Belize City which was a full day north and then from there it was to be another bumpy road trip further up the coast to a holiday resort back over the border into Mexico.

Colm explained patiently that they were still in a very precarious situation and there were some desperate people who would do anything to find them. 'However', he said with a grim smile, 'they wouldn't be expecting us to take a boat trip and so this should shake them off which will allow us a little breather before the next phase of the plan'. Ridge was too tired to ask any further questions and he too fell asleep up on deck with the warm sun and the cool breeze carrying him off to a better place.

The next thing he was aware of was Colm was poking him awake and he jumped out of his skin. Momentarily confused, he quickly remembered where he was and he growled quietly, his displeasure at being awoken quickly being replaced by the sheer and utter joy of being out at sea on such a beautiful day. The others were awake too and were hanging out over the side of the boat trying to wet their hands and in the main just doing what all those unused to boats always seemed to do.

Ridge laughed and he could feel a genuine lifting of spirits in the group. The sea was becoming choppy and Juanita was a little green looking but was adamant that she was okay. It seemed strange to Ridge, but she confided that she had never, in fact, been on a boat before in her entire life. She stared disbelievingly when Ridge told her that he had almost been *born* on a boat!

The reason Colm had woken up Ridge seemed almost as unlikely – he was feeling seasick! Amazingly for such an apparent all round tough guy, Colm didn't travel that well on water and he pushed Ridge along the deck to where he quickly explained the autopilot mechanism and left Ridge at the helm which compared to what he was used to made him feel like Captain Jack Sparrow. Orla would have laughed at this he thought, she fancied the arse off old Johnny Depp! 'The boat would more or less look after itself', he had said. 'We are hugging the coast line and as long as we don't hit anything it should be child's play'.

As Colm went below deck for a quick lie down, Ridge couldn't help himself and quickly switched off the autopilot. The boat surged forward as Ridge felt the enormous power of the huge Perkins diesel underneath him. He heard Colm cursing his dubious parentage up at him in no uncertain terms and he slowed her down a touch, smiling away to himself like a buffoon.

The sun continued to sparkle off the water and they all took turns just to sit and marvel at the way the light bounced amongst the waves from the forward rushing of the boat. Colm and Ridge shared the helm duties and they apportioned out the bountiful picnic that had been contained in the capacious rucksack. There was a sense of optimism at that moment and none of them wanted to break the spell. There was little conversation, each of the four of them content to withdraw from their mutual predicament for a short while.

It was Ed who began to get anxious as to what was going on and he and Colm stood talking at the helm for a couple of hours both of them making judicious use of some mobile phones hastily obtained just prior to embarkation.

Juanita was happy to just sit and look at the sea. Such a fresh and exciting new experience for her, she drank in the sounds and the smells and as the wind blew her hair back and the afternoon sun warmed her face, she felt happier than she could ever remember. She knew they still faced insurmountable odds and yet she was content. She could face the end, she thought calmly, as long as she could hold this moment in her heart for ever.

Sitting looking at her, her beatific face revealing her happiness far more profoundly than words, Ridge was again struck by her beauty and he remembered their first days together as if watching a romantic film, warm and fuzzy yet curiously detached. He would always think of her as she was now on this beautiful boat and no matter what was to happen next he was glad to have met her and proud to have played a part in freeing her from those monsters.

Curious about what was happening, Ridge took a stint at the helm and asked the other two what they were talking about.

'Marshalling our troops! That's what, son. Turns out your brother in law knows a hell of a lot of useful folks out there, almost as many as you and me!'

Ridge didn't follow and so between them, Ed and Colm described the plan for the next few days. Apparently, through his old work contacts, Ed was aware of a big meeting between Ramon and his most powerful lieutenants which was taking place within the next week and so he and Colm were arranging to meet up with some other like minded people. Colm looked to Ed and then across the boat to Ridge with his serious face back again.

> 'We're going to crash their party. Then we will be after wiping that infamous smile off *El Cocodrilo*. Permanently…'

Chapter Twenty Three – The Hummer

A black Hummer raced through the small village, making no allowances for the narrow roads. Tiny children were quickly picked up out of the hot red dirt and chickens loudly shooed away from the deadly path of the enormous vehicle. No-one noticed the blacked out windows, each head remaining bowed as the dust, wind and overpowering noise assailed their senses in a momentary preview of the inferno of hell that awaited them if they were to cross paths with the occupants of this car.

Maximiliano was in a foul mood. For a man whose normal demeanour could be described as malevolent at the best of times, this was not good. If he was completely honest, he thought angrily, he was lost. *Lost in more ways than one*, the devil on his shoulder muttered accusingly. He didn't know this part of the country well at all and he was desperate to find a main road again before Ramon got wind of the situation and things would really get out of hand. As it was, Ramon was one jumpy motherfucker right now and Max was under strict instructions not to stop the armour-plated Hummer until they got to the rendezvous. Of course, wise-ass Max had gone off route whilst trying to track down some information that he thought might please the boss and had proceeded to get them lost.

Until recently he would have been considered Ramon's number one guy and it was usually Maximiliano, 'The Hummer', who would guard Ramon and be privy to high ranking decisions and information. He was feared by all who knew him and he knew there were precious few in the organisation who would have a good word for him and that there were many more who would gladly see him dead. He was proud of this however and he had felt assured that he was the best man for this most prestigious of roles. What was more, he knew that Ramon had thought the same way about him. Ramon had encouraged the reputation of his right hand man as both his very own dark angel of death and as an invincible protector of his mighty leader, *El Doctor*.

That was *before*, he thought morosely. His position had been dealt a massive blow by the loss of the *puta* with the big eyes last week in that tourist hell hole. He had not been happy about babysitting the girl from the start. It had been an impossible state of affairs for a man of his position; taking orders from her, knowing that she was deliberately putting herself in a dangerous situation, not being able to just slap her and lock her in a safe-room and worst of all having to suffer the jibes from the men behind his back.

More serious than that though, was the manner in which she had been taken. Ramon had been angrier about that than anything else. Max had never seen him so enraged; he had been literally foaming at the mouth like some rabid prairie dog. Max was positive that if it had been any other man who had been in charge that day, he would not have escaped with his life. If they had been hit by a professional team, which was a theory Max still wouldn't buy into for sure, but if they went along with that, it would have to have been their most audacious enemies, the Cali cartel. Then why had a body not been found or a ransom demanded? Ramon wanted to talk about a level of revenge proportionate to his fury and Max could sense a further ratcheting up of the already merciless war between themselves and the Cali among others.

What had been unusual in this case had been the relatively low body count. There had been only one casualty throughout the whole operation although young Juan Jose, who had been expertly executed with a single efficient bullet to the temple, was a favourite cousin of the boss. His death would have to be avenged. But why had they not walked into the courtyard and emptied an AK47 into the lot of them, including himself?

But the most unusual part of all of this was that it seemed to have been contracted out to a bunch of *gringos*. Not only that, but to Maximiliano's thinking, they must of been a bunch of amateurs! After he had left to inform Ramon personally that the girl was gone, he had been in constant communication with his men on the scene. Desperate for positive news that might alleviate his own pain at the hands of the boss, Max had been pleasantly surprised that they had come back with a positive lead within only a few hours of the abduction.

One of the gringos had been an ex DEA agent who had done some favours for the organisation some years back, when Arturo was running the show. He must have been given a better offer or been threatened perhaps. It had been easy for his men to trace the guy and they had last called in to say they planned to hit the guy's house and either collect the girl or torture the occupants until they gave up her whereabouts. Either way, the situation was under control and they would call back with the good news within a few hours.

It was the next day before Maximiliano could get another team to the location and all they found was the still smoking, burned out shell of a house. The authorities had pulled out three bodies, two men and a woman. Strangely, they said, the two men appeared to have been handcuffed inside the house. None of the victims had been identified. Whilst it would have simplified matters if it had been the girl, it seemed that the bodies were too badly burned to tell who they were at this early stage. His men confirmed that the body was that of a small female and so it was very possible that Juanita had perished. *One less problem to worry about*, Max had growled to himself, although he would not have dared express such an opinion to Ramon.

Maximiliano gripped the steering wheel tightly and the dark ink tattoo of the titular Hummer vehicle became even more conspicuous than usual against the bloodless marbling of his tense hands. The fire was obviously not an accident and the whole incident was very troubling for Max.

In some ways it seemed professional but in other ways it was a complete mess. Why would you rescue a kidnap victim and then take her back to your own house? He seriously wondered if his men were being totally truthful with him. When he had berated them for their

265

initial slowness in pursuing the fleeing SUV they had said that either there had been a police stinger placed across the road or someone had shot out the tyres of their leading vehicle. Max had looked at the car himself before leaving and the tyres were indeed shredded. There was no trace of any such device on the road and so it was a mystery. Could it have been down to poor driving on the rough road? Dreading how he was going to tell Ramon about the kidnap and fearing for his own life at this point, his last words had been that there had better be a positive outcome on this or he would have their throats cut.

He wondered if the whole story about the house had been a cover and if they had just burned down a *gringo* tourist house to put an end to the matter? It was not that bad an idea, in some ways, but he decided to keep these thoughts to himself.

The way things were going these days, he'd be keeping a lot more thoughts to himself. He couldn't shift a feeling he had in the back of his mind that there was something going on that he was not party to and he had a sneaking suspicion that Xavier might have something to do with it. The two men had been like brothers in the old days under Arturo but now he could smell something different. Could Xavier be about to change sides? It was unthinkable, but there it was. The fool must know that not even the Cali could protect him from the wrath of Ramon.

It was not the only problem that Ramon was struggling with at this time. Max was aware of some ambitious plans involving overseas contacts that were not going as smoothly as Ramon had expected. Even more so than his brother and his father before him, he was very ambitious and Max was fine with that, after all lots of business is done globally these days. But then Ramon would get angry when respect was not paid to him as it was at home and he would go off the deep end. Even Max could see that there were bigger fish in the sea and he worried that Ramon would blow it for all of them. He didn't have the nous of his father and he could never command the respect of the country in the way Arturo had. It pained Max to see Ramon posturing about being the great don, *El Patron*, on one hand and then disrespecting the memory of Arturo with all his whoring and drug excesses.

In his wilder moments Maximiliano saw himself as the natural successor to Arturo but he would never challenge Ramon. If things were different however, he used to think that Xavier would have made a fine number one but now he was not so sure. In any case he had put out a strong message to everyone in their organisation and beyond; the police, the army and all their informers at every level of society - find this *gringo* agent and there would be a handsome reward for his head whether it was connected to his body or otherwise. Maximiliano smiled thinly to himself. The man was a walking corpse. It would only be a matter of time.

Chapter Twenty Four – Bitch Soldiers

As they made their approach slowly and quietly towards Belize City, Ridge was struck by the low slung aspect of the place. The warm glow of the first flickering of an early sunset further accentuated the rich red of the rooftops and there was a flat horizon over the city just as if you had been looking in the other direction out towards an open sea.

But the tranquil façade was soon shattered as they drew closer. Now they could hear the cacophony of noise crashing across the choppy water as the bustling city became alive with the discordant sounds of taxi horns competing with the aggressive roar of old buses. Underpinning everything else was the deep menacing throb of larger vessels and industrial machinery.

After the quiet solitude of the voyage with just the breeze for company, it seemed a frightening prospect for Juanita. All her fears came rushing back, pulsing through her veins like a powerful illicit poison. She gripped tightly to the handrails and looked to Ridge for some reassurance but was only met by a wary and tight lipped face.

The frenetic activity had only served to further increase his own growing anxiety and he felt a cold wraith-like hand grasp ever tighter around his insides forcing his breathing to become shallower and his head to spin.

For several hours he had been agonising over what he should do next. He wanted to see this through but couldn't shake the fear that he was hopelessly out of his depth. He had been trying to pluck up the courage to question Colm a bit more deeply as to what they were actually going to do. He could remember when Ed first mentioned something about a 'phase two' back at his place and he had definitely said that they themselves would be having nothing to do with any of it, that it was all in the hands of the professionals and that it would be 'suicide' for them to become involved. Yet…, that seemed to be *exactly* what was now on the agenda. It wasn't that he particularly valued his own life but more that he didn't want to be part of someone else's personal suicide mission. He was good enough at that sort of thing himself without requiring assistance from anyone else.

He had been looking at maps and he knew that they were to get off here and then drive a bit further up the coast. When he had asked Colm why they couldn't just sail the boat up further he had been told that it would be far easier to sneak into Belize City under the radar than at Chetumal which was very touristy and was tightly patrolled by drugs agencies. 'Besides', he warned, 'there is a hurricane coming and you don't want me spewing to add to our problems'!

Colm showed them all the white swirl of pixellated carnage which was heading North West on the monitor. 'Say hello to Hurricane Tina guys'! He explained that it was shaping up to be a Category 5 and if caught, they would be tossed onto the shore like an empty beer can.

'This has been a bad coast for hurricane damage', Colm went on, 'and the last bad one about five years ago, Hurricane Dean caused a lot of destruction. There were winds of up to 175mph! This place, here, has been levelled a few times, so it has!'

They were closer now and they could see the tumult of excited faces staring out at the incoming vessels from open windows and all along the waterway. Ridge could see they were about to go up a narrower looking channel a bit like a noisier more colourful version of the canals back home. He couldn't understand how they could go much further as there seemed to be a low passenger bridge up ahead which was way too low for the large yacht ahead of them.

'Keep quiet!' Colm hissed. 'Either go below or keep your heads down! And don't make eye contact with *anyone*!'

Despite himself, Ridge couldn't help looking around and he was amazed to see the rusty yellow bridge suddenly divest itself of a multitude of people who began teeming off to either side as the bridge began to swing round to allow them passage.

They shadowed the larger boat past the bridge and as he glanced up briefly, Ridge could see a sweating man busily turning a large wheel which he guessed must be controlling the huge bridge. 'Not too shabby…' he thought, impressed, as he made his way below deck, Colm scowling darkly at him.

Ed was busy counting out a wad of damp US bank notes, the sweat dripping off his nose as he silently mouthed the numbers. He passed the money up to Colm and after a few minutes they berthed the boat and they were being ushered off. It was a sombre moment for all of them as they reluctantly left their maritime sanctuary.

The three of them stood huddled closely together on the dark, deserted quay and as their heads turned quickly from this place to that, the light from their frightened eyes flashed brightly in the gloom. Ridge could just make out Colm standing with another man, some way off, and he imagined that he saw cash change hands. Colm whistled them over and as they bundled themselves into the stifling heat of an old car, Ridge felt sure he could see a pitying look on the dark face of the man as he folded the notes into his pocket and turned away, shaking his head slowly.

'You're never going to believe me, but we'll be after going through a place tonight called 'Orange Walk'! It's feckin' true an' all!'

Colm laughed as he jammed his foot on the accelerator and the car lurched forwards into the dark. Ridge thought about Scotland, certain parts of which seemed depressingly at times to be riven with religious intolerance and it all seemed so petty and inconsequential compared to the mess he was in now. He would guess the majority of his fellow Scots didn't go to church anymore. Yet every summer there could be bitter recriminations between Protestants and Catholics surrounding the 'Orange Walk' and the celebration of events such as The Battle of the Boyne which had occurred over three hundred years before.

He remembered how terrified he had been when he and his dad had been caught up in a march in the Gallowgate in the east end of Glasgow. The look of vituperative hatred on some of the faces had given the innocent island lad nightmares for weeks after.

Nobody was saying much during the short journey although Ridge did try to get Colm to open up a bit more. Sitting up front again, his curiosity was eating him. Nothing made sense anymore. He could accept that his own story was bizarre to say the least, but he did have some kind of reason for the mess he was in. What the hell was going on with his brother-in-law and what was he doing here, driving him around Central America being chased by bandits? He only got another small piece of the puzzle, *nothing new there*, he decided.

It turned out that Colm had been interested in this country a long time before Ridge had ever stumbled across the Mexican border. 'It's complicated,' he said mysteriously and he seemed reluctant to continue. He sighed deeply.

'Soon after I went undercover, it became obvious to me that the Real IRA had been getting in to bed with other organisations on a regular basis and I found out that part of that had involved groups over here like your man Ramon for example.'

Ridge had expressed some scepticism

about this and Colm had retorted angrily.

'Listen to me when I'm tellin' you!
These guys are all the same!
There's no cause that will unite all these
wee bastards better than hard cash!
At the end of the day that's all any of
them are interested in nowadays.
United Ireland is just a pile of shite as far
as most of the provos are concerned, they
know that politics is always going to get
in the way and so they are happy to
shelter under the guise of being 'freedom
fighters,' allow themselves to get royally
supported by ignorant tossers in the US
and meanwhile get on with the business
of being a criminal organisation.

It's a whole lot worse with the guys over
here. They're not just drug gangs
anymore, guys like Ramon are
controlling millions of dollars, they have
their own armies and they have
aspirations far beyond what we give
them credit for.'

'But, surely the IRA are not really buying
drugs all the way from here are they?' Ridge was
very tired but even so, he was having difficulty
swallowing this idea. Colm was sounding
exasperated.

'Would you just wise-up for a wee
moment! I'll spell it out for you, so I
will. It is not about drugs!
It is about money and about power!

273

The whole world has all gone to shite since the breakup of the Soviet Union and the Warsaw Pact countries and there's guns floating about all over the place. Himself over here wants guns and other armaments and so do the boyos back home. Guns give them power and/or money. Ramon and his like are rolling in so much cash that they can't get rid of it quick enough!

But it's like operating a good trucking business. You don't want to be returning with an empty truck.

So Ramon will try to ship massive quantities of cheap drugs to our boys, they in turn will use the drugs as currency to acquire guns and bombs from Ukraine, Bulgaria, Lithuania, Albania and so on and then they will pass on some of these weapons to the drug cartels back over here.

In addition, the Real's will get themselves a cushy wee consultancy job. When they bring the weapons back over, they then teach the numpties over here how and when to use them to their best advantage.

Being the vicious wee fuckers they are, they also teach them lots of nasty new tricks so they can get one over on their rival drug gangs or maybe take over an entire country!'

Little more was said as Ridge sat dumbfounded. He could understand the cold logic of what Colm had told him. It just sounded so mad that somehow the crazy situation that he had got himself into by dating the wrong girl in San Francisco, could be inextricably linked to the job of his 'secret-agent' brother in law in Ireland. Quietly, he had mumbled words to that effect and Colm in turn just looked at him with a wicked smile on his face and laughed. 'Well, listen to you! Jesus! It's going to get a whole lot crazier before this day is done! That, I can promise you!'

Ridge slid wearily back in his seat, unable to process any more information that night. The others were trying hard to doze off as the old car bounced around in the dark, somehow managing to stay mostly on the rough road.

Ridge had faded before they reached 'Orange Walk' and just as he had settled into a deep sleep they arrived in Chetumal. The others were awake and Ridge realised that Juanita was leaning forwards with her arms draped around each side of his neck and he could feel her excited breath on the back of his neck and in his ear. It felt alright and he guessed he was still dreaming until she exclaimed loudly, 'What about that one?' Ridge turned quickly to see a plush looking neon lit hotel. 'Los Cocos', it might have said. It looked fine to him anyway.

'Too expensive! Plus, we need something a wee bit less obvious, I'm afraid. You'll love it, I promise! It's come highly recommended, so it has!' Despite his tiredness, Colm was obviously having a good wee laugh to himself and Ridge had a strange feeling that he was up to something.

The 'new' Colm had been so deadly

serious but Ridge knew he could have a wicked sense of humour. Little could he imagine the carnage that was shortly to ensue...

Moments later they drew up at another dimly lit hotel and Colm expertly pulled in through the narrow entrance. He quickly jumped out and before they could muster the energy to get out themselves, he was back and they drove through into a gloomy gated car park.

The intense heat was still everywhere as they all tumbled out onto the dusty concrete. The hotel was painted an acid turquoise and it enclosed the car park in a series of rusty old quaint New Orleans style balconies and right beside them there appeared to be an extremely dingy looking pool. Colm was nowhere to be seen again and so the others just stood leaning wearily against the car taking it all in slowly. They could hear what sounded like a thrash metal band rehearsing in the next building and the traffic noise from the main street was pleasant in comparison. Not that sleeping was going to be an issue, yawned Ridge as he looked over to his dog-tired companions. How right he was although he didn't know it yet.

Colm came literally bounding around the corner and with a massive grin across his face he grabbed Ridge's shoulder with a strong hand and pulled him back towards the watery light. 'Come here, son! I've got someone who's dying to see you again!' Before Ridge could mutter a word, his beleaguered brain already spinning madly, a long dark shadow began to shorten towards the corner and as it turned into an even larger black shape silhouetted by the dim lights, Ridge lifted his tired eyes up to see, as if dreaming, the imposing figure of Thaddeus!

Thad stood there impassively for but a second or two, his eyes shielded behind mirror shades, legs in a wide stance, head slightly cocked and his huge arms folded in an overtly aggressive posture and in that brief moment Ridge felt himself shiver with a cold dread.

But then as Thad laughed and jumped forward, whipping off his glasses, his eyes flashing bright and true as always, Ridge felt a wonderful surge of warmth and happiness as he was bundled up in the big man's embrace. Brushing away the tears, and still not believing or understanding what the hell was going on, Ridge screamed mad questions while Thad carried him up onto his powerful shoulders and spun around making as if to drop him into the dark pool.

'How did I know where you'd gone? How did I know? I'll just say two words, my friend, two…little… words…, then we'll make that the end of it, ok!'

Ridge just stared at him in joyous disbelief as he was unceremoniously dumped back on to the concrete.

'American…Express…!'

'Ah!' Ridge gulped. 'I forgot about that! I only used it twice…, in emergencies!'

'Dude! Enough, already!
Do I look like I give a shit?
Lemme' tell you, if that had been me, I
would have spent that much on the first
day, so don't sweat it!'

Ridge would never have been able to
stem his tears if he had known that his big
friend, upon discovering the missing card, had
actually doubled the spending limit just in case it
had been needed.

Juanita was quickly given the grand bear-
hug treatment and she was very happy to meet
Thad again. Unaware of his past involvement in
her 'situation', she nonetheless had quickly
sensed he was not here on a vacation and like
Colm, he seemed to have that air about him, that
confidence that anything could be possible. She
allowed herself to dream for a second of a life
beyond this, a secure life full of sunshine and
warmth but then slapped herself back down
again, *'there can be no hiding place that he will
not find'*, she reminded herself morosely.

Without realising what she was doing,
she found herself leaning into Colm for comfort
and he gently put an arm around her as they
watched and laughed with Thad and Ridge as the
pair of them monkeyed around and tried to
involve a bemused Ed.

'Hey what about the name of this place
then?
Pretty cool, huh?
When Colm told me about it, I said we
just *gotta* have it man!'

Ridge looked blankly at Thad and then over to a grinning Colm.

'Oh! Jaysus! I was so looking forward to winding him up about that, so I was, but in all the excitement I clean forgot. Ridge! See if you can't read that there sign up there...'

Ridge strained his eyes to peer up through the gloom to a rusty old sign, its neon tubes long burnt out. It was a short word running vertically downwards. 'Ucum...?' he muttered hesitantly.

'Yeah! You got it man!
The Hotel U-CUM!
And maybe you will, *amigo*, maybe you will!'

With the hilarity over with, an awkward silence was looming and before anyone else could stop him, Thad had taken charge of the group. He seemed to have come to a decision of some kind and he was adamant that they should stay and wait for him in the car park for a moment or two longer. He darted off but not before he turned to Ridge with a twinkle in his eye, 'and you're not the only dude with kick-ass buddies, my friend!'

Ridge paced up and down the car park, his fevered mind struggling to process this latest strange, but not unwelcome, development. Thad had been gone for ages and he couldn't get Colm to explain how Thad and he knew each other and why Thad was actually here. He knew that Thad could probably be very useful in a punch-up but that couldn't explain what he was doing thousands of miles from home with this bunch of miscreants. Ed and the others were sitting against the car whispering conspiratorially to each other and when Ridge barked over questions to Colm, all he would say with a knowing look in his eye was, '*all will be revealed, all will be revealed in good time*', like some phoney palm-reader!

They were all tired, but nothing would have prepared them for what was to follow. It was just after midnight and the thrash metal guys had given up for the night. First Ridge, then the others suddenly picked up their heads and tried to work out what the sound was just about to come around the corner.

It was faint still, but sounded unmistakably like the deep tones of gentle a capella singing. *It is*, thought Ridge, and he thought he could make out some words.

'*Hey sister! Go sister! Soul sister! Go sister...!*' The voices grew louder and deeper.

'HEY SISTER..! GO SISTER..! SOUL SISTER..! GO SISTER..!'

They all picked up on it just at the same time and as they stared incredulously at each other and collectively wondered if they had finally lost their minds, then the next few seconds stamped that thought indelibly onto their tortured brains.

Thad came prancing around the corner waving his hands in the air whilst swinging a large coral blue feather boa and singing '*Mocca choco-lata ya ya,*' at the top of his voice! He swung an arm down and backwards in an exaggerated theatrical bow and shouted 'Let's hear it for the DIAMOND DOGS!'

They could hear the others clearly now and the three of them exploded into view in a riot of colour and sound!

'HE MET MARMALADE DOWN IN OLD NEW ORLEANS...

STRUTTIN' HER STUFF ON THE STREET...

SHE SAID '*HELLO, HEY JOE, YOU WANNA GIVE IT A GO?*'

Like insane fireworks they spun and jumped around in front of the bedazzled travellers whilst screaming out the lyrics to some raunchy 'Moulin Rouge' song!

Juanita was spellbound. She had never seen anything like it in her life! Performing in front of her very eyes were three dark skinned statuesque goddesses! With high heeled boots, basques and suspenders, exotic furs, enormous coloured wigs and way too much make-up it took her far too long to work it out.

Ed may have been dazed but he twigged in a flash whilst Ridge and Colm just stood speechless with cartoon open mouthed expressions. As they strutted and high kicked, the three girls were not too adept at hiding their modesty. They hooted with laughter as they locked their large bejewelled eyes onto their audience to see the moment when they realised.

Juanita had been the best, they all agreed later. She had suddenly screamed and brought her hands up to her face before accepting the fact that she was now THE show as she collapsed to the ground in a crimson faced heap laughing her head off!

It was too hot still for any further dancing and to a man, they all flopped down beside an astounded Juanita. Even sitting, the three 'dogs' dwarfed the young girl and she just sat silently in awe of them, noticing how an arm rippled like black steel rope as one of them, in a coral pink wig and black velvet basque, smiled warmly and asked her to help unpeel some long matching pink leather gloves. Thad felt it was incumbent on him to make the introductions and he quickly retrieved a large case of ice cold beers from a dusty black SUV that Ridge hadn't even noticed before.

'OK Guy's! That was a blast!
Grab a beer and then we can get the team organised and I guess some of you might want to sleep in a bed for a change, yeah? Not you though Big Boy! You gotta big night ahead of you yet!'

Ridge realised they were all looking at him and he also felt he was blushing, but he had no idea why. 'What the fuck!' He gratefully poured the beer down his parched throat and it felt good.

Thad jumped up again and got everyone's attention.

'OK!
It's time for me to introduce my dear, dear friends, who have taken time out of

their busy schedules to come down here and kick some ass for us!
Firstly, in the fetching fur robe, all the way from Boston, let's hear it for 'Barbarella' or Joey 'Badman' Barbarossa to give him his Sunday name.'

A large man in a shock white wig jumped to his feet, taller even than Thad, he must have been 6'4 and over 200lbs yet he was as lithe as a ballet dancer. Bowing gracefully and then with his hands over his knees, he smiled coquettishly á la Monroe. He then kissed the end of his right forefinger and then mimed the firing of a pistol straight at an obviously dubious Ed who was quietly downing his beer and shaking his head. He just couldn't hold back what was going through his head.

'Let me get this fuckin' *straight* here, if y'all pardon the expression. You 'Can Can' dancers are here to help *us*? To do what? Hump the bad guys?'

They were all on their feet now and before anyone else could blink one of them had Ed by the throat. He gradually lifted Ed upwards until his feet were barely touching the ground.

'Listen here motherfucker!
We *is* the bad guys!
Nobody is gonna hump nobody unless we say so!'

'Easy DJ!

Motherfucker didn't mean nuthin' now,
he just scared by your *sheer animal
sexuality*, that all! Ain't that so, my
friend?'

Ed just rubbed his sore neck and
glowered at the other man who seemed to be the
leader. Easily the tallest and strongest built of
the trio; the man flicked back his luminous green
wig hair away from his face incongruously with
a spade-like hand. Underneath the theatrical
make-up he had a jaw which resembled the front
end of an army Jeep and his black eyes were
buried deep under a heavily muscled brow
which right now was flexed tight and scored by
deep dark lines. It was time for some mediation
from Thad.

'Hey guys! Take it easy, OK!
It's been a tough day for everyone here,
let's all just take a chill-pill and relax
already!
Guys! Ed, you've already met
'Guadalupe' or if you prefer DJ 'Wild'
Cherry and last but certainly not least, it
gives me great pleasure to introduce my
old friend 'Lady Marmalade' AKA
Patrick LaBelle!'

The two men smiled and holding hands,
they performed a perfect curtsey before turning
to face each other. Side on now to their
'audience,' they folded their arms and turned
their faces simultaneously to the front, each with
an exaggerated wink and a puckered kiss.
Colm strongly suspected that was still

not his real name but he broke the ice by grabbing Patrick in a firm manly handshake and making some small talk. Looking straight into the eyes of the other, he had an equally overpowering suspicion that there was a whole lot more to these guys than burlesque costumes and despite the make-up and perfume he was sure detected the unmistakable whiff of the soldier about them.

'Nice show, *girls*' he said, smiling and then 'so who did you serve with?'

'That obvious, huh?' muttered the other man.

'Well, I was involved with the British Army, so I was, well y'know, sort of, and so you get a feel for it after a wee while, I suppose. Though I was never after meeting any boys in bras, neither I was!'

They all laughed at that and as DJ wriggled out of his basque revealing a rock hard torso, he sidled up to Ridge and pulled off his pink wig. He turned his head and pointed to a small tattooed scroll, just readable over the bunched muscles behind his left ear.

''*Semper fi,*'' Ridge read quietly, 'what's that then?'

All three men turned and spoke as one.

'Semper fidelis, man!
US Marine Corps!
At your service!'

They went on to explain that their motto, Semper fidelis meant 'always faithful' and how the shortened version meant even greater loyalty in particular to each other, to comrades in arms.

Ridge made the mistake of asking innocently how long had they been ex-marines for and again the response was strong and pre-programmed.

'Once a Marine, always a Marine!'

Three pairs of eyes drilled into his and he nodded in silent reply before grabbing a fresh beer for something to do. The stories were now bouncing back and forth between them all and after recent events none of them were coming up short on the drama stakes.

Chapter Twenty Five - Boys and Toys

'Let's go, guys!

It was getting late and Thad started to herd up the tired travellers.

'We'd better get these rooms before they give them to someone else.
DJ? You on first my friend?
Pat, we'll catch up with you at the truck in a half hour or so OK?'

'Sure boss. We gotta do a lotta' sorting anyhows. I guess we won't be transporting too much in that?'

The big man gestured dismissively towards the rusty wreck which had steadfastly taken the four refugees from Belize City.

The hotel proved to be a surreal experience almost at risk of putting the car park theatrics in the shade. A seriously grumpy old man showed them where they were staying; Ridge was to share with Thad, ominously, with just one additional room for the other three to share. When Ed protested at the fact there were only two beds, the situation was quickly defused when Colm happily agreed to sleep in a hammock provided by Thad. 'Thanks be to Jesus!' Colm exclaimed when he sat on one of the beds.
The walls of their room were painted a

vivid mustard colour and each bed had the headboard actually painted onto the wall. The beds each had a snarling tiger bedspread and the chequered tiled floor was straight out of an old-fashioned seaside public toilet.

The crowning glory had to be the little television which sat on a concrete table and was totally enclosed in a heavy metal grilled box! The overall ambiance made Ridge feel as if he had stepped into a David Lynch movie and this wasn't helped when he walked into Thad's room. Initially relieved that his big friend had also resolved to sleep in a hammock, he sat heavily onto the double bed and surveyed the room. With similar style-defying décor as the others, this one had additional features that posed an obvious question, *what kind of people stayed here?*

The walls were decorated with large cast iron hooks and Ridge could see the door was like Thad's own apartment door back in San Fran. Outwardly clothed in flimsy wood like the rest, but to an experienced eye and from the inside, it was plain to see that this door was double reinforced with steel plate and Thad was also fiddling with what turned out to be a double tumbler lock. Thad explained that this particular room was favoured by savvy tourists and others who may often be travelling with excessive amounts of hard cash. There was an innocent explanation for the hooks, of course, which were only there to tie the hammocks onto.

'Were you hoping I was gonna strap you to the walls?

You'd need to take a long shower first,

amigo!
But not now OK! We gotta lot of stuff to talk about first. Let's go!'

Ridge jumped up after his friend, surreptitiously sniffing his armpits as he did so, the results confirming his worst fears; it had been a while since he'd had a decent wash and it seemed that adrenaline didn't smell too damn sexy after all!
Thad tapped quietly on the door next to theirs and Colm stepped out. He confirmed the other two were asleep and followed them out. Ridge saw DJ perched uncomfortably on a tiny wooden chair at the end of the dingy corridor and when he threw Thad a questioning look, the reply had been comforting.

'You guys will have an armed guard around you 24/7 until this whole situation has been resolved to our satisfaction. And trust me; they don't come much tougher than old Loopy here. He ain't called '*Wild*' Cherry for nothin' isn't that so my old friend?'

'That's for damn sure' was the laconic reply.

It was still clammy outside and they walked quickly around to the car park where the other two 'dogs' were sitting on the tailgate of the SUV, patiently waiting. Big Patrick handed them each a cold can and then seemed to stand back a little allowing Thad to take centre stage. Ridge was extremely curious to see this as he would not have imagined these guys accepting orders from his friend, capable though he was. He resolved to dig a little deeper when the opportunity arose. For now though, Thad seemed to be strictly business.

'OK, guys! Let's get our shit together and then we can kick-back awhile before we bring the rain down upon our little Mexican bandidos!
Barbarella! Show us what you've got baby!'

'First off, let me make this quite clear to y'all. With me being the Ordnance bitch of this here detail, I do not want to find any of this shit walkin' after we is done, OK?'

Joey Barbarossa locked his eyes, first on Thad, then menacingly over to Ridge before staring pointedly at poor Colm, who coughed guiltily and spluttered beer froth right across the face of his accuser. 'Sure and I won't! Jesus!'
Joey showed no emotion whatsoever as he wiped his hand over his face, at no time taking his eyes off Colm. At that, he turned and pulled a heavy black tarpaulin off the piles of hardware inside the truck.
Showing off like a ten year old boy, Joey quickly dropped his 'Badman' personae and instantly transformed into a smiling, happy person as he introduced his toys to the other boys crowding round to see what he'd got. The next hour or so was a complete revelation to Ridge and he couldn't even pretend to understand half of what was being said but right

then it all sounded good to him. Colm, it turned out, was fairly nifty around the old guns and bullets scene but even he was looking impressed at some of the weapons they now had at their disposal.

'Welcome to my world, guys! Now, don't be no *shy* motherfuckers here!

None of this shit is loaded just yet and after, *but only after*, I have shown you what the fuck to do with it, you are invited to get up close and personal with all of it. You can stroke it, lift it, cock it, hell you can lick it if y'all wanna but just don't jerk off none! You here what Ah'm sayin'?

Do not be afraid to ask a dumb question, that is how you will learn.

It will be TOO LATE to ask when the motherfuckers have put a round through the front of your head!'

'Good point, Joey!' interjected Thad.

'Can I just say something quickly which may just help focus our minds here? We know that this is a new experience for some of you and so what we decided was to divide up the roles that each of you will play over the next few days according to your experience or aptitude. This obviously has a bearing on what you are about to see. Joey, you will keep me right here, OK?'

The man nodded. 'Copy that.'

'OK. So it will go like this.

I will be in overall command of this operation from now until completion of our objective.

Joey, here, will look after all weapons and ordnance, DJ will handle security and communications and can brief us in the morning.

Patrick will lead the assault on the *finca* and now we just need to sort out what Ed and you two will do. It seems…'

'Hold on just a wee minute!' Colm said quietly but firmly, his hand raised as if to ask teacher a question. 'I can do this…but on my own!'

'What the fuck!

No way man! Who the hell do you think you are?'

A furious Patrick stood nose to nose with Colm, who just quietly reiterated his point, 'I've *have* done this sort of thing before…alone.'

'Listen,' said Thad quickly. 'Take it easy! Pat! Stand down, amigo!' The big man turned away growling like a grizzly bear with a thorn stuck in his paw.

'Ever heard of 'Operation Enduring Freedom'? We was part of the vanguard unit - me, Joey and DJ. You know what went down, kid! Tell the ungrateful fucker.'

Thad gripped the man tightly on the

shoulder and forced him to look right back into his eyes. 'Yes, I remember. Only too well. You were not just *part* of the vanguard, my friend, you *were* it!'

He turned to face Colm and Ridge.

'Pat here led the Marine Corps Strike Force and they took the airport against overwhelming odds!'

Ridge just stared blankly back and Thad could see he didn't have a clue what they were talking about.

'Afghanistan...!
The US Marine Corps took Kandahar Airport from the Taliban in an air insertion mid-December 2001.'

Joey whooped, 'Hell! We had ourselves one motherfuckin' Christmas!'

Thad looked uncharacteristically melancholic for a moment. 'Yeah! I bet you did! Me, I had a lonely one, another one. ' Ridge was about to say he remembered it on the news and then play acting the attack at school when Patrick shouldered him roughly out of the way to square up to Colm again.

'So who the fuck *are* you?
What makes you think you are better than the US Marine Corps; the few, the proud?'

Colm stepped backwards with his hands

up in a gesture of surrender.

'Okay! Okay! Jesus Mary and Joseph! I'm not after saying I'm better than *anyone*, far from it. I can't tell you what I've done or where on God's earth I've done it.

It's classified. I'm only after saying I'm not used to doing this sort of stuff with other people. I would be honoured to be part of this team, so I would. Honestly, anything to stop my eedjit brother-in-law from getting his head blown off!'

As everyone scaled down the testosterone and exchanged a few grunts and slaps, Ridge pondered once again about what the hell he had got himself into. And what was Colm on about? Was he playing some mad game of 'my willy is bigger than yours,' or is there still a heap more to uncover about Orla's brother than he had thought? And then there was the obvious question, what was the connection between Thaddeus and the 'Diamond Dogs' and why would these rough tough Marines be happy for him to be commanding what sounded like a full-on military operation?

Joey had jumped back into the driving seat again and he was discussing with the others about who should do what.

'OK, Colm! So now you is some kind of motherfuckin' James Bond! Yeah? Well, what does that make you good for here?

We know all about Ed, so we're cool there.

Ridge, have you ever even seen a

motherfuckin' gun before?'

Looking over at the assortment of weapons still mostly hidden amongst the gloom of the pickup, Ridge stuck his chin out proudly and told them how he had shot a .22 air rifle often as a boy as was common on the island. He could shoot a rabbit from almost 200 yards, he told them. Joey's eyebrows rose dramatically at this and Ridge was sure he was impressed. Colm also professed an interest in long range work.

'OK, guys! Let's see what Joey has to show us, then we can apportion out the kit.
Joey! Take it away!' Thad stepped back again and listened with the others.

'Gather round my friends!
What have we got here?
OK! Colm and Ridge we got you guys a couple of USMC M40A5's. Real nice sniper rifle. You may have heard of it before as the M24. This will do a half mile real easy and we got some nice telescopic sights too.'

'Half a mile, is that so? I think this is modelled on the Remington 700 hunting rifle, is it not. I see you have the latest A5, the one with the bigger suppressor,' said Colm as he expertly shouldered the gun and ran his eye down it admiringly.

'Hey! We have a guy who knows his motherfuckin' guns! I apologise for dissin' you earlier, my man.

295

Hell! You may well *be* James Bond for all I know!

Now for each and every one of us I got a M4A1 Carbine which to you, Ridge, is the *Daddy* of Assault Rifles. This is the all-rounder of battlefield weapons, it is manoeuvrable and compact with great handling and pretty cool rail mounted optical sights.'

Ridge picked one up and it still felt big and heavy compared to an air rifle.

'Is this like a submachine gun?' he asked innocently.

'Yeah, kinda...

The cool thing about these is you can switch real easy between semi-auto and fully automatic fire. It's not as powerful as a submachine gun but it's lighter, y'all can fire from the shoulder and it will still do 1000 feet easy.'

'I was trained by the Brits on the M16, so this is just a more advanced model isn't it not?' asked Colm. Patrick agreed with him and the admiration was there in his eyes now too.

They looked at several more guns of various types including a few pistols, some Heckler and Koch submachine guns, RPG -7's and three 'DMR' guns that Patrick and DJ seemed most taken with. There also seemed to be a high-tec crossbow of some kind which apparently Colm had requested personally.

Ridge could not fathom what this could be needed for and the whole weapons thing was all becoming a tad confusing. His attention was drawn to a much larger contraption at the back of the truck and with help from Patrick and Thad; they lifted it out and onto the ground. To the untrained eye, it looked to Ridge like a Star Wars droid and he had muttered something to that effect.

'Hell no! This here is a Starstreak MANPADS!
To you, it is a man portable air defence system. Still no clue, huh?
How about a hand held surface to air missile system?'

'No fucking way...! He's joking right, Thad?'

'He is deadly serious, my friend!' said Thad laughing as Ridge stood back slightly, his eyes wide as saucers.

'Yup, this little beauty will fire short range heat seeking missiles and it is *muy rapido*!'

'What the fuck do we need that for?' gasped Ridge.

'Remember, our *amigo* has a lot of dough! He is having a golf course built for him. I ain't joking!
Alongside the course he is laying a short runway. We already know from recently

purloined aerial shots of the Santa Ana estate that he has a helipad and so he could have a helicopter hidden away in an outbuilding.

From what Ed has told us, backed up by some fresh Intel, we know there will be other sleazeballs, important to Ramon's organisation, arriving at the *finca*. It's not that far from an international airport and so helicopters will probably feature on the day.

Remember, these guys are goddamn jumpy right now, things haven't been going to plan and none of them are comfortable in this part of Mexico.'

'Thad..., how do we know all this stuff?'

Thad sighed deeply and spoke with only a vague trace of irritation in his voice. 'It's a long story, Ridge. One we just don't have the time to go into right now, OK? Later, dude, I promise.'

As they lifted the Starstreak and kit back into the truck, Ridge asked if this was not going a wee bit over the top and would they not need to have a pick up truck just to house this on it's own. He made a joke about getting a Toyota Hilux, the terrorist's pickup of choice, which only Colm seemed to get.

'This ain't so heavy, man!' Joey retorted brightly. 'It only weighs about 45lbs and Patrick here can carry that and still run faster than you! But the best bit about this motherfucker is that it is easy as pie to operate. Just wait until you hear a bleep on your 'phones and press the goddamn button. Even you could do that, my friend!'

'And…' interjected Colm, 'I think you'll find that it's made in Belfast, so it is, boys! And that reminds me, if you've finished now, can I throw in the one wee gun that I like to use?'

'Give the man a cigar! Sure Colm, you can bring your 9mm to the party. We all eyeballed that dude in the first five minutes!'

'Oh this?' Colm looked down almost forgetfully. 'No, Joey, not the pistol. I *always* have that with me. No, I have something upstairs in one of my backpacks. I'm after thinking it'll have you coming in your pants, so it will!'

'Go ahead!' said Patrick. 'You got me drooling already! We'll get the rest of this kit packed up.'

Colm returned quickly and Ridge dragged himself back onto his feet, weary and not a little scared by all this gun stuff. Colm soon had pieces of gun lying out on a large canvas and within moments had his rifle assembled. The others had just closed up the truck and they turned and literally stopped in their tracks.

'Wow! Check out the man!' said Patrick whilst Joey actually simpered up to Colm and asked for a hold. 'Is that really an Accuracy International?' he asked, seemingly awestruck. Not for the first time on this hot dark night was Ridge totally baffled.

'Yep! It's an AI L115A3 sniper rifle. I have an adapted version, so I have, with larger bullets than normal so it doesn't get deflected so easily. I have used it, successfully mind, on a target over a mile away! I think the record with this gun is over a mile and a half.'

They all turned around as Ridge slumped back down against the truck, more in shock than fatigue. 'I suppose my 200 yards doesn't really float your boat does it?' he gulped in astonishment. Joey gave out a high pitched excited laugh. 'Hell! Don't you worry 'bout nothin'! I figure you gotta yourself a regular super-fly spy guy in the family!'

Patrick gently edged Joey out of the way and picked the gun out of his arms. He looked down the barrel, one eye closed.

'Nice feel to it man. Shit... I wish we had had stuff like this when we was still in the Corps. That a five-round magazine, I'm thinking?
Not that you would need it, right? Is that kinda range considered to be good for a kill shot?

'Sure as hell it is Pat,' exclaimed Joey, whose voice was still two octaves higher than normal.
'I've read all about this gun, man! It can go that far and still hit like a motherfuckin' 44 Magnum! Are WE feelin' lucky? I am *so* lovin'

this gun!'

Chapter Twenty Six – A Man Who Can

'Stop the goddamn car!' shouted a panic stricken Ed. 'He's gonna go this time!'

Colm pulled over abruptly, slamming on the brakes as the vehicle skidded to a halt. The huge 80's saloon car seemed to have only two operational braking modes; full on lock or nothing at all. He looked at Thad and they both laughed quietly as a feverish and trembling Ridge fumbled at a back door and literally fell out onto the ground.

'If you just slowed down some it'd be okay! Heck, it feels like the Indy 500 in here today.
You're makin' us *all* feel like puking!'

Ed was looking at a pallid faced Juanita as he spoke and she smiled weakly towards him in thanks. He had been very grumpy ever since they were all rousted early from their much needed slumbers and he had been vociferously campaigning for a rest day or two. Maintaining the view that they should be spending more time planning the whole operation, he had initially refused to be part of this ridiculous 'transvestite cavalcade.'

There was a very real reason he desperately wanted to stay away from the *finca* for a few days more. His deal with the devil, which had greatly worried him, even before

Mandy had been taken from him, now burned painfully through his belly and corroded his every thought. Colm had 'acquired' a boat-like old Cadillac for this leg of the trip and Ed's earlier attempted sabotage of the brakes had mostly failed although it could probably be held accountable for the current 'rest break.'

'Let's get us some air!' he exclaimed to Juanita and she gladly jumped out after him. Ridge had wandered a hundred yards further back through the heat haze of late morning and the big black truck was stopped an equal distance ahead of them. No-one else had shown themselves and Ed reached in through an open front window to grab a bottle of water. 'Think I might top up the water while were waiting for him to puke.' Colm was talking quietly with Thad and he fumbled under the dashboard, nodded to Ed and popped the catch.

Feeling only slightly less ropey after his tactical puke in the bushes, Ridge talked his way into the front, the large bench seat affording plenty room for a skinny Scot to join the other two. Putting a still shaky pale hand onto an enormous thigh next to him, he leaned hard against Thad. 'Seeing as it's all your fault that I stayed up ALL night and drank too much beer, I think the least you can do is tell me a story to take my mind off how bad I feel! Maybe that way, I won't want to throw up all over you and we won't have to stop again.'

Thad gave a resigned sigh and seemed to accept the warped logic of his strange little friend.

'OK... Where do you want me to start?'

'I dinna ken, pal...
Why no just start at the beginning?
We've got, how long, four or five more
hours? That should cover it, what do you
think? And if we still have some time
left, maybe we could let my brother-in-
law have a wee shot too!'

'If you think you can take it, *amigo*!'

Thad spoke quietly and there was a new
and gentle sadness to his voice that Ridge had
never heard before. He told them how his father
had been brought up in Hawaii, of mixed
Japanese and Hawaiian descent and that he had
been just a baby when Pearl Harbour was
bombed in 1941. This event and the subsequent
privations his family suffered, had shaped his
entire life. Young Tadashi Kamaka spent most
of his formative years watching the rebuilding of
the base and by the age of 19 he had established
his own successful construction business. After
seeing how much money had been spent
rebuilding Pearl Harbour he could see early on
that military contracts were the way to go. He
wasted no time in pursuing this goal. Still only
in his twenties, Tadashi was in Vietnam
overseeing the building of bases like Khe Sanh
and the airport at Da Nang.

The Vietnam conflict had been very good
to his father. One of the biggest problems out
there had been logistics and so he invested a
large chunk of his new wealth in part ownership
of an airline company which then went on to

specialise in moving military personnel and cargo across the Pacific. By the late 60's his company owned a fleet of eleven Boeing 727's.

Even as events began to turn sour in the war, Thad's dad pulled off the biggest PR coup of his life. In March 1975, he was awarded the US government contract to make evacuation flights from the beleaguered Da Nang airport which up until that time had been his largest ever construction project.

The situation all around Da Nang was perilous and worsening and Thad was sure his dad like most people had no idea what was to happen. The very first flights had gone fine with mostly US personnel and families being uplifted. The South Vietnamese were starting to panic however that perhaps the Americans were going to abandon them and many, too many, were beginning to gather at the airport. The US government cancelled the contract after only three flights and Tadashi had apparently been furious. He always said in later years that his motivation was purely humanitarian, but Thad was fairly sure his father was still thinking about his revenue stream.

Tadashi personally ordered three of his 727's to fly to Da Nang to continue the evacuation; women and children in particular. This was highly irregular and against the advice of both the US government and the military. Two of the three planes never landed but the third plane managed to land with difficulty at the base. On board this plane was Tadashi himself plus a gaggle of the world's top press and photographers. Thad told how he had met some of the Marines who had been there and how at the time they had viewed this landing as complete madness. There were South Vietnamese soldiers and civilians all over the airport and it had literally become the rule of the gun.

The jet could not land on a proper runway because of so many people running around and when they eventually took off again they had to take the taxi runway which was too small but was the only one useable. Meanwhile, US military personnel were scurrying around just trying to get hold of enough fuel to keep the planes and choppers airborne. Apparently something like two complete infantry divisions of South Vietnamese soldiers had simply evaporated over a couple of days and everyone wanted to get on a plane.

'Everyone knows about the fall of Saigon which happened just after this, right?' Thad nodded towards the other two. 'Well this situation in Da Nang was equally tragic, man.'

Thad explained how his father had been adamant that they would fly out regardless of any orders to the contrary. So what was to be called 'The last flight from Da Nang' received massive world-wide media attention. Rockets and artillery fire pounded the airport and hundreds of South Vietnamese soldiers armed with rifles and grenades fought their way onto the plane. There were now thousands of others flooding into the airport and, in desperation, people were lying down in front of the aircraft to keep it from leaving whilst others had climbed all over it.

The plane finally took off with soldiers mobbing the runway, some actually firing directly at the cockpit of the plane. Thad's dad had admitted later to his wife, Tia, that he had been very worried they would not get away and that he had been very forceful with the pilots, telling them that if they didn't make the takeoff then they would surely all die within minutes. As it was, he may have been correct but Thad knew he had been having recurring nightmares about the incident for the rest of his life.

The official story, documented all over the world, was that they had rescued over 300 people and Tadashi and his airline had been presented as heroes, particularly in the US where positive stories concerning Vietnam had been sorely needed. Allegedly hit by grenades, they had prevailed against the odds and whilst dodging bullets, they had been the last western aircraft to leave Da Nang before it was seized by the Communist forces.

In truth, Tadashi had told Tia that most of the aircraft damage had not been caused by grenades but by contact with multiple objects on take-off, that is, with people. He reckoned they had probably run over up to 20 people before the plane left the ground and many others had fallen from the wheel wells and cargo hold once airborne. Tadashi himself saw the body of a soldier still in a wheel well after they had landed at Saigon.

Ridge could see there were tears welling up in his eyes as Thad spoke about his father. He told how he had hated him for large portions of his life but now as an adult he could see the complexities of the man and he had accepted his father as a flawed genius, as capable of great good as well as terrible wrong and he was only now in that place where he could love him unconditionally.

Thad told how, only a week after the Da Nang airlift, Tadashi directed a daring rescue of almost 60 Vietnamese children, all orphaned by the conflict and flew them from Saigon to California. Again heralded as another act of courageousness, gratefully trumpeted around the globe, the real impetus for this action had been to attempt to assuage the terrible guilt that was wracking through the young man. This time, he had not attempted to orchestrate any publicity, he had no need to. Lionised by the media, he could have had no idea the effect this one mission would have on the American people.

Overwhelmed by the tide of events, cognisant always of the political implications and possibly feeling distinctly second-string to the heroic Tadashi, the President of the United States, Gerald Ford, immediately sanctioned a massive airlift programme.

'Operation Babylift' would bring almost three thousand further Vietnamese orphans back to the safety of the US. Of course, every single plane in Tadashi's fleet was contracted to assist and the resulting publicity did the airline company no harm at all.

Thad had to give him some credit, he explained, as he very quickly sold his interests in the airline business after that. However, his overwhelmingly positive media exposure, even in the military sphere, now guaranteed that he would be successful in obtaining virtually any construction project that he could ever wish for.

'And that's why I have lived out of a suitcase for my whole life, can speak five languages and have an unhealthy liking for leather shorts!'

'Probably explains quite a few things…!' laughed Ridge. 'So, leather shorts…were you in Germany or what? And what about Scotland? There used to be a big US base in…'

'Faslane! No! I was never there but I know Pop has been to Scotland, nuclear subs right?
But, yeah, we all lived in Germany, more than once. My mom was German, well half German and half Brazilian to be exact! My dad was particularly keen on doing Marine Corps bases, so he has done practically every one there is.
He figures he would be dead if it hadn't been for the courage and resourcefulness of the leathernecks around him in Da Nang.
Mom was working with IBM near a Marine Corps base at Boblingen and the rest was history.
I have two older 'German' sisters who were born there. One lives in Berlin and the other is into politics in DC and helps Pop a lot, I guess.
Myself, I was nearly Japanese! We were all in Okinawa at the time but there was a pregnancy complication, I guess I was too big or something and Mom got flown

to LA instead.

We flew a lot, naturally. I used to travel with my dad as much as he would let me in my teens; otherwise I would never have seen him. This way, I sometimes got to spend time with him, but not often. I guess he was just a busy guy.

We were both in Afghanistan when I first met the 'Dogs' up there in front. Pop had sewn up the contract to rebuild Kandahar airport whenever we had 'liberated' it from the Taliban and there was so much money for him to make in the new 'War on Terrorism', he just couldn't stay away. Pretty fuckin' stupid looking back on it but at that time we didn't think Afghanistan was going to take two years, never mind ten. Mom had been killed the year before in an auto crash in Germany; worst snow in a decade. The girls had all split and I guess I needed to be near Pop.

The Marine Corps led the attack on the airport and it was a great success; particularly where my Dad was concerned because they didn't bust the place up too bad, not compared to the Russians anyway! So, afterwards, with my Dad being such a USMC groupie and all, I met Patrick, Joey and DJ. Pop must' a pulled some strings and they got lumped with baby-sitting me for a while. I guess I had a crush on all three of them but somehow, with a lot of pushing from Pop, I was encouraged to apply to join the Marine Corps!

You may joke, Ridge! You try it! It was a lot fuckin' harder than watching *Full Metal Jacket* that's for damn sure! Anyway, I enrolled at the Marine Corps Officer Candidates School at Quantico where I completed the ten week course top of my class!'

'You? You were at Quantico?' Ed spluttered himself awake. 'I did some stuff there too, son. DEA training facility. Hell, those jarheads were mean sons of bitches! I owe you an apology, buddy! Maybes we *can* kick some butt after all!'

'Thanks Ed! Did you see the facility just next to your DEA area? The Marine Corps Research Center? Did you see the name of it, the T. Kamaka Research Center? Named after the old man! He put a whole heap of cash into it, probably was a tax write off or something like that, but a very astute move. The business he must' a gotten from that…unbelievable.'

'We got ourselves an A-list celebrity here! I take it that's how you got to be top of your …?'

'No, fucking way, dude! Come on, man! You gotta know that's bullshit.
If anything, it made life harder for me, no drill sergeant wants to look like a pussy

at Quantico. I hated my name back then; the pressure was 24/7, almost too much to stand. Half the men envied me and the other half despised me but it did make me a stronger candidate for damn sure.'

Thad had twisted himself back around to Ridge and Colm, leaving Ed nodding quietly behind them. The older man seemed to be re-appraising the personnel on this mission and by his relaxed composure it looked as if their stock was slowly rising.

'So there I was, a second lieutenant, United States Marine Corps. It was a bitter sweet time for me. The graduation had been a watershed moment where it hit me that there was nothing I couldn't do if I set my mind on it, but there was no way I was going to spend the rest of my life as a leatherneck. I had also come to terms with the fact that I was queer as hell!

I got specially selected for Special Ops training where I learnt a whole lotta good stuff and even got a medal. Pop was real proud of me which made it even tougher on him when I quit the Corps after six months and officially 'came out'!'

His flawless hazel cheeks turned deathly pale as Thad quietly told how, until recently, his father and he had not spoken for several years. His words were clipped and his handsome jaw became lowered as he explained how he had changed his surname and become one of the top male cover models in the US. He had been in touch constantly with his two sisters and they had told him that at no time had his father even allowed them to mention his name.

'But hey! You actually did something useful for once, you punk-ass Scotsman!'

Ridge had the feeling this wasn't much of a compliment but he could feel the beginnings of a warm glow of redemption deep inside, the same kind of feeling he could remember getting from a 15 year old island malt, only rarer still.

Thad spoke more quickly now, the reason for his obvious happiness now evident.

'When I came back from New York and found your note, it didn't take a brain surgeon to work out where you were going to. I had lied to you, Ridge! I am real sorry but it was to protect your dumb ass and in particular it was to dissuade you from doin' exactly what you went an' did!

So I kinda panicked. I knew what a shitstorm you were going into and that you were goin' in blind so I figured you needed some back-up. I tried getting in touch with my buddies, upfront here, but they were all incommunicado and for all three of them to be unavailable at the same time meant only one thing; they were on a job!

As I said, I was real worried for your ass and so I took a deep breath and called my dad. He was a goddammned saint. He cried, I cried. I shouted a little. I shouted a lot, actually. He took it all and then he did what he does best; he put aside his not too hot part-time dad persona and unleashed the mean, motherfuckin,' 'don't mess with me,' kick-ass 'Mister Fixer!

I'm tellin' you guys! Love him or loathe him, my dad really is a man who can. Within 24 hours, he had spoken with 'the dogs,' who were actually on vacation together plus he had a fix on your exact location at that time!' Ridge had discovered later that the boys were on a wee spot of 'r and r' after another particularly outstanding mission.

'Not only that, he had spoken to Colm here also!'

Ridge began to feel queasy. *What was going on here?*

'It's was nothing, really, neither it was! I was after surfing some websites that your man's da' here looks at. Sometimes, I might just have been sneaking a wee look at some that I shouldn't have been allowed into and so we made contact, so we did, to exchange information and such like. *Gossip* mostly...!'

'So!' Thad jumped in again quickly as Colm shrugged sheepishly. 'My dad has basically bank-rolled this operation and procured most of the weapons. The guys are doing this as a favour to both my dad and me and the only two provisions Pop has made are that I have to be in charge of the mission and that once this is over, he wants to see us all in DC. I get the impression he thinks you are my boyfriend, Ridge!'

Chapter Twenty Seven – Santa Ana

The oppressive heat wrapped itself around Xavier as he stepped from the air-conditioned sanctuary of the gun range. He had only just removed his protective headphones and his ears were still too sensitive to appreciate the rap music blaring from the speakers all around the pool area. He sat down and contemplated the menagerie of young girls flouncing licentiously in the shallow water, all clearly stoned. They were local girls, barely pubescent, brought up to Santa Ana to satisfy the ever increasing appetite of the boss.

They displayed a naïve charm, he allowed himself to admit, as they thrust their hips provocatively in time to the music and pouted towards the young drivers and lower ranked men. But to Xavier, they held no allure. He considered himself to be a red blooded man but he felt nothing but pity as he observed their crude attempts at coquetry.

The object of his all-consuming passion had more style and class in her little finger than these wet playthings. He knew now that his was not some fleeting capricious infatuation. That he loved Luisa, he understood with every atom of his being. Now his recent discovery that she felt the same for him, filled him to bursting point with both hope and also with dread.

He allowed the drooling men to posture and show off for a short while but, when they began to cut up lines on a glass table in clear view from the rear verandha of the house, he decided he had seen enough. He jumped up snarling like a cage fighter, his plastic chair flying across the tiled floor and into the pool. The girls screamed in terror as he charged over to the men, most of whom stood stunned.

One man appeared not to notice and continued to bend over the table, his nose noisily continuing its gluttonous consumption of the white powder. Xavier grabbed a handful of oiled hair and smashed the young driver's head through the mirrored glass table. Then, as his bloodied and powdered face was brought forcibly up, it was met by the tapered point of a switchblade only millimetres from his right eye.

'You need those eyes, motherfucker! Don't let me find you getting high in public again or I will feed them to the dogs! You know the rules.
If Ramon himself had come down those steps over there, you would be a corpse by now!
Tidy this fucking mess up, *pronto!*'

There was a brief frenzy of chairs and tables being scuttled across the floor, glass being swept and the clacking of stiletto heels and then suddenly there was silence around the pool.

Xavier looked all around and then smiled slightly, he was alone. It was like being a schoolteacher sometimes, he thought, with a small degree of pleasure. Perhaps soon he would be the Head Teacher. Sitting back down in the shade, he wondered what the next days would bring.

He was certainly impressed with the new guns they had recently acquired. If these few were of a representative standard, then he would certainly look forward to receiving the full consignment from their overseas contacts in Europe. There had been problems, he was aware of that. Luckily, Max had been more involved in the negotiations with the Irishmen and Xavier was confident that he was going to be able to use this situation to his great advantage.

Unfortunately, there had been a little too much reliance on luck, Xavier appreciated. He would have been happier if his current good fortune had all been as the deserved result of careful thought and considered planning, as it would have been in the days of Arturo.

In the old days, there was little margin for error when battle plans were drawn. For that was the mindset of Arturo, it was always a war; a war against the authorities, against the rich and in particular, against the insidious interference of the *norteamericanos*.

With Ramon, it was ugly avarice, instant gratification and senseless violence. That was why he had to go. Xavier was becoming increasingly convinced that most sane people would agree with him, whatever their respective allegiances. He likened himself now to a Senator, an honourable Roman, of ancient times, plotting to overthrow a corrupt and evil Caesar.

Ramon was in a ferocious temper as usual these days and Xavier was content to sit in peace for a while longer. Despite his haranguing of the men just then, Xavier knew that Ramon rarely spent much time around this pool. With the ten car garage along one flank and the gun range along the other, the large house linked the two with the partially covered pool separating them. It housed the lesser ranks and was situated nearer the front of the Santa Ana estate. There was a much larger mansion house further back which formed the heart of the newly acquired headquarters for the organisation. Adjacent to that was a massive outdoor pool, half shaded by a beautiful pergola threaded with bountiful vines. Ramon had fitted out the small pump house by the pool with the latest gadgets so that he could lounge by the pool but still watch his plasma TV's and pluck ice cold drinks from his huge coolers.

Xavier knew that was where they would all be sitting right now, enjoying the faintest of cooling summer winds that played across the estate at this time of the afternoon. He had to think like Arturo now, to play this like a game of chess. He would take his time, only move when all the options have been weighed carefully. He had planted a tiny seed earlier in the day and had skilfully avoided Ramon ever since then. It was vital, in his careful estimation, that he should not be seen to be orchestrating events in the unlikely situation that things did not pan out the way he had intended. The unbelievable good fortune that had befallen him in the last few days was also the primo reason for Ramon's savage disposition.

There was the matter of the girl naturally. That the circumstances of her disappearance had troubled Ramon more than his actual feelings of loss, Xavier like Max, had grasped fairly early on. A relieved Luisa had confirmed his suspicions when she told him that he had not altered in his sparing attentions towards her during the entire episode and she was confident that Juanita had already been supplanted by another. Initially dubious about the sanity of aiding her abduction, Xavier could not have anticipated precisely how well it had consolidated his current position.

Poor old Max had been forced to shoulder the blame and although he had survived physically unscathed, he was no longer the unassailable fortress of previous days. Particularly since the Irish deal appeared to be cracking under the strain and this was where lady luck seemed to be playing exclusively for Xavier.

Maximiliano had been assisting Arturo with the Irishmen before his untimely demise and so he continued to broker much of the dealings as even he had known that these guys would not put up with a crazy *loco* like Ramon.

The sample shipment had been brought over by the two main Latin American contacts, Murphy and O'Callaghan. They had been well received and despite himself, Xavier could find no faults with the weapons no matter how hard he had tried earlier today. The problem was that the two men seemed to have vanished off the face of the earth. Ramon was being accused of foul play from the Irish whilst at the same time he was scouring the country looking for them and trying to ascertain which of his many enemies had had a hand in their disappearance.

In the absence of any firm intelligence, the Cali cartel were the obvious suspects in the way that Al-Qaeda get the blame for any terrorist activity directed against the West. Only Xavier knew for a fact that the Cali were not responsible but he could not divulge this for fear of jeopardising his own position. There was no way he could explain being custodian of such information and besides, he was enjoying the play and he was working hard to be the only one who would benefit from the fallout.

Ramon meanwhile, was apoplectic. The Irish had steadfastly refused to honour their side of the bargain until the fate of the men had been established. Just at a time when these new weapons could have been most useful, they were being denied him and it was the thought of anyone dictating terms to him, the great don, Ramon that had him completely incensed.

The top men of the whole organisation had been summoned to Santa Ana for a weekend of meetings and gratuitous partying. Max and Xavier both knew this was not a company reward situation rather it was both a vehicle with which to engender loyalty and discipline in a organisation creaking at the seams plus a covert attempt to root out any disaffected gang members or even possible informers.

All Xavier had to do was to time everything just right. If he could be allowed to spin these plates for a little longer then he could pull off a stunt worthy of the most accomplished don. He knew this had to be his moment. A just reward for all of the hard years of servitude, bathed in the blood of those wretches unfortunate enough to have crossed his path in this abattoir of a land. Years mired in the bestial violence which, until very recently, he thought had anaesthetised any genuine sensitivity he might have to the human condition. It was not going to be without its difficulties, of that he was certain. There was going to be a brief but concerted period of uncompromised bloodletting before order would be restored. He knew he must steel himself to be merciless in the field of battle.

It was the personal treachery that he found the most iniquitous. Max was in serious trouble already and like a once mighty beast of the plains, he was too strong to be defeated by a single wound or a sole adversary. However, unbeknownst to him, he was going to be brought down by a number of disparate foes, not the least of which was plain bad luck.

If the chess board had looked different today, then Max could have been his greatest ally but due largely to the circumstance of fate he had been fatally weakened. Thus, in their primitive domain, Xavier had no choice but to exploit his former comrade in arms who had now, expediently, become a sacrificial pawn.

Towards Ramon as a man, Xavier felt nothing, only the age-old guilt of treason gnawing at his bones, an unshakable feeling that to depose your leader by violent treachery must be inherently wrong. But, no! It was not wrong to think that this man is a disgrace to his position, Xavier told himself. It was the only rational way to think and if he could hold this thought at the forefront of his consciousness, he would be strong and he would prevail.

Galvanised into action by his quickened heartbeat, Xavier leapt up and headed towards the marble steps of the house. It would only be a couple of days, he told himself, before the authorities descended upon the estate and it would all be over. Xavier would be the only lieutenant left alive or not incarcerated and a new period of stability and progress would ensue. As he strolled casually past the men he had recently shouted at and down the front steps he tried to shrug off any lingering doubts about the possibility of a double-cross by the DEA.

It was inconceivable, he told himself! He had given them so much already and the capture of Ramon would be such a feather in their cap that they wouldn't give a fuck about who was left to mop up the pieces. Now, all that remained was to ensure that the next few vital moves proceeded as he had planned.

The air was still warm as he walked across the large courtyard, skirting past the grand entrance to the main hacienda and then over towards the new outdoor entertainment area where most of the men were situated. The afternoon light was beginning to fade but he could see Ramon striding up and down in an agitated manner with several of the men fawning behind him.

Ramon was normally fairly stoned by this time in the day and Xavier was surprised to see him looking as invigorated. Something must have riled him yet again, he decided, and he contemplated doing an about-turn just as Ramon looked over and gave him a commanding wave of his arm.

Maximiliano smiled grimly over at Xavier, his wary eyes betraying a lesser degree of bonhomie than usual. Xavier seemed to have walked into a full scale argument and to his delight it was concerning the very topic that he had planned to casually introduce himself. Most of the guys were quietly lit and it was only Ramon who was uncharacteristically articulate and he wasn't wasting the opportunity.

'You are all a bunch of old women!' He turned toward them, sneering.

'We *have* to do this!
When will you fucking see that...? When it is too late?'

He laughed sarcastically, his red eyes hungrily searching for a victim, for eyes to lock on to, to pull down and to devour.

'Easy for you to sit on your fat asses and pull in less and less each month!
Who will you come crying to when some other cocksucker has taken the food from the mouths of your children?'

'Of course, Ramon! It is has always been a excellent idea...'

Max tried to placate his boss.

'But maybe we are too stretched right now and with our new base here, we are too far away to make sure it runs ok, are we not?'

'Too fucking far from anything,' whispered Jose, a young boss from one of the northern states. He smirked at some of the others. There was not a man there who wasn't at least a little drunk or stoned, but some of them could handle it better than others. The old hands knew instinctively when to straighten up.

'What you say?
You fucking laughing at me?
What the fuck have you been doing the last few months?'

'He's not laughing, boss, I promise. He's knows I'd kick his sorry ass all the way back to Chihuahua, that sewer of a town he calls home!'

Ramon stopped abruptly and slowly a smile appeared across his fat pock-marked face. He bared those infamous yellow teeth, betraying the evil that lurked within his head and just for a moment, all present bore witness to the vile portrait of El Cocodrilo, the crocodile.

'I tell you what we are gonna do my *amigos*!
Maximiliano! You are to leave tonight and make this problem go away.
I am counting on you so do not think of letting me down, AGAIN!
Do you understand me...?'

Max could see there would be no reasoning with the boss tonight. He was wound too tight for any rational argument, besides which, he was obviously grandstanding in front of the younger men. It was the last thing Max wanted to do. Go all across the country only to be recalled in a couple of days when something else cropped up.

But maybe it would be good to get some fresh air. It was difficult even to breathe around Ramon these days. He also relished the opportunity to make right the situation between the two men by showing Ramon, once again, that it was he, Maximiliano, who could get things done. No one else but me, he sighed inwardly.

He nodded his head in acquiescence. 'As you wish, *El Patron*. I will leave immediately.' Had he noticed the quick glances between Ramon and Xavier, he might not have felt quite so relieved as he strode across the courtyard. Xavier, for one, was mentally cheering at this welcome development. With the ultra capable bodyguard out of the picture for the foreseeable, Xavier knew that Ramon had unwittingly signed his own death warrant. No one could save him now, not even Xavier should he even desire to do so. Upon taking control of the reins of power, Xavier would then be in a position to deal with Max also, one way or another.

Ramon stood proudly as he watched his closest friend stride purposefully away from him. Despite this pretence of masterful leadership, behind the façade of uncompromising power, he felt somehow that he had just made an error of judgement, that he had been deftly manipulated. He looked across at a smiling Xavier but couldn't make the connection.

'And take this laughing coyote with you! Before I have him put down for his insolence!'

But Max did not hear him however, as he

had marched some distance across the courtyard.

'No way, boss!' exclaimed Jose, smashing his drinks glass across the paving stones. The looks of incredulity and the imploring eyes only served to embolden the young man in his expensive suit.

'Please, don't team me up with that old cunt...'

'SILENCE!' Ramon boomed.

'*Vete a la chingada*!
I have heard ENOUGH from you...!
I will not have you disrespect us in this way! Give me your belt.'

None of the men moved so much as an inch to help Jose. He was a dead man and they all knew it. However and whenever it happened, he was already marked down for a body bag and they did not wish to be tainted by any allegiance to the young fool. They all stood dumbstruck as their little dictator strutted up and down in front of them, all the time screaming at the dazed Jose.

'Hurry the fuck up! What's the problem eh? Hands shaking?
Not laughing now! You little *coño*!
Hector! Strap his fucking hands behind his back, *pronto*!
Now, Roberto, take off your belt too!
It's OK! I give you one of mine in a moment.
OK Hector, now strap his ankles. Make it

real tight now!'

Jose tried to fall over to hinder the activity at his feet but Ramon was on to it and held him by the shoulders. He was babbling about how sorry he was and how it was the cocaine talking and he never meant any disrespect.

'Shut the fuck up!' Ramon socked him hard in the face and he fell heavily onto the imported granite paving stones.

'Help him up!' Ramon screamed. Jose stood falteringly, his nose broken and his tailored
suit now drenched in his own bright red blood.

'Now! Quick! Carry him over there!' He pointed in the general direction of the pool.

'So, just swim across to the other side... then I will forget the whole affair. OK? Pardon? Did you have something else to say?
Not so funny now, cocksucker!
Throw the fucker in the pool!'

The men had no choice as they grimly carried the wailing man over to the pool and with Ramon practically exploding with rage, they reluctantly dropped him into the still water.
The antiseptic blue calm of the pool quickly turned a turbulent crimson as Jose attempted to turn one way and then the other. He tried in vain to tread water using a crude jacknife

motion but each time he sank down it was deeper than the last. Ramon stood directly above him, sweating and red faced, venting his anger.

'Not laughing now, you fucker! What? Can't hear you!'

As the man began his last desperate spasms, he finally understood what it meant to be taken by *El Cocodrilo*, dragged down to the depths and slowly rolled. Ramon's men looked at each other and at their leader, waiting for the call or a simple gesture that would mean enough was enough, that he had been punished adequately, it was time to pull him out, he had surely learned his lesson. All of the men apart from Xavier. He had sat back down and lit himself a cigarette. He alone knew. The call never came.

'OK Guys!
Mosquitoes are starting to bite now. Let's go in and have dinner, we have a lot to talk about tonight! And Xavier, make sure the pool company get all that shit cleaned out tomorrow morning, OK!'

It was dark now and none of the men would have noticed the faint glint of two pairs of army binoculars way over beside a newly constructed bunker by the 18th green. The two men had witnessed the entire pool episode and they sat and stared at each other, Thad shaking his head sadly. Now he truly understood the calibre of animal they were dealing with but he felt that to even call him that was disrespectful to animals, or even reptiles. As they worked their way back off the estate, Colm smiled suddenly. As horrific as all that had been, it had however, given him a cracking idea.

Chapter Twenty Eight – Smoke on the Water

The late morning sun was beating down relentlessly and the designer sunglasses did little to help her see the target which glimmered in the heat some two hundred yards away. Still, she was holding her own against Ridge, who earlier had boasted of having had a gun all through his boyhood. Ed was secretly very pleased with both of them and with a little more practice he felt comfortable with them having a restricted range of small arms, with the vital proviso that he was never actually in front of them at any point.

'Be cool, Ridge. Don't hold the gun so goddamn tight, that's why you're gettin' so much of a kick-back all the time. See, how Juanita does it, nice and smooth every time, *tranquilo.*'

Ridge held up the .45 calibre Colt M1911 pistol, his right arm outstretched but still relaxed. He tried hard not to grip the gun too tightly. Holding his breath, he closed his left eye and ignored the resulting relocation of the liquid frustration that was rivulets of his sweat trickling from his eyebrow down to the end of his nose.

As it dripped, he pulled the trigger. This time, to his astonishment, the old bottle exploded and Ed was jumping in the air with excitement.

'You did it kid! You're good to go on that one!'

'Hey Neeta! I'm catching you now!' Ridge turned grinning madly at the girl only to stop in amazement as Juanita casually swung back on her heels and sprayed a line of nine or ten bottles with a custom M4 assault rifle.

The girl smiled happily and ran the back of her arm across a sweaty oil streaked face. She was enjoying herself! Each time she pulled the trigger she became more empowered and was even starting to feel that maybe they could just pull this off. She had shot Ramon, Max and the other thugs many a time this morning, each time the reverberating thrill of revenge becoming stronger and pulsating deeper inside her. She had decided it was the best therapy a girl could get!

Across the dusty field, in the old abandoned farm shack, Joey and DJ were making final preparations for the assault on Santa Ana. They had planned to make the initial attack in the late afternoon while the sun would be low in the sky and more importantly behind them. From what Thad had seen the previous afternoon with Colm, he reckoned the estate guards weren't up to much anyway but there was no point in taking extra risks. But as Colm had pointed out, it might have been a wee tad distracting having to endure one of their own being tortured to death in the swimming pool. However, he had returned much later that night for a thorough recce of the site and he professed to being more than happy with the layout.

Patrick and the other two had been gone since first light and as DJ had just received their latest report, all seemed to be going well. The plan was for the truck to leave in three hours and rendezvous with the other three half a mile from the Santa Ana estate. Joey had the weapons prep well in hand and it looked like Ed and the two civilians would make up some useful additional firepower after all. There could be no passengers on this trip and both DJ and Joey would have preferred that they had deposited Ridge and Juanita somewhere safe in Villahermosa.

Like all of them, DJ had found Juanita captivating and notwithstanding his old gay heart he had become smitten by her natural open beauty. He joked that she had the saddest big eyes he had ever fallen into. In the few days they had spent together, they had become like sisters and he was determined that he would not be responsible for delivering her to be offered up for slaughter.

He had been brutally forthright with Ed earlier that day when he told him that unless they could shoot to an acceptable standard by noon then they would be dropped off at the edge of the city. He knew that this was directly contradicting their existing orders but as Ridge had protested, he had shouted them all down. On the ground DJ was in charge of their security and therefore, he had told them, his word was law. He was unyielding on this matter and so Ed had been faced with the seemingly insurmountable task of teaching them the rudiments of modern warfare in less than one day.

As far as Ed was concerned, this was yet another valid reason to delay for a few days and so he had begun his task with the sole intention of falling at the first fence. But he couldn't help himself. He knew that he cared for this young girl more than anything else still living on this miserable rock.

He could barely live with himself knowing he had so casually cast aside his true feelings for Mandy on the last night of her life. He knew he had been instrumental in bringing a cruel and undeserved death to her doorstep. Yet somehow, he felt if his love for Juanita remained strong and pure then it somehow meant something more than just a lustful infatuation and his betrayal then became a more justifiable mendacity amongst the numerous other lies that lacerated his brain.

Besides, he had a love ripped savagely from him once, he was not about to let it happen a second time. So, he found himself teaching her to shoot as if it were the most important thing that he had been put on Earth to do. Which it most certainly was.

Juanita had responded well to the care and kindness and against all the odds she had shaped up to be a pretty good shot. Even the hapless Scot had punched above his weight, not that Ed could give a damn for him when compared with the girl. He did have a great respect for the boy and along with Joey and the others he continually marvelled at how Ridge had actually survived this far. Listening to him recount some of his recent escapades the night before, Patrick had actually summed Ridge up best when he said, 'that guy is a walking good luck magnet and I for one am keepin' Mr Serendipity close to me tomorrow!'

The foul smoke continued to drift across the estate, it's only saving grace the fact that it moderated the full intensity of the midday sun. *But what a price to pay*, thought Ernesto, coughing deeply again as he paced the new road, choking with the smell. These guys are fucking animals! He had only taken this job a fortnight ago and he was already regretting it. The money was good, better than he had ever known and his wife was happier than she had been in a long time, but he was in the depths of despondency. Surely it does not please God for him to live like this, with these evil monsters.

His anguish was only worsened when he was told he would be working the front left quadrant today. He had heard what had happened at the pool and he did not want to be responsible for that part of the estate this morning. Not only did he have to deal with the grisly pool cleaning, but to make matters worse, the bosses had deliberately placed the fire to the left of the pool area, just before the start of the new golf course. That meant with the summer winds blowing from the East, the acrid haze would be pushed all the way across his patch, over the pool and barbeque area, straight into the front of the hacienda.

The poor bastards would have woken from their hellish slumbers, shaking and hungover, to be confronted with a Dante-esque nightmare of swirling mephitic grey smoke and the ghastly realisation that this was the smouldering remains of one of their own. It was a diabolic and calculated act that would serve as a potent reminder of the monstrous power wielded by their psychopathic leader.

It had come as a relief then, that the body had already been removed from the pool before the cleaning company arrived. He had invented a story about raw meat for the barbecue party the previous night having inadvertently fallen in and stewed in the pool all night. From the distance Ernesto could see the pool guy was very tall which meant it wasn't either of the two normal guys. *That's cool*, he thought, as he walked over, *I won't have to get into too much conversation.* The guy was a real skinny *negrito*, which was very unusual at the Santa Ana *finca* but there had been more and more coming over from Jamaica in recent times and as long as he was no trouble, Ernesto could care less.

> '*Hablas Ingles*? *No hablo Español*! What I say, mon? *No entiendo*!'

Ernesto didn't speak many words of English but he could understand the basics, so nodded eagerly.

> 'Stevie alla time good worker. You don't need to stand alla time. I no thief, mon! I drum-drum angry, mon! *No me gusta*!'

The language barrier was perfect. He didn't have to get into anything and the guy was obviously not happy about the mess so Ernesto determined to leave him to it for the rest of the day if need be. 'Ok, *adios compañero*.'

What with the filthy pool and the smoke,

it seemed that the bosses were all staying in the big house today which suited Ernesto well. He only had a couple of hours left and then he was away. That was still two hours too long. He had determined to tell his wife that that was it, he was not going back. He figured she would go *loco*, but if he told her what had been going on, then surely she would relent. They had two *niños* already and one on the way which was why the money was welcome but what would be the point of him getting killed, then where would they be, he thought morosely?

Several miles away from Santa Ana, a white petrol tanker bearing the red triangle and green logo of Pemex was carefully guided off the long straight road into a lorry bay. The driver was cursing under his breath. *Holy mother of Jesus!* This was not good. He didn't have a clue who the two men were but one was a *gringo* and they both looked very serious and official.

The two men stood for a moment to allow the dust to dissipate slightly and then gringo walked up to his side of the cab and gestured for him to wind down his window. Miguel was under strict instructions not to stop for anyone and never to get out of the cab unless he was loading or unloading, but today, curse the gods, he had his little brother Angel in the cab with him which was totally against the rules. He slowly wound the glass down whilst grasping for his little baseball bat with his free hand.

The gringo pushed back his teamsters cap and looked up at Miguel smiling. His face was the insipid pale pigmentation of a Band-Aid and he had thick hair of a hue Miguel had never

seen, *diablo rojo*, he decided to call it later. The
man spoke up to him clearly and firmly in
perfect Spanish.

'*Buenos*. Would you please climb down
out of the cab? You have nothing to fear from
us, I promise you.' Miguel cautiously descended
to the road, nervously looking back over his
shoulder at his brother. 'Can I please ask your
co-worker to step down also? A little young to
be driving a petrol tanker, is he not?' Miguel
swallowed nervously and nodded. '*Si*, he is my
brother, he should be at school today.' Miguel
cursed inwardly, *why did I let him talk me into
coming today*? He could picture his poor
mothers face. Had she not suffered enough?'

Colm tried to keep his face straight as a
skinny young boy no more than 13 or 14
clambered awkwardly out of the tanker. The two
Mexicans were sweating profusely and Colm
could see the real fear in their eyes. It was a
sharp reminder of his life back home and he
shuddered briefly. Not one single vehicle had
passed in the few minutes the tanker had been
stopped. Fuel robberies were rife in this area and
Miguel had already figured they were going for a
long walk home, if they were lucky.

'Can I ask you how much fuel you are
carrying, *amigo*? Three quarters full? Good, that
is very good. Can we both jump up on top and
have a look? I promise you we will not harm you
if you just answer my questions.'

Thad stood in the welcome shadow of

337

the tanker with the young boy. Even then the suffocating heat reflecting off the white paint of the vehicle was fierce and Thad tried to relax his breathing and to manifest an aura of calm authority. He did *not* want to have to chase after the boy in this heat. There was some intense conversation going on top of the tanker and they could here the clanking of valves being opened and metal banging against metal.

After a few more minutes Colm led the man down and then waved over to the pick up which had been parked inconspicuously off the road. Patrick jumped out and it became immediately obvious to the two terrified Mexicans that this had to be some kind of *Federales* operation. Part time transvestite or not, there was no hiding the military bearing of the big man.

'OK, *amigo*. I am going to borrow your truck for a while. You say you service the Santa Ana estate? You know what goes on there, right? OK, well I don't need to tell you that you must keep this little matter between us. My big friend here will take you to the next town north from here and there you must stay for the rest of the day. Here is 2,000 dollars for you and your brother. It is yours to keep, in payment for your silence. You will have to say you were robbed by bandits, OK? We could just tie you up and throw you into the bushes, at the mercy of the coyotes. You would also lose your job for taking your brother on the job, am I right?

But this way, you are the innocent victims of a robbery, you have made a little money and if this matters to you, you have also helped in the fight between good and evil. It is important that you should know, today, we are the good. However, if you ever speak about what really happened here, then I will hunt you down and I will kill you. *Entiendo? Muy bien*!

Oh! There's just one other thing.' Colm looked straight into Miguel's worried eyes.

'I want you to take off your clothes...'

Miguel's face crumpled and he pulled his little brother closer to him, his brain accelerating into overdrive. 'Please *Señor*! No!' He had heard that the *norteamericanos* were a sick people but he never expected anything like this to happen to him. As Colm dropped his trousers, Miguel considered his chances in a fight situation. He knew instinctively that he wouldn't make it but maybe young Angel could be spared the horrors that were surely to befall them. Patrick, sensing trouble, took a deep breath and drew himself up to his full height, his massive chest jutting out like an enormous headland on the far horizon.

'I just need your Pemex overalls, *amigo*! You are about my size and you will need my clothes or you will end up in a jail cell!'

The relief on Miguel's face was comical and the men were all smiling despite themselves as Colm struggled to squeeze himself into the tight overalls. He had been somewhat flattering to the smaller man. Patrick handed Angel the money and told him to keep it safe. The two men stood aside for a moment while the others conferred quietly. Angel could see them all looking at their watches and then they shook hands solemnly.

Colm turned to climb up into the cab and Patrick ushered the others towards the truck. 'Hey Pat!' Colm suddenly stopped and turned. 'We nearly forgot…' Patrick looked blankly up at him. Colm made a gesture with his head towards Miguel. A light came on in the big man's eyes and then he grimaced momentarily. 'Oh shit, yeah!' In one instantaneous movement he glided round and punched Miguel hard in the face. The stunned Mexican dropped to the dirt and they all heard one of his teeth ping against the metallic body of the tanker.

'Sorry, *amigo*!' Colm apologised as Thad and Patrick helped the dazed man back onto his feet.

'We had to do that. You've just been robbed remember! Don't want anyone thinking you were a pussy now do we! Your story wouldn't hold water without some form of evidence.'

Miguel nodded disconsolately as he rubbed his bruised jaw.

Chapter Twenty Nine – The Reptile House

It was getting darker as Ernesto walked across the courtyard to his car. He nodded briefly towards Jesus whose big frame had set off the security lighting as he ambled over to the main house to check in for the night shift. He disliked the big man and the feeling seemed to be mutual. Jesus was soft, overweight and lazy and had always preferred the nights as there was never anything happening.

Ernesto looked disinterested tonight also, Jesus mused, but he just had to catch the little *pendejo* quickly and save himself a walk down to the pump house, it was still way too hot right now for that kind of shit.

'Hey! Ernesto! Wait up man! Did you like the barbeque today?
I know... Fuckin' far out! Is that the delivery for the pump house?
Are they refilling the drums too, man?'

'I guess. They only came in just behind you. I'm off now, go check yourself you fat fuck!'

'It's OK! I'll take your word for it, amigo.'

Ramon surveyed the large oak panelled

room and belched with the deep satisfaction of a man who not only commanded the respect of all in his presence but whose very name was synonymous with achievement, power and great wealth across the whole world. At least that was the way he liked to be thought of, but these days, he was not so sure.

It had seemed so much simpler in his father's time, everyone knew where they stood and the battle lines were clearly drawn with each side acquitting themselves to the best of their ability whilst still managing to adhere to the precepts of the game.

Admittedly, the young Ramon never had to endure too much of the business side as it was always taken as read that he would be unlikely to ever be holding the reins of power. He had always had the gnawing realization that none of the family actually considered him capable of controlling the many scabrous factions of their fast growing empire. With the death of their father, quickly following the untimely murders of their other two brothers, Alfonso and Carlos, it had befallen Arturo, by far the most capable brother, to assume dominion over the organisation. He carried out this task admirably with his trademark planning and attention to detail. Perhaps, his only failing had been his lack of fraternal care towards the embryonic monster that was to have the temerity to live long enough to succeed him.

But, now he, Ramon had proved them all wrong! He turned away from the long meeting table which was encircled by anxious looking men all talking at the same time and walked slowly over to the drinks cabinet by the window.

As he looked out upon the crimson sky of his new playground, he struggled to stifle a wicked laugh. He was very happy with the way his lieutenants were working so hard to please him today. Maybe I should market my new management incentive scheme, he thought darkly. *First, marinade and then barbeque* your problematic staff member, then sit back and watch closely as the graph of your business performance goes through the roof. *Repeat as often as required.*

He grabbed roughly at one of the young girls standing attentively by and pulled her onto his knee as he sat down heavily onto the sturdy throne-like chair at the head of the table. 'Well, my sugar. Let's see if they have made a decision yet, shall we?' As Ramon slipped his hand up the inside of girl's tight tee-shirt and absentmindedly rubbed a small hard nipple, his men all squirmed in their chairs and now tried not to be the first one to speak.

Ramon had known Max would be furious on the phone when Ramon had boasted of his treatment of Jose. From the other man's perspective, it was a major character flaw in the boss that he could never anticipate the consequences of his actions and Maximiliano was always the one who had to act as a 'shit-filter' between Ramon and the others. Without this essential component in the management structure of the organisation, there would have been widespread mutiny long ago. Now, on top of sorting out this crazy boat scheme, Max would need to find a replacement for Jose before the Chihuahua region became lost to a rival cartel.

Ramon knew he had been out of control and that he needed the stabilising influence of Max to cool the insane rage that erupted without warning more and more often. He sensed that Xavier had secretly approved although he never found it too easy to read what the quiet man was really thinking. Perhaps Max was getting soft! It certainly seemed to have been a sound idea of Xavier's to get Max to deal with the issue on the far coast and when he then suggested they get Max to drop Luisa and the children off in Mexico City enroute then that sealed the deal as far as Ramon was concerned.

He could do some hard business as planned but be freer for the more pleasurable things in life. He would never have considered sitting at an important meeting with a *puta* on his lap if Luisa had been in the vicinity. There was only so much that she would take.

His father had been known publicly for his tough as nails approach to business and yet privately for his warm gregarious personality and there was no way he would ever have lost it so publicly, so childishly, as Ramon had the day before.

Whilst his brother Arturo was by no means a puritan, he had always managed to keep the business side separate from his family life and like his father he had been an inspirational character, a true leader who had led by example. *What example am I setting*, he thought as he watched the craven antics of his men, all trying to second guess his unpredictable moods.

He could see it in their eyes; the naked fear, the wariness of how each word or deed could be misinterpreted and their fate sealed. He was regarded by many, he imagined, as one would regard a wild beast, a caged animal. He had initially enjoyed his reputation as *El Cocodrilo*, but lately it had lost its bite somewhat.

He had realised this only just recently when he noticed a subtle change in the way people looked at him. It was not just base fear that he could see now, it was that morbid curiosity people have when they slow down to see a badly injured casualty at the scene of a traffic accident, the feeling you will get watching a mighty bull slowly, inevitably, succumb to the repeated wounds of the matador. As his mood became darker he recognised that to many, he had become the human equivalent of the twin towers of Manhattan just seconds before that infamous second violation; arrogant, tragic and proud, awaiting inevitable destruction, exposed time and time again by the savage and unrelenting media in the ultimate manifestation of schadenfreude.

'*A la chingada!*'

The men all looked up in various stages of trepidation. The girl fell off his lap as Ramon took to his feet, cursing.

'I've had enough for the time being. I will see you in a couple of hours.

Keep at it! I want those distribution points nailed down tonight!

You three! Come with me upstairs. I need to relax awhile.'

The girls exchanged glances and fixed their smiles to the 'on' position before stumbling after him in their unfeasibly high heels of their *botas de cuero*.

Most of the men at the meeting table fixed his stare to the rear of whichever of the girls he thought the most desirable and there was a palpable exhalation of air as the door closed behind the last one. Each present visibly relaxed and it was possible to see a brief flickering of prurience, sympathy or even outright revulsion cross the faces of the hardened drug peddlers. Although there was not a man over the age of forty five in the room, there were several who had children of their own no older than these unfortunate girls who were to be tonight's executive stress toys for the boss.

Barely an hour later, *El Patron* was passed out on top of his large bed, his fat hairy stomach wobbling in time with his loud snores. The three girls in various stages of undress were huddled together by a cooling window in a far corner of the room, fixing up each others' acrylic nails. Learning fast, like all creatures in the wild, they had succeeded in rendering him incapable after providing him with an extremely potent joint and a rough hand job. Looking forward to a peaceful few hours, they were pleased with themselves and they joked quietly and giggled over at the sleeping ogre.

It was around midnight and it had become much darker and cooler now and the girls cuddled up to each other, limbs interlocked, feeling sleepy and safe together. One of them gazed lazily out at the full moon and felt her heart ache as she wondered if her parents could see the moon just as she could.

As her heavy eyes began to droop she saw a beautiful shooting star curving high into the black night. *Holy shit*, she thought after a second or so. It must be a firework or a flare or something and she wriggled free of her two companions. From the window she could see it was still arcing in the most perfect parabola the girl had ever seen and as it began to descend somewhere over by the boundaries of the estate she shrugged her narrow shoulders and turned to rejoin her sleeping friends.

But then, for a stunning moment, the whole room in front of her was violently illuminated as if by the reflection of the brightest bolt of lightning. Ramon's bloated belly was rendered white by the acid intensity of the flash and the two dozing girls became purified for that second as if made of perfect alabaster.

Expecting only a crack of thunder, or at best another fork of lightning, she turned around for a better view just as the world outside exploded with a thunderous explosion and the walls shuddered with the impact. A blinding fireball ate up the sky like an angry sun, its voracious tentacles reaching far out across the estate. She instinctively raised her arm across her face and crouched quickly as the full cataclysmic force of the eruption shattered the window, showering the room with shards of glass and pieces of debris.

Ramon jumped up in terror, his rotund stomach streaming bright hot blood from a gaping wound.

'QUÉ DEMONIOS!'

Chapter Thirty – Light into Darkness

Not since Ridge had his impromptu leaving school party in the lee of the 17th at the windswept Blar Mor, had a golf course been subjected to such a rag-tag bunch. Not that this bore much resemblance to Sorsay, Ridge mused. That watershed moment between school and the-rest-of-his-life had been marked, or perhaps marred, by a riotous frolic at the head of Ardalanish Bay overlooking the impressive stack of McPhail's Anvil rising out of the choppy waves like a mighty black fist.

They had drunk their fill of cheap booze and cried out to the gods; some moving on to college imploring good fortune or those remaining on the island cursing their already narrowing prospects. All of them sensing that life would never again be quite be the same. *But here I am*, he thought, umpteen years later, hiding out in another bunker.

It was almost midnight and Ridge had been waiting for what seemed like hours for the rest of the team to arrive. His stomach clenched with that familiar pre-competition tension he remembered from his boyhood running days, only he was sure nobody had tried to shoot him then.

He had been in the second wave with Ed and Juanita, once the Diamond Dogs had ascertained that the area was safe. Like Ridge, they had all been fitted out with some tricksy communication devices courtesy of DJ with a tiny pellet in one ear and a simple pendant style transmitter and receiver wired to a unit strapped to a waist belt. They had been warned not to speak unless it was absolutely necessary and there had been some complications due to Joey setting up a jamming device throughout the centre of the Sana Ana estate to prevent any use of mobile phones.

It was DJ who was babysitting them and the others were due at any moment. Apparently Patrick had already 'taken out' two of the sentry guards and Ridge hadn't wanted to know any details. DJ looked down at the three worried faces and grinned, his perfect white teeth glinting in the near pitch darkness.

'Hey, dudes! Cheer the fuck up will ya!' He brandished a large automatic weapon. 'Y'all gonna' be just fine. You got a nigger on the trigger!'

Just then, as the cooling breeze blew in their direction, they heard the unmistakable sound of a vehicle rumbling through the silence and it seemed to be getting louder. Juanita attempted to burrow into Ed's armpit and the others froze. 'Relax!' DJ whispered. 'It's just the others.' To everyone else's amazement, out of the murky gloom appeared the dusty black pickup, straight up what purported to be the fairway, all the way to their bunker! Making as little noise as possible, Colm, Thad and the two remaining Dogs jumped out and began unloading equipment from the truck. 'It's OK, guys' said Pat, seeing the obvious concern on the faces of the 'civilians', 'We got this zone neutralised, it belongs to us now, we is cool.'

Ridge looked at Colm accusingly, his trembling voice revealing just how scared he was, 'Where have you *been* all day? What happened to 'we strike at sunset, to catch them with the sun in their eyes'? It's pitch fucking dark and we've been here for ages!'

'Come on, now! Relax. It's OK.
There was too much to do in the timeframe and way too much going on at the ranch, so there was.
DJ was after doing an infra red on the main building earlier and there are even more of the wee fuckers than we could have dared for!
This is goin' to take all night. We won't be finished until after daybreak so I hope you've all got your party pills. I've been a wee bit busy meself, so I have, so don't you worry about a thing.
You're goin' to fucking LOVE this! I'm tellin' you, you'll fucking shite yerself!'

Joey and Pat were handing over weapons and ammunition as per earlier rehearsals and barking out various orders to anyone who was listening. Thad took Ridge and Juanita aside.

'You two, just stick as close to Colm and me as you can OK! Keep your head down and don't take ANY chances.
This is not a game.
These guys can take care of themselves.
Ed. That goes for you too if you want.'

Ed put a comforting arm around Juanita.

'Roger that. You just lead the way; I'll stick to you guys like glue. Let's kick some ass!'

Pat quietly put his hand up and all of a sudden everyone stood still and in the eerie silence, Ridge had that ominous feeling like they all knew what he was going to say next.

'OK guys. This is it now.
Colm is gonna show us his party piece and then it's full on in there like a fuckin' train.
You all got your orders.
Keep safe you hear?
I hear you kids did great today, so just remember what Ed showed you and keep out of trouble, OK?'

They all nodded meekly and Ridge tried to swallow but it was no use. His heart was thumping out a heavy bass rhythm under his ribs and he wrapped his hands around his M4 and clutched it to his chest as if was some lucky charm. He looked around at the others and was met by apprehensive yet determined faces and it was only then he realised that both Joey and DJ had vanished into the night.

Colm hoisted up a large cross-bow and carried it up to the lip of the bunker where he could see the lambent lights of the main house to the left and the smaller house and garages straight in front over from the pool area. Back down in the bunker, the others looked up at him with confusion replacing fear in their eyes. 'OK Colm, you are good to go when ready.' Patrick nodded up to the Irishman and muttered to the others.

'As soon as I give the call we are goin' to run straight forwards as far as the pump house area. Use all the cover you can.
If this works, we is gonna have the advantage and they will be running about crazy style.
What was it you said Colm?'

'Like ninnies' was the terse reply.

'Yeah! They is gonna run about like ninnies!'

Colm had the cross-bow primed and ready and satisfied that the wind was as predicted and with the distance accurately plotted, he was ready. He had spent hours practicing earlier and he felt confident he could hit target from this distance.

Turning to Patrick one last time, he looked down and flicked his thumb up and out of his closed fist twice. The big man stared back up at him uncomprehendingly. 'A feckin light, Pat!' Patrick twigged and performed a rapid search of his many pockets, to no avail. Just as his normally impassive face began to show signs of cracking, he received a quiet nudge from Ridge. 'Is it a lighter you need?' Pat exhaled loudly and nodded whilst Ridge lobbed his lighter up to a tense Colm, his face set cold and hard in the dim light. 'What's that for?' Ridge whispered to Ed, next to him. 'Dunno kid.' Ed shrugged.

Straining their eyes upwards, they could just see Colm cupping his hands around the cheap lighter until he had managed to light a larger taper like object which Ridge suddenly realised must be a high tech arrow! *A flaming arrow?*

Colm quickly re-positioned himself and silently pulled the trigger. The arrow shot high up into the night sky with a gentle swooshing sound, *surprisingly high*, Ridge thought, expecting the faint glittering light to go out at any second. But upwards it continued, in a long smooth arc and as they watched in awe, it seemed almost to hover there motionless in the moonlight. It was at once beautiful, serene and endlessly pure while all the time having the innate capacity for great violence.

A poisoned arrow? But what good is a bow and arrow when we have all this other hardware? His head throbbing with anxious questions, Ridge watched in perplexed silence as the arrow gradually began its inevitable descent becoming much smaller but picking up greater speed.

'Here we go….' whispered a crouching Colm, almost to himself.

Just when it looked as if the arrow had struck the ground to no effect, the sky lit up with a massive explosion, a huge ball of flame enveloping the buildings of the Santa Ana estate. Seconds later they heard and felt the force of the explosion. Thad leapt up screaming at the top of his voice. 'Let's go guys! Come on!'

Patrick was already sprinting ahead and the others stumbled after Thad and Colm. There was still a huge fire burning ahead and Ridge could see smaller outbreaks of fire all around the central compound. It was only as they got closer that Ridge finally guessed it must have been the pump house that had been hit. He still didn't understand what had happened and as they all hunkered down into small groups, eyes competing with the flames and smoke, he could swear the pump house building was still more or less intact with maybe just a missing roof. They had all studied photos of the layout and everything seemed to be more or less as normal. There were lots of broken windows on the two main buildings; the smaller house had a fire in the roof but what was causing the huge fire near the, right by the... Ridge rubbed his disbelieving eyes hard and blinked again. The pool! The fire was in the swimming pool!

There was no time to think as dark shapes were stumbling out of the buildings, temporarily stunned by the force of the blast and blinded by the fierce fire burning in the centre of their compound. Juanita screamed as the sharp bursts of rifle and automatic fire echoed loudly off the stone walls and she gripped Ridge tightly as they listened to the harsh reality of the confrontation.

Patrick had run the full length of the combat area, along the new runway and golf course road and he had then fallen back slightly to afford himself greater protection behind the ostentatious stone arched gate. Colm could see that he was trying to provide backup for both the Dogs who were heavily involved in a deadly conversation with the occupants of the smaller building, the continuous barrage of sound being the only real evidence of the intensity of the exchange.

Colm gestured across to Thad and shouted into the intercom that Thad should stay put and keep Juanita and Ed with him so that when the break out opportunity arose they could assist Patrick and the Dogs. He would take Ridge and keep the occupants of the main house from breaching the empty courtyard and joining the main group.

'We must stop them getting the cars out! Leave Ramon to me! He's not going anywhere for the time being. Once you guys get control of the hacienda and the hired help then you can come over and we will be strong enough to get into the main house.'

'Ridge! Keep close to me! And don't be after sticking you feckin' head up like that!'

Ridge shot Juanita a quick glance before scrambling after Colm. There had never been the time to say the things he had wanted to say and he knew he would probably never get the chance now. He caught the look on her wretched face as she turned to follow Thad and it was the eyes that transfixed him. Those huge eyes that teemed with the anguish of a love unreconciled, unalloyed emotions cruelly pushed aside by the greed and stupidity of others.

For a brief second he was both overwhelmed and confused by this until he saw that she was directing those headlamp eyes past him and directly at Colm who was crouched to his left. He nodded impassively and then ran. Ridge zigzagged after him, falling over debris and tripping on his own feet until they found temporary cover behind a couple of upturned tables. Colm let loose a barrage of automatic fire and grabbing Ridge he leapt up and they sprinted to the smouldering pump house.

'We should be OK here for a while! As long as they keep missing these here drums of petrol, that is!'

They were close to the burning pool now and for the first time Ridge understood that the flaming arrow must have ignited something in the pool to create an explosion, although Christ knows how Colm actually managed to do that! The two stone pillars were providing great cover for the guys who had poured out of the main house but the temptation to sprint across the courtyard to the other building was proving too strong for some. Ridge watched in shock as Colm picked off one then another. He wiped the film of sweat and dirt away from his eyes and stared dully ahead.

Despite the heat coming from the fire nearby, Ridge shivered violently. He could see flickering clouds of insects lit up by the blaze. Not really thinking now, his brain already becoming numb to the reality of what he was doing, he swung his own gun up to his shoulder, just as he had done dozens of times earlier that day, *it feels different now,* and trained the sight on any black shape delineated so cruelly by the flames.

Bullets whistled just above his head and he ducked quickly as Colm cursed darkly in Gaelic. Then he saw him. A short plump man edging his way slowly across the dusty courtyard, the most direct route to the other building. He could have not had time to dress completely and his dirty vest had ridden up exposing a fat belly.

Ridge had seen enough pictures of Ramon to last a lifetime and he found himself aiming the gun, his breathing slow and controlled as the man continued to slide forwards as if he somehow thought he had acquired invisible powers. With his finger squeezing gently on the cold oily trigger and momentarily frightened by what he was contemplating doing, he glanced across at Colm hoping his brother-in-law would take the shot before he had the chance, *or the bottle.* But Colm had laid his gun down and was fiddling with some other piece of equipment.

Realising that they could lose possibly the only chance they might get to take out one of the most powerful criminals on the planet, Ridge clamped his eyes shut and fired. The recoil was manageable and he looked into the distance. The man was now lying prone, a small pool of bright red liquid becoming impatiently larger, embraced by the parched brown earth. Exhilarated and yet sickened at the same time, he felt the adrenaline course powerfully through his body like a black tidal wave of raw aggression, pulsating in both his groin and under his arms. He turned to Colm, screaming hoarsely, 'I did it! I fucking did it! I got Ramon!'

Colm had shouldered a massive RPG type gun and he looked over quickly at Ridge, 'Nice one kid, to be sure, but keep 'em coming, that's *not* yer man!' With that he discharged the weapon and Ridge felt his cheek flush from the heat and a second later half the front entrance disintegrated in a second orange and yellow fireball, large chunks of masonry crashing all around them and the smell of charred flesh causing his queasy stomach to spasm and release its meagre contents over his shaking hands.

'Jesus! What was that?' Ridge mumbled, wiping vomit across the back of his trouser legs in a vain attempt to hide this latest indiscretion.

'*That*…was one I prepared earlier!'
'Now! Follow me!'

Colm took off and once more Ridge struggled to keep up with him. They were running straight ahead, right for the main entrance of the big house. It seemed crazy to Ridge but perhaps this would be the place they would expect them the least. Maybe, he thought optimistically, they were all dead and this could all be over.

'OK! Let me go in and finish off the rest, there will only be a few in here so there will, then we can go help the others. Don't follow me too far in, stay close to the entrance and if you see any of the fuckers trying to get out, pop them just like you did back there. OK?'

Ridge nodded, suddenly feeling nervous about being left on his own. Colm disappeared into the smoky interior and Ridge tried to make sense of the tenebrous surroundings.

He was kneeling on what seemed to be a large marble floor occupying the frontal area of the house at the bottom of a large flight of steps sweeping up to the main part of the living space. He felt very vulnerable being so close to the gaping maw of what was once the grand entrance. From above him he heard a couple of gunshots, the echoes far louder than he expected, drowning out the busier but more muted sounds of gunfire coming from over the way.

Ridge was scared beyond all reason yet he felt like he should be somewhat responsible for Colm as he was part of what was left of his precious family. So despite his fear, he raced up the steps, not considering for a moment what he might find up there, just knowing that his destiny was not to sit alone doing nothing. Apart from the rasp of his laboured breathing it was quieter now and he found it hard to locate the source of the shots he had just heard.

Feeling his way rightwards, he found his way into a large high ceilinged room with a grand meeting table strewn with masonry rubble and papers. The windows were gone and acrid smoke was being sucked inwards to combine with the smoke from Colm's latest stunt to produce an eye-watering fusion of noxious fumes.

There was a noise under the table and before Ridge had a chance to react, a man

359

appeared from the muddled heap of furniture with his hands held up in that universal symbol of surrender. If he had chosen a more aggressive course of action, Ridge would have been the loser as he was so stunned he had not even raised his gun above knee level. This he then did awkwardly and so the two men stood there silently face to face as the smoke swirled angrily around them.

The man smiled nervously and as his thin lips pulled back he reminded Ridge of a shark, a Great White, just as it closed in upon his victim in those gory Attenborough documentaries back home. With this in mind, he tightened his grip on the trigger and levelled the gun at the man's face. 'Don't fucking move, OK! Don't move!'

'American! Yes? You should have waited!

Please, I ask you, do not shoot.

I am Xavier, you are going to need me and I am the only person who can save your life!'

'What the fuck are you talking about? Stay still, understand! If you move I will use this! I'll fucking shoot you, I don't care who the fuck you are!'

'If you shoot me, you will be dead as surely as if you pulled the trigger yourself, this Xavier can promise you.'

'Who are you? What are you talking about?'

'I told you. I am Xavier. You don't need to worry about me. I am your friend. Who is in charge of your operation? Bring me to him, immediately!'

'Listen pal! Right now I'm in fucking charge, got that?
If you try anything, I'll shoot your fucking heid off! Now tell me what the fuck you are on about or I'll fucking banjo you right here!'

'You could not keep to the plan?'

'What fucking plan?'

'Why are you early? You were not supposed to be here for another day at least. I haven't had enough time!'

'What do you mean early? Did you know we were coming?'

'Of course I did! This was all MY IDEA! I will kill Ramon for you. It will not be a problem! But this is all too early, he is still alive. You may kill him yourself if you prefer, it is all the same to me. Just don't hurt me, that is what you agreed.'

Ridge shook his head wildly, trying to make sense of all this. *How could this guy have known they were coming? Worse than that, he was welcoming it*! He heard noise from outside the room and instinctively edged backwards until he was against the wall. He looked over his left shoulder, keeping the gun pointing at the Mexican, praying that it would be Colm and that he could make sense of all this. *What to do*? He knew he should have knocked the guy out, or tied him up at least. Now he was going to be stuck in the middle! *Fuck! Fuck! Fuck!*

'Hey, easy lad! I've got it, now. Good work.' Colm stepped into the room, his gun pointed straight at Xavier, each foot carefully placed, his eyes adjusting to the smoky room.

'YOU! *Lo mató! Madre de Dios…!*'

The pistol spat silently, as it had done often before and as Xavier dropped to the floor, Ridge clearly saw the brief spark of recognition in his eyes, before a momentary confusion metamorphosed to calm demeanour as the senses abdicated their earthly authority to that of death's dominion.

'Quick! Follow me! We haven't found yer man yet. Come on!'

Ridge was too scared to argue. *What had just happened*? He was positive that this Xavier guy had recognised Colm but *how could that be*? Had Colm done some kind of deal with him in advance? If that was true then why did they have to go through all this guerrilla warfare stuff and why did he kill him outright in cold blood?

'Quickly now! We haven't much time. I've searched the whole house and unless he has hidden under a floorboard like the vermin he is, then he is outside of here right now or more likely he's scarpered over to the other building and will be trying to fuck off in one of the cars.

I'm after placing a charge of C4 which should demolish most of the interior so if he *is* still here then he's brown bread, so he is!

I just want to do a quick run round the outside of the house to make sure, especially round the back.

Can you run fast and watch my back?

Sure you can, right? Quick then! We haven't got much time.'

Ridge was worried about who was going to watch *his* back now. There was something that smelt rotten about all of this and he prayed that he had been mistaken just then and that his brother-in-law was not involved with these guys. *Come on, get real would you,* he told himself.

Colm had come over to visit Orla and him when they were in the Southside and an unexpected memory lanced through his brain. The three of them had been in high spirits and he had taken them to a hoary old Irish bar called Malachy's. Rubbing shoulders with a filthy rundown general store and a bookies, it was completely at odds with the rash of designer bars which had mushroomed south of the river. He had never been there with Orla and in truth he had always been slightly intimidated by its reputation as a probable republican hangout but he innocently thought it might give Colm an authentic Irish feel to the night.

The pub had been steaming by the time they went in and there was no likelihood of a seat unless you were prepared to be the life and soul. Colm had been such a revelation that night! The jokes and ribald comments that flew between them and the inebriated locals were the best and before long everyone in the bar was Colm's best buddy.

Richard's only ever previous visit had been an afternoon one with his best man and they had never drunk a pint of Guinness so fast in their lives. They had sat silently supping, two bookends, arms folded tightly like a pair of old maids and the visit had been so short that a visit to the gents had never been an issue.

The *craic* this night had been the other extreme entirely and he and Colm had been doubled over in hysterics along with half the clientele when Orla, her face blazing red, had stomped back from the toilets and bawled out, 'Ye might have fookin' told me there was no Ladies bog in this god-forsaken pigsty!'

He had kept pace, his gun crashing against his raw and bloody knees every few steps and with his lungs screaming for some cool fresh air. They rounded the back of the building and Colm suddenly held up his arm which Ridge careered into practically decapitating himself in the process.

'Look! Over there! Do you see something?'

Ridge peered into the darkness. He could vaguely see something move and more than that he could just make out the faint sound of a high pitched engine, it sounded like a 2-stroke outboard at full pelt or maybe one of the wee hairdyer-engined mopeds that were so popular back on the island.

'That's HIM!' Colm shouted. As quick as Ridge could shoulder his M4, Colm had fished a sniper rifle out of his backpack and dropped to a prone position. Ridge fired a couple of shots more in hope than anything else. He knew he just didn't have the range. The guy had to be a mile away by now, it was surely hopeless.

The ground suddenly rocked with the force of an explosion behind them and as Ridge fell to his knees, Colm turned his head in savage fury. 'Bastard!' The curse had no sooner left his lips when the night sky became darker still and the charred remains of the overgrown sentry guard Jesus hurtled through one of the overhead windows and crashed onto Colm with a stomach-turning thud, knocking him out cold.

In a panic, Ridge jumped up and tried to lift the dead body off. It was a gruesome sight as the man had left his head behind but this had probably saved Colm's own head from being pulverised as the man had landed so perfectly over Colm's body it looked almost like Colm wasn't there.

He shook Colm hard but there was no sign of life and his own heart was pumping so hard that he couldn't work out if there was a pulse or not. It was obvious that something was wrong as he could see that Colm's left arm was bent back at the shoulder in a position that was not natural and there was blood gushing out from his chest. Whose blood he couldn't tell.

Fearing the worst, his only thought was

to find Thad! Grabbing his gun, he ran as fast as he could around the back of the building and around the corner, straight into the blinding glare of the fire and in full view of the continuing gun battle. Before he even had time to think about crouching down and with no Colm to help him this time, he heard a sharp crack and his head exploded into a myriad of fireworks as he cartwheeled into the dust.

Whining like a injured animal he inched a hand up towards his heart and it was hot and wet and then everything went silvery. He awoke and found himself back at home on Sorsay, lying carefree in the Big Field with the delicate snowflakes falling gently onto his face and he allowed himself to drift away carried along by the haunting melodies of the cursed pipes.

Chapter Thirty One – To Stop Is To Die

His nose must have been broken in the fall he realised, as he could only breathe, with some degree of difficulty, through his mouth which was fixed open in a grim rictus of discomfort. Myriad swarms of insects splattered against the abraded skin of his face and his red eyes wept tears of defiance and rage. He held on as tightly as he could with his good hand. Luckily it was his right hand which was still uninjured and so he could keep the throttle fully open while his damaged left hand attempted to keep some pressure over his ripped stomach. *Qué chinga*! He smiled to himself cheerlessly.

The gods had not forsaken him after all he thought. He might be the only one to emerge from that battle alive! Thanks be to God that he had bought Juan, his eldest, this new dirt bike! It was only sized for a seven year old and at best it was only as fast as a man could run but right now it was the only thing keeping him alive.

The smell of his blood cooking as it dripped down on to the hot little engine was nauseating and he knew he only had a short time left unless he found sanctuary. He had felt the bullet speed past him and there had been only the one. He dared not look away from the dark road ahead but he had heard the second explosion and he sensed that no one was chasing him.

He was not sure yet who had perpetrated

this audacious act but he would know soon enough and then they would pay! No one does this to Ramon! He would bring Max and together they would bring down a dark rain of vengeance on those who had sought to destroy him.

It was the stinging pain which tore him back to reality and he cried out with it. The sound of gunfire was intense but Ridge could tell that the locus had moved slightly away from where he was lying. Not feeling able to stand, he tried to drag himself through the dirt. His left arm was not responding and he knew he had been shot either in the arm or more probably the shoulder, right now he didn't care which. He was in agony but the pain was coming slowly in hot waves and was less sore than his recent elbow break. He felt sure he could survive assuming some bastard didn't find him lying out in the open asking to be shot again.

He presumed that he had been left for dead which made him think suddenly about Colm. Not knowing how long he had been out for but guessing it had only been a few minutes, he hoped Colm had similarly awoken and was able to get himself safe. Most of the fighting seemed to be around the front of the small house and on the side nearest the main gate. He guessed it was the cars that were the prize now and if he could get himself mobile the best course of action would be to go around the back of the building which would bring him round to the side which housed the garages.

Pushing himself up with his right arm he

staggered drunkenly over to the building, dragging his gun behind him and as the dizziness lifted for a moment he found himself leaning against a rough stone wall which became smooth modern glass from around chest height. Inside was darkness and he decided that just in case anyone was looking out he would try to keep himself below that height.

Just then the world went sideways again and he found himself flat out, staring at the ground. *OK, maybe I'm hurt worse than I thought.* Panicking now that he would bleed to death before he could find the others, he pressed his forehead into the cool earth and wriggled his body into a seated position supported by the wall. He spat dust out of his mouth and then his body heaved up the remaining contents of his stomach. He tried to think when he had last eaten; all that was coming up now was bitter tasting bile which burned the back of his throat.

Without warning his shoulder became excruciating and he frantically tried to tear away the neck of his shirt, picturing tiny maggots of pain burrowing their way into his raw flesh. He saw enough of the injury to convince himself that it was serious, certainly away from his heart which was good but most definitely involving bones which was bad. The effort of ripping his shirt only a little had been enough to send electric bolts through his body and he tried to muffle his cries with his good hand as the pain intensified.

Of course!

He should have remembered from his running days that it had probably only been around thirty minutes maximum since he had

been wounded. He was still benefitting from that
'golden' period when the soothing effects of
adrenaline pumping through the body tended to
mitigate the severest symptoms of an injury.
That meant he had perhaps twenty to thirty
minutes at best before this torture was going to
ramp up to a whole new level of hurt.

Come on! He told himself angrily.
You've not come this far to bleed to death here
alone tonight. He thought of his parents,
oblivious to his suffering and pangs of guilt
added fresh flames to the pyre of his anguish.
What would Dad say right now he thought?
Ridge closed his eyes briefly and there before
him stood his father, sleeves rolled up, one foot
on his garden spade. His face was creased with
worry and he flung his spade down in anger. *'Is
this what you wanted? Are you happy now? To
leave us wi' nothing! Looks like you've got
yourself into a right palaver, as usual. Have ye
no hud enough adventure, eh? Time to get a grip
son, come on. Come on hame before your Mum
hears aboot a' this. She'll have a hairy fit! She
misses you, son, we both do, that's a' I'll say
aboot it.'*

Tears running down his face, Ridge
reached out but he was gone. His dad had
seemed so real, he could smell him; that unique
scent, the creels, his hand rolled tobacco and the
raw salt earth of the island. He wanted to be
back on Sorsay so much, he realised, and he
made a pact with himself right there and then
that he would make himself get through this. He
could not put his folks through all that again.
Gavin's death had been punishment enough for
any family to stand and now it was time for him

to rejoin the living, to sweep away the last vestiges of melancholy, rebuild a positive future and for the first time since the tragedy on Cruachan all those years ago, *to truly live*!

Pushing with his legs he slid up the wall onto his feet as a fresh spasm racked his body. He doubled over in pain and looked at the redundant gun lying beside him. Inspired, he reached over unsteadily and grabbed at it, groping for the safety catch. Pointing the gun downwards, he extended the stock, leant forward and let his armpit fall onto the butt of the gun. As a crutch it was way too short but it supported his weight and allowed him to use it more like a walking stick to keep him from falling over when the dizziness struck.

Cursing without restraint or inhibition, he lurched his way around to the back of the building, falling only twice but each time feeling as if he had come off a roof as an unelected government of pain issued its merciless edicts to every constituency of his ravaged body.

Keep moving, he told himself, *to stop is to die*. The adrenaline effect must be wearing off he realised, as any movement, however slight, was sickeningly sore. His other biggest problem was his eyesight. As the agony had increased, he was finding that his body was slowly shutting down, no doubt in a misplaced effort to stay alive. He was sweating, his face burning up with wild delirium, yet his body had become cold and increasingly numb with his limbs obstinately refusing to obey his commands. His vision had blurred and intermittently he became lost in a spinning technicolour world of blazing colours more vivid than any chemically induced episode he had ever experienced.

He staggered resolutely onwards.

Right foot. Left foot, *come on...*! Left...
Fuck! Left foot..., good, now right.

He felt so dizzy that shutting his eyes
seemed to work better. He realised he had turned
a corner as a slight breeze crossed his fevered
face and the rough ground had given way to
smooth tiles. Feeling reinvigorated for a
moment, he pressed on. I must be close to the
others now, he thought. Over the pulsating,
relentlessly throbbing machine noises in his head
he could hear the sounds of gunfire, less frantic
than before, but surely louder.

With his next step forward the ground
wasn't there at all and he pitched helplessly
forward. Opening his eyes as he fell he could
only make out unreal swirling patterns and
before he could stop himself he was falling into
cold water, slipping ever deeper, swallowing
huge mouthfuls in his panic and thrashing
impotently with the one hand. He was in the
other pool! Images of burning petrol scorched
his frantic mind. The water tasted of chlorine
and he opened his eyes, kicking strongly with
both legs. Through the red haze he could make
out some vague lights above and he burst onto
the surface gulping air into his aching lungs.
Making his way to the edge, he stood for a
moment to compose himself. To his amazement
he found that he was standing more easily than
when out of the water.

The cold water had brought him back to
reality. He looked down at his shoulder as the
water swirled around his wound, gently
cleansing it. As the coagulated blood began to

dissipate, he could see where the bullet had struck him, tearing away a large piece of his upper chest and almost certainly breaking his collarbone. No wonder it was so fucking sore! As a cross country runner he had seen many a hard man sob with the pain of a snapped clavicle as it was one of the most sensitive bones to break.

Moving towards shallower water, he could see over the lip of the pool and he was looking directly at a row of garage doors. He could hear frantic shouts and the occasional gunshot but the fighting had slowed a lot over the last half hour or so. He ducked back down into the water and considered his options.

He couldn't stay there any longer as already he was getting very cold and he worried that the wound would start bleeding heavily now it was so wet. He'd lost the gun somewhere in the pool and wasn't about to start looking for it in the depths of the dark water. That meant walking wasn't a great option either. He peered back over the edge of the pool. They must be holed up in a garage! But, it could just as easily be the drug gang, how could he know? There must be around ten garage doors there, but did that mean ten separate garages or was it all one big open plan garage inside?

He had no choice. *To stop is to die*, he knew that instinctively. He had to try and find the others. He moved easily through the shallow water and gently walked up the low tiled steps and out of the pool. Surprised at how good he felt, he walked slowly over to the garages and listened carefully through a heavy metal door. He could hear nothing at first as he hobbled along, each door bringing him nearer to the house. Then he saw through the glass verandha of the back of the house. It was dimly lit but in his heightened mental state, to him it twinkled like a shopping mall and it afforded the occupants no protection as compared to the darkness surrounding him. There were up to half a dozen Mexican guys that he could see and they were moving quickly around inside the building as if in a hurry to do something.

That meant the voices he imagined through the garage doors *must* be our guys, he reasoned. He wished he had learned Morse Code! I could just tap anything on the door he thought. No! That was a sure way to get shot. I can't shout either in case the guys in the house hear me. So why don't I just open a door and find out. He reached down and grabbed a handle. Pulling with as much strength as he could muster, the handle refused to budge. Bastard! It must be locked. That explained why the bad guys were not too worried about keeping watch down through the pool area.

Ridge slid despondently down to the ground. He could make his way around the back of this flank of the building to the front of the garages; it was no further than he had already travelled. As a burst of lightning seared through his weakened body, he knew he wasn't strong enough to do it over again. Besides, he didn't actually know what he would find round there and he had already paid a heavy price for running round a corner without thinking first.

As he thought what the others must be doing, it hit him like a train. Feeling foolishly happy for a second he fished in his left ear with

374

his right hand pinkie. Of course it was still there! What a prick! What about the rest of it? He pulled up his bloody and torn shirt to see the transmitter and receiver still attached around his waist. It had become switched off somehow and he quickly fumbled to switch it back on. A faint red light glowed. Praying the frequency hadn't been altered, he whispered hopefully, 'Hello... this is Ridge here! Can anybody hear me?'

He instantly heard a flurry of activity behind the garage doors and a shrill voice in his ear.

'Ridge...? Motherfucker...! It's DJ man! You're alive...! Where the fuck are you, dude?'

'I'm on the other side of these garage doors! I can hear you! Can you open them? I'm OK but I've been shot in the shoulder and I'm pretty weak.'

'He's OK guys, he's OK! Were all cool Ridge. I got Joey, Ed and Juanita here, Colm is busted up bad but still squawking, Pat just gone to git him right now. Thad's holed up in the garage next door, hurt but OK also. Motherfuckin' doors are locked at the back, open at the front. We just fixin' to bust Thad out when Pat gits back.'

'Do you want me to stay put then?'

'Ridge? This is Joey. Can you make it round the front?'

'I dunno'. I'm really struggling pal. I'll

try but it might take me a wee while.'

'How long do you figure?'

'30 minutes or so.'

'Too long, *amigo*. You need fixed up before then and we have to get Thad before these fuckers go back for him. They got him handcuffed to a goddamn car. I have a plan. Pat! Are you getting this?'

'Roger that, Joey. I agree, we gotta move. I will be with you in 5.'

'Copy that chief. We will go so as to be already moving when you get here. We will rendezvous at position A. Can you utilise the second surprise package?'

'Will do.'

'OK! Ridge listen up. These garages are spilt into two 5 garage blocks. We are in the far block, Thad in the next door block nearer the front of the house. I want you to go to the furthest door of the far block. I will blow that back door and you will come through it, OK. I can't risk blowing the wall separating our block with Thad's as he is chained up adjacent to the wall.
We will then exit through a front door of our garage block and back in through a front door to Thad's block. The front doors all appear to be unlocked.
Has everyone got that so far? We will

need to have point duty on the back door after we blow it and Pat will create a diversion at the front to enable us to get round to Thad.

OK! We are good to go. Ridge stay ten metres away from the door and I will blast on a count of three.'

Ridge put his good arm over his head and huddled up as much as he could, steeling himself for the explosion. He prayed that he had understood the instructions and that he was in the right place. 'I'm about that far from the last door anyway, so I'm ready when you are.'

'OK. Three…two…one…'

He gasped as the last door of the row immediately blew across the tiled floor and into one end of the pool. The blast was less severe than he had expected but the roaring in his earpiece was proportionately louder. 'Go, go Ridge!' He hauled himself up and shrugging off the pain, he dragged himself towards the smoking garage entrance. Joey was already crouched in position, raucous fire blazing from an automatic weapon.

As he fell through the gap, Ridge felt his body being carried by a multitude of hands and before he could protest they had him lifted right off the ground. Sidestepping up through the parked cars they carried him carefully towards the other end of the block where there was an empty car space to lie him down.

The next few minutes were hazy and afterward all he could remember was a sea of anxious faces peering down at him as DJ had his

377

shirt off and had expertly applied a field dressing on him before he knew what was happening. DJ gave him a shot for the pain and sat him up against a car wheel.

Even in his woozy state, Ridge could see everyone else was pumped and playing an active role in the proceedings. He slapped his face hard and already he was beginning to feel better. Juanita was behind them, providing Joey with ammunition and a variety of weapons. Ed reached down and roughly put his big paw of a hand through his hair. 'You done good son... just keep it together, we ain't through yet...here, this might help...' and he reached into his shirt and brought out a small bottle of tequila. He was surprised when Ridge shook his head. 'I'll pass on that if you don't mind.' The others all had a slug and shuddered, in turn, at the bitter taste.

Pat had located Colm who was talking but otherwise in a bad way, so the big man had carried him around to the front left of the main house where they could safely see across the courtyard to the hacienda, the garages and the main gate. The enemy attention was being directed mainly from the front of the hacienda with some action at the back, towards the garages. It was time for the next stage of the plan - to rescue Thad and to secure their exit.

'OK Guys. Colm and I will initiate kill package two. That should give you enough cover to get out of your garage block and into next door and recover Thad. I will not, repeat not, be able to provide you with cover fire as I will dragging Colm's sorry ass over to the pump house. Once we git there and you have Thad, then we go to stage three. DJ did you recover comms for Thad?'

'Negative chief. But he knows we is a comin' for him.'

'And you confirm he is cuffed to a Mitsubishi Trojan?'

'Copy that. There are two identical trucks in here. I've had a good look at them. I will have her hotwired in a minute and the handcuffs will be no problem. Then we is gone!'

'Roger that buddy. We go in 2...'

DJ looked around at the others and smiled his usual, *what the fuck* smile. 'Ready, *amigos*, ready to run like the motherfuckin' wind?' They could hear him humming gently, '*Hey sister, go sister, soul sister, go sister...*' Ed helped Ridge up and together they crouched, the nervous anticipation running through them like electricity. Ed shouted back to Juanita, 'Hey girl! Come up here quickly!' She looked at Joey who nodded briefly. 'I've got your back, girl!' he said determinedly as he unclipped a grenade from his jacket.

Pat looked down at Colm and he was worried. He had seen it many times before in the field of battle. The man had lost so much blood it was unlikely he would make it. The shock alone would have killed most guys by now, he reckoned. But they would not leave him behind. *Semper fi, man, semper fi.*

He would just have to do this bit alone.

He knew he could hit the target easily from there. What was it that Colm had said? If you wanted the best effect, hit the Primacord directly and this will ensure the bigger primary blast doesn't stop the fun stuff going off. The detonation cord is so fast, Colm had said, it goes at four miles per second, that the explosions will appear almost simultaneous. Pat shook his head sadly as he thought, *as always these days, the others guys get all the good shit.*

The rusted brown oil drum had been placed there at the front right corner of the hacienda the night before along with the one Colm had already detonated. Like its boisterous sibling, it had been filled with a lethal cocktail of truck oil and petrol. Immersed in this incendiary special brew was a waterproof sack, the contents of which Colm had earlier described as '*the dogs bollocks, no offence, lads.*' Joey had been generous with the plastic explosive and added to this was an unhealthy mixture of loose gunpowder, commercial fireworks and numerous small foil bags of various metal compounds.

The drum was half buried in the dry red dirt and the remains of Ramon's crew were literally standing next to it. The top had been sawn off and then carefully replaced. It was amazing that they had not noticed it as there had been no time to add any camouflage. Pat surmised that they had obviously not been trained in the ways of observation that he had been. The fact that they were unacquainted with

380

the location, it was still dark and they were shit scared and leaderless probably had something to do with it also. There was perhaps a dozen of them situated around the front right of the hacienda and from the regular gunshot sounds maybe a couple around the back.

Nobody was moving right now that he could see. Some of the men appeared to be gloomily surveying the sombre landscape of death set out before them. It was a glowering moon that cast its bleak light across the smoky courtyard area littered with dead bodies and fragments of dark bloody flesh. It was truly an apocalyptic hell that had been visited upon them that night. They were not even aware that he and Colm were there, watching them, waiting. In the grim silence, he again shook his head slowly and his trademark stoic features betrayed just a rare hint of emotion, fleetingly perhaps, as a look of pity crossed his face.

He fired.

Even although they were expecting it, the magnitude of the explosion surprised them all. They had the garage door propped slightly open to give them a quicker start and so it felt that they had just been hit by a B52. As the first explosion went off, DJ and Ed pushed up the door and out they ran as a crimson flashlight rent the sky, momentarily blinding them. Instantaneously, they felt their eardrums scream with a piercing pain as the force of the seismic blast tore up the earth all around them and a thunderous whirlwind of dust, stone and human flesh spun them to the ground.

The sky was incandescent with eruptions of yellow, red and orange and all the while white hot concussive bangs lit up the entire area. A huge grey mushroom cloud had risen slowly with ominous majesty from the frenetic carnage below. Luminescent white for brief sickening moments, it was like a monstrous serial killer caught in flash-light, its horrific image seared into the consciousness of all who were unfortunate enough to witness it.

At that point there was no opposition from the remains of the cartel and as Joey lifted up the garage door they could see Thad lying handcuffed by the car, a large pool of blood rendered an unreal tacky brightness by a sudden explosion of light flooding in behind them.

'Hey Guys! What took you so long? Sounds like you're having fun out there! Don't worry 'bout me none, I'm having a ball in here.'

DJ was immediately crouching down over Thad as the others crowded around him expressing their worries over the extent of his injuries.

'Hell, bro! You should have told us you'd been shot, man!'

'Sorry, DJ. I figured you'd get here as soon as you could anyways and I didn't want you to take any unnecessary chances, I know what you guys' are like. Then I think the damn blood seemed to short out the comms transmitter.'

'Blood my ass, dude! This thing took a

bullet! Probably saved your damn life!'

They all turned suddenly as Joey sprayed automatic fire out of the garage door.

'I need some back up here guys! We got bogeys coming from both sides and we gotta keep them from movin' else they'll git over to Pat and Colm.'

He glanced sideways for a moment and seemed to address his next comment more towards Thad and Ridge.

'Pat says Colm is hurt pretty bad. I am sorry guys, it doesn't sound like he's gonna make it.'

He crouched down on one knee, slamming a fresh magazine into his assault rifle and straight away his gun was barking rounds left and right. 'So git movin' guys! Lets not let him die for nuthin' OK!'

Ridge stumbled forwards as if in a waking nightmare. The news about Colm and the sight of Thad's bloodied torso had really taken the wind out of him and he truly felt as if they were not going to get out of this after all. He could hear himself shooting but he felt numb and he knew he was not hitting anything. It was still carnage outside, there were small fires burning all over the area but there had to be sufficient numbers still surviving out there as they were being fired on relentlessly.

The burning oil drum was now acting against them as the Mexicans could shelter behind its bright flames making it impossible to see who to shoot at. Meanwhile they couldn't be lit up better without spotlights. Ridge stepped back deflated and it was then Juanita screamed and pointed to the roof. Fragments of the oil drum explosion must have landed on the roof and it was now burning ferociously.

They were all shouting at the same time and the panic levels were increasing with every second. DJ was looking very worried as he attended to Thad. Not only did he have a bullet wound through his side but the hand that was handcuffed to the truck had also been demolished by a large calibre round and DJ was not sure if he was going to be able to save it.

'Just leave me guys! You don't have the time for this, that roof is gonna fall in any second!'

Joey shouted back angrily, as much at all of them, as just Thad.

'We are NOT leaving you Thad. That is not a motherfuckin' option. Now git movin' guys. COME ON!
Ridge…! If you can't use a fuckin' gun then help DJ! Ed, you take the left.
Juanita! I need some grenades. NOW…!
DJ! What's happening bro?'

'You gotta buy me some time Joey! I gotta stop this bleeding before I touch the hand. If I try to cut the handcuffs, his motherfuckin' hand is gonna come off with it! Sorry Thad. Ridge, tear up that shirt and make a tourniquet.

Put it tight around his wrist so we can at least stop that bleeding then maybe we can do the cuffs.'

The roof material was burning fast and it was all moving towards their end of the garage.

They could hear excited voices from the other side of the breeze block wall. DJ started cursing under his breath. He shouted 'Guys, we gotta split, real fast! I think these guys are going to blow the wall! I can hear them! We is toast!'

Joey looked round at him. Pat was shouting through the comms. 'They will have Colm's backpack. I repeat they will have his backpack!'

'Shit!' Joey exclaimed. 'Who knows what motherfuckin' stuff he had in there! We gotta move, NOW! DJ can you just wire the car and we can just crawl outta here dragging Thad?

'Not without killing him we can't!'

Thad suddenly sat up straight, upsetting DJ's careful bandaging. 'Sit still asshole, I'm almost done here if you don't jerk off like that.'

'I've got an idea!
We don't have time for this!
Ridge! We gonna do a *Joe the Lion*'!

DJ looked up at him angrily. 'What the fuck you talkin' 'bout?'

Ridge just sat looking at Thad, open

mouthed, the blood draining from his face as his big friend became more and more animated.

'Come on man! It'll work! You know how we always wanted to do this? I was against it back then 'cos I didn't want to jeopardise my modelling career. Well, that's fucked now isn't it?
And anyway, I just lost my Levi contract to a goddammned 17 year old! It would buy enough time for the others to get free! Come on! They won't know what hit 'em!'

'It would be suicide…' Ridge said quietly, yet at the same time he knew in a mad way that it made sense. Thad couldn't fight, he was injured himself and if they could somehow create a diversion then the professional soldiers should be able to overcome these assholes and get out, taking Juanita with them.
He would be killed and so would Thad but it struck him that maybe that was what all this was really about. It wasn't about him saving his skin at all. If he *was* to truly live then perhaps he would first have to die.

'Fuck it! Let's do it.'

Everything then seemed to happen at once. Joey and DJ were shouting at Thad who in turn was reminding everyone that he was actually in charge. The roof was falling in dangerously close to Thad and DJ and then there was an almighty blast and the wall exploded right next to them, flying rubble smashing both side windows on the truck and miraculously missing all of them. Joey, moving fast jumped clean over Ridge and lobbed a grenade through the gaping hole just as the muzzle of the first gun began poking through. There was a deafening crump and then silence.

'Motherfuckers!' Joey screamed with all his force.

'We need to go! There will be more of them now they know they have an in!

Thad, if you wanna do this, do it now! I don't think we have enough time but what the fuck do I know? You're in charge…!'

Ed was still guarding the front and he alone felt the breeze from the helicopter flying quickly overhead. He knew what it meant. They would be safe after all, but only if they could survive the next few minutes. He also knew in the pit of his stomach that his part in all of this would become known. He knew what he had to do. He could save them all.

He reached into a pocket and brought out a pair of ladies panties, stolen that night, that terrible night before Mandy died at the hands of these bastards. Without a backward glance, he pulled the panties onto his head and over his face. Grabbing a fully loaded M4 Carbine he stepped out into the blinding glare of the fire. Inhaling deeply the musky aroma, he began to walk slowly, finger pressed hard over the trigger and hell-fire poring from his gun. He didn't hear the sound of the gunfire. He couldn't hear the shouts of Joey and the others behind him. All he could hear was the sweet voice of Mandy and he walked slowly towards her, step by step.

The beleaguered cartel foot soldiers were initially stunned. Out of the smoke and the flames there came this demonic apparition. It was like something both ancient and holy yet also like some hideous underworld creation unleashed from the very gates of hell they had prised opened here tonight. Two of the men turned in panic and simply ran. The others stood motionless, realising somehow that this was the defining moment of the whole confrontation. *Do or die.*

As bullets ripped mercilessly through them, those still standing shook themselves and began to return fire. The target was easy to hit yet their bullets seemed to have no effect. Another of their group turned and fled, a bullet entering the back of his skull as he ran, lending a more gruesome effect to the front of his terrified face as hot red blood gushed from his eye sockets as he fell.

Ed continued to walk, inhaling deeply. The bullets drove into his body like wild birds diving speedily and efficiently into an ocean. He felt nothing. His legs began to buckle and his breathing became laboured, but still he walked on. The men were questioning their sanity as they continued to fire upon a man with *underwear* on his head? What kind of madness was this? He was closer still and they could see the wildness in his eyes as still he continued to fire. Many of them had been killed, and still he kept coming.

A bullet hit Ed in the throat and a terrible

rush of blood poured from his mouth soaking through the cotton underwear. The effect was terrifying. As the evil poured out him, purging his soul, in his dying seconds he may have looked as would the dark lord of Hades himself and several of the men crossed themselves emphatically as he finally fell forward and was still.

For a moment all was eerily still until their worst nightmares were re-awakened by the blood-curdling vision that crashed through the flames. Those few left who were still able to comprehend what they were seeing then dropped to their knees in full and final acceptance of their admittance to hell as they acquiesced to their inevitable death at the hands of these monsters.

'Yaaarrgghhh!'

Thad screamed like a feral beast as Ridge expertly reversed the truck one handed out of the garage and headed straight for the oil drum.

Handcuffed on one hand and the other hand strapped on with the remains of his bloodied shirt, Thad lay across the back of the vehicle in a spread-eagled position, his black and red torso slathered in blood. Joey and DJ ran alongside firing furiously. Ridge swerved past the drum and stopped, jumping out amazed to be still alive. The resistance up to that point had been non-existent as the enemy had been too shocked to move. They looked on the verge of surrender as Pat began attacking them from behind. Ridge took up a defensive position just as one of the men following them chucked one of Colm's grenades and next moment Ridge was airborne.

Juanita ducked her head momentarily behind the safety of the truck then jumped up to begin untying Thad. The crazy move seemed to have been successful in buying them a few seconds and DJ was also attending to Thad, unpicking the handcuffs. The girl spoke quietly as if to herself and lifted her head to see where Ridge was. There in front of her was one of the cartel, crouching in the shadows, inching closer.

Realising he had not been seen by the others, she grabbed the automatic pistol stuffed down the back of her jeans and looked directly into Thad's eyes for a second. He nodded imperceptibly as she rose up and emptied half a magazine into the man's surprised face. Turning, she dropped the gun, muttered inaudibly and resumed her efforts on the twisted rope.

He wasn't sure if he was alive or dead. The pain had vanished and all around him he could hear the crashing of waves, enormous sweeping breakers thundering down onto the rocks at Ardalanish Bay.

But he knew he hadn't found his way home. This was somewhere else entirely. Feverish heat was coursing through his body, ecstatic currents of torrid plasma streaming wantonly into his brain like the dizzying rush of his first orgasm. That was it! So it must be true. The final curtain call ends as his life began, in a frenzied moment of ultimate consummation.

He heard movement above the swooshing waves and looked over to see the vaguely familiar back of a man sitting beside him. Was it Colm? He was still alive? The sun was coruscatingly bright and his mouth was too dry to speak. Everything seemed to shimmer in the baking heat and he summoned up the strength to nudge the man with his knee.

Ridge gasped in horror as John turned to smile at him. His yellow teeth only momentarily distracted him from the impossible vision of a man with a dusty black eye-patch over his right eye and an additional green eye shining out from the middle of his forehead. John gestured across the dry desert bowl of China Lake with a sweep of his arm, 'Hey kid! You here to fish or what?'

Before he could muster the strength to respond he was aware of throaty coughing to his left and he turned to find Crawford leaning against his dusty car, smoking a cigarette. 'How's it gaun, pal? Only fair tae say like, it's pure went sideways, has it no?'

Ridge smacked the side of his head in disbelief as Soterrana stepped gracefully from the back of the car and stood looking down at him, shaking her head in a silent reproach. He heard the car door slam on the other side and young Fabio came bounding round, his eyes gleaming with pleasure at meeting up with his hero again. 'Look Ridge! Look over there!' He pushed himself up on his elbows and tried to follow where the boy was pointing, across the flat dusty desert.

Fabio was beside him now and gesturing impatiently. 'See? Just there!' Ridge squinted, his tired eyes struggling to achieve any focus and he scanned the vista for any signs as to what the boy was meaning. Then he saw, just faintly, an outline. Undulating in the intense heat, he could see the black outline of a man walking in their direction.

He was still far away yet there was something familiar about him. *Perhaps he is the devil, come to escort me personally*, he thought. Then he screwed up his eyes further. *Wait.* Was that someone else, behind him? Just then, the rushing sounds in his head intensified and the lake seemed to sink in on itself to be replaced with a roaring wave of dark water and then everything went black.

He awoke to the thunder of explosions all around him and the hot air rushing into his face seemed charged with a primordial and wretched anguish. *This is finally it!* Darkness enveloped him and as he looked up in the vain hope of a last minute divine intervention, he was aware of a tall dark shadow looming over him, the hazy outline of an automatic rifle swinging over to point at his head. He squeezed his eyes tightly shut and held his breath. He felt himself being roughly kicked and when he opened his eyes he saw a gloved hand reaching down to him. At this point he knew he had passed into the next world as a once familiar voice shouted down to him.

> 'Hey lover, don't be giving up on me just yet!
> It's after being a long time since anyone read me a bit of poetry!'

It was Orla…

Ridge passed out.

Chapter Thirty Two – Line Of Sight

He awoke with the sound of laughter ringing in his ears. He felt very queasy and carefully opened first one eye and then the other. The first face he saw was that of a smiling nurse gazing down at him and the fact that she didn't appear to have any unusual features, such as a third eye, encouraged his optimism that he might actually be alive.

The room was cool, brightly lit and smelt comfortingly of disinfectant. Looking up he saw a large fan rotating slowly and silently, the gull wing blades reminding him of the massive wind turbines that towered majestically out to sea way beyond the Anvil. His shoulder ached as he struggled to sit up and the nurse whispered soothingly, in perfect English, that he must take things slowly and carefully. As he looked beyond the foot of his bed, he saw the source of the laughter; three happy faces all beaming madly at him.

'Hey dude! Welcome back!' Thad shouted over, waving a heavily bandaged hand at him. Unrestrained tears streamed down his face as he smiled back at his friend, his mouth as yet unable to find any words. In the bed next to him, Colm was sitting propped up by pillows and bolsters with Juanita standing alongside. Colm seemed to be fine although he had significantly more tubes and apparatus surrounding him than could be healthy.

There was only one question; *there could*

be only one question that he wanted Colm to answer. As he struggled to articulate this, his brother-in-law looked back, deep into his eyes, his own welling up uncharacteristically, and his head simply nodded repeatedly. Not daring to believe him, he glanced from face to face and saw each of them doing the same thing, nodding, crying and grinning like idiots.

Turning to the nurse, whose face was much closer, he managed to whisper only, 'Is it true?' Before the woman could reply, she looked up and the light in her eyes spoke for her. He turned his head to see Orla striding towards him across the tiled floor, a water jug in her hand.

Her short red hair was now long and black as coal, but he could never mistake those eyes, shining wet now; they were of the most vivid emerald green he could ever remember having seen and she was directing them straight into his very soul. Her words tumbled out madly and all he could do in response was to smile inanely.

'Richard! Oh Richard! How are you feeling? It's grand to see you awake; you're after being asleep for 36 hours now. You're so *thin*, so you are! Listen. I'm so, so, sorry for all of this, it's all my fault, so it is, and I never *ever* thought that anything like this could happen, sure I didn't! I've been a right eedjit so I have, there's no doubt about that but I didn't know *what* the feck to do. I'm so sorry my love. I should'a trusted you, I know that now, but it just wasn't like that, sure it wasn't. I didn't know which way to turn and I couldn't feckin' well breathe without someone questioning what I was doing and why. I was only trying to do the right thing, so I was… Will you ever forgive me?'

Struggling to take in the fact that his wife, *presumed dead*, was actually sitting alongside his bed, he had squeezed her hand hard to see if he was just dreaming again. Right at this moment, *that alone would have been enough*, he had thought. But Orla had returned the gesture and gripped his hand tightly with both of her own.

He had still to make any discernible sound beyond an intermittent popping more commonly associated with fish and he blinked hard through the tears. '*But why?*' was all he could breathe. He felt his head birling and then, as her face began to swirl in front of him, there was an unbroken sound of waves crashing onto sand and then everything went silvery.

He could hear Orla repeating his name over and over as he plunged down into a pitiless black whirlpool, her voice becoming fainter and his last thought was that he had lost her…, again.

'Richard…RICHARD…Richard…Richa aard…'

He came to with the same voice drawing him up towards agreeable warm sunlight and he felt her fingers, hotter still, palpating his clammy hand. Opening his eyes cautiously and fully expecting to find someone other than Orla sitting there, he was amazed to see her grinning at him, her infectious smile bright and cheerful, completely at odds with her mane of jet black hair. 'S'at real?' he asked groggily, a finger raised weakly towards her.

'Mother of Jesus! Is that all you're after asking about! You're as bad as him over by,' Orla indicated towards her brother with a flick of her head. 'Yes, it's real! But maybe if you get lucky I've still got a little bit of the real deal down there to show you. Mind, you'll need to get your strength up before then!' He actually blushed as he saw that familiar glint in her eye. 'Now how about sitting up a wee bit and taking some of this soup here. It's good old fashioned traditional so it is, just like home.'

'Where are we?'

'We are in a 'private' hospital in Belize, so we are, courtesy of my new best friend Thaddeus over there, or his daddy, if the truth be known.'

'The *truth*... I don't know if I can take the truth right now. But do any of you actually know what the word means, by the way?'

Sad bleak eyes surveyed the room penetratingly and the hurt was clearly displayed, enough for them each to feel it, uniquely. Orla and Colm exchanged a brief look and Colm nodded.

'OK grouchy!' Colm replied bluntly as he attempted to sit himself up a little higher.

'You're hungry and disorientated.

Fair play to you.
Eat some food and then we can talk, for we have a lot to talk about, so we have. You can feckin' well keep the disparaging comments until then.'

Colm screwed up his eyes with a savage intensity that defied any contradiction and Ridge felt himself compelled to look away. He took temporary solace in the warmth of the first proper soup he had tasted in the best part of a year. As he accepted being spoon-fed by Orla, swallowing gratefully, he wondered how they had managed to get soup so much like homemade soup here in Belize. He looked up into those beautiful eyes and attempted to divine the answer to this and the many other deeper questions that plagued his weary soul.

Despite his mental anguish, he was powerless to resist the fervent passion that radiated from those sparkling jewels. He fought against the current for perhaps a few seconds before allowing himself the sybaritic pleasure of just floating there, wantonly basking under the outpouring of genuine heartfelt love, cascading down upon him like a sensual waterfall.

As he felt all his worries wash away a deeper understanding opened up inside him like a spring flower and there passed between them the knowledge that everything that had led them to this place had been necessary and that their mutual bond forged in the fiery depths of hell could never be diminished from this moment onwards.

Juanita looked at the faces around the

room and shook her head, smiling to herself. Who could ever predict what their lives were going to turn out like? Just over a year ago, she was a carefree young girl with a vague romantic notion concerning her long-standing crush on the infamous gangster Ramon. *Well that didn't turn out too good now did it?* She shivered all over, realising that, for her, this wasn't yet over – Ramon was still out there somewhere and he would be looking for her. Terrified as she was, she also knew that it could never be over until one of them was dead.

A year ago, she would have considered herself a chaste, self-contained kind of a girl. Her yearnings for Ramon had not been public knowledge and she had not been the type of girl to give herself freely to just any skinny boy flashing a cheesy smile. *Yet look at me now*, she scolded herself with a smile.

She had to agree that Ridge, (or Richard as Orla seemed to call him), was still a beautiful dream that she would always be happy to have had, despite everything else that had occurred. He would recover physically and she knew that locked away somewhere in his heart there would be a little piece which would have her name engraved upon it. It was never going to be anything more than a blissful escape and she was relieved to have discovered that he too had felt the same way and when the wild eyed Orla had made her dramatic rescue it all seemed to fall into place.

The last few days had been a time of wonder for Juanita as she had spent much of it quietly listening to Orla and Colm, learning all about the strange lands they had come from, not unlike her own in many ways; ruled by violence, greed and corruption but also passion, honour and fidelity.

Watching Colm quickly recover from his injuries with a remarkable stoicism, she had thought a great deal about what it was about him that fascinated her and why it was that she seemed to be attracted to men of action, of violence.

Her own grandfather had died at the hands of a violent state. She decided that this had probably planted not only the perfectly natural seeds of insecurity that she felt slowly choking her throughout her childhood but perhaps intertwined with this was the pernicious desire for revenge; a bloody, liberating deliverance that would slice through the insidious feelings of vulnerability and set her free. Before, she had thought perhaps the rebellious Ramon could be her instrument of retribution but he had turned out to be just another of the malignant weeds which were spreading like a relentless cancer across the land.

She looked at Colm, quietly sleeping. He was different to any man she had ever met. It had taken a while for her to notice it and she remembered the delicious sensation that had gently wrapped itself around her as she had watched him confidently pilot the boat; despite the maelstrom that enveloped them, she had felt protected and safe in his presence. But more than that, with Colm by her side, she felt empowered, she felt as if finally *she* could make a difference.

Even when the others thought he may have been killed, she never gave up hope and she had fought on as if he was beside her, casting his cloak of invincibility around her. She in turn, never stopped talking to him, whispering through the comms. When out of the blue, he spoke back to her, her heart took wing and she must have looked to the rest of the world as a woman possessed, smiling madly through the smoke and the ear-splitting gunfire. Despite his faltering replies she had continued to coax him, to cajole him and it was probably apposite that it was during the heat of battle that she declared her love for him.

Watching him now, she understood that for him too, the war was not yet won. Colm had warned Thad to keep out of things; that from now on it was personal and that he would end it his own way, the only way. He opened his eyes, startling her and they both laughed. Juanita leaned forward and kissed him softly on the forehead and he sighed happily before asking her to help him sit up properly.

'Ah Sis! Will you give lover-boy there a wee shake and let's see if we can get him to move his lazy arse so I'm not after having to shout over all the rest of the day.'

Ridge still had his left arm in a sling and so Orla took hold of the other and helped him stand up. Despite her calm demeanour, he could tell she was very nervous and he felt her body trembling as she helped walk him across the floor. For his part, he was anxious to get to the nub of what was really going on here.

He felt annoyed that somehow he had not been given the same script as everyone else and that consequently he had been blundering through making error after error and generally making a hash of things. Until all of this he would have considered himself to be a successful young man who generally had everything under control. It could be argued that his life had been fairly mundane up until he married Orla, give or take the odd family tragedy, and he had been used to the majority of things going to plan or at least following a path that he was comfortable enough to meander down in his own individual manner.

That had all irrevocably changed in a single moment in time, one ground-shaking shattering event, the fallout from which he had been attempting to deal with ever since. His pain had never subsided whilst the persistent and head spinning confusion only increased as his previously insulated world hurtled along its violent collision course, with bone-jarring regularity, into the shocking alternate realities he was now forced to endure. Each new iniquity serving as yet another nauseating reminder of just how precarious his previous life had been.

Sitting heavily into a large comfortable chair, Ridge swallowed nervously as he prepared himself for the worst. *How bad can it be?* He searched each face for clues but was none the wiser for it. *My wife and her brother are wanted IRA terrorists? I think I've guessed that much,* he thought angrily. *But what else is going on?*

'OK, my love. Maybe I should go first.' Orla cleared her throat, took a deep breath and began.

'You mind back to when we used to jaunt over all the time back home and all over the place?' Ridge just nodded.

'And how me brother here never was around much. We used to wonder what he was at and we joked about this and that and then there was that time we got a visit from the Special Branch, mind?

Well...

That was the day all of this started.'

Orla reached over and took hold of Ridge's right hand and squeezed it hard. He held on tightly and returned her steely gaze with as neutral an expression as he could muster. He didn't miss the exchange of nods between her and Colm.

'I swear I didn't have a notion what was going on, but you saw what these shites were like. On and on and on..., 'bout Colm being in the IRA and that. What did I know? Well, you know how long they were after questioning me. Three feckin hours!

It didn't take them three minutes to cop on to the fact that I knew nothin' at all! They let you go pretty quick didn't they, the bastards?

That's when this other guy came in. He told me that it was my duty to help him. He said that if I agreed to do the 'right thing' I would be helping to save countless innocent lives, that...'

'In other words, they fed you the same bollocks as they gave to me!' Colm interrupted angrily.

'Yeah… they did. The bastards!
But I *believed* them Colm…, but if I had
just told them to go an' take a flying fuck
to themselves and had come and spoken
to you then none of this would have
happened.'

'You've lost me guys…' Ridge looked
from one face to the other.

'Are you saying you are *both* working for
the good guys, that *neither* of you is a terrorist?
Do I have a fuckin' zip up the back or
what!
I may look-'

'HEY…! Just *hold on* a wee minute, will
ye!'

Colm began coughing and his face went
an angry purple colour. Until this point he had
been making an extraordinary recovery
considering he had a punctured left lung, a
shattered left shoulder and numerous broken ribs
thanks to the close affections of the weighty
Señor Jesus. In addition he also had a bullet
wound in his left thigh.
Juanita's face paled as she coaxed him to
drink some water. Ridge had not seen Colm look
so agitated since the pair of them watched
Scotland thrashing Ireland at Lansdowne Road.
Colm pushed her arm gently aside and continued
talking.

'Sorry Orla! I didn't mean to butt in like
that, but just let me do this wee bit 'cos it really

403

is all down to me in the end. I'm the one who could have nipped this in the bud if I hadn't been so feckin blind! It was *never* your fault nor this eedjit husband of yours here either!

The answer to your question, Ridge, is... *Aye and no.*

We were *both* working for the good guys as you put it, but I'm using the term, *good,* loosely in this context, so I am. The complication was that we were still not really on the same *page,* as they say. To answer your question fully I would have to say that, *yes,* I was, in fact, a terrorist. For a while, I had *no choice* but to carry out terrorist activities to ensure my cover remained intact. I was actively encouraged and assisted by *your government* to do this. I thought I had already made my position crystal clear on that matter.'

'Let me explain better Colm. What my brother says is not wrong but he does like to play the drama queen, so he does. When I was talked into helping the authorities, what I meant was the 'proper' authorities. The ones that most people have heard of, you know, MI5, Special Branch, the police and the like. They convinced me Colm was an active member of the IRA and they said that if I didn't help them they would either have him killed or frame him as a tout and let the 'RA do the dirty work for them. Now here's the real problem... The bastards that Colm was working for, the FRU, *must* have been aware of my

role at some point as they had access to all the security forces' data.
Yet they never told my guys to back off or not to waste their feckin' time having me checking up on Colm as he was actually one of ours working undercover! So they had me sneaking around reporting on the movements of me own brother!'

'There was no *line of sight*, is the official position' interrupted Colm.

'They didn't give a shite about you, Colm!
The FRU were happy to use your services and if in the 'unfortunate' course of events you were eliminated by the authorities or bumped off by the Real's it didn't matter, 'cos your never bleedin' worked for them in the first place, not *officially*.
These guys were operating on the kind of 'need-to-know' basis that makes Al Qaeda look like a Blackrock bridge club! Meanwhile, the bold boy here starts to get suspicious of his wee sister and does a disappearing act on us all.
Great!
I thought he was after being killed. How did that make me feel Richard?
Shite! *Really* shite, if you want to know. I wanted to talk to you about it, so I did, Richard.
But I couldn't think straight and believe me when I say, Richard, I was prepared
405

to lose you rather then have you killed too!'

Ridge stroked her hand and said sadly. 'Richard's dead, baby. Richard's dead...'

'I'm sorry love. I really am...
I did think that maybe I could get out now that Colm had gone. Don't be so feckin' stupid girl! You don't walk away from these bastards. By this time I had infiltrated myself too well and they wouldn't hear of me giving up. This time it was *me* they were threatening, no doubt about it, and Mam and Da' too.
They had used my Scottish connections to get me involved in a plot to destabilise the peace process and get back at your 'Tartan Tories' by setting off a bomb outside the Edinburgh Parliament. I panicked and decided that my only way out was to fake my own death!'

'But why didn't you just TELL ME all this at the time!' Ridge implored.

'I TRIED to tell you!
That day in the tearoom! It wasn't easy. Being with these people so much, I was kinda half indoctrinated into their ideals anyway by this time. Then when you seemed so ready and willin' to accept the fact that I had been at the very least a Provo sympathiser, I tell you, I feckin' *hated* you for that!
I was half for doin' meself in for real, at times, so I was.

But underneath, I *did* still love you,
Richard, and I knew that we would never
be together unless I did something
drastic.
I had it all worked out.

We would run away up the West Coast
to somewhere like Applecross and you
could keep doing your computer stuff
online and I would have babies and...'

Orla stopped suddenly, tears running
down her face.

Ridge gripped her hand tighter, his own
face wet and his head spinning madly. *If only he
had known*!

'Could you not have given me a SIGN or
anything to TELL ME you were ALIVE!'

'She DID give you a feckin' sign, you
eedjit! It was bleedin' obvious.
I realised it straight away, for the love of
Jesus.
Why didn't you?'

Ridge stared at the two of them
uncomprehendingly, his face ashen white. Orla
could only nod mutely through the tears and then
it became too much and she broke down in
anguish, her head thudding into Ridge's
shoulder as she howled and howled. He held her
head and stared furiously over at Colm.

'What the fuck are you taking about?

What sign?'

'The bleedin' watch! That's what. Did
you not think it was a bit queer that she died
wearing a broken Timex that she'd had since she
was twelve? Did you not wonder why she wasn't
wearing that beautiful solid silver watch you
bought her when you proposed to her in Toledo
in lieu of an engagement ring? The watch that
YOU proudly told me, she NEVER took off, not
even in bed? The one she's got on right NOW!'

Ridge lifted Orla's head up for a second
and there it was on her wrist, glistening wet
under a deluge of tears. The watch which had
been a symbol, both of their love and of their
modernity, eschewing an engagement ring to the
abject horror of both families.

He stroked her face as she sobbed hard
into his wet neck. How was she to have known
he would be in London when the bombing
happened? He hadn't been anywhere beyond
Hadrian's Wall without her in years. It would
have been inconceivable to her that he would be
on a different continent within a few hours of the
blast. He had studied the US papers for a couple
of days only but even then, the level of detail
was nothing like it would have been in Scotland.

Orla sat herself up, blew her nose and
continued to talk, through the tears.

'I realise now that I wasn't thinking too
straight. I thought you'd guess I was still alive. I
thought you knew me better than that.

The jacket too. It was your old jacket,

one you gave me when we first started goin' out together. The watch was in the pocket and the jacket was well folded so it was.

I gave it to the wee bitch wrapped up like that on purpose. It was allegedly in case she got cold but I knew she wouldn't put it on. She was a cold-hearted cow, right enough, a right wee hoor. Did the world a big favour getting rid of her, so we did. You should have heard her! How many people she hoped to kill that day, how grateful she was to take my place in the van!'

'So what did you do?
I mean how did you pull it off?'

'It was easy enough to rig the timer. I told them I would wait for them round the corner as an additional backup plan. As I said, I wasn't thinking straight. I was totally paranoid that someone was on to me and I was positive I was being followed. I hid out in a festering hole in Larkhall. Watched TV all day.

Kept calling your mobile, not knowing where you were, too scared to go anywhere near the flat. Bleedin' torture so it was.

After a week or so I decided you must have been picked up and were probably lying in a ditch somewhere. I was starting to do the rounds of the local chemists, stockpiling the pills when Colm came knocking on me door!'

Orla broke down once more, her shoulders rising and falling with the intensity of her sobbing. Ridge simply held her, too choked to speak. He tried to console her and to his surprise heard himself crooning softly in her ear.

409

Colm saw Juanita was also crying quietly and he tried to disperse the cloud of despondency that had descended over the room.

'Was that not a good day's work I did, my wee blister? You were in a terrible state, up to ninety so you were. Mind you Ridge, I never saw a change in anyone like I saw in this girl here when I told her you'd skipped the country! I'd not a notion where you actually were at that time but you'd conveniently left your Blackberry at Schipol which was a good start.'

'Just to know you'd got away from those bastards. That was enough for me!' Orla mumbled through her tears.

'So… what do you think would have happened to me if…y'know… I'd not gone to the States and gone back to the flat?'

One look from Colm said it all.

'That's enough talkin' fer now. We all need a wee bit of time to take all of this in, so let's rest up and take it nice and slow, OK? '

Colm made to stand up before falling backwards a little, Juanita jumping up quickly to steady him. 'Whoaa! Easy girl, easy… Thad?' He shouted over. 'Have you got any news for me?' He smiled thinly and shuffled away leaving the rest of them, still too emotionally drained to move from their seats. It was much later, as the sun was setting, that Ridge and Orla made their way back over to the other side of the room.

Over the next few days, the rest of the story began to fall gradually into place. It seemed to be Colm who had pieced the jigsaw together first and it had been easy enough for him to track Ridge to San Francisco, notwithstanding the dodgy molar.

For her own safety, Orla had been cruelly kept incommunicado and Colm had hidden her with an elderly couple who lived in a lodge house on the Balmoral estate far away from prying eyes. The area was regularly swept by Royal security. The couple who had been former spooks, back in the day, had promised Colm that no-one would ever know she was there and that no harm would befall her.

Forbidden to contact anyone on the outside, Orla had to be content to wait it out patiently which had not come naturally to her. She was now however, an expert in cryptic crosswords and could recite each episode of Dad's Army word for word.

The need for complete security was not just paranoia. Her trusted associate who was to have collected Ridge and brought him to rendezvous with Orla enroute for the North Highlands was found washed up on the beach at Ballantrae Bay just south of Girvan.

Presumably his killers had tossed him into the sea either from or immediately prior to embarking on the Belfast ferry at Cairnryan. The Ayrshire police had considered him an unusual suicide case. It was not easy to do a 'jumper' when you'd forgotten to bring any knees.

Colm confessed that by this time he had

411

already been completely under the radar for a good while. As he had explained to Ridge during their panicked flight from Lake Atitlan, he'd already known he was a security threat to his former handlers who, after all, had been content to sacrifice him prior to Orla's involvement, so he knew they would have no qualms about eliminating him now.

Unfortunately for them, they had no idea of who or what they were dealing with. The monster they had created was more terrifying than their worst nightmares and over the next few months he had rained his vengeance down upon them with a merciless fury that shook the very foundations of the security establishment.

During an enthusiastic apprenticeship with his shadowy employers, Colm had availed himself of every opportunity to develop and expand his knowledge and capabilities. His extra-curricular activities had only served to increase the arsenal of pain he now had at his disposal and this, in turn, had greatly increased his worth to those that valued such skills.

Sitting in the cool sanctuary of the hospital, it all seemed unreal to Juanita, as if they were talking about people and places that did not exist. She wanted to know the truth about Colm, however painful that might be, but he would not allow himself to be drawn on what should actually be on his unorthodox resume. He only quoted a phrase that Ridge remembered from an earlier conversation.

'He who pays the piper, calls the tune...'

It was through his international

reputation that the connection with Thaddeus had been made. After Ridge had disappeared from Thad's apartment, it had been obvious to his friend where he was headed. Despite his unerring ability to cross national borders without official sanction or record, it had been simple to track his rough location through the occasional credit card transactions.

There had been nothing to indicate that Ridge was in too much danger initially and Thad admitted he had been only slightly concerned when he decided to enlist the assistance of his father. As usual, his dad had taken a belt and braces approach to the problem and had immediately used his considerable resources to do a background check on Ridge and everyone who had ever been associated with him. It had been with utter surprise when his name had cropped up in highly sensitive files relating to an internationally wanted ex-British agent.

It was only after an exhaustive and convoluted dance lasting many days that they eventually confirmed that Colm was himself in Central America. Thad had also been in contact with his old friends from the Marine Corps who had further substantiated the rumours of a relentless phantom spewed from the hostile swamps of the 'Irish problem.'

Colm had then reluctantly agreed to meet Thad. But first, he had let him sweat for two endless days in an anonymous border town whilst he carried out a detailed surveillance of the area, checking and rechecking every last detail, before breaking cover.

'And the rest is history, as they say!' It

seemed that Colm was only too happy to draw a veil over everything else.

'But, did *you* know that Orla was still alive Thad?'

There were still far too many unanswered questions as far as Ridge was concerned and he was still unsure who in this room, this other-worldly afterlife, he could fully trust, if he could ever trust again.

'No way, dude! Not until she almost landed on my sorry ass!'

Ridge thought Thad was trying *way* too hard but he turned his attention back to Orla for a moment.

'How did you get here? I thought Colm said you were cut-off from everything that was going on?'

'Ah… well now. That's true enough. But let's just say the Brigadier and I had a bit of a thing goin' on, so we did an' then me an' old Tadashi became rare pals on Skype. He seemed to be worried about the attack on Santa Ana 'cos of some information he had about your man, Ed Foster, doin' some kind of deal with the DEA. In the end we decided that I shouldn't take any more chances with my eedjit husband and Tadashi didn't want to lose his son again, perhaps permanently, so we gatecrashed your party!'

Juanita stood up abruptly, her huge tear filled eyes looking round at each of them slowly in turn.

'*Muchas gracias* Orla!

I think it is the right time for *me* to speak, now...

I have listened to you all talking and I need to say to you all a big, big thank you. My English is too bad, I know and I don't understand all what you say about, but,' she turned to Colm with a huge smile, 'I am even understanding your crazy accents a little better.

What I hear you *all* say is how BAD you think you have done and how stupid you are. I say to you that the time for crying is OVER.

Maybe, for some of us, our troubles are still waiting out there but we *must* be proud of what we have done. Each one of you sitting in front of me has saved a precious life.

It is not important what went wrong with your lives before you came to Mexico.

In coming here you have brought salvation.

Ridge, you rescued me. Nobody else would have been *loco* enough to do it!

Yes! We have all suffered, it is true.

But know this, my *amigos*, as Jesus suffered and died to redeem us from our sins, so you have paid a ransom for your own deliverance.

You should go from this place with your heads high, your faces to the sun because we have *all* found liberation have we not? It cannot be only me who will never be the same again?'

Ridge looked around the room at the ashen faces. Juanita sat down, laughing and crying at the same time and as Colm put his good arm around her, Ridge detected an unfamiliar look of relief or release on his face. Juanita's words had affected them all considerably and there was a moment of peace as each of them slowly understood their own part in the whole episode. Juanita may have a weaker grasp of English than the others but she had always had an unerring ability to cut through the bullshit and get to the meat of an issue.

Ridge, who didn't possess a pious bone in his body, nevertheless had felt a wave of ecstasy surge through him akin to what he imagined to be a religious cleansing, an emancipation from his feelings of worthlessness and guilt stemming all the way back to the death of his brother, Gavin. He looked up at Orla and returned her tender gaze, thinking about home and family and hoping that the two of them could somehow be part of that life together again.

For some reason he thought of Ed Foster and how out of all of them, he had truly paid the 'ultimate sacrifice,' as the newsreaders liked to call it, when the endless parade of bodies was returned from miscellaneous oil rich war zones.

'What *was* Ed up to, Colm, do you know?'

'To be honest Ridge, I had not a notion what he'd done for us, although I was aware that he'd been compromised in the past. We see it all fine now.'

Colm turned towards Juanita, his face grave.

'He did it for you, my lass. He sold Ramon to the DEA to save you back in Antigua.
But they betrayed him and his wife died as a direct result. He saved you again four days ago. He saved us all.'

Ridge felt his head swim as he stood quickly. Trying not to stagger, he made his way across the darkening room towards a huge window. Sterile frosted glass was gradually turning to a sensuous flaming umber as the first fingers of sunset caressed the building. He gasped for air and realised he had not seen unfettered daylight for many days. Pushing the windows forcibly open, he anticipated the draught of a cool fresh breeze that normally accompanied such an action. He drew himself up tall and prepared to fill his lungs only to be assailed by a wave of stifling heat and exotic fragrance. *Idiot*! He laughed quietly to himself and jumped slightly as he felt Orla sidle up to him, her arm gently curling around his waist.

He looked down at her then across towards the fading light above the trees. He remembered one time, the two of them standing fearlessly at the lip of the Witches' Cave high above the tumultuous thunder of the high tide crashing on the rocks underneath the steepest face of the Anvil.

For the islanders it had always been a symbol of outstanding bravery, or foolhardiness, to attempt the black mouth of the cave. For the two of them it had been an act of faith. For even as they stood, arm in arm, shrieking in horror as the foaming water smashed down only metres from their kayaks, they had understood the simple truth that it was because of, not despite, their wild and reckless love that they could never have come to any harm. It may just have been their youthful optimism, he considered sagely, but standing here this night, Ridge could feel that protective aura envelop them once more.

He felt his body relax for the first time in months and as he embraced the suffocatingly warm evening air. Smiling ruefully he raised his good hand in a silent toast to all those who had given so much to save them both from the perilous rocks.

Get it up ye...!

Chapter Thirty Three – Only those who deserve to die will die

The normally tumultuous roar of traffic was pleasantly subdued at this early hour and the warmth of the sun made little impact through the tinted windows of the little sports car. He squeezed his foot harder on the throttle and a wave of pleasure rippled through him as the controlled power of the engine vibrated quietly and the car increased its velocity with capable ease. Ramon felt strong and powerful this morning. He was unused to being awake so early and he felt very pleased with himself; this was the new Ramon, the new improved version that was going to make Mexico and indeed the world, take notice.

This beautiful new Porsche 911 was just the start. He had only collected it an hour ago in Cardenas but already he felt the benefit. Sure, he thought, I have a fleet of ancient Rolls Royce's in Mexico City gathering dust but they are the old Ramon; slow, ponderous and inefficient. This car is fast and lean and is a symbol of my new stripped down organisation.

Deep down he knew that he was too scared to go anywhere near his property in Mexico City and that most of the scaling down of his cartel had not been through choice. But today would be a good day, he decided. He was heading up highway 37 for Morelia where he was to establish a new business relationship and from there he was going to personally oversee the plans for the first wave of retaliation later in the week.

He had lost a lot of good men in Villahermosa, including Xavier. But he took heart from an early memory of his old father showing his sons how to be brave after a loss such as this. He had taken a bucket of water and put his hand deep into it, right up to his wrist. He then asked Arturo, who was no more than twelve or thirteen, what would happen if he took his hand out of the bucket. Arturo had looked at his father, confused, as they all were. 'Simple,' his father had said. 'Watch closely. I take my hand out and the water quickly fills the space just as if my hand was never there. That is what happens when we lose a member of the organisation.'

Since the bloodshed of the previous month, many of his men had defected to rival cartels and he was haemorrhaging money on a daily basis. He consoled himself with memories again. Not long before he died, his father had once told him, in confidence, that he could lose close to 90% of his drugs shipments and yet still be in profit. What did my father start with all those years ago? *Money is nothing. Power is everything.* His father had drilled this into his sons but Ramon had somehow missed the point until now.

He remembered a time when he was a very young boy, around ten or so when he had been alone with his father and they had suddenly had to leave the place they were in and go and hide in a different place, in the basement of an old house he was unfamiliar with. It had been for a day or two, he thought, and it was very cold, especially at night but it wasn't safe for them to go out to get wood for the fire or even for food. His father had a bag of sweets which kept him happy enough apart from the biting cold.

He remembered his father taking out huge bundles of notes from under the floorboards and tossing them into the hearth to burn. He was sure he remembered his father saying later that they had burned over two hundred thousand Yankee dollars just to keep him warm in that basement but that it was only paper, something that can always be replaced. The important thing, he said, is that my children are kept safe and that my wife is loyal to me.

Ramon winced as he thought about his own family. He had to stay away from them until he could be sure it was safe. Luisa had not spoken to him for weeks now and he wondered if she was now a lost cause as far as he was concerned. He had never known her to be so dejected. Still, he would make it up to her soon, he decided.

There were great plans afoot. He mentally listed the carnage he had planned; a judge who had issued a warrant against him was to be blown up, several reporters who had written unpleasant reports about the Villahermosa massacre were to be shot, many of the security forces were to die as a warning that Ramon would not tolerate any future attacks on his organisation. *Only those who deserved to die would die*, he thought. There would be no wanton destruction anymore. Each action would be carried out for a reason or to achieve a goal.

He was going to think like Arturo from now on. The houses of the rich would burn as a lesson that he must be treated with respect and that it was to him that they must turn to for protection. He had paid good money in bribes to ensure he could move freely but the consequence must be that if he or his cartel is attacked then blood must be spilled. *They always had a choice*, he rationalised to himself. It was the rule of *plata o plomo*, they could take his silver or they could take his lead.

He was worried that Maximiliano was still out of contact and he anxiously awaited some encouraging news regarding the maritime venture and also if there had been progress with the Irish. He had hired a group of young girls for the weekend and he hoped Max would be able to meet him in Morelia where they could catch up on business but have a little fun also. He glanced at his new diamond and gold Rolex and gunned the Porsche harder as the highway stretched out ahead of him.

When his cell phone began to ring he was confused for a moment as he thought it sounded different in this car and did he not have it switched off in the back pocket of his pants? Without taking his eyes off the road for more than a moment he reached over and deftly lifted the phone, putting it to his right ear. As he went to press the button to answer the call, he didn't notice an incongruous couple standing by the edge of the highway.

The man was unusually tall with a thick mane of red hair and he had his arm around a small dark girl. If he had looked over he might have found it strange and unnerving that the couple seemed to be straining their eyes to look directly at his car, at him, as he sped past;

perhaps they were covetous of the Porsche, maybe they had just broken down.

Ramon always waited a split second before speaking, to let the other party speak first. If no one spoke he would normally just hang up. He pressed to connect and the tiny charge of plastic explosive rebounding off the phone had just enough power to penetrate through his right ear, through his skull and out through his left ear leaving an exquisite blood spattered snowflake crack on the blue tinted glass of the driver's window. He may just have had time to appreciate the neatness and clinical efficiency of his demise, before the remaining Semtex hidden under his seat blew his legs off, turning the sports car into a speeding fireball.

The strange couple who must surely have witnessed the entire incident, appeared to be unmoved by the horror of what they had seen and they simply turned to face one another, and smiled quickly. Without exchanging a single word, they lifted their eyes to the bright morning sun, as if noticing it for the first time that day, and they walked hand in hand, away from the burning wreckage towards the light.

Later that day, the DEA intercepted a strange mobile call originating in Mexico City. Considering the recipient of the call, the conversation was unusual in that it was longer than would normally be considered safe, the quality was extremely good and there seemed to be no attempt to jump between phones or disguise the subject matter with obtuse code-words.

'*Bueno! It is me*, El Gaitero.'

'*It is done, I hear?*'

'*Of course. But the fee is now double. There have been... extras...*'

'*You have been very thorough, and it has been noted with great satisfaction. You have wiped them out.*'

'*I also took care of the two... Irish 'periodistas...' That was for free. To remind you to keep to our original bargain. No shipments. *'

'*We assumed that had been you! A nice touch. Our local friends were not amused, I think. We will not deal with your brothers*, amigo. *On this you have my word.*'

'*The fee is ten million US. Direct transfer as before.*'

'*It will be done within one hour.* Adiós.'

Chapter Thirty Four – And, in the death…

Capitán Muñoz was irritated, *as per usual*, he thought. He was chief officer on this vessel, a Polaris II class patrol interceptor, yet he felt it might as well be captained by a monkey from the zoo, for all the respect he got from those above him. He was still a young man, not yet thirty and his glossy black hair shone in the bright sunshine as his vessel ploughed through the rough seas at a respectable fifty knots.

The rapid response capability of his ship was part of his problem he acknowledged to himself, ruefully. He had worked hard to earn his position as a Capitán in the Mexican Navy and the four stripes sat proudly upon each side of his broad shoulders. Yet here he was heading out to sea when in fact his vessel had completed it's duty shift and should instead be tying up alongside the quay away back, in the opposite direction, in the harbour at Salina Cruz.

He was attending a big family wedding in Acapulco tomorrow morning and his wife Maria was going to kill him if he didn't get home in time to help with the preparations. He shrugged and laughed quietly to himself as he looked across the waves, *maybe this was not so bad after all.*

There had been an unconfirmed report of a capsized vessel 200km off the southwest coast of Oaxaca and he had been ordered to investigate. He had argued that it would have been better to have this checked out by the next scheduled helicopter sweep of that area later in the afternoon but his protestations had been ignored and he was now leading a group of similarly disgruntled and hungry men away from land.

There were many small craft foundering in this region, most of them small fishing boats but sometimes there would be an overfull boat desperately trying to make it as far as the Baja, it's cargo of illegal immigrants optimistically hoping to get beyond the border itself and into the US. Slow and cumbersome at best, they were easy to spot onscreen and even easier to catch. Muñoz had resisted this mission as he knew if the boat had capsized then there would be little point in rushing as the occupants would have perished long before he could possibly get there and so he would have the hassle of tying up the stricken vessel and towing it, slowly, back to base.

It wasn't long before he got the shout up from a 2nd Petty Officer that the vessel had been located onscreen and that they would be alongside within a short while. He also said it appeared to be much larger than reported. Muñoz had been cheered by this as it could mean the boat had not actually capsized and so if they could pump her out quick enough then the return voyage could be made all the faster.

As it began to appear out of the summer mist, it only took him a second to realise he would not be heading back anytime soon. The late afternoon light was fading fast and he and his crew members strained their eyes to make sense of what they were looking at. The vessel, a small tanker, was indeed capsized and her heavily rusted underside was protruding up out of the water revealing a damaged drive system. But no-one was paying too much attention to the ship. Thick mist shrouded the stricken vessel giving it the appearance almost of being suspended above the water and all around her the men could see bodies, hideous bloated bodies, floating towards them. Several of his men, hardened sailors, were violently sick over the side as the carcasses became closer still. Shoals of silvered fish, their feeding frenzy interrupted, swept through the water as the patrol boat eased alongside. Muñoz had to shake himself hard to take it all in. He crossed himself, as he saw others fearfully doing.

There were dozens of them; men, women and young children, blackened eyeless faces staring up at them, fixed in a grotesque rictus of agony, each one having seemingly suffered the same excruciating fate as for some reason their bellies had burst violently open.

Divers were sent down and their grim account was beyond human understanding. Trapped in the belly of the vessel they discovered literally hundreds of decaying bodies, all burst open at the middle. Finding around ten tonnes of cocaine in large bales had been no real surprise but the first tentative investigations of one of the bodies had revealed that each one had been stuffed with several small plastic bags amounting to perhaps two kilos of pure heroin. The men estimated that there must be at least twenty million dollars worth of drugs floating inside their decomposing repositories. Muñoz would have to wait for the experts to arrive but he was already trying not to formulate any further the sickening thought that this could all have been a nightmarish error and that once the bags of heroin had begun to split with such appalling consequences, the poor peasants had simply been abandoned.

The divers had mentioned yet another gruesome discovery under the water. Next to an obviously ransacked safe, they had found a large hand which was handcuffed to a steel table leg. The men had remarked that the jagged flesh around the wrist looked as if it had been hacked off crudely with a blunt knife and that despite being nibbled by fish they could still see a distinct tattoo on the large hand.

It looked like a car... a big black car.

Made in the USA
Charleston, SC
03 March 2016